MORE PRAISE FOR *CRIMINAL JUSTICE*

"A GOOD WRITER . . . HITS THE HIGH POINTS."
—*Washington Times*

"NOBODY PLOTS MORE GENEROUSLY THAN PARKER."
—*Kirkus Reviews*

"PARKER ONCE AGAIN SHOWS THAT SHE IS AN ORIGINAL, FRESH TALENT." —*Fort Lauderdale Sun-Sentinel*

"AN INTRICATE AND SUSPENSEFUL TALE."
—*New York Law Journal*

"REALISTIC DIALOGUE, GRITTY DETAILS, AND PLOT MOMENTUM!" —*Key West Citizen*

"WRITTEN WITH LOCAL COLOR AND GUSTO!"
—*Miami Today*

PRAISE FOR BARBARA PARKER'S
BLOOD RELATIONS

"A SCORCHING, FAST-PACED LEGAL THRILLER . . . A REAL PAGE-TURNER WITH A CLIFFHANGER ENDING!" —*Florida Bar Journal*

"A LEGAL THRILLER THAT SIZZLES . . . PARKER SCORES AGAIN!" —*Columbia State*

"TAUT, LIVELY, COLORFUL SUSPENSE." —*Chicago Tribune*

"THE PACE NEVER FLAGS FROM THE OPENING TO THE KNUCKLE-WHITENING FINALE!" —*Publishers Weekly*

"STYLISH WRITING, GLAMOROUS CHARACTERS, AND AN INTRICATELY CONSTRUCTED PLOT—*THERE'S* A FORMULA FOR SUCCESS!" —*Booklist*

"IF YOU'RE A FAN OF JOHN GRISHAM AND SCOTT TUROW, YOU'LL FIND A LOT TO LIKE HERE. . . . PARKER DOES HER HOMEWORK!" —*Charlotte Observer*

"PARKER KNOWS HER WAY AROUND A COURTHOUSE!" —*Miami Herald*

PRAISE FOR BARBARA PARKER'S
SUSPICION OF GUILT

"PROVOCATIVE, BREATHLESS . . . WILL SURPRISE YOU!" —*Cleveland Plain Dealer*

"EXCELLENT! Fully realized characters turned loose in a darkening setting . . . Parker has a natural storyteller's gift of grabbing our attention and never letting go." —*Chicago Tribune*

"SIZZLING . . . Provides plenty of good twists in this story of corporate greed and old-guard pretentions." —*Orlando Sentinel*

"MARCIA CLARK, MOVE OVER! Parker delivers a thriller combining forgery, murder, and legal shenanigans . . . great fun!" —*Indianapolis News*

"Deftly shifts the puzzle pieces, building tension to a slam-bang conclusion." —*Booklist*

"COMPLEX AND TOTALLY INVOLVING . . . THE ACTION NEVER FLAGS TO THE UNFORGETTABLE CLIMAX . . . A TOP-FLIGHT READ!" —*Romantic Times Magazine*

"A SPLENDID, PUNCHY READ . . . some of the best reading in the current thriller scene." —*Tulsa World*

PRAISE FOR BARBARA PARKER'S
SUSPICION OF INNOCENCE

"The very real and complex characters set this book apart from other legal thrillers."
—*New York Law Journal*

"STYLISH . . . A SUN-DRENCHED . . . variation on the work of Scott Turow and Patricia Cornwell, whose fans will welcome this newcomer."
—*Library Journal*

"DEFT, SEXY . . . Parker makes excellent use of Miami." —*Kirkus Reviews*

"Rises above the pack by virtue of a distinctive heroine, terrific South Florida setting, and a wonderful plot." —*MLB News*

"MURDER, GREED, AND SIBLING RIVALRY . . . solidly paced . . . a writer to keep an eye on!"
—*Chicago Tribune*

"A well-spun tale of intrigue." —*Orlando Sentinel*

"A BRIGHT NEW TALENT . . . a real find for those who love taut, highly literate yarns."
—Tony Hillerman

AND THE RAVE
REVIEWS CONTINUE ...

"SUPERB, MASTERFUL SUSPENSE . . . HOT, SMOLDERING AND TANGY." —*Boston Herald*

"A STUNNING PAGE-TURNER . . . SIMMERS WITH INTRIGUING TWISTS AND TURNS, RAISING THE HEAT NOTCH BY NOTCH."
—*Detroit Free Press*

"COMPLEX FAMILY DYNAMICS—OLD MONEY, OLD SECRETS, SEX, BOOZE, AND DENIAL . . . PARKER CAN TELL A STORY!"
—*Miami Herald*

"EXHILARATING . . . A SIZZLING PAGE-TURNER THAT STEAMS WITH MIAMI HEAT." —*Publishers Weekly*

"A FAST-MOVING THRILLER CHARGED WITH FLORIDA ATMOSPHERE, EROTIC LOVE . . . WORTH THE TRIP!" —*San Francisco Chronicle*

"DAZZLES . . . MORE TWISTS AND TURNS THAN A ROLLER COASTER . . . A LEGAL THRILLER THAT SPARKLES LIKE A DIAMOND AMONG RHINESTONES." —*Albuquerque Journal*

BARBARA PARKER

CRIMINAL JUSTICE

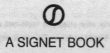

A SIGNET BOOK

SIGNET
Published by the Penguin Group
Penguin Putnam Inc., 375 Hudson Street,
New York, New York 10014, U.S.A.
Penguin Books Ltd, 27 Wrights Lane,
London W8 5TZ, England
Penguin Books Australia Ltd,
Ringwood, Victoria, Australia
Penguin Books Canada Ltd, 10 Alcorn Avenue,
Toronto, Ontario, Canada M4V 3B2
Penguin Books (N.Z.) Ltd, 182–190 Wairau Road,
Auckland 10, New Zealand

Penguin Books Ltd, Registered Offices:
Harmondsworth, Middlesex, England

Published by Signet, an imprint of Dutton Signet,
a member of Penguin Putnam Inc.
Originally appeared in a Dutton edition.

First Signet Printing, January, 1998
10   9   8   7   6   5   4   3   2   1

 REGISTERED TRADEMARK—MARCA REGISTRADA

Printed in the United States of America

PUBLISHER'S NOTE
This is a work of fiction. Names, characters, places, and incidents either are
the product of the author's imagination or are used fictitiously, and any
resemblance to actual persons, living or dead, events, or locales is entirely
coincidental.

BOOKS ARE AVAILABLE AT QUANTITY DISCOUNTS WHEN USED TO PROMOTE
PRODUCTS OR SERVICES. FOR INFORMATION PLEASE WRITE TO PREMIUM
MARKETING DIVISION, PENGUIN PUTNAM INC., 375 HUDSON STREET, NEW YORK,
NY 10014.

If you purchased this book without a cover you should be aware that this
book is stolen property. It was reported as "unsold and destroyed" to the
publisher and neither the author nor the publisher has received any payment
for this "stripped book."

For Andrea Lane
my daughter
and future attorney-at-law

ACKNOWLEDGMENTS

Authors are often asked where they get their ideas. Most of mine are handed to me like gifts when I research a novel. To all of the people who generously shared their time and their stories with me, I say thank you.

For taking me into the music business, I am most grateful to Alex Kane, rock guitarist and songwriter; Mike Carr, Fantasma Tours, Inc., Darlene Delano, Long Distance Entertainment; Pamela Douglas, Warner-Electra-Atlantic; Sean Gerowitz, Billy Velvet, and Randy Bliss of the Underbellys let me sit in on rehearsals. Glenn Richards, WVUM; Louis Vaiz, tour bus driver for Rancid; and sound engineer Orazio Spagnardi. And thank you, Kelly Chang and James Lane.

For answers to my legal questions, thanks to Beth Sreenan, Richard Gregorie, Milton Hirsch, Richard A. Sharpstein, and Stephen B. Gillman.

Thanks also to Ron Cacciatore, formerly with the Broward County Sheriff's Office; Charles Intriago for insight on money laundering; Bill Brewer, Arvida Corporation, for the dragline; and Richard A. McMahan, O.S.I, for the advice.

Andrew Geist, diver and spear fisherman, took me underwater; and my sister Laura Parker kept me afloat during the long months of writing.

CHAPTER 1

Two men stood looking out past the ruined terrace into the blazing light of a Sunday afternoon. One man held a pair of binoculars to his eyes; the other peered through the long lens of a telephoto camera. No one across the lake was likely to see them. The shadow of the roof and the overgrown trees cast the interior of the house into an unnatural darkness.

The room was silent except for the clicking of a shutter.

Along one wall a folding table held recording equipment. The woman sitting there jotted notes on a clipboard. The glow of a small lamp reflected on her face. Her movements were precise and unhurried. At her feet electrical cords were routed to a junction box. Another line ran along the wall, then across the living room, held down by strips of duct tape.

Elaine McHale walked in hearing the slight echo of her own footsteps on the bare concrete floor of what had once been a two-million-dollar lakefront house in a development in one of those vast tracts northwest of Miami. Elaine had driven up to check out the surveillance operation. The agent in charge, Vincent Hooper, had opened the garage for her so she could park her car out of sight. As far as the neighbors knew, the place was being renovated for the new owners, who lived out of state.

The woman at the table looked up from her notes. Daisy Estrada, petite and auburn-haired, could have been any of the wives who might be found lunching at the Lakewood Village country club, except for the pistol holstered at her waist. She greeted Elaine by name.

Elaine knew one of the men at the windows, Carlos Herrera, a Colombian-born agent with a graying mustache. They exchanged a nod. The other man was younger, with a dark blond ponytail. She extended her hand. "Elaine McHale, assistant U.S. attorney."

"Glad to meet you. Scott Irwin." The knees of his jeans were ripped, and his black T-shirt had a picture of a guitarist with spiked hair. His one earring was a silver skull.

She took all this in, finding it impossible not to smile. "You're the agent Vince put undercover at Coral Rock Productions. You have to be."

Carlos patted his stomach. "Because the rest of us are too old or too fat. Scott, show her your navel ring." The younger man pulled up his T-shirt. A silver ring pierced his skin.

"Ouch," Elaine said.

Vincent Hooper put a foot on one of the steel chairs and lit a cigarette. "Scott plays bass guitar, fits right in. He's getting his arms tattooed next."

"Not even for you, sugar pie." Scott pulled down his shirt.

The DEA had planted an agent at a music production company because the man who lived across the lake, Miguel Salazar, was using the company to launder money for a drug cartel based in Ecuador.

From where she sat by the tape recorders, Daisy Estrada said, "What about the wiretap? We're ready to roll."

Elaine said, "The warrant should be signed any moment. They have your number here."

Scott laughed in disbelief. "What's the problem? Salazar's been making calls all morning. He's walking around in there with his phone stuck in his ear."

"Take it easy. We've got time." Vince watched the younger agent go sit down by the windows. Then he turned his head to look at Elaine.

She felt a sudden weakness in her chest, a catch of breath. Vince had said nothing at the door, just opened it and let her in. She hadn't expected that seeing him would get to her. Vince had been undercover in Ecuador since before Christmas, back in Miami for more than a week. She wanted to stare at him, to soak in the subtle changes; Vince always came back changed in some way. Following him into the room she had noticed that his skin was more deeply tanned. His shirt seemed tighter across his shoulders. He had a beard, neatly trimmed but full enough to cover the scar on his jaw where last year a cop in Panama had clubbed him with a rifle butt. There was some gray, not much.

Elaine walked to the sliding glass doors that formed the west wall of the living room, facing the lake. One of them was broken out, replaced with plywood. She slid another back to get some air. This house stank of decay and desolation. On the patio, the screening was gone. Leaves and algae choked the pool, whose tiles had blackened with mildew.

This time of year, late January, air conditioning wasn't necessary. She doubted it even worked. The former owner, who had been charged with securities fraud, had broken everything in the house rather than let the government seize it. At trial he had ranted how federal agents had set him up, lied to him, led him into a trap. Before the guilty verdict came in, he had punched holes in the walls and ripped out the wiring, sloshed motor oil onto plush carpeting, shattered every sink and toilet, then poured cement down the drains. His wife had already run out on him, so what the hell. Then he went into their bedroom, bit down on the barrel of a .38 revolver, and blew his brains out.

Beyond the glittering blue lake Miguel Salazar's mansion soared upward, an expanse of glass and peach-colored stucco under a red tile roof, with a tennis court on one side and a pool on the other. Purple bougainvillea twined through a trellis shading the terrace. Tropical flowers bordered the brick walkway that led to a white gazebo, then to the lake, where a catamaran had been pulled to shore.

On the terrace women in bright dresses were tying balloons to the backs of chairs set at circular tables. The balloons danced in the light breeze, and the tablecloths fluttered. Children played in the grass, laughing and shouting. A young girl came out of the house carrying a box with a ribbon on it, which she put on a table already stacked with presents. Elaine heard music—a salsa melody. Rhythmic, pulsing, fading in and out.

She turned her head slightly. Vince stood beside her. "It's a birthday party."

"I didn't know Salazar had children."

"A teenage son, but he's in boarding school. He has some relatives living with him. A sister, cousins. The party's for his niece."

"What about his wife?"

Vince took a last drag on his cigarette and flicked it into the pool. "His wife is dead. She was a girl from the country, married him at fifteen. At the time of her death they lived on his ranch outside Quito. Salazar found out she was pregnant by his foreman. He shot her. The foreman lived, minus his *cojones*. That's the story, anyhow."

Elaine let out a breath. "Good Lord."

Vincent Hooper could repeat these horror stories without a flicker of emotion. He had told her worse than that, inventing nothing, and there were more things he refused to tell her. They had left their mark. He thought of himself as a soldier in a nasty war, the last line of defense. And yet Elaine had seen tenderness in this man—not often but enough to keep her from losing hope.

She noticed a Mercedes-Benz flashing in and out of view among the big houses on Salazar's street. A minivan appeared after that. Both cars turned into his driveway, then were blocked from view by the house. More guests. A few minutes later a couple came out onto the terrace with a little boy, who ran off to join the others. The parents sat in the shade with the adults, and a woman in a maid's uniform brought a tray of drinks.

"Just another happy family Sunday in the burbs." When Elaine didn't respond, Vince said, "What's the matter? You're pissed off because I haven't come to see you."

"Don't make it sound so petty."

His lips barely moved. "And don't be bitchy, Elaine. I couldn't get away."

She didn't speak. It wouldn't do any good.

To the south she could see white mounds of earth and the boom of a dragline moving slowly back and forth, digging up muck and limestone, making lakes and dry land out of what had once been Everglades.

Elaine said, "I got another call from your informant at Coral Rock Productions."

"Not my informant. I didn't put her in there. I was out of the country."

"But she is working for you, Vince, and she doesn't like it."

He made a short laugh. "Well, I'm sorry as all get out."

The DEA had been using a female rock guitarist to gather information about the same company that Scott Irwin had infiltrated. The young woman, whose name was Kelly Dorff, had been given a choice—help us or go to prison for possession of heroin. She had called Elaine twice already to complain that she couldn't do it anymore.

Elaine spoke quietly, making sure no one else in the room could hear her. "Look, Vince. What else can Kelly give you that you don't already have? If you keep leaning on her, she could lose it. She's not stable. If she tells Salazar what's going on, you're going to blow your chance to get him."

"She's not going to do anything," Vince said. "Don't worry about it. Scott's keeping an eye on her. She doesn't know he's DEA." He added, "You know what Miss Dorff's problem is? She's dating a guy who may well end up as a defendant in this case. A former buddy of yours. Daniel Galindo."

Elaine looked at him.

"She says he's not involved with Salazar, but I think she's lying to us. What's your opinion?"

"You can't be serious. I know you hate Dan's guts, but really."

"I don't hate him, Elaine." Vincent smiled slightly. "That would be a waste of energy. I only look at the facts. Dan Galindo is sleeping with a girl arrested for trafficking. The girl plays in a band that Salazar is promoting. She works part-time at Coral Rock Productions, which Salazar is using for money laundering. Coral Rock is owned by Galindo's former brother-in-law. Don't tell me he doesn't know what's going on."

"I'm not going to argue about it," Elaine said.

Before resigning from the U.S. attorney's office, Dan Galindo had lost a case against a major drug dealer. Vincent suspected that Dan had blown the case deliberately, that he'd been paid off.

Scott Irwin stood up, raising his binoculars. "Here comes Leon."

Across the lake the sun flashed on the windshield of a Jeep Wrangler turning into the driveway at the side of the house. A skinny man with long black hair got out the driver's side. His passenger, an older man wearing sunglassses, carried a box wrapped in pink paper.

Vincent grabbed the extra pair of binoculars. Carlos swung the telephoto toward the driveway. Daisy Estrada came over to look.

"Who are they?" Elaine asked.

Daisy said, "The driver is Leon Davila. He's a drummer in the same rock band as Kelly Dorff, but his real job is playing courier for Miguel Salazar. He's on your list of indictments, right? The other guy . . . I don't know."

"He's a banker," Vince said. "Executive V.P., Banco Nacional de Quito, the branch in downtown Miami. I wonder what's in the package."

Daisy laughed. "Freebasing Barbie?"

Carlos's finger pressed the shutter, and the camera clicked on automatic. The two men went inside, and the door closed after them. Scott trained his binoculars on the house. "Okay, I see Miguel in the living room. Handshakes, pat on the back. Now they're on the stairs. His study's up there, but the curtains are shut."

They watched for a few more minutes, but Salazar did not reappear.

The cellular telephone rang. Vince Hooper walked to the table to pick it up. His voice was indistinct. After a few seconds he looked at the others. "That was Paxton. We've got the wiretap warrant."

"Finally." Daisy flipped switches on the tape recorders and pen register, then put on a pair of headphones and sat down.

Vincent Hooper stood by the open glass door. His dark eyes were fixed on the house, as if by will alone he could see beyond the curtains at the upstairs window and the glare of sun on the tinted glass.

For another half hour Elaine waited for something to happen, but only two calls came through. As soon as Daisy determined they were not relevant to Salazar's business, she disconnected. There were four tape recorders, one for each line at the Salazar residence, plus a pen register to record the telephone number of every call going in or coming out. The lights on the machines stayed stubbornly dark. Finally Elaine checked her watch and said she ought to be getting back to Miami.

At the door to the garage she heard footsteps behind her, echoing in the dim hallway. She turned.

Vince Hooper had followed. "Leaving already?"

"I've seen the operation."

He smiled. "Is that why you drove thirty miles?"

"Get off it, Vince."

"Come here." He went into a room off the hall, standing just beyond the open door, waiting for her. She looked back toward the living room, wondering if the other agents knew where he had gone. "Come here, I said." He held out his hand.

They walked deeper into the house. Bits of smashed Italian tile grated under her shoes. The room they entered was—had been—a beautifully decorated study. Now green silk wallpaper hung in shreds. The blades of a ceiling fan lay twisted on the parquet floor, which had been gouged and hacked. Sunlight filtered in a crazy pattern through broken wooden louvers.

Vince pushed her against the wall. "You think I didn't miss you?" His knee pressed between her thighs.

She was breathless. "Liar. How many *ecuadoreñas* did you sleep with?"

"Fifty teenage whores, and thought of you every time I came." His mouth came down on hers, and callused fingers slid under her pullover top and closed on one breast. She knew he wanted to pull up her skirt and take her standing against the wall, her legs around his waist. Crazy. She knew she would let him do it.

There was a noise in the hall, someone stepping on glass. They looked around. The young agent, Scott, stood in the doorway with his gaze fixed on the ceiling.

"Sorry. Daisy wants to know who's supposed to stay tonight."

"She can stay till the shift change at eight o'clock." Vince had not moved his hand.

The other man left.

Elaine pulled away. "Damn."

"Don't worry about it." Vince laughed softly. "He'd die before he'd say anything. Any of them would."

"They guard you like Rottweilers." She brushed her hair back with trembling fingers. "I'm leaving."

"When can I see you?"

"Now you ask."

He ran a finger down her cheek, under her chin. He kissed her gently this time, and his beard prickled her skin. "I was going to call you, Elaine. Tomorrow. To take you to lunch." In the semidarkness his eyes were almost black and so close to her they blotted out the room.

She said, "What about tonight?"

"Can't. I'm going to be busy."

He kissed her quickly, then walked away. Elaine didn't say his name. Not to have him turn around and explain that he had something to do with his wife tonight that he couldn't get out of, and that tomorrow was the best he could do. Sorry.

She leaned against the wall, eyes closed, and heard his footsteps fade. Then faint voices. Already he was back with the others. She could find her own way out.

CHAPTER 2

As the bubbles cleared, Dan Galindo looked up through his dive mask. The boat's pointed shape bobbed on the surface, and a line of yellow polyester rope angled toward the bottom, ending at a grapnel hook sixty feet down, caught on a pitted white ridge in the reef.

He inverted, kicking slowly with his fins. A school of chub eyed him, then shot away, their sides glinting silver as they turned in unison. Dan moved along at a shallow depth, ten feet or so, till he ran out of air. At the surface he blew sea water out of his snorkel, took a few deep breaths, then went under again, deeper. A few seconds with his ears above water had been enough. The girl he'd come with had turned the radio to a rock station. Of her Dan had glimpsed only scraggly blond hair and a bikini top. She was up there getting some sun, opening another beer.

At ten o'clock this morning Dan had staggered out

of bed, panicked. What trial had he forgotten to show up for? What judge had he pissed off this time? Monday mornings were God's revenge. He'd phoned his office. Alva—sweet Alva—told him he'd missed an appointment with a client, but she had covered for him. She read him some phone messages, but there was nothing on his schedule he couldn't put off.

The day half gone already. He thought of the paperwork left over from last week. There was always that. Then Kelly poked her head out from the covers. *Let's have lunch in the boat. It would be fun.*

They drove across the causeway from Miami to a marina on Key Biscayne, where he kept his boat, a twenty-foot Mako. Dan put his dive gear aboard while Kelly bought food at the marina store. Once into the bay they headed due south, leaving behind the congested waters close to shore. A few miles farther along, with the mainland reduced to a line of green in the west, Dan guided the boat through the narrow channel at Sands Cut, just north of Elliott Key, then headed east toward Triumph Reef. The depth finder held steady at thirty, then went to forty, fifty. Dan slowed. At sixty he cut the engine. Their wake caught up to them, and the boat rose and fell. Another quarter mile out, the bottom would drop quickly to a depth of hundreds of feet. He tossed the anchor over the side and cleated off the bow line.

For a while they sat quietly, water gurgling on the hull. The winter sun blazed from a cloudless sky. They ate sandwiches and drank beer. Then Kelly started telling him about the demo tape her band was doing, and the keyboardist who was trying to take over the vocals. Dan closed his eyes behind his sunglasses and wished he was alone. It was when she started fiddling with the dial on the radio that he clipped the dive flag to a pole, then stripped off his sweatshirt and jeans and got into his wet suit. It covered him from neck to knees. He zipped up his rubber booties, put on fins, gloves, and weight belt.

He told Kelly he'd be back in a while, don't go away. He lowered his mask, bit down on the snorkel, and jumped in. The sea closed over his head in a froth of bubbles, and he sank into perfect silence.

Dan kicked slowly, moving along, watching a queen parrot fish with its beaklike mouth. The fish was bright turquoise now, but bring it to the surface, the color would fade as life ebbed away. Visibility was good all the way down. Patches of sand appeared bone white among the grayish rocks of the reef. The uneven terrain dropped into rocky holes between outcroppings of coral where purple fan grass waved in the slight current. The reef was alive with fish. Dan spotted a long-nose butterfly, a blue tang, and gray angels. Rolling over, he took the snorkel out of his mouth and blew air. The bubbles floated upward, rocking side to side, then were lost against the bright surface of the water. He wanted to follow them, to climb back into the boat, sit in the sun and think of nothing at all.

Coming up again, Dan pushed his mask to his forehead and looked toward the boat. Kelly was dozing on the bow with the radio blaring. Her forearm was over her eyes, and one foot moved to the beat of drums and a screaming guitar. Her swimsuit top was off, and rosy nipples pointed skyward. There was a valentine tattooed on one breast.

Dan spat into his mask and sloshed it with sea water. He began to breathe deeply. Slowly. Pulling air into expanded lungs, then pushing it all out, purging the carbon dioxide. He was going to the bottom. He counted fifteen long breaths, took a look at his watch, then did a one-eighty.

On Dan's long, lean body, his weight belt, eleven pounds of lead, would allow buoyancy to fifteen feet. Any deeper, he would sink. When he felt the subtle shift he stopped kicking. He glided down, eyes closed, ears popping. It would take about twenty seconds to reach bottom. He felt water flowing past, colder now. The mask pressed into his face, and a few bubbles squeaked out of his wet suit. He tongued the snorkel out and pressed his lips together.

There was a time when he'd been good at this, when he could stay under for a minute and a half. He wondered if he could still do it.

His father had told him to close his eyes—the brain consumes less oxygen that way. Dan didn't know how it worked, but it did. On land Raul Galindo had been as ungainly as a wading bird. Underwater his body had achieved a sort of grace, his long fins curling, uncurling, flowing behind him like the tail of a fish.

The light through Dan's eyelids dimmed, and he

sensed the bottom. He flicked his eyes open once, then again. His watch showed twenty-five seconds had elapsed. With thirty to get back up, being careful, he would have thirty-five more to lie here. He settled on his stomach in a patch of sand, gloved fingers hooked on a rock to keep from drifting. The only sound was a slight buzzing in his ears.

To stay under a minute and a half would be difficult but possible. As a kid he had nearly grown gills, catching tropicals for spending money in high school, or going spearfishing on long weekends in the Keys. There were more good fish then. Big, meaty snapper, grouper, and yellowtail. Gradually, though, overfishing and fertilizer runoff reduced their numbers. The new residents, with even fewer fish, were saying what a paradise they had found.

Dan clamped his teeth together and tightened his throat. Already he needed air. He opened one eye. The second hand on his watch gave him twenty-two seconds. Twenty-one . . . twenty.

The thought of not going back up drifted morbidly through his mind. In two weeks he would turn thirty-five. The number was somehow portentous. The halfway point. The zenith. And then what? Between hangovers and periods of generalized funk, when he dared to reflect on the tattered state of his psyche, Dan slammed up against the horrifying vision that he would never get beyond that ratty office where he worked now, with its cheap, cigarette-burned carpet and wheezing air conditioner. That one day he would be washed up, living on memories of better days, like the old lawyer who owned the place. If he drowned, what difference would it make, really? He had life insurance. His ex-wife's mortgage would be paid off. Their son, Josh, would go to college on the proceeds.

Dan's chest involuntarily heaved, and his lungs were burning. What if he hooked himself to the anchor with his dive belt? Kelly would haul on the rope, and there he would be, limp as a gaffed squid. Dan checked his watch. He tried to focus, to remember where on the dial it would reach thirty seconds. He decided to count down from fifteen. A black grouper came closer, checking him out, magnified slightly by the dive mask. Its undershot jaw opened and shut, and when Dan made a slight motion with one hand, the fish vanished into the coral.

Thirteen seconds left. Twelve . . . eleven. He closed his eyes again, seeing little dots of light that whirled and exploded in the darkness like miniature fireworks.

When Dan was ten, he and his father had gone spearfishing, Dan's first time with his own gun. They were in the water off Marathon when a bull shark saw them, an eight-footer. Sharks usually swam on by. This one didn't. Raul Galindo extended his speargun at arm's length, pivoting, motioning for Dan to stay behind him. The shark glided closer, and he nudged it in the head—easy, not wanting to make it mad. With a flip of its tail, it scooted away. And then came back. Fast. Raul fired, hitting it just above the eye. The shark was a thrashing, twisting piece of meat, leaking red. Back in the boat Raul said they should leave the area because of the blood, but as soon as they anchored somewhere else, they would go back in. Dan screamed, *No, Dad, no,* but his father threw him in anyway. *Don't be afraid, I'm here.* Two years later, Raul Galindo had been driving home from Key Largo when a drunk crossed the center line.

Dan felt dizzy. His entire body ached. He was sixty feet underwater. The height of a six-story building. If he passed out, he would stay down here, weighted by his belt, until his body bloated and the currents lifted him away.

Eight . . . seven.

Josh was seven years old. Brown hair and eyes. *Like mine,* Dan thought. Same neat haircut, though Josh's was longer, flopping into his eyes when he ran. A sweet kid. Small for his age. He'd been premature, had to catch up. Played soccer. Lisa had mentioned a game tomorrow. Dan hadn't planned to go, so Josh didn't expect him. What a hassle, dealing with Lisa.

Dan remembered he'd promised to take Josh fishing this winter. Never got around to it. *Son, I want to show you how to use a speargun. You're not too young.*

That was weird, Dan thought. The voice in his ears—it sounded like Raul's voice.

His watch had stopped. Dan looked closer. No, another second ticked by. Why not go fishing? Not the bay, forget that. Too tame. They'd go to the Bahamas. Cat Cay. So many fish there. Beautiful. They'd go to Eleuthera, feel the sun and wind on their faces. The boat skimming over the water like a pelican with out-stretched wings.

Dan's vision dimmed. Oh, Christ. He was going to die. Heart slamming in his chest, he pushed off and began kicking frantically. The surface seemed dark now, impossibly far away, the boat tiny as a matchstick. He rose, feeling the pressure subside. No. He wasn't going to make it. It was too far. He was too heavy, too tired. He would black out before he reached the surface and fall back to the bottom.

Dan thought of Joshua, and his chest lurched, almost a sob. Air burst from his lungs and he gagged on water. Too late, too late. His gloved hands fumbled for his weight belt. With his teeth he tore one glove off. He grabbed for the plastic clip. Then the belt dropped away and Dan kicked, no strength left, but the silvery light getting nearer.

There was a splash as he broke through. He dragged in a breath. The rush of oxygen made him drunk, almost euphoric. He rolled over, wheezing, barely keeping his face above the surface. The sun blasted his eyes. He kicked steadily for the boat, reached for it, then a wave lifted it away. When the boat fell back, Dan curled his extended fingers over the gunwale and hung on.

"Kel—!" He tried to scream her name over the music and went into a spasm of coughing. "Kelly, for God's sake, would you wake up!" He pounded the hull.

She sat up squinting, looking around, not seeing him. "Dan?"

"How stupid can you be? You have to pay attention when someone's diving!"

"What happened?" She looked over the side and finally saw him bobbing in the water near the rear of the boat. "Oh, my God, did a fish bite you? Are you hurt?"

"I almost fucking drowned!"

"I'm sorry! Dan, I didn't know!" Wearing only her bikini bottoms, she clambered through the gap in the windscreen.

Dan spat salt water. His aching sinuses were full of it. When he was fairly sure he had enough strength, he told her to move, he was coming in. He handed her his flippers and mask, stepped on the dive ladder, and shakily hauled himself up past the outboard engine and over the transom, scraping his shin. He flopped to the bottom of the boat, his sides heaving.

She crouched beside him, pushing her long hair behind her ear. "Dan? I'm sorry, okay? What can I do?"

He retched. After a while he sat up, leaning against the rear bench seat. All his life diving, he had never dropped a weight belt. He had never come that close. He took off his remaining glove and his booties.

"Let me have a towel." He dried his face and hair, and when he had stopped shaking, he peeled off his wet suit and put his clothes back on. Kelly hustled around picking up beer cans and repacking his dive bag, not saying much. Dan caught her by the hand.

"Kelly, I didn't mean to yell at you. I was scared. It wasn't your fault."

She hugged him around the waist. "It's okay."

"Come on, let's go back," he said.

The outboard engine roaring, Dan turned the boat north. He stood up behind the wheel and let the wind rush into his lungs. The sky was incredibly, intensely blue, the water a sheet of silver. The boat danced over it. A gull dipped, then swung away. Dan laughed out loud. He was thinking of Cat Cay again.

CHAPTER 3

At the marina, a forklift raised Dan's little outboard from the water on padded steel arms as if it were a toy. Dan stood on the dock watching. The driver backed up the machine to reach a garden hose at the rear of the marina office, a small, flat-roofed building with mildewed white paint.

"You have a good ride?" He was a young Cuban named Ramon. He aimed the nozzle at the boat and sprayed salt water off the hull.

Dan said they'd had a great time, thanks, and gave him a ten as a tip. He walked around the boat, taking a close look. The hull was in decent shape. He'd had the engine overhauled last year. For fooling around on Biscayne Bay, the boat was fine, but for a longer trip, living aboard? Not a chance.

"Hey, Ramon, do you know of a cruiser I could rent for a week or so? I want to go to the islands to do some fishing."

Ramon gazed past the chain-link fence at the dry storage shed across the weedy road, then studied the motley collection of boats tied up at the wooden docks. A rotting houseboat lay on its side under the mangroves. "Maybe. I know a guy has a real nice Silverton." Ramon flipped the hose back against the building and turned off the water. "Thirty-two-foot, twin engines, insurance, gas . . . You probably get it for three thousand." He dried his hands on a towel.

"For one *week*?"

"Includes the captain."

"What do I need a captain for? I can operate a boat."

"You kidding?" Ramon laughed. "You gotta have a captain. Nobody give you his boat for a week if he ain't on it, man. Why don't you fish around here? Don't pay nothing. That's what I do."

"No, I want the Bahamas. This is special."

With a shrug Ramon hopped on the forklift, cranked the engine, and drove it across the road, the boat still dripping water.

Dan turned around to see Kelly sipping beer from a paper cup. He took the one she offered him, but didn't feel like drinking. She was smiling, squinting into the sun. "So. A trip to the Bahamas."

He hesitated, then said, "Well, this is for my son. I promised to take him fishing."

"Oh, I get it. Doing the guy thing." Kelly bumped him with a hipbone. She had put her jeans back on. Her bare shoulders had turned pink. "Let's walk down to that end of the dock. Somebody just told me that a manatee comes over there sometimes."

Dan looked at his watch. "It's almost two-thirty. I want to go by my office this afternoon."

"It's not that late," Kelly said. "You can spend five minutes. We're here already."

Through the forest of aluminum sailboat masts Dan could see the skyline of Miami glittering a mile across the bay. His office was just north of downtown, not in one of the high-rent glass towers, but in a relic from the thirties on Biscayne Boulevard. Kelly was strolling along the dock already, her rubber thongs slapping the wooden planks. She gazed into the brownish water and sipped her beer. Her hair hung in tangles past the thin strap of her bikini top.

With another glance at his watch, Dan followed.

Kelly kicked off her thongs and sat down. Leaning back on her arms, she tossed her head to get her hair off her face. The first time they'd gone out, she told him that her family came from old money. She had the look: delicate bone structure, big green eyes, thin lips. The gold nose ring had been made from an heirloom locket. Dan had once found it erotic. Now he didn't know what he thought.

"I love the sunshine," Kelly said, swinging her feet. "Did you ever notice how musicians only come out at night? That's why we're pale. Not like you. You're so brown. Except for your butt. I did notice your butt is white." She laughed, then reached into her straw bag for her cigarettes.

Dan smoothed his hair and resettled his ball cap on his head. "Listen, I called my secretary this morning before we left. She said Rick Robbins wants me to call him. Do you have any idea what that's about? Anybody arrested lately for DUI? Possession of pot? Some major crime that requires my legal expertise?"

Between gigs and practice sessions, Kelly worked part-time for Dan's former brother-in-law, the owner of a music production company. They'd had a falling out during Dan's divorce, Rick taking his sister's side, but since then Rick had sent a few cases his way. It was unusual, however, that Rick would make the call himself. He would generally give the client Dan's phone number.

Kelly frowned, thinking about what Rick might want. "Martha Cruz. Bet you a dollar that's it."

"Who's Martha Cruz?"

"I told you. You weren't listening, were you?" She took a drag on her cigarette. "Martha plays keyboard in my band and sings backup. She was arrested on South Beach outside a club a few weeks ago. She hit a Miami Beach cop." Kelly tapped ashes into the water.

Dan laughed. "Was she drunk? Or just suicidal?"

"No, she was just, like, trying to tell the cop to leave this guy alone, that all he was doing was drinking a beer on the sidewalk or something. I wasn't there, but that's what she told me."

Dan had never met these people. Kelly had played him a tape, but she had said not to come to the rehearsals at the studio. The other musicians didn't like strangers around.

Kelly looked up, shading her eyes with one hand. "Martha has an attitude, you know? I'm almost sorry I let her in the band. What I think is, Rick lets her get away with it because Martha's boyfriend Miguel just spent like ten grand on promotion, so naturally Rick can't tell him to butt out, and she's taking advantage of the situation. Don't you hate people who do that? Martha and I are friends, but she's starting to be a pain."

Dan looked toward the skyline again. "Kelly, I've got to go."

"Why? You don't work for anybody. You can take the whole day if you want to." She suddenly sat straight up and pointed. "Shh! Look. There they are."

He stepped closer, saw a shifting under the surface. Manatees. A female and her calf, peaceful gray creatures with rounded horizontal tails and dangling flippers. Algae grew on the mother's broad back. This one had several nasty scars—boats hitting her before she could lumber out of the way. She raised her head for a breath, blowing air out of flared nostrils. She fixed her tiny, patient eyes on Dan for a moment before submerging again. The calf stayed close by. Latticed sunlight played on their bulky shapes as they glided away. The water was murky, and soon they were lost to view.

"Manatees are so adorable," Kelly said.

He wondered, standing in the blinding light of a Monday afternoon, what he was doing with this girl—besides getting laid. She had wandered into his law office about a month ago about a traffic ticket, and a half hour later he was asking her out. Why, for God's sake? Out of nowhere Dan felt a leap of anxiety in his gut, the same lurch as in the recurrent nightmare he'd had lately—walking into court for opening argument and he couldn't remember what the case was about. He poured the rest of his beer into the mangroves and flattened the paper cup.

Dan picked up his dive bag. "Sorry, Kelly, but really, I have to go."

The area of Miami around Biscayne Boulevard and Thirtieth Street, a few blocks south of the expressway leading over to Miami Beach, had once been prime business property. Some of the royal palms that had lined the boulevard were still standing, but most of them had made way for storefronts, gas stations, and cheap motels.

The law office where Dan rented space was a one-story building with a Spanish-style facade and Moorish columns across the front. A sign on the front wall read, LAW OFFICES OF CHARLES DUNAVOY. Below that had been added, DANIEL R. GALINDO, ESQ.—Criminal Law. Dan drove around back and went in through the rear door, after unlocking the security gate. Bars kept out the occasional crack addict wandering through.

He picked up his mail and messages from Alva Dunavoy's desk. She was married to Charlie. Dan waited to speak to her until she had finished typing a letter. In theory his rent included her services, but she had made it clear whose secretary she was—Charlie's—and anyone else could stand in line. Dan shuffled through the envelopes. Bills, pleadings, notices of hearings. He went through his messages. A bail bondsman notifying him that a client had skipped town. A court reporter wanting payment for a transcript. And the message to call Rick Robbins. Now there was a second message attached. URGENT.

Alva kept her half-rim glasses pointed toward a steno pad, and the ball of an old IBM Selectric clattered across the page. She had a puffy bleach-blond hairdo and dangly gold earrings that bounced with the staccato movement of her fingers. Her long nails clacked on the keys. A few decades ago, she had been a hot number, as they used to say. Charlie had showed him a 1962 edition of *Playboy*. Girls of Miami Beach, posed around a pool at the Castaways. There was Alva by the waterfall, her hair in a platinum-blond pageboy with bangs straight across her forehead. Big smile, nothing on but red high heels and a beach ball.

Dan spotted a *Miami Herald* in the trash can next to the copier table and retrieved the classified section. He turned back the page advertising boats for sale. *1971 25' Bertram Bahia Mar*, $39,000. Probably leaked. *1988 Sea Ray Express, 34'*, $47,500. Good price. Dan circled that one, wondering if a bank existed in Miami that would front him the down payment.

Hearing a low burble of Spanish, Dan walked over to slide back the frosted glass window a few inches.

Three people sat in the small waiting room—a middle-aged couple and a teenage boy.

Alva pulled the finished letter out of the typewriter. "Well. Mr. Punctuality."

"Hi. Where's Charlie?" Dan walked back to her desk.

"He's not here."

"I noticed."

She relented, smiling a little. "He's at a real estate closing. He'll be here soon."

"Who are those people in the waiting room? Not mine, are they?"

"No, they came in about ten minutes ago. They asked to speak to a lawyer, and I said Mr. Dunavoy was expected momentarily." She added, "You wouldn't be interested. They're walk-in's."

"Well, what do they want?"

"They bought a used car from a neighbor, but the title was bad, and the police came and towed it. Now the neighbor says he can't pay them back."

"Oh, great."

Alva dabbed some correction fluid at the letter she had just typed. "So do you want them?"

"Let Charlie do it. I have some paperwork to catch up on." He held up the messages from Rick Robbins. "Alva, did Rick say what he wanted to talk to me about?"

"No, he just said call."

"Didn't give you a hint?"

"Honey, if they don't tell me, I don't ask." She pulled a file from the bottom drawer of her desk and stiffly straightened her back. Her radio was on at low volume. Frank Sinatra finished singing "My Way." Then an ad came on for pre-need arrangements from Levitt-Weinstein Memorial Gardens.

Dan said, "Why do you assume that I never want to see walk-in's?"

She glanced at him as she cranked an envelope into the typewriter. "Because you told me, 'Alva, I don't want to see any walk-in's, unless they just got run over by a drunken doctor in a heavily insured Cadillac.' "

"I didn't say that."

She shrugged.

Dan looked at the waiting room door, then went over and opened it. "Hi. I'm Dan Galindo. You folks want to come in?"

It was exactly what he had expected: The case wasn't worth the time a lawyer would need to put into it.

The teenager translated for his parents. The father drove a truck; the mother was a maid in a Miami Beach hotel. They had saved for months to buy a car, then the police said it belonged to someone else. How could this happen? Dan told them all they could do was file a claim against the neighbor who had sold it to them. No, don't hire a lawyer, it would cost more than the car was worth. They could file the case themselves in small-claims court, get a judgment, put a lien on the neighbor's property. Dan went through the steps with them. The statement of claim, the summons, what to take to the clerk's office. He gave them directions to the courthouse. *Next time see me first.* The father wanted to know how much he owed for the consultation. Dan almost told him *nada*, no charge, but saw the pride in the man's face.

After they were gone, he counted out the bills on Alva's desk. She looked up at him. "Thirty bucks?"

"Just put it on my rent account, okay?"

She pursed her lips, lines appearing in her coral pink lipstick, which extended past the natural line of her mouth.

The back door slammed. A few seconds later, Charlie Dunavoy came in, suit coat over his arm, briefcase in his hand. He was a big white-haired man with a red face and broken veins in his cheeks.

Dan said, "Charlie, got a minute?"

"Yeah, sure." He picked up his messages from his wife's desk and rattled off some instructions to call one of the probate judges about resetting a hearing. In his office, he tossed his briefcase onto a brown vinyl sofa.

Dan came in behind him. "Charlie, if I were gone for a week, would you be able to cover my schedule?"

"Yeah, I guess I could do that." Charlie hung his jacket on a wooden hanger behind the door. His stomach strained at the buttons of his shirt, and suspenders held up a pair of trousers going baggy in the seat. He asked, "What've you got? No trials, I hope."

"Routine stuff," Dan said. "No trials. There might be a motion or two. Most of it can be reset. I want to take my son fishing in the Bahamas."

"Oh, now, isn't that a lucky kid?" Charlie leaned back in his chair.

"Say, do you still have that Sea Ray twin outboard? You told me you went down to the Keys in it, remember?"

"Oh, I sold that sucker. Engines were shot anyway. Must've been, jeez, five or six years ago. I bought a little flats boat that I keep down there at the condo."

Before Charlie could tell him about bonefishing off Islamorada, Dan shook loose and went back to his own office.

Two years ago he had been making over seventy grand a year as a federal prosecutor, living with his wife and son in a new house in a good neighborhood—before he resigned. The career went, then the marriage, then his concentration. In a city saturated with lawyers he went from job to job, scrabbling not to fall behind on alimony and child support. He worked part-time, a degrading experience. Then a friend, Elaine McHale, gave him the name of a lawyer her family had known for years, a man in his sixties who needed someone younger to help out, preferably someone with trial experience.

Charlie Dunavoy had never asked Dan why he'd left the U.S. attorney's office. Elaine had probably filled him in. The answer was, Dan had blown a major prosecution against an Ecuadorian drug trafficker by refusing to use the DEA's confidential informant. The guy was dirty. True, many of them were. After all, what upstanding citizen would be involved with dopers? But Dan had good reason to believe the guy was flat-out lying. Dan went to the judge. *No way can I put this witness on the stand, Your Honor.* The defense team was jubilant. The lead DEA agent on the case smelled a payoff, as if Daniel Galindo would ruin his reputation for a murdering slimewad thug. No, Dan's real sin had been blabbing about it to the media, embarrassing the office. A week later he got the news: he would be handling slip-and-fall cases from V.A. hospitals or claims filed by postal customers run over by mail trucks. He would prosecute picnickers caught with a six-pack at Everglades National Park. Within an hour Dan's resignation letter was on the U.S. attorney's desk.

Coming into this office six months ago, walking out of the blazing August heat into that tiny waiting room, past a man in a gas station uniform and a woman with her hair in dreadlocks, coming in and seeing the rundown furniture and the dusty fan whirling on the filing cabinet, Dan had seriously wondered what Elaine McHale thought of her former colleague, that she would send him to such a place. Or what he had thought of himself, that he had taken Charlie's offer. But he had survived. He was paying his bills.

The ten-gallon salt water tank under the window was humming, bubbles coming out of the aerator. Dan kept blue and yellow rock beauties, which he had caught off West Palm Beach. He gave them a few pinches of food.

Putting the box back on the shelf, he noticed the photograph of Josh—his first-grade picture, a dopey smile, his new front teeth making him look like a rabbit, glasses halfway down his nose. Dan touched the photograph, sliding his fingers across the silver frame.

"Hey, bud. We're going fishing. You and me."

CHAPTER 4

That afternoon Dan drove to Coral Rock Productions, finding his way through tourist-season traffic to the flat-roofed building in Hallandale, just over the county line. He hadn't seen the place in months. The small lobby had a new collection of music posters on the walls and a different set of tunes on the receptionist's radio, but otherwise it looked the same.

The receptionist told him to go on back, Rick was expecting him. Dan remembered the way to Rick's office, a windowless cave at the end of the hall.

They had met in college, then gone in separate directions, Dan to law school, Rick into the music business. He had become successful at it, booking national tours into local venues, managing acts, and producing shows anywhere from gospel to acid rock. After Dan left the U.S. attorney's office, Rick had offered him a job as general counsel. *Entertainment law? Nothing to it.* What he had really wanted was somebody to be the hardass, to rein in musicians who trashed their hotel rooms or ignored their contracts. Dan had said no. The offer had smelled like charity. Last summer, when Dan had sunk about as far as possible financially, Rick started referring cases to him. A booking agent charged with DUI. A country singer caught with a pound of weed. Then a slip-and-fall, a burglary, a sexual battery. Dan didn't like it, but at the time he was in no position to refuse. As his practice improved, he accepted fewer of them. The last was a spike-haired punk rocker arrested for peeing into a mosh pit.

He found Rick on the telephone, leaning back in his chair. His hair was a little thinner, and a bald spot had worked its way through. He turned around when Dan rapped lightly on the open door. He held up a hand, don't go away.

"Yeah, I told them we'd fax an offer. . . . Twenty for her. At least, which is a deal. She's gettin' anywhere from twenty to thirty. Like she wants thirty for L.A., plus a limo ride, *plus* a suite . . . The venue's a theater, should be okay."

Dan mimed drinking a soda, and Rick nodded.

In the tiny kitchen, Dan was taking a Coke out of the refrigerator when his peripheral vision caught a Bonnie Raitt tour T-shirt and tight black jeans. He turned his head and looked down. Rick's wife.

Sandy Robbins smiled up at him, a petite woman with aggressively frosted hair. She handled publicity for Coral Rock. "Hey, Dan. How you been?"

"Great. How about yourself, Sandy?"

She pushed the door shut. "Rick said you were comin' up. What did he say to you, why he wanted to see you and all?" She had a voice straight out of the Georgia hills, more twang than drawl.

Dan shrugged. "Rick didn't say. You don't know either?"

"Shoot, he won't tell me a blessed thing. He says he wants to give you a case, but it's got to be more'n that. You and Rick ain't laid eyes on each other in a long time. So why's he calling you now?"

Dan popped the tab on the soda can. "What do you think it is, Sandy?"

"I honest and truly don't know. It's a feelin', like when we got in trouble on the payroll taxes. Lord, you know about that, I guess. What's the little bonehead done now?" She tapped her long fingernails on her crossed arms. "I think Rick's into some shit he don't want me to know about. He don't give me straight answers about the money. He's playing cute with the books. I'm scared the IRS is gonna knock on the door and take everthang we own. You gotta make him tell you what's goin' on, Dan."

He put a hand on her shoulder. "Sandy. I don't do tax law. Nor do I intend to get involved with Rick's business. The man makes me crazy. If you have the slightest inkling that Rick is dicking around with the IRS, call somebody who can help you. I could give you some names."

Sandy's temper flared, and she slapped his hand

away. "Go on. Turn your back. I know y'all had a fallin' out, but I'll tell you one thing, mister. He helped you plenty when you didn't have a pot to piss in or a window to throw it out of."

"Fine. Jesus." Dan left the can beside the sink and went to see if Rick was finished. He could hear Sandy's boots behind him.

Rick was on another call, phone under his chin, reading from a computer printout. "Tampa on the fourth, travel day on the fifth, Athens on the sixth, and Atlanta on the seventh and eighth. . . . Well, they're only playing one date in the north, St. Paul on the fifteenth. . . . You're gonna be in touch with the record label, right? Call Sandy, she can give you more information than I can. . . . Nothing on the tenth, that's a Monday. . . . The Civic Auditorium, that's what I've been told." He noticed Dan, who had come in and dropped into a chair. "Listen, I've got to run. Call me later in the week, all right?"

Sandy had come in as well, standing about five-two in her red leather cowboy boots, glaring at her husband.

He took a tweed sport jacket off a hook. "Hi, sugar. Dan and I are gonna grab a bite. Then I'm going to the studio. The band is putting a couple of songs on tape tonight."

"I'm not invited to dinner?" Her smile was brittle.

"No, you're not."

"I'll follow you in my car, Rick. I swear. Whatever's going on, I'm not gonna be cut out."

"Out of what? I'm talking to him about Martha's assault and battery. I told you."

"You lie to me, I'll by God make you wish you hadn't."

"Come on, Dan, let's go. I wish my lovely wife would stick to her own job, and let me do mine."

"Rick would sooner run us into bankruptcy than admit he don't know his pecker from a tire pump."

"Yes, dear. Bankruptcy is exactly what I have in mind." Rick zipped his cellular phone into its leather pouch. "Sandy got her MBA from Yee-Haw State, did you know that, Dan?"

Dan said, "For the love of God, will you two shut up?"

Rick left black marks coming out of the parking lot, then headed his lemon yellow Mustang north on U.S. 1 past strip shopping centers, a car dealership, mom-and-pop motels flying the Canadian flag. *Nous parlons français.* The sun was dropping behind the trees.

"She's a piece of work. Tell me why I stay with her, I can't fuckin' figure it out."

Neither could Dan. He had seen battles in the halls of Coral Rock Productions. Screaming. Throwing things. Pushing and shoving. But it hadn't taken the heat out of their romance, apparently.

Dan grabbed the handle over the passenger window as Rick's car hurtled down the road. "So. Martha

Cruz. The keyboard player in Kelly's band. Arrested for battery on a Miami Beach cop."

"Yeah, a couple of weeks ago. I told her to go to South Beach to catch this rave band out of New York, and she winds up sitting in on the last set. After that, outside the club, some fan gets hassled and Martha opens her mouth. The cop pulls an attitude, tells her to butt out, yadda yadda, you heard it before. Arrests her for interfering, battery on a police officer, assault, whatever he can get her on, just to be a prick." Steering one-handed, Rick opened a roll of Tums with his teeth. "What I want is, get this cleared up for her. The band doesn't need this shit. The record labels don't like it. An arrest, a trial—it's bad news, Dan."

"I can't make it go away."

"Maybe some kind of probation. If it would help, tell Martha to apologize to the officer—although with Martha that would be a stretch." Chewing on his antacid, Rick said, "But she's smart. She'll do what she has to. All she cares about is her career."

"Is she any good?"

"Oh, yeah. Martha's so good it's scary. Don't get me wrong. So is Kelly. Kelly's a terrific guitarist, and the bassist and drummer aren't half bad either. But Martha's the musician in the bunch. She's the engine. I don't say that to the others, of course." Rick lifted the console and pawed through a disorderly pile of tapes and CD's. "I don't have anything current. Wait. This is Martha before she joined Mayhem. She was in this group called Two-Tailed Lizard." He slid the tape into the tape deck. "Yeah, the name sucks. Before that it was Electric Iguana. And overlook the sound quality. It was mixed in somebody's bedroom."

A bass drum thudded out of the speakers, followed by the crash of guitar chords. "All right, the keyboard's coming in. A step beyond techno, hear it? That's Martha. Okay, the guy's gonna sing, ignore that part. Wait. Here it comes."

Dan heard a wail, a scream. A female voice coming from a place he couldn't imagine. The words were impossible to make out. He finally said, "That's . . . pretty bad, Rick." He hid a grin under a knuckle, elbow on the windowsill.

Rick flipped the power off, leaving only road noise and the growl of the Mustang's big engine. He turned his sunglasses toward Dan. "You know your problem? You're still stuck in that eighties New Wave crap. Duran Duran. The Cars. I bet you knew all the words to 'Candy-O.' "

"No way. I listened to Bad Company and Zeppelin."

"Did you or did you not have a poster of Flock of Seagulls in your dorm room?"

"Yeah, for the girls," Dan said.

"Oh, man, you too?" Rick laughed. "I had the Police. I'd take that down and put up David Lee Roth for the metal chicks." He put on his right blinker signal. "The Lobster Shack is over here. You feel like seafood?"

Brake lights ahead of them went on. A Lincoln sedan with a Quebec tag began a slow turn into the parking lot. Rick said, "Come *on*, puddin'!" He swerved around the car. "Another fuckin' Canadian. Jesus, I'll be glad when it stops snowing up there."

A fifty-gallon salt water tank was built into an inside wall of the restaurant. Through the tank Dan could see another section of dining room, distorted by the glass. Fish swam in and out among fake sea grass planted in neon orange rocks. A clam shell opened and shut, releasing bubbles. A miniature shipwreck had spilled gold plastic coins and strings of pearls. The fish were the usual fish-tank variety: angels, a clownfish, a butterfly.

The waitress brought two beers.

Rick put on his glasses to read the menu. "You been okay?"

"Sure."

"I should have called, you know, kept in touch. The business has been nuts. I turn around, it's next month." Rick took a swallow of beer. "You're doing okay, though."

"No problems." Dan lifted his mug. "What about you? I noticed a new BMW in Sandy's spot in the parking lot."

"Oh, jeez. If I've got it, she spends it. Women are that way. Don't tell her I told you, but she also got her boobs lifted."

"Really?"

"I told her she didn't need to. She's forty-two, you believe that? Six years older than me, still hot."

Dan drank some beer. "My birthday's coming up. The big three-five. I'm halfway there, Rick."

Rick looked over the top of his menu. "Halfway to what? Croaking?"

"It has to make you think. You ask, what have I accomplished that's worth a damn? You wonder if you should run wild or get serious, or if it makes a difference either way. You didn't think about that?"

"No, I was busy that week." Rick turned a page. "They do a good blackened tuna."

"I don't like tuna. What I thought of is, I'd take Josh fishing in the Bahamas. Cat Cay, Eleuthera. Sleep on the boat, swim naked, walk on the beach. We'd do the father-son thing. I'd get back in touch with what's important, you know? I'm not sure Lisa's going to go for it, though."

"Sounds great. That's what I need, a vacation. You want a deck hand, call me."

Dan turned around to see the list of specials on a chalkboard. "They've got mangrove snapper, ten-ninety-five."

"Try it. Get whatever you want, it's on me." Rick gave the menus to the waitress, told her what they wanted, and put his glasses back into his breast pocket. "You know, Dan, I think she's still got feelings for you. Seriously."

"Who?"

"My sister, who do you think?"

"What does that mean, she wants me back?"

"It doesn't mean anything," Rick said. "But since

you ask, yeah, I think she'd take you back, if you play it right."

"Jesus. A year ago you paid for her divorce lawyer. I was lucky to come out with my balls intact."

"I was upset with the situation at the time. You didn't make it easy."

Dan turned his beer mug in the wet ring on the paper place mat—a map of the Caribbean. "Has Lisa said anything to you?"

"Not directly, but they don't always say what they mean."

"I wouldn't go back," Dan said. "Too much has changed."

Rick said, "Hey. Learn from the past, right? Look at Sandy and me. We fight. We yell. We're still together. And you can't get along with Lisa, a genuinely classy woman, a great mother to Josh? What are you doing, hanging out with Kelly Dorff? She's a cute chick, but come on."

"You didn't bring me here to talk about that, did you?"

"No. I'm sorry what happened, that's all I'm saying."

The waitress came with a basket of hush puppies and two salads. Rick's cellular phone rang. He turned it off.

Dan said, "Tell me about Martha Cruz. If she was arrested two weeks ago, she's got a court date coming up soon. She hasn't talked to a lawyer?"

"I said I'd find her one. Okay, I dicked around, I was busy. Then I thought of you over the weekend."

"Thanks a bunch. What if I say no?"

"Don't do that, man."

"Battery on a police officer. Tell her to plead no contest. They'll give her probation."

"What if they don't? I can't screw around with this."

"It's no big deal, believe me. It's one of those petty cases filed to show who's in charge. Tell her to kiss the cop's butt, she'll be fine."

"No. No, listen. I promised Martha's boyfriend I'd find her a good lawyer. I called him yesterday, said let me get Dan Galindo, my brother-in-law. Formerly a federal prosecutor, very tough, very smart, now a top criminal defense attorney in Miami—"

Dan laughed.

"Okay, I might have exaggerated somewhat, but do I need to hire Roy Black for this? As if I could afford him."

"Martha's boyfriend," Dan repeated. He recalled what Kelly Dorff had told him this morning. "Miguel something. He's bankrolling the band."

"More or less. His money, my brains." Leaning on one forearm, Rick dug into his salad. "Miguel Salazar. Miguel wants Martha to go places, but what he has in mind for her is crossover pop, like Gloria Estefan. That's so far off. Right now, though, I've got to keep Miguel happy, so help me out, will you?"

"Rick, what's going on? Are you in trouble with the IRS again?"

"What are you asking me that for?"

"Sandy talked to me."

"Oh, Jesus. That chick is so paranoid. No, I am not in trouble with the IRS. I'm a little late, but when I get a few items squared away, we'll be in good shape."

"I don't want to hear about it."

"You brought it up," Rick said.

Dan asked, "Who exactly is Miguel Salazar—in addition to being Martha Cruz's sugar daddy?"

Rick speared a cucumber slice. "Who is he? You mean, like, what does he do? He's from Ecuador. He runs an import-export business in Miami, mainly exporting CD's and videos to South America, importing clothing, flowers, coffee. It's very diversified."

Dan looked steadily across the table until Rick glanced up at him. "Is Miguel Salazar into importing anything else?"

"What do you mean?"

"Don't play stupid, Rick."

"No. Jesus, would I get involved with a trafficker?" He glanced around as if someone might have heard him, then said, "Miguel's a successful businessman, that's all. Lisa's met him. He lives in Lakewood Village. His kid or something plays on Josh's soccer team, in fact. If you'd stayed, you'd be neighbors, practically. Miguel's into music because he likes the life— hanging out with the artists, being able to say, yeah, I know Madonna, I know Willy Chirino, I met Trent Reznor. He thinks he's a producer, but he has no ear and no sense of the market."

"How'd you get to know him?"

"Through Martha. She joined Kelly's band about a

year ago, and Salazar knows the drummer. I think Miguel and Martha met that way and sort of fell in with each other. Then Martha told me that Miguel wanted to help out, and I said okay—a very stupid move. Then one thing and another, blah, blah, he lent me some money for the office. Maybe—if you are feeling generous with your time—you could assist me in getting Miguel off my back, when I find the money to do it."

"Does Sandy know about this?"

"God, no, and I'd appreciate it if you didn't enlighten her. Soon as I get the band signed, I can pay Miguel."

"Signed? Just like that?" Dan laughed a little, stopping when Rick looked at him darkly.

Signing a deal with a major record company was so rare as to be statistically impossible. Rick had never even come close. He had signed a couple of bands to local labels. He had put money into one that showed promise, but as soon as they got a whiff of success, they blew him off and hired a manager from L.A.— and then fell apart before Rick could get a lawsuit going. He was known in the entertainment industry in South Florida, but that didn't mean jack to New York, Nashville, or Los Angeles. Except for Latin music, Miami didn't exist.

"Let me ask—not that I want to pursue this—how much did Salazar lend you?"

For a while Rick considered the question. He sucked a tooth and stared vacantly across the restaurant. "About a hundred grand." When Dan let out a breath of astonishment, Rick said, "If we get the deal—if this works out—they could be big, Dan. Very big. Music video. Feature stories in *Billboard* and *Rolling Stone*. An opening slot for the next Stone Temple Pilots tour, if STP is still around next year. Or think of this—opening for U2. It could happen."

Dan stared across the table. As a manager, Rick made fifteen to twenty percent of everything his artists earned. If a band took off, broke the charts, went platinum, and generally survived past the usual life expectancy for new bands, a year or so—Rick could make millions. But that never happened. More likely, if Rick got them a deal at all, it would be for a $25,000 advance. The recording budget might be $125,000, but the label would take it off the top before the band saw a nickel. Their one and only CD would eventually wind up in the cut-out bins at Wal-Mart.

"Jesus, Rick. What are you doing?"

Rick reached across the table to grab Dan's arm. "I flew to New York last month and talked to a guy at Capitol Records, Joel Friedman. He does A-and-R. That's artists-and-repertoire to you. A talent scout, okay? As a breed, they are the most cynical, bitter, and manipulative SOBs you'll ever meet. But Friedman owes me a favor. He was here a few months ago, he likes to bet sports, so I set him up with the right people, and he lucked out. He's grateful. So I go to New York. I play him a tape of the band—a live performance, mind you, not even studio quality. I watch his hands. You can always tell. The way he's tapping the rhythm on the chair, I knew I had him. But Friedman is a very cool guy. He says he's coming down on vacation, and he'll try to catch the concert if he likes the demo tape. The band is playing at the Abyss. Not as the headliner—that's Bone Dog—but Mayhem will be opening. They're going to make it." Rick closed his eyes and dropped his forehead on his hand. "Please, Jesus, just let them make it." He moved back, blinking, when the waitress put their dinners on the table.

Dan said, "Kelly played a Mayhem tape for me. Rick, I don't want to pop your bubble, but are you sure they have the talent for this?"

"Listen to me, you know so much." Rick pointed his fork at him. "Where is it written that success has anything to do with talent? When Smashing Pumpkins found their bass player, she was still taking bass lessons, okay? All the talent in the world won't get you there if the timing's wrong, or if the record company doesn't click with what you're doing. That's my job. Selling the band to a company who will turn around and market the band to the public. Success is whether anybody buys your stuff. Period. And it's tough. There's a gazillion singers and musicians, all wanting to be stars and make the money, and most of them have talent. Can I guarantee that Mayhem is going to make it? Of course not. But I have an ear. I can tell when something is possible or not. I listen to Mayhem and they shimmer, like pure gold."

As he spoke, Rick's voice grew raspy. "All my life, fifteen years in this business, I've never been this close. I might never be again. I've got to get Martha's case taken care of, and I don't want to hear any of your bullshit about oh, isn't this just so petty, battery on a police officer. You're coming up on thirty-five, and you're cryin'. Well, excuse me for not sharing your pain. You skated through college and law school. You had a beautiful wife and kid and a home. Then you fucked up at the U.S. attorney's office—not because you weren't good enough, but because you thought you were too good for what was required to get along. You want to help me with this, fine. If not, screw you."

Dan felt a wave of heat flooding through his body. He wanted to walk out of there. He wanted to punch Rick in the mouth. Or come back with a remark to shut him up. But there wasn't one. There was too much truth in what he'd said.

Taking a couple of slow breaths, Dan stared at the tropical fish weaving in and out among the plastic sea grass. "I didn't say the case was petty."

"You implied."

"You know what?" Dan looked straight at Rick. "It is petty. It's stupid. Tangling with a cop—a Miami Beach cop, no less. She's lucky he didn't break her arms."

"How much do you want for this?"

"Who's paying? Her rich boyfriend?"

"No. I told Miguel I'd take care of it. Call it good P.R."

"For you?" Dan looked at Rick. "A thousand for a plea, five if it goes to trial."

"What the hell? You said it was no big deal."

"It is after I had to pay twenty grand to a divorce lawyer."

Rick glowered into his beer mug. "All right. I told her already you'd do it."

"Then do this for me. I'm going to talk to Lisa about taking Josh fishing. If she says no, I'll call you. You have more influence with her than I do."

Spreading his palms, Rick shrugged. "I'll see what I can do."

"Thanks."

Rick waved the waitress over. "You have key lime pie tonight? Good. We'll each have a slice after dinner. And give the check to my friend here, I don't have my wallet with me."

CHAPTER 5

Josh had a soccer game the next night at the field behind the elementary school. Dan called Lisa to say he would come by to pick up Josh and take him to the game.

The curving, landscaped road through Lakewood Village led past four or five other gated residential areas before Heron Hills. There were no hills, only long green mounds of earth planted with shade trees and serving as barriers between traffic and houses. All this had been wetlands ten years ago, with nothing on it but sawgrass and alligators.

At the gate Dan automatically showed his driver's license to the security guard, who glanced at it, then ran his finger down a list of names on a clipboard. "Galindo . . . Galindo. Here it is. Six-thirty." He checked his watch. "It's six-oh-five."

"And?"

"We're not supposed to admit you till within fifteen minutes of the time stated."

"Are you serious? Come on, you know me."

The level brim of the guard's Boy Scout leader hat shaded his face from the setting sun. "We've been told to tighten up on procedures, sir."

"What am I going to do, run to your boss?" A horn tooted. Dan glanced in the rearview mirror. There were two cars behind him.

The security guard's mouth tightened. He turned to his computer, which was bolted to a rolling cart. An extension cord ran through the door. He tapped the keyboard and a piece of tractor-feed paper rolled out of the printer.

"Now what?"

The guard handed it through the window. "This is your entrance pass. Please stay on the main road. Your exit code appears in the lower corner. Punch it in when you leave to raise the exit gate. Enjoy your visit."

The house Dan used to live in was a warm beige color, like the others on the street. A short concrete walkway, bordered with pink and red flowers, led to a white door flanked by a glass panel through which he could see an artificial topiary tree and the fringe on a Persian rug. The dog that Lisa had bought after Dan moved out, a cocker spaniel, watched him through the glass. Dan rang the bell, then stood with his hands in his pockets. Ex-husband waiting on the porch.

The door opened. Lisa put a hand on her hip. "What a surprise."

"I said I'd be here."

"You say a lot of things." The cool gaze lasted a second or two, then Lisa sighed and stepped back into the foyer. "Come on in, Dan. Would you like something to drink?"

"Thanks. Where's Josh?"

"Putting on his uniform. He'll be out in a minute."

She strode through the living room, then around the corner to the kitchen, the dog right behind her, its nails clicking on the tiled floor, tags jingling. Dan had forgotten its name. He thought it was a male. The pooch had set her back $500.

Lisa had the confident walk of a woman who took care of herself—tanned from tennis, slim from lunches of salad and mineral water with her friends at the real estate office where she had her license. She was pretty at thirty-two—more than pretty, even in jeans and a Lakewood Tornadoes team sweatshirt. Her pale blond hair, trimmed precisely at shoulder level, glimmered when she moved. Dan had stared at her the night Rick introduced his sister at a rock concert, this blue-eyed college girl from Florida State. *This is Lisa. Did I tell you she was gorgeous, or what? Lisa, this is Dan. He just got his acceptance to law school.*

Lisa opened the refrigerator. "I have iced tea, soda . . . wine?"

"Iced tea, thanks."

She fixed him a glass and set it on the counter, then

pivoted toward the dishwasher, her hair swinging. Rinsing plates and pots from dinner, she told him about the neighbors across the street. They were moving back to Ohio. Bob got a promotion. Meredith was just sick about it, because they hadn't been getting along, the counselor wasn't helping a bit, and the kids had so many friends in Lakewood.

Dan felt awkward sitting in this kitchen, watching Lisa tidy up, listening to stories about people he never saw anymore. Their old life hung like wisps of cobweb in the high ceilings, visible but out of reach.

"Lisa?" When she looked around, he said, "I came a little early because I wanted to talk to you about taking Josh fishing in the Bahamas with me for a week. This would be a real adventure for him. For both of us. Cat Cay is a paradise for divers."

She had a handful of silverware. "You want to take him diving? Joshua doesn't dive. He's only seven years old."

"Sure, he's small for scuba tanks, but he could handle a snorkel. The reef fish are so pretty over there. I'd get him a small speargun and we could hunt hogfish. They beg to be speared. Good eating too. I know a lagoon, not deep, that would be perfect for Josh. We'd go over on a boat and live right there at the marina, or moor wherever we wanted."

"What boat? Not your Mako."

"No, I'd borrow something with a cabin. Or rent one. I don't know yet."

She aimed the silverware into the dishwasher basket. "What about school?"

"He's in first grade, how important is it?"

"Dan!"

"Okay, we could go during spring break." Dan suddenly laughed. "The craziest thing happened yesterday. I was free-diving off Triumph Reef, sixty feet down, trying to do a minute and a half like I used to. Lisa, I nearly didn't make it back up. It was scary as hell, coming that close. A lot went through my mind. I thought about Josh."

She poured soap into the dispenser. "So that's where this sudden streak of parental involvement came from."

"Don't say that. I've been involved."

"Involved is not a phone call, Dan. Involved is coming when you say you will. Spending time with him."

"Am I not here? I believe this is his father sitting here, isn't it?"

Her eyes went past him at the same moment Dan heard the clatter of soccer cleats on the floor. Josh sped around the corner and into the kitchen. "Dad!"

The cocker spaniel leaped up off the rug beside the back door and ran in circles, barking.

"Hey, bud." Dan swung Josh up and kissed him, then held him on his arm. "How's my boy?"

"I have a game tonight!"

"That's why I'm here. You gonna be on the starting lineup?"

"Probably not, but you know what happened last time?"

"What?" Dan straightened Josh's glasses on his nose.

"I got an assist for a goal. I set it up and we scored. It was stupendous."

"Wow. I'm sorry I had to miss it."

"It's okay. We lost that game."

"Oh, well," Dan said.

"Oh, well." Josh repeated Dan's shrug. His uniform was a little too big. His white shorts were baggy and his red socks were turned down over heavy shin pads.

Dan ruffled Josh's hair. "Guess what? We're going on a fishing trip."

"Really? Where?"

"To the Bahamas."

"Way, way cool!" He bounced up and down on Dan's arm.

"If it's okay with your mom," Dan said.

"Mom! Say yes!"

Lisa shot Dan a look across the kitchen. Then she smiled at Josh. "What fun. But Daddy isn't sure yet. We'll talk about it."

At the soccer field the sun had set, leaving stripes of purple and orange in the west. Parents stood along the sides or sat on the small set of bleachers. The other team gathered across the field. Josh and his teammates huddled near the coach for a pre-game pep talk.

Lisa arrived a moment later, carrying a folding chair.

Dan caught up to her. "Lisa, you know I wouldn't take Josh on a trip without your approval."

She kept walking. "Are you taking your little friend along?"

"What friend?"

"The one with the nose ring. Rick told me about her."

"No. This trip is for Josh and me."

She arched her brows. "Well, don't assume he's going."

"I'd like to take my son fishing, Lisa. A normal request for a father to make."

Putting down her lawn chair, she said, "It's so easy, isn't it? You make promises to him—which you may or may not follow through on. But if I don't say he can go, I'm the meanie."

"Fine. I'll tell Josh I have to find a bigger boat first. That should give you some time to think about it."

She sighed. "Dan. You are so screwed up." She picked up the chair and went to sit with her friends.

After a moment he zipped his jacket and wandered off. The evening was chilly, in the mid-fifties. He watched the game for a while and talked to some of the other men, fathers of kids on the team. He knew a few of them. Two were talking about investing in emerging growth funds. He got into a conversation with another about the Miami Heat, heading for the basement this year. When Lakewood drove the ball into the net, everyone cheered. Dan scanned the field for Josh, then found him among the kids still on the bench. They were giving each other high-fives. Josh turned around and Dan made a thumbs-up.

At halftime Dan paid a dollar for a cup of soda, then walked over to talk to Lisa. The other women in the group looked at him out of the corners of their eyes. They knew who he was. He sat on his heels beside Lisa's chair. "I had dinner with Rick yesterday. He wants me to take a case for him, a girl in a band he's managing. Her boyfriend lives out here, and Rick says you know the guy. Miguel Salazar."

Lisa crossed her legs and slowly bounced one sneakered foot. "I've met him. His niece plays soccer with Josh."

"Right. That's what Rick said. What do you know about him?"

"Well, he bought a house recently in the Estates section, an incredible piece of property. He has a business in Miami, something with videos and CD's. I think he's starting a chain of music stores in South America."

"He's . . . legitimate? As far as you know?"

"Of course he is. Stop being so suspicious of people. He's a widower. His son is in boarding school. His sister and her family live with him, and I believe a few other relatives. He comes to parent-teacher meetings at the school. He plays tennis at the club. If he's here tonight, I'll point him out. He likes to watch Anita play." She leaned a little closer. "I've met Martha Cruz. What was she arrested for?"

"She hit a cop." Dan shrugged.

"Really."

"Keep it to yourself, though. Where did you meet her?"

"At Miguel Salazar's house on Sunday. Joshua went to a birthday party for Anita." Lisa pointed. "There, the one with the red ribbon on her ponytail. Miguel's niece."

The teams lined up for the kickoff, and all the parents moved closer to the sidelines. Standing beside Lisa, Dan asked, "Is Martha Cruz living with Salazar too?"

Lisa crossed her arms to keep warm. "I don't know. I'm not even sure what's going on between them. He introduced her as the daughter of a friend of his. She doesn't seem his type. I hardly got a word out of her at the party. She reminds me of a cat—very quiet, just sits around watching what's going on. I guess she's pretty—if you can overlook the tattoos."

She had her eyes on the soccer field, where the coach had called a time-out. "Look, Joshua's going in." She cupped her hands and yelled, "Go, Joshua! Tornadoes, yaaay!"

Dan whistled through his teeth. Josh looked back and waved. He ran downfield, his hair flopping on his forehead. He kicked the ball a couple of times. The kids thundered by, a jostling herd of red and blue. The other team tied the score, and a subdued groan rose up from the parents on the Tornado side, then polite applause for a good play.

Lisa touched Dan's arm. "There's Miguel. Do you want me to introduce you?"

He hesitated. A dark-haired man about forty stood a little off to one side watching the game. Dan had an appointment to meet Martha Cruz at Rick's office tomorrow, but Rick hadn't said whether Salazar would be present.

"All right. Don't mention Martha's case. This is supposed to be confidential."

Lisa ambled over to speak to him, and Dan followed. "Miguel, hi!"

Miguel Salazar looked around, then held out his hands. "Lisa!" He pulled her closer and gave her a quick Latin kiss on the cheek. "I missed the first half. What's the score?"

"It's tied, three all. The Tornadoes are kickin' up a storm tonight." She had her Miss America smile on. "Dan, this is Miguel Salazar. His niece plays on Josh's team. Miguel, this is Josh's father, Dan Galindo."

"Of course." Salazar's eyebrows arched. "The lawyer from Miami."

"That's right." Dan shook his hand—the man had skin as soft as a woman's and a surprisingly strong grip. One strand of Salazar's hair had come out of his short ponytail and curled down his temple. Indian blood showed in the high cheekbones and dark, slightly pock-marked skin. Not a handsome face, but with the full lips, good build, and monogrammed white cashmere sweater, the whole package was pretty compelling.

"I understand you live in Lakewood, Miguel."

"Yes, Lisa's brother—you know Rick—he recommended it to me. A beautiful place. I lived in Miami before, so much noise! And traffic!"

Lisa said, "Miguel was born in Potopaxi, a small town in the mountains in Ecuador. Elevation four thousand, two hundred meters."

He laughed. "You remember!" Lisa beamed when he put a hand on her shoulder. Gold flashed on his wrist—a heavy link bracelet.

Dan felt a stirring of jealousy, a reaction that occurred too fast for him to slam the door on it. Habit, he thought. Lisa had been his wife for nine years.

The upward-tilting eyes turned back in his direction. "My friend Rick says to me, Miguel, I have a good lawyer for you, to help Martha." Salazar said to Lisa, "You remember Martha? A Miami Beach policeman pushed her out of the way after a concert, and she pushed him back. I said, oh, my God, Martica, you have to show respect to the police! Maybe Dan told you about this? Yes? That's all right."

Lisa said, "Dan is an excellent lawyer."

"I hope so." Salazar smiled at both of them. "Please, come to my house after the game. Martha will be there. Have a drink with us. And bring Josh, of course. Anita loves to have her friends visit."

"Tonight?" Lisa seemed a little surprised.

"Yes, why not?"

"Well—" She glanced sideways at Dan.

Dan said, "You can take Josh home if it's too late for him. I'll go. I'd like to meet my client." He gave her a subtle look that used to mean only one thing between them: *Stay out of this.*

Lisa smiled at him, then turned to Salazar. "We'd love to come—but only one drink. It's a school night."

"Marvelous." Again the eyes were on Dan. "I think we will have a lot to talk about."

Across the soccer field, in an unmarked van parked along the street, Vincent Hooper asked Carlos Herrera if he had gotten a shot of Salazar shaking hands with Galindo.

"I have it," Carlos said. He was still looking through the telephoto. The camera clicked and whirred through half a dozen more frames. "I didn't know Galindo and Salazar were friends."

Vincent trained his binoculars on the three figures. "This could be a problem, Carlos."

CHAPTER 6

Lisa had taken Dan aside and said it was just too weird for them to go in the same car. Josh would only be confused. Her minivan followed Salazar's black Lexus, and Dan came last with Josh.

At the gated entrance to Lakewood Estates, Salazar's window slid down, then the guard waved all three cars through. Dan had never been in this area. The road curved past the golf course and around lakes, silver in the moonlight. Sprinklers fanned out on the greens like vaporous ghosts. After a mile or so, Salazar's blinker came on, a right turn onto a narrow road leading to the Isles of Lakewood. Another guard shack, another gate.

Josh talked about the game, which the Tornadoes had won by two points. He had spent most of the game on the bench. Dan reached over from time to time and patted his shoulder.

That a public elementary school soccer team had

brand-new equipment and a professional coach was due to the generosity of parents and local businesses. The schools here were the best in the county because the Village residents supplemented the measly budget with books, computers, teachers' aides, and tutors. The kids were multicultural—mostly white or Hispanic, with some Asians and a smattering of black kids. Anybody could live in Lakewood who had the money to afford the real estate. Dan had never thought of seeking custody or asking Lisa to sell the house. If Josh lived in Miami, he would be thrown into a dusty, overcrowded public school with a metal detector at the door, where too many of the kids could hardly speak English, and Josh would get his little butt kicked.

"Are we really going fishing?"

"Yes, we're going. I don't know when, exactly, but I promise, we'll go."

"The Atlantic Ocean is really, really deep, right?" Over his glasses, Josh's brow furrowed.

"Yes, son, but we're going to a shallow lagoon. You can touch the bottom." Dan took his hand. "Would I let anything happen to you, bud? We'll have a great time. You might have to skip school, though. Could you stand that?"

"Skip *school*?" Josh stared up at him. And then laughed. "Okay."

On Alamanda Way the houses were spaced out on huge lots. Each seemed more imposing than the one before, with two-story porticos and chandeliers glowing through high windows. He turned into the Salazar driveway, paved in fake cobblestones. The construction was no different from the houses in Heron Hills, only there was about ten times more of it.

A short-legged woman with braided hair opened the door. Salazar spoke to her in fast, idiomatic Spanish. *Tell Martha to come downstairs and bring the papers. The lawyer is here.* Josh went with the woman to find Anita, who was waiting in the playroom.

Salazar led Dan and Lisa through a massive marble-floored living room with ceiling fans and indoor trees and white furniture, then into a room done up in wood and leather. Salazar asked them what they wanted. Lisa took a glass of dessert sherry and Dan a single malt scotch on the rocks.

Black leather sofas faced each other across a glass table mounted on curved animal horns. Beneath it lay a rug woven in what Dan guessed was an Ecuadoran Indian design. Lighted shelves featured a collection of pottery. Lisa explained, with the authority of one who had been here before, that the pieces were from tombs in the Andes. Dan noticed a squat male figure with overdone private parts and a necklace of hammered gold.

A stereo system and video screen took up the wall opposite the French doors. Salazar opened a set of them. Beyond the terrace Dan saw the long rectangle of swimming pool, an acre or so of grass, then a lake.

Lights from houses on the other side shone on the black water.

Dan declined a Cohiba cigar from Havana. Salazar lit up with a gold lighter, and the aroma of expensive tobacco drifted across the room. Sipping his scotch, Dan decided a comment on the house was in order. "Impressive place you've got."

"Thank you. For many, many years, in Ecuador as a young boy, I dreamed of the U.S., to come here and start a profitable company, and to have a house like this one. God listened to my prayers." He laughed modestly, then his attention shifted across the room. "Martha, come in."

She was young and slender, wearing a jersey wool dress to mid-calf and a pair of flat-heeled boots. A long sweater had been pushed to her elbows. Black hair curled around her face and strained to escape the tight braid that hung heavily down her back. Her only jewelry was a pair of silver earrings and a narrow black bracelet on her right wrist. Her lips were lush and full. Her dark eyes settled on Dan.

"Mr. Galindo? Hi. I'm Martha Cruz." Her voice was low, and the words were clearly enunciated. She stepped forward with an extended hand. The fingers were delicate and cool. Dan noticed that what he'd thought was a bracelet was a tattoo of tiny leaves. Salazar asked Martha if she remembered Lisa Galindo, and she said she did. "Hi."

Lisa smiled at her. "Nice to see you again."

Salazar asked if she'd brought the police report with

her. He held out his hand, and she gave him some folded sheets of paper from her pocket. "We'll discuss this in a moment," he said, and put them on the bar. "Would you like a drink?"

With a small shake of her head, she sat on one of the leather couches, one leg underneath her, the other foot swinging.

Lisa sat beside her. "We didn't get a chance to talk at the party on Sunday. Are you from Ecuador too?"

"I was born in Miami. So were my parents."

Lisa's smile didn't waver. "My brother says you're very talented. How did you get your start in music?"

She shrugged. "I learned piano when I was little."

Salazar squeezed her shoulder. "This woman learned music before she could talk. It's in her blood. Martha will be very big in the U.S. and Latin America, even Europe. But I think she should change the name of the band. Mayhem. I don't like it."

While Lisa gave her opinion, Dan wandered to the bar and set down his empty glass. He was reaching for the police report on Martha's arrest when he noticed something he'd missed before—a big color photo on the wall. Several framed photographs hung there, but this one showed a silvery blue sailfish hanging by its gills from a gaff hook, and beside the fish, a bare-chested Miguel Salazar in shorts and sunglasses. At the dock was a Bertram sportfisher, the name *Basilón*—Spanish for good time—painted on the stern. Forty-two, maybe forty-six feet of gleaming white fiberglass and chrome. Ladder to the flying bridge, tower above that. The salon was just visible through the open door. No shag carpeting or plastic flowers. This baby was made to run.

"A big fish, no?" Miguel Salazar walked over, drink in hand.

"I was looking at the boat, but yes, a very nice fish."

"He weighed ninety-five pounds." Salazar gestured with his cigar.

Lisa walked over to see. "He's huge."

Dan came in closer. "Ninety-five? Did you weigh him? I doubt he'd clear ninety."

"He was ninety-five."

"You caught him off the back of the Bertram there?"

"He fought for over two hours. He was very tough." Salazar laughed. "A macho fish."

"Yeah, ninety-five's pretty common, fishing with a hook and line," Dan said. "I got a fifty-eight-pounder once, but I was free-diving with a speargun."

"A speargun," Salazar repeated.

Lisa gave Dan a warning look.

"Two pounds off the world record," he added. He noticed that on the sofa Martha Cruz was smiling, biting her lower lip. He said, "That's a great boat, though. Is it yours?"

"Yes. I keep it in Coconut Grove."

"I'm going to take my son fishing in the Bahamas. A boat like that would be ideal."

"Oh, you don't have a boat?"

"Only a twenty-foot runabout."

Martha said, "Why don't you lend him your boat, Miguel? If he wins my case, let him borrow it."

"You want the boat?" Salazar asked.

Lisa said, "Wait a second."

Dan looked at Lisa, then at Salazar. "No. I couldn't do that." Nor wanted to. Accepting Salazar's offer would be indebting himself to this man.

"Yes, I insist. If you win Martha's case, you can borrow my boat."

He felt his resolve slipping. "Thanks, Miguel, but Rick's already paying my fees."

From the sofa he heard Martha Cruz say, "Take the boat while you can, Mr. Galindo. Miguel hardly ever uses it."

Lisa held up her hand. "Excuse me? I'm Josh's mother. I have a say in this."

Salazar looked at her, surprised. "And what do you say, Lisa?"

"Yes, fishing's loads of fun, but Dan wants to take Josh *spear* fishing."

"And you're opposed." Salazar took her empty glass from her and went back to the bar and uncorked the sherry for a refill. "Why?"

She glanced at Dan, who made a slight shrug. He wanted to see where this was going.

Lips compressed, Lisa widened her eyes at him—*traitor*—then said to Salazar, "Joshua is only seven years old. A rod and reel is one thing; a speargun is entirely different. The blood attracts sharks. It's very dangerous."

"But, Lisa—" Salazar poured sherry into her glass. "We have to teach our boys to become men. When my son was eight years old, we went hunting in Costa Rica, each of us carrying a rifle. We saw a wild pig, and I let my son have the first shot. He hit the leg, so I had to finish it. I showed him how to hang an animal from a tree and cut its throat to drain the blood. We built a fire and ate until we couldn't hold any more, and we slept in the forest that night." He held out the glass to Lisa; she was staring up at him. "You don't like the sherry?"

"What? Oh." Lisa took it. "Thank you. Yes, it's very good."

Miguel Salazar looked over at Dan and took a puff on his Cuban cigar. "So. Tell me what you plan for Martha's defense. This case could be very bad publicity. Rick said he explained that to you."

Martha unfolded her legs and stood up. "We're going to go outside and talk, Mr. Galindo and I."

Salazar frowned. "You can talk here."

"No, the lawyer has to speak to the client alone. That's how it's done." She went over to the bar and grabbed the papers. "Tell Lisa all about me, why don't you?"

Martha walked out onto the terrace. Dan said to Salazar, "Excuse us." He looked at Lisa, whose expression clearly said she wanted to get the hell out of there. "We won't be long."

The moon shone brightly, nearly full. A hundred yards or so south, long mounds of white indicated where a dragline had been digging another lake, throwing the rock into piles. The behemoth machine sat idle now. Apparently this part of the Isles of Lakewood was still under development. The lot next door was vacant, and beyond that lay barren ground.

They walked past the pool. Palm trees marked the perimeter of the terrace. At the far end Martha Cruz threw herself into a chair.

"Sorry he's such a jerk," she said, putting one booted foot up on the railing.

"Don't apologize," Dan said. "Lisa will think spearfishing is sissy compared to eating a wild pig. Did he cook it first?"

Martha smiled, then held out the papers. "This is a police report and a notice that I'm supposed to show up next week for an arraignment, whatever that is."

"That's part of the routine." Tilting the report toward the house lights, he could make it out. There was nothing he hadn't expected. *Subject verbally threatened officer and attacked him with her fists—* "Were you intoxicated? On any drugs?"

"No," she said firmly. "It's B.S. The cop was trying to arrest somebody for drinking a beer, and I told him to stop. He shoved me and said to shut up, bitch, and I hit him. I'd do it again." She got up and leaned on the railing, facing the lake. "No, maybe not. I don't need this."

Dan glanced at the paper again, looking for her birthday. "How old are you?"

"Twenty-one."

He folded the report to fit into his jacket. "I might work out a deal, get you probation. There shouldn't be a problem. Then in a few months, you keep yourself out of trouble, we'll move to seal the file and have your arrest record expunged."

"And that's it?" She turned around and stared at him.

"Well, if the officer has it in for you, he could cause us some grief, but I can't see the judge giving you any jail time."

She nodded and closed her eyes for a moment. "Good. What I'd really like is to get out of this jail."

"This house, you mean?"

"The house, the neighborhood. Lakewood Village. Miguel tells me how lucky I am to live here. I hate it. People are zombies out here, and they don't even know it. They hire guards to protect them. From *what*?"

"Why don't you leave?"

"Well, I don't pay rent. I've got my own rehearsal room and recording equipment." The moonlight turned her skin silvery, and the earrings shone against her long neck. "You used to live here, didn't you?"

"Not in this section," he said. "Heron Hills."

"Why are you with Lisa? Aren't you divorced?"

"Yes, but we were at our son's soccer game at the same time, and Miguel invited us over. We get along all right, Lisa and I. Most of the time."

"I met her at Anita's party. She was jonesing on this

house. 'Oh, Miguel, what a lovely home!' 'Wow, I just love the kitchen.'"

"Don't make fun of her. Lisa is truly a good person."

Martha sighed. "Yeah, right. My mother was like that. A saint. Nothing you do is enough. I wrote a song. It goes, *Purely, goodness. Give me mercy. Kill me, darkness, let me go. I'm here dyin', on the altar—*" Her quiet voice, husky and melodic, suddenly stopped. "Oh, well. Whatever." She pointed at him. "Hey. You really liked Miguel's boat, didn't you? You're a fisherman. I can tell. You have those little squint lines around your eyes. I hope you get to go. Miguel can be unpredictable. He brought you here to check you out, you know. He isn't sure he wants you for my lawyer."

"I'm not representing Miguel," Dan said, "and he's not paying my fees. It's up to you."

"Up to me, huh?"

"We were going to meet at Rick's office. Why don't you come to mine?" He took a business card out of his wallet. Martha read it, then slid it into a pocket of her sweater.

Dan asked, "What's with you and Miguel?"

"Why?"

"I like to know my clients."

Martha stretched her arms out on the railing, a boot propped behind her. "I'm his hobby. He wants to see me on TV."

Dan let it go at that. He asked, "Are you going to get there?"

"It's the only thing in this world I am sure of." Her

generous lips parted in a smile, revealing perfect teeth. "I liked that, what you said to him. You caught a fifty-eight-pound fish with a speargun."

"I did."

"I believed you."

Hands in his pockets, Dan shrugged. "It was pretty silly. My fish is bigger than your fish."

She swung her upraised knee side to side. "You haven't come to any of our rehearsals. Why not?"

"You don't mind? Kelly told me the band doesn't like strangers at the studio."

"Oh, that's dumb. We have visitors. You should come listen to us. I hereby invite you."

"All right. Maybe I will, then."

Martha Cruz walked farther along the railing. Dan followed. She asked, "Are you a good lawyer?"

He took awhile to answer. "I get the job done when I have to. Is that what you mean?"

"Kelly told me you used to be a U.S. attorney."

"That's right."

"Why aren't you anymore?"

"The office and I had a philosophical difference."

"What does that mean, they fired you?"

"I resigned."

"Why?"

Dan said, "You're pretty direct, aren't you?"

"I like to get answers."

"The answer is, it's personal."

"If you resigned—whatever—is the judge in my case going to listen to you?"

Dan realized that she honestly didn't know. Like many people, this girl had no idea how the system worked. He said, "I'll be defending you in state court, Martha. I used to be a prosecutor in the federal courts. It's a different ball game."

"*If* I hire you," she said. "You said it was up to me."

"Well? Do I pass?"

She tilted her head and looked at him sideways. "You'd be my attorney. Not Miguel's. Not Rick's. Mine."

"Correct."

"So . . . if I told you something, it would be confidential. You couldn't tell anyone. Is that right?"

"Yes. Like a priest."

A smile played across her lips. "Whatever."

"Is there something about this case I should know?"

"Does it have to be about this case?"

"Not necessarily."

Martha searched his face. "Kelly says you're not like a lawyer. Not like most of them, I mean."

"Is that supposed to be a compliment?"

"From her it is."

"Well, then. Am I hired?"

"Sure." Martha Cruz held out her hand, and they shook on it. She laughed suddenly, an unexpected burst of gaiety. "My lawyer. This is too cool."

"You want to tell me what's on your mind?" Dan

asked. "The 'whatever' that doesn't necessarily relate to the case you hired me for?"

She faced the lake again and grabbed the terrace railing. She leaned back, arms extended, and her black braid swung. "Not now. Maybe when I see you next week." The sweater fell open. Under the jersey dress her breasts moved as if unconfined, and her slender waist was supple and firm.

Dan took a step toward the open French doors. "We should go back inside."

Martha Cruz exhaled and turned around. Her dark eyes swept over the high stucco walls, the red-tile roof, and the glittering windows. If her gaze had been napalm, the house would have gone up in one immense fireball.

CHAPTER 7

It was close to ten o'clock when Dan arrived at his apartment in a small building a few blocks from the bay. Turning into the parking lot, he saw Kelly Dorff's old green Thunderbird under a tree along the street.

Coming up the walkway to his front entrance, he could hear music rattling the glass louvers in the windows. He unlocked the front door and came inside. Kelly's purse and denim jacket were tossed on the kitchen counter. He went to the bookcase and turned off the stereo. Beside it was a metal stand with a salt water aquarium. Someone had left a cigarette burning in a saucer on top of the tank. He crushed it out.

"There you are." Kelly stood in the open archway to the kitchen, putting a square of cheese on a cracker. "I was getting worried." She was barefoot, wearing only underwear and a T-shirt.

"I went to my son's soccer game." Dan held up the

cigarette butt. "I wish you wouldn't smoke in the apartment. I don't like it."

"Okay, sorry. Why are you being such a grouch?" She popped the cracker into her mouth and came to kiss him.

Dan walked past her into the kitchen and put the saucer in the sink and the cigarette butt in the trash. He turned around and said quietly, "Kelly, do you recall my telling you that if you wanted to come over, to ask me first?"

"I called! Check your answering machine if you don't believe me. I got out of rehearsal and I called, but you weren't here. So I decided to surprise you, okay? I brought some wine and a movie." She came over and put her arms around his waist. "I thought we could stay home instead of going out. We could act like we have a relationship."

As it sometimes did—and he usually managed to ignore it—her voice achieved a balance of accusation and self-pity. "It's late." Dan unzipped his jacket and headed for his bedroom. On his double bed one pillow was bunched up, and her shoes and jeans were on the floor. He hung up his jacket in the closet.

Kelly came in and leaned against the door frame. Dan glanced at her without speaking and put his car keys and wallet in a tray on his dresser.

"Aren't you glad to see me? At all?"

He hesitated. "Kelly . . . let's go sit down in the living room for a minute."

"Why?"

"Because we need to talk."

"What do you want to tell me? I should leave? God forbid I drop by like a normal girlfriend. You never come to my place. What am I supposed to do, wait till you call me?"

He stood by the door and held out his hand. "Kelly, come on."

She sat on the edge of his bed and pushed her hair back. "I got here and it was dark, and I brought this bottle of wine, and I thought you'd be here any minute—"

"Kelly—"

"A fucking twenty-five-dollar bottle of wine! What did I do wrong? You don't give me a *clue*, then you say we need to *talk*. Like I don't know what that means."

He sat down and put his arm around her. "Listen. I admire you very much. You're very talented. Very pretty. But we're going in different directions. Neither of us expected anything long-term."

She put her head on his chest. He could see the part in her blond hair, wandering unevenly through the tangles. "If people want something bad enough, it has to work out. I mean, we have fun together, don't we?"

"Sure, but there has to be more than that. You and I just aren't suited for each other."

"We are! I thought you cared about me."

"I do. I care a lot about you."

She started to cry. "That's a horrible thing to say! What's next? Let's be friends? Please, Dan." She held his face. "You're so sweet. The nicest man to me. Everybody I've ever known has been such a loser. Please don't be like them. Just tell me what you want me to do, I'll do it. Let's go to bed, okay?"

He stood up. "I'm sorry. Look, I have to be up early—"

She flinched as if he had struck her. "Thanks for the good time, there's the door?"

He picked up her jeans. "I'll give you a call tomorrow or later in the week."

"Why? Like maybe when you get all horned out?" She laughed. "You're not that great a lover, believe me. I've had better." She grabbed her jeans and put them on.

"Right." Dan opened the bottom drawer of his dresser. "You've got some things here you'll probably want to take with you."

"Well, keep the box of condoms for the next idiot." She stepped into her shoes.

He tossed her T-shirts and underwear on the bed. "Kel, please. You know it's for the best."

She rushed across the room, shoving him so hard he fell. Dan held up his hands. She screamed at him. "Fuck you! User! You suck! You made me think you actually gave a shit!" She kicked his nightstand into the wall. "I hate you! Son of a bitch user!" The lamp went over.

"Kelly, stop it!"

She ran out of the bedroom. Dan scrambled to his feet and went after her. His dive gear was stacked in the hall. She pushed over an air tank, which rolled into his spearguns. He leaped over them as they clattered into his path.

She shoved his aquarium as she went by. It rocked on its metal stand, water sloshing. In the kitchen Kelly flung open the refrigerator and grabbed a heavy green bottle—the wine she'd brought—and threw it at Dan. The bottle smashed against the wall.

Grabbing her jacket and car keys, Kelly ran out the front door. He heard the screech of her tires and saw her taillights disappearing down the street.

CHAPTER 8

Just outside the rehearsal room, Vincent Hooper looked down the corridor with its stained brown carpet and the walls plastered with rock posters. A fluorescent light buzzed overhead. Where the hell was Rick Robbins?

The band had arrived already. They were outside with a six-pack.

Vincent lit a cigarette.

Music was coming from behind other doors, a chaos of styles and rhythms. DEA was using Manatee Studios because the owner had been caught dealing up in Fort Lauderdale. In exchange for staying out of jail, he agreed to keep his mouth shut about who was renting the studio. The building itself was in North Miami, one of a row of warehouses containing, among other marginal businesses, a builder of cheap kitchen cabinets and an auto repair that the DEA, in nosing around, had discovered to be a chop shop. As soon as this operation was over, they would pass that information on to the local police.

As Vince smoked, he could hear the crash of drums and cymbals behind him—Arlo Pate filling in for the sound check. *Bam, bam, ching, ka-bam*, a beat like a piledriver. Pate lived over Salazar's garage, keeping the grass mowed and the dogs fed. First time he'd spotted Vince, Pate had filled the hall with his shoulders, a low-watt intelligence flickering in those sunfaded eyes. Vince had smiled genially. *I'm waiting for Mr. Robbins. My name is Victor Ramirez. My company is recording the demo tape for Mayhem.* Pate had stared at him, then moved aside. *Yeah. Okay.*

Vince dropped his cigarette butt into an empty soda can in the trash and went the back way into a dimly lit control room. The ceiling and walls were covered in gray foam soundproofing. Cables and wires—the recording engineer called them snakes—ran in all directions. A big Mackie console took up half the room. A reel-to-reel, ADAT, and CD backup were within easy reach. The engineer's hands were moving over dials, buttons, and switches. Vincent had insisted on hiring Willy Silva, a top-flight man out of New York. He wasn't DEA, but they could trust him.

Willy flipped the talk-back button. "Arlo, that's fine. Stay where you are. Looks like the bassist isn't here yet. Scott, can you give us a sound check on 'Rainbow Baby'?"

Scott Irwin, the undercover agent at Coral Rock, was plugging in an amp. "Sure, hang on a second." He picked up a bass guitar from a stand, put the strap over his shoulder, and turned a knob. Arlo Pate clicked the sticks together to set the tempo, then Scott came in as the sticks crashed down on the drums. Bass notes thudded like a huge heart.

Scott had gone more radical with his hair. Shaved it up the sides, dyed the rest of it blue, and combed it over to one side. He wore jeans with a rip in the seat and a ragged T-shirt from DisneyWorld. The guitar hung low, resting on his thigh. Scott moved to the beat, facing the drummer. He and Arlo Pate were jamming.

Willy saw Vincent standing beside him and spoke loud enough to be heard above the studio monitors. "Hey, Scott's pretty good. If he wants another line of work, I could line him up some gigs."

Vince smiled slightly. "Don't count on it. He's DEA to the bone."

"Looks like a rocker to me." Willy turned a dial and cut the volume. "I gather Rick hasn't showed up yet."

"No. Maybe Arlo Pate told him I was here. Looks like Rick is avoiding me."

"Relax, Vince. What can you do? Either Salazar comes through or he doesn't. It's not up to you."

"Jesus, I hate waiting. I'd rather be shot at than have to wait around." Vincent cracked his knuckles, a bad habit, but he'd broken so many bones in his hands over the years that it felt good loosening them up.

The music suddenly stopped.

The studio door had opened. The band's drummer,

Leon Davila, came in. He set down his can of Mello-Yello, peeled off his leather jacket, and motioned for Arlo Pate to get out of the way. Pate took his time, reaching down to pick up a long-neck beer in one big paw. He stood up slowly, towering over Davila by a foot or more, making him wait.

"Move it, man." Davila's voice sounded distant on the open mikes. He jerked his head to get his shoulder-length hair out of his face. He wore an unbuttoned black vest, and his body, corded with muscle, had an emaciated, hungry look to it. Tattoos circled his biceps like armbands. His legs were sticks in black jeans, ending in filthy red high-tops.

A month ago Leon Davila had been photographed coming out of a motel near the Miami airport dressed like a tourist, a travel bag over his shoulder. He got into the passenger seat of a waiting Grand Cherokee with tinted windows, which the DEA then tailed to a branch of the Banco Nacional de Quito on Brickell Avenue downtown. The car turned into the parking garage, and a security gate came rattling down. A confidential informant at the bank said that the bag had contained $275,000 in cash to be laundered by Miguel Salazar for the Guayaquil cartel. When the U.S. marshals served the arrest warrants, Davila's name would be on the list.

Willy said, "Check it out. See how he's wiping his nose? He must've stopped in the men's room for a bump. He keeps a little bag in his undies. By the time we quit tonight, he's gonna be ripped." Willy leaned back in his chair and put one foot on the edge of the console. "I don't know how Rick Robbins is going to keep this group together. Kelly skipped out early last night. Now the bass player's late—again. They all play this game—it's a race to see who's last."

The two women finally wandered in, Kelly Dorff and Martha Cruz. Kelly was a skinny blonde. Martha had some curves. Her black hair stood out in wild waves. Baggy jeans hung off her hips. She had three silver rings in her navel, and the chain looping through them ran up under a cropped T-shirt. If she had a bra on, Vincent couldn't tell.

"That is one sexy chick," Willy said. "Come on, Vince, admit it."

Vince smiled and smoothed his mustache into his beard.

Martha Cruz spoke into the studio mike. "Willy? You there? What about that chord change in 'Last Man Out'? Did you get that on tape?"

"Wait a minute!" Kelly looked up from plugging in her guitar. "Excuse me? I wrote that song."

"Yes, Kelly, but listen to the progression. It goes nowhere." Martha's hands came down on the keyboard. "See what I mean? Now listen while I do it the other way."

The chords were drowned out by the buzzing shriek of Kelly's guitar.

After a moment of complete silence, Kelly threw her hair back over her shoulder and said quietly, "We are not a techno band."

"It isn't techno. Would you just use your ears? It's totally new."

"What are you trying to do? Be different just to say you're different?"

Martha stared at her. "You really don't get it. You don't even hear it."

Leon was bouncing on his seat behind the drums, laughing at the girls. Martha Cruz yelled across the room, "Leon, shut your—" Her curses disappeared under a barrage of drum volleys. *Bam, ka-bam, ching-ching, bam*— More complex than Arlo Pate's steady thuds but just as loud.

In the control room Vincent asked Willy, "What do you think of this stuff?"

Willy turned around to look at him. "The music?"

"Yeah. What the hell is it?"

"Man, you need to get out more. It's brilliant. I'd say it's . . . well, sort of a rave core, add some blues, like the bastard son of Thrill Kill Kult and John Lee Hooker. Love it or hate it, man. They're great. Martha's phenomenal. If I wasn't working for you guys, I'd love to record this band."

Vince glanced at the studio door, which was opening again. Rick Robbins came in with another man close behind. About six-two, one-eighty. Brown hair and eyes, early thirties. Jeans, sneakers, blue pullover sweater.

"What in hell—" Vince moved back from the window.

"Who's the guy with Rick?" Willy asked.

"Long story." Standing out of the light, Vincent watched Rick Robbins take Dan Galindo over to talk to the musicians. Leon Davila put down his drumsticks long enough to shake Galindo's hand. Kelly Dorff stayed where she was, not speaking to him. She went through some fingering on her guitar with the volume turned off. Her glance moved for an instant to the control-room window. She made a tense, wide-eyed shrug. *I don't know what he's doing here.* Vincent didn't believe that.

He had last seen Dan Galindo two years ago in a gray pinstripe suit outside a federal courtroom. He might have beat the shit out of him if another agent hadn't pulled him back. Now Vince was fifteen pounds heavier and wearing a beard, but this operation would be over if he were recognized.

Second problem—Kelly Dorff. He wanted to shoot the idiot desk jockey who had picked her for a CI on this case. Kelly had been at a party last year when a DEA raid went down. Luis Barrios—now deceased— had been there as well. Kelly had promised not to mention this to Dan Galindo. She knew what would happen if she did. *Ms. Dorff, I will personally escort you to the Atlanta federal pen. You will not jeopardize this operation. Do we understand each other? You will not mention the name Barrios to Mr. Galindo; nor will you allow him to attend your rehearsals.*

Now Galindo was here. He wouldn't be able to see much more than Willy at the mixing board, the lights flickering on the recording equipment, and his own reflection thrown back at him. Even so, Vince stayed well away from the window.

"Willy, there's nothing I'd rather do than stick around and see what's going on, but if I have to run out the back door, make my apologies."

Just then Rick Robbins stuck two fingers in his mouth and whistled for Leon Davila to be quiet on the drums. He looked around at the musicians. "We're short-handed tonight, people. Bill-E got an offer to play with a band in Atlanta. He says it's starting to happen there, and he has to go. Don't worry, we'll find another bassist."

"*Ay-yi-yi,*" Willy said.

"Is that bad?" Vincent asked.

"Bad? If Robbins isn't about to cry right now, he's the biggest B.S. artist I know. It's real bad."

The musicians stared at Robbins, who kept smiling. "Soon as we find a replacement, we'll lay in the bass tracks. No problem. You guys are fantastic, okay? You can work around this. Come on. Do I hear a yes?"

They all looked at each other. Martha Cruz said, "We can do it. We have to."

Leon Davila did a drum roll. "And when we get signed, Bill-E can kiss my ass."

Kelly Dorff said, "Rick, we can't rehearse without a bass!"

"Let's try it with a click," Martha said. "Where are the headphones?"

Kelly swung around, glaring at her. "I know what you're trying to do. You're saying that my time sucks."

"Don't be so insecure, Kelly."

"I'm not the insecure one."

"Let's just get it *done*. We'll worry about the bass later."

"Stop ordering everyone around! It's not your fucking band!"

Leon was banging on his drums, drowning the women out, playing his double-kick pedal, crashing the cymbals. Rick yelled at them all to shut up.

In the control room, Vincent asked, "What's a click?"

"Essentially a metronome," Willy said. "They all hear it through their headphones. It's usually for the drummer, or if somebody doesn't have a good sense of rhythm. For Martha to suggest it is an insult to Kelly. They've had a running argument on the subject."

Martha Cruz hit the keys, and the sound of a bass guitar came out of a speaker. "How's that? We can use that for now."

"It's inhuman," Kelly said. "We can't play with a damned machine."

"It could do lead guitar too."

"Martha!" Rick pointed at her. "I said be quiet. We don't need this right now." His finger, still extended, swept around the room and stopped. "You! Scott."

"Me?" Scott Irwin straightened up from where he had been leaning against the wall.

"You jammed with Rage when they came through on tour. Right?"

"Yeah, but—"

"Get your guitar and come over here." Everyone

stared at Scott. Rick said, "He knows the tunes. He's been listening to you play long enough. Let's try him out for tonight."

Vincent could hear Scott's incredulous laughter over the studio main.

Martha crossed her arms, a hip cocked to one side. "I'm not playing with him," she said. "He's too Van Halen. This isn't the eighties."

"So what? He's got the rhythm," Kelly said.

"Rhythm? Is that all? But what do you know, you don't even read music."

"I *said*, it's okay for *rehearsal*! We can't rehearse without a bass!"

"Be honest, Kelly. *You* can't."

"Shut up!" She threw the first thing she could grab, a beer bottle, which flew past Martha's keyboard and hit Leon's high-hat cymbal.

"Hey!" That brought Leon out of his seat. "*¿Qué haces?* You gonna break my fuckin' drums, bitch!"

"That's it!" Kelly took her guitar off and dropped it on the floor. It bounced and squealed.

Willy looked around at Vincent. "Kelly's freaking out tonight."

Rick Robbins rushed over and put his arm around her. "For the love of Christ, what is the matter with you people? Martha, keep your remarks to yourself, will you? The only thing that counts now is getting the demo tape done. Come on, you guys, please!" Even from the control room Vincent could see the sweat on his face.

Scott said, "You want me in or not?"

Martha shrugged. "Fine—for rehearsal." Leon did a roll, going across the drums, ending with a bass thud.

"And we don't need a damned click track," Kelly said.

Looking through the window as if he were watching a movie, Willy whooped. "Scott's in the band! I do not *believe* this!"

Robbins held up his hands as if to a dog about to bite. "Okay? Everybody all right now? All taken care of?" They nodded. "Good. You're terrific. Okay, guys, what do you want to do first?"

Kelly picked up her guitar. "Let's do 'Miss the Point.' Willy! Wait till we run through it with Scott a couple of times. Ready, Scott?"

"Let's do it."

Leon made four clicks with his drumsticks, and on the downbeat Kelly hit a foot pedal and slammed her right hand across the strings of her guitar. Scott came in, then Martha. Kelly leaned forward and screamed the lyrics into her microphone. Leon's arms were a blur, and his hair danced on his shoulders. Scott focused on his fingers climbing up and down the frets. He shook his head as if he'd missed a few notes. Martha glared at him, but the band kept going.

"Smokin'!" Willy said. "Vince, he's gonna resign from the agency, what do you think?"

Vince had his eyes on Dan Galindo, who had sat on one end of a broken-down sofa in the corner. So far he hadn't moved.

When the music ended, Rick Robbins sank to his knees, arms raised. "Yes! Yes! Thank you, Jesus." He grabbed Scott Irwin's head and kissed him on the cheek. "Not there yet, but it's coming. You're going to be brilliant. It's going to happen. Go over it again while I speak to the engineer."

The musicians huddled for a talk, then started fooling around on their instruments, making a racket. When Robbins came inside the control room, Willy wheeled around. "Your new bass player kicks major butt."

"Think so?"

"Yeah, no lie. You going to use him for the demo?" Behind Robbins's back, Willy winked at Vince.

"I might have to, if I can't find anybody else. At least he's got a steady beat. Kelly gets lost without one, and Leon can't give it to her." Robbins slit open a roll of antacids with his thumbnail. His hands were shaking slightly. He brought his eyes up to Vincent, who was leaning against the back wall out of the light. "Hey, Victor. I saw you through the window."

"It's been awhile since we talked, Rick."

"What do you think of the band?"

"Rock and roll—it's not my thing, man." Victor Ramirez, born in Puerto Rico, spoke with an accent. "You have an answer for me, Rick?"

"Just about. I'm still working on it. But it looks good."

Vincent tilted his head toward the studio. "Who's the guy that came in with you?"

"Him?" Robbins looked through the window. "He's my lawyer."

"What's he doing here?"

"Checking the place out." Robbins spread his palms and made a small laugh. "Is there a problem?"

Vince said, "Does he know about us?"

"More or less. But he's cool."

"I don't want him in here. Out there, okay. But not here."

"Fine. Whatever."

There was an extra chair against the wall. Vince sat in it and crossed his legs. "Rick, I think you're playing a game."

"Not at all."

"What's the problem that you have no answer from Miguel? We're waiting two weeks already. I got funds coming in. If Miguel wants to take care of it for me, okay. If not—" He shrugged. "You pay me for the work on the tape, find some other studio."

"Believe me, Vic, I'm not trying to jack you guys around. He's cautious. He doesn't know who you are."

"Who could we be?" Willy asked.

"I don't know, maybe he thinks you're DEA." Robbins laughed.

Willy and Vince laughed too, then Vince looked up into Robbins's face. "I'm going to ask you, are we doing business or no? I want you to be sure. If you're not sure, Rick, you tell me, all right? Now. You don't waste my time."

"I'm okay with the deal. It's Miguel that's not sure."

"What do you think, Willy? Maybe Rick wants to get the demo tape, then he says, fuck you guys."

"No. Absolutely not. I can't make the man's mind up for him, can I? But I'm telling you, it looks good."

Beyond the glass Vince saw Dan Galindo analyzing the routing of the cables from Martha's computer to her keyboard, and Kelly's effects pedals to the amp, then to the shoulder-high speakers behind them. Then his eyes went to the control room. He walked across the studio.

"Your lawyer's coming. I told you, I don't want anyone in here."

Robbins went to the door as it opened. For an instant Galindo's eyes focused on Vince. Then Willy stood up, casually blocking Vince from view. Robbins motioned for Galindo to step back; then they went out, closing the door. The noise from the band diminished.

Willy glanced around at Vince. "Now what?"

"I'm going to split. If Galindo asks any questions, handle it."

CHAPTER 9

In a bar near the airport, a neighborhood tavern whose clientele consisted largely of baggage handlers and machinists, Vincent Hooper had a couple of drinks and waited for Scott Irwin. When Scott arrived, his blue-dyed hair was under a Marlins baseball cap and his skull earring was gone. It wasn't a place a rock musician could walk into without arousing comment.

Scott sat next to Vincent at the bar and ordered a bourbon. The handful of patrons in the place were watching an NBA game on the television at the other end. Vince told the bartender to bring another vodka and soda as well, and put the drinks on his tab.

He asked Scott what had happened at the studio after he'd left.

"Not a lot. We took a break around eight-thirty, and Martha Cruz went outside to talk to Dan Galindo. I don't know what they talked about."

Vince said, "According to Rick Robbins, Galindo's in on this deal with Salazar."

"Willy told me. I haven't seen Galindo around Coral Rock, though."

"Check it out for us," Vince said. "You're closer to the action now. Lucky break for us, the bassist taking off for Atlanta."

"Very. And completely unexpected. I spoke to him yesterday. He didn't mention Atlanta. He was completely into the band. And then boom. Gone." Scott looked around at Vince, studied him for a moment, then put down his drink. "Hooper, what did you do?"

"Like you said, a lucky break." Vince couldn't keep his face straight. "All right. A guy I know on the Miami narcotics squad did me a favor. Willy was going to recommend you as a replacement, but Rick Robbins made it easy."

Scott shook his head. "Amazing."

"But I'm worried about you, Irwin. What if you like it? Fame and fortune could be too tempting."

"Uh-huh." Scott picked up his bourbon.

He was a good kid. Vince had to remember not to call him that—kid. His fake ID said he was twenty-five, but he only looked young. He was almost thirty. A good man. He'd go further than Vincent in the agency because Vincent despised the bureaucrats who ran it and had told them so. Scott had more sense. Already a G-11. It had taken Vince seven years to get there, even with a drawer full of commendations, and another ten to work up to G-13, and he doubted he'd go any higher. The next level was supervisory anyway, a desk job. A few more years he could take early retirement. Then what? Open a security business. Work for one of the South American intelligence agencies that had made offers. It pleased Vince to know that Scott paid attention, but he still had a lot to learn.

"Another thing I want you to do," Vince said, "is keep an eye on Kelly Dorff. Be careful. Don't give her a chance to suspect who you are."

"I know."

As Vince talked, he had been breaking a plastic stir stick into pieces. He tossed them into the ashtray. "Galindo came close to seeing me tonight. If he gets any closer, it's Barrios all over again." Vince finished his drink, then signaled the bartender for two more.

Scott waved his off. His glass was only halfway down. "One's enough. I have to be in court in the morning."

"In court." Vince smiled. "What do they do, give you a sobriety test at the door? Learn to hold your liquor, my friend—"

"I can hold my liquor just fine."

"Because you're going to be in a situation, believe me, where you have to drink with the enemy, and if you don't know how to stay in control, you could be in trouble." He laughed. "It takes years of practice."

The bartender set down Vincent's drink, picked up his empty, and wiped the bar. He went back down to watch the game, crossing his big arms over his stomach. The light from the TV flickered on his face.

Scott said, "How did you know that Galindo threw the Barrios case?"

Watching the television, Vincent said, "I didn't. That's the truth. At the time I highly suspected." He picked up his drink. "Dan Galindo was an experienced prosecutor. It's like a top contender slipping on the mat, going down. You can't believe it could go that way. Galindo said the C.I. was dirty. No snitch is lily white, he knew that. A prosecutor has a duty, and that duty is not to be the judge or jury. That's the problem, see. The worst traitors aren't the ones who have the guts to draw down on you. You know where you stand with them. No, you have to watch out for the ones who whine about truth and justice and the American way, then complain when we have to take up the slack."

Vincent took a swallow from his glass, then said, "Barrios. As I say, when Luis Barrios walked, thanks to Galindo, it just didn't smell right, and I've operated on gut instinct so many years that I *believed* he threw the case, and I came out of that courtroom wanting to kill him for it. Well, not literally. I would have done some damage, you might say. After I cooled down, I could've let it go. Sure. But now?" Vincent shook his head, smiling. "Don't ever believe in coincidence. You'll live longer."

Scott pivoted around on his stool and put his elbows on the bar. "Barrios did some deals with Miguel Salazar, did you hear about that? The FBI seized documents from the Bank of Quito, and there it was."

"Yes, indeed. Let's give the Feebies their due on that one," Vince said. "Consider. Barrios, Salazar . . . Galindo. No, I can't *prove* anything. I don't *know*, in the strict sense of the word, but it does give me pause. Indeed it does."

Scott caught the bartender's attention and pointed at his glass.

The clock over the bar said 11:15. Vince had told Elaine McHale he might be by tonight, but don't wait up. Now it was too late. He would go home, catch a few hours, then be up early. He had to give a deposition in the morning, meet with a federal prosecutor about another case, then go back to the office and do paperwork. And tomorrow night, a stakeout in Key Largo. The schedule had killed his first marriage and was putting a strain on his second. He didn't know what could be done about it.

When Scott lit a cigarette, the match flared, and Vince noticed his hand.

"What'd you do?"

The flesh on his fingertips was ripped open. Blood had dried under his nails. Scott flexed his fingers. "This is from playing guitar for four hours. Bleeding for the cause, Vince."

"Oh, Jesus." Vince coughed on some smoke, then laughed. "Playing a guitar. Wait till you take a bullet, then talk to me about bleeding for the fucking cause." He unbuttoned his cuff and pushed up the sleeve, working the fabric over his bicep, turning his arm around. "Mexico, August 1991. I got another one in my back, just missed my kidney. We were tracking a shipment through Quintana Roo, and the Mexican *federales* in the area were working for the dopers. Customs knew it. The CIA knew it. Did they tell us? Fuck, no. And after we limped home, did Congress raise hell? No way. Don't disturb NAFTA. Don't piss off our trading partner, even if half the government of Mexico is paid off by the cartels. Look at Salinas, the fucking president. You think our government didn't know what he was doing? Not only do you have to fight the bad guys, you have to dodge the morons in your own agency."

He felt his pager buzzing and reached into his pocket. "Somebody—don't ask me who because I can't remember—said the greatest danger to a republic is the absence of war. Well, we are in a war, my friend. We are in a fucking war here, don't doubt that for a minute."

Looking at the screen, Vince expected to see Elaine McHale's number—again. She would want him to call her back, tell her where the hell he was, when he was coming. He frowned, turning the pager more toward the light.

"Who is it?"

"Our favorite C.I., Kelly Dorff. You have any idea what this is about?"

Scott shook his head. "Call her."

CHAPTER 10

The task force on Operation Manatee met every other Friday at the U.S. attorney's office in Miami—prosecutors, DEA, FBI, and representatives from four local police departments. There were coffee and donuts on a side table. Four dozen donuts—two dozen glazed, one jelly-filled, one plain. In six months it had never varied.

The smell of sugar and grease made Elaine McHale want to gag. She sat at one end of the long conference table with a bitch of a hangover and tried not to breathe.

Everybody was arguing over when to serve arrest warrants. DEA and FBI disagreed—as usual. Leaning back in her chair, Elaine doodled in the margin of her legal pad, staying out of Vincent Hooper's line of sight. She couldn't bear to look at him. Last night she'd had too much to drink and made a perfect ass of herself on his voice mail. Finally he called. Five seconds to tell her he wouldn't be there, stop calling. Elaine woke up at dawn on the sofa, fully dressed, with her drink overturned on the floor. Not a weekend. A workday. It had scared the hell out of her.

The agent who ran the show for the FBI was a guy named Tom Braslow. She didn't like him. He had a red, ugly face and a tight collar. She drew a caricature of him on her legal pad.

He was saying, "Any more delay, there's going to be a leak somewhere. You'll start seeing these guys take the next Avianca flight south, and it's hell trying to extradite them back here."

"No, let's nail Miguel Salazar first." Vincent Hooper's voice came from over by the windows. "He's being coy, but he's interested. If we start busting his contacts now, we could lose him." Elaine could guess what Vince was thinking. *Damned Feebies. Out to run the show and claim the credit.*

"Salazar's not the only target in this operation, Hooper. We've got a list of Brickell Avenue bankers and major narcotics traffickers to take down."

"We need him," Vince said. "The cartel he works for has run over a hundred million dollars in drug money through South Florida in the past five years. Salazar goes after legitimate businesses. When he's finished with them, they fold. The man is a cancer."

"We're aware of the statistics." Braslow's face had become even redder. "While you're busy running after Salazar, we could lose the major dealers and distributors."

"We're not going to lose them," John Paxton said. This was Paxton's meeting. He was the senior prosecutor on the operation. "We have time. This office wants Salazar along with the others, but we need more evidence. Most of it has been supplied by informants. Dopers and couriers. Guys trying to keep their asses out of prison, if they're not there already. Any defense lawyer who isn't asleep at the wheel would try to make every one of those witnesses look like the self-serving scumbags that they probably are—*truthful* scumbags, but the jury won't see that, will they?"

Vince said, "As soon as we put this deal together with Salazar, he's ours. What about his bank accounts? Do we have a subpoena?"

"We'll have that early next week, I should think." There was a pause. "Elaine?"

She sat forward until she could see Paxton at the other end of the table. "I'll ask the grand jury for the subpoena this afternoon."

"Excellent."

For the past month Elaine had been presenting evidence to a federal grand jury, and so far the government had obtained indictments on sixteen targets of the investigation, including drug dealers, bankers, and a variety of couriers and go-betweens. She was still working on Miguel Salazar. Much of the cartel's income was routed through his hands.

Braslow turned around in his chair and eyed Scott Irwin, the DEA agent standing by the windows next to

Vincent. "You're the one in the band? The guitar player."

"Correct."

"Well, my goodness," Braslow said. "We can't move on the warrants till after the show. Agent Irwin is having a debut with a rock band. I heard you dyed your hair blue. Take the hat off, let's see it."

Scott Irwin said quietly, "I'll get you tickets to the show if you wear your leather."

Braslow looked at him, then snorted a laugh. "Smart-ass." The Metro-Dade detective next to him snickered.

While the rest of them talked about subpoenas to be served on downtown banks, Elaine studied Vincent and his latest sidekick. They stood apart from the group, more by choice than exclusion. The same casual slouch, the same blank look that hid whatever was really going through their minds—in Vincent's case, boredom and disdain. Elaine knew what he thought of these interminable meetings. He was ready to go out and do his Latino thing today, gold chains and a guayabera. The loose shirt would hide his semiautomatic pistol.

She found herself doodling again and put away her pen.

Daisy Estrada, the woman on the DEA team, was in the middle of a story. "Guess who Robbins brought to the studio? Dan Galindo—his lawyer. Oh, my God, I wish I'd been there, it must've been so funny. Vince was afraid Galindo would recognize him, and he had to hide in the control room."

Laughter went around the table.

"And this tells me ... what?" Paxton spread his hands as if she might toss him an answer.

"Ah. Then Robbins says that Galindo knows about the deal with Salazar. This is supported by information we received last night from our C.I. at Coral Rock."

Paxton seemed a little stunned. He exchanged a look with Elaine. She leaned forward to see around a detective from Broward County. "What C.I.? Do you mean Kelly Dorff?"

From his post by the window Vincent said, "Kelly Dorff corroborated what Robbins told me—what he told Victor Ramirez, rather. I talked to Ms. Dorff last night. She said she overheard a conversation between Galindo and Robbins outside the studio during a break. I had already left at this point. They were discussing Salazar's deals through the company, Coral Rock. Galindo was asking Robbins how much he expected to make on the next one. That's all the C.I. could hear distinctly."

Paxton said, "Good God. Do you think she was being truthful?"

"She was dating Dan Galindo for a while, and she just broke up with him. In a situation like that, you always wonder if emotions are involved. I don't think so because of the other evidence." Vincent made a quick nod in Braslow's direction. "The FBI has just established a connection between Miguel Salazar and Luis Barrios. Two years ago, Galindo prosecuted Barrios and threw in the towel before it got to trial. This past Tuesday night we spotted Salazar, Galindo, and Galindo's ex-wife at a soccer field in Lakewood Village. The ex is also Rick Robbins's sister. We trailed them to the gatehouse, then went to the surveillance position across the lake. They had a few drinks and talked until around ten o'clock."

Across the table, Braslow said to Paxton, "So there's an ex-federal prosecutor in on this. Interesting, John."

"Wait a second before you draw conclusions," Elaine said. "No one knows what we've got at this point, and we shouldn't speculate."

He smiled at her. "*Au contraire*, Ms. McHale. If a former assistant United States attorney—who has jumped the fence to join the ranks of criminal defense lawyers—if that man is friendly with one of the biggest money launderers in South Florida, I'm going to speculate the hell out of it."

She smiled back. " 'Friendly' doesn't mean anything. And if Dan Galindo is Rick Robbins's lawyer, he can't inform on his client. It would be unethical."

Daisy Estrada took a last bite of donut. "You used to work with Dan Galindo, didn't you?"

Before Elaine could respond, Paxton was waving a hand at Daisy, telling her not to draw conclusions like that. "Dan had a lot of friends in the office, myself included, and we all regret what happened."

"Regret? Luis Barrios murdered two of our agents and dismembered their bodies."

"Yes, yes, yes. And Luis Barrios is dead now too. I'm trying to be philosophical here, Daisy. Let it go."

The conversation turned to other topics, and it was finally agreed to allow more time to see if Miguel Salazar would take the DEA's bait. When the meeting was over, detectives and agents milled around for a few minutes talking, then slowly filed out. Elaine waited until Vincent Hooper had left to gather her notes and stand up.

"John, could I speak to you for a minute?"

Paxton looked back at her. "All right." He finished what he was saying to one of the detectives, then closed the door. "What's up?"

Elaine told him she wanted to talk to Kelly Dorff. "Do I have to go through the DEA for this?"

"That question says you don't want to."

"Exactly. Kelly might be more open if I spoke to her alone. Here's my concern. This allegation about Dan Galindo and Miguel Salazar bothers me. It's not so much a question of Dan's guilt or innocence, but of Kelly Dorff's veracity. They've been intimate. Say she's angry and implicated him falsely. I need to know that. Or perhaps she told the truth. If so, she betrayed the man she slept with. I don't care what anybody says, a jury would hate her for it. Before we use her testimony—or continue to use her as an informant—I'd like to know her motives."

"Good point." Paxton frowned at the floor, his eyes half hidden under heavy gray brows. "You could add another ingredient to the mix. The DEA are convinced that Dan sabotaged a case they spent a year building. They could be predisposed to judge him guilty. Of course, a lying informant shouldn't be put on the stand, but Dan refused to consider any other course of action. He went to the judge. He shot off his mouth to the media. That's what really ticked everyone off."

In one intemperate blast to TV reporters after the Barrios case had been thrown out of court, Dan had criticized the policies of the DEA, the U.S. attorney in Miami, and the Justice Department. Elaine had seen him on the evening news standing on the steps of the courthouse, wind ruffling his hair. His wide brown eyes. His righteous, stupid response. *The government didn't lose today. We made the system play by the rules. Winning is never as important as defending the truth.* Elaine had moaned and buried her face in a sofa pillow.

She said to Paxton, "I can't believe that Dan Galindo would get involved in money laundering."

"You don't *want* to believe it, Elaine. I don't either, but you and I both know that not every person we prosecute is a career criminal. We've seen good people have terrible lapses of judgment. Look at it from Dan's point of view. He has no love for us after what happened. We kicked him in the teeth for doing his duty. His law practice is marginal. His ex-wife is probably after him for alimony and child support. He was sleeping with a girl arrested for possession of heroin. What does that tell you? Answer this: Why should a man in Dan's position go on believing in a clear line between right and wrong? What's it brought him so far? He ought to start looking out for himself. He trusts Rick Robbins. They're friends. If he could do this one deal—just one— Oh, yes, Elaine. It does happen."

"I could find out from Kelly Dorff," Elaine said.

After a moment Paxton shook his head. "No, I wouldn't advise it. She's the DEA's informant. Let Vince deal with her."

Vincent Hooper was waiting in the corridor outside, leaning a shoulder against the wall. He nodded at Paxton as he passed, then spoke quietly to Elaine. "Are you okay? You seemed a little dragged out in the meeting."

"I didn't sleep well, that's all."

"Sorry I couldn't come over last night," he said.

"Forget it."

"What about breakfast in bed tomorrow? Sleep late. I'll wake you up."

At the end of the hall the other agents were talking with one of the prosecutors. Scott Irwin glanced their way. He knew. Elaine was becoming certain that everyone knew, and it made her queasy.

She said quietly, "Vince, if I asked you—please—to ignore my messages on your voice mail for a while, would you?"

He drew his fingers down his beard. "Are you asking?"

"I should."

"Why do you get so worked up, Elaine?"

"Because it's lousy. We're lousy for each other."

"Well, my love. Who isn't, when you really think about it?"

"Don't say that." She made a short laugh. "Even if it is true."

"That's why we get along. We understand each other." He squeezed her arm. "See you tomorrow."

"No. I need to work."

He looked at her for a moment longer. "Whatever you say."

In her office, Elaine closed the door and sat down, willing herself not to go after him. If she hurried, he would still be in the lobby outside, waiting with the others to take the elevator downstairs. She counted off seconds until it was too late.

CHAPTER 11

Elaine met Kelly Dorff at a Denny's restaurant near the beach in Hollywood, and they found a booth in the back. Elaine unwrapped the scarf at the neck of her suit and took a menu from the waitress. She told Kelly to order whatever she wanted.

"Just some coffee."

"That's all?"

"I'm not hungry."

"The same for me, then."

Kelly Dorff slumped into the corner of the booth. The fur-trimmed hood of her jacket pillowed her shoulders, and hair parted in the center framed a narrow face. The rims of her green eyes looked as if she'd either been crying or smoking dope.

"Are you wearing a microphone?" she asked sullenly.

"No." Elaine had to smile. "This is just you and me."

"Sorry. I feel like everything I do, they want to know about it."

Elaine had debated calling Vincent Hooper for clearance in speaking to Kelly Dorff. Aware of her resolution not to call him at all, she had decided to tell him later. Or not, depending.

Kelly unzipped her jacket and took it off, folding it on the seat. Her collarbones showed at the neckline of a thin pullover, and her hair fell to cover her small breasts. She hesitated in reaching for her purse. "Do you mind if I have a cigarette?"

"Go ahead."

The purse was leather with brass trim, an expensive make. Battered and scuffed now, but still good. She lit a cigarette from a book of matches and slid the ashtray closer.

"How is everything with you?" Elaine asked.

She exhaled smoke. "How am I? Oh, simply marvelous, thank you. Did you ask about getting me off this case? I called you two weeks ago, and you never said one way or the other."

"Well, it's really up to the DEA," Elaine said, "but I did mention to agent Hooper a week ago that you had cooperated fully, according to the terms of your plea agreement. I don't know what else they could want you to do."

"I can't do this anymore. I can't. If anybody ever finds out— Oh, my Go-o-ood. Kelly Dorff, a snitch for the narcs? Good-bye. I might as well shoot myself."

"I suppose the music business isn't very forgiving."

"Oh, generally people don't care what you do, but this? Uh-uh. I should have taken my chances in court.

The guy I was with jumped bond, did you know that? And I'm stuck in this nightmare."

Eight months ago Kelly Dorff had given a ride to her German boyfriend at two o'clock in the morning, a condo in Coconut Grove to a club on South Beach. A patrol officer had spotted her running a stop sign. The boyfriend threw a kilo of heroin out of the window. Kelly claimed she didn't know he had it, but he said it was hers. At the station a narcotics detective recognized the name of Kelly's employer, Coral Rock Productions, and called the DEA.

Kelly was staring out the window. The sun had gone down, and the road was a steady stream of taillights. Elaine could see a pale face reflected in the dark glass. When the waitress came with their coffee, Kelly turned around and picked up the little metal pitcher. She asked Elaine if she wanted cream. Elaine said please, and Kelly poured as if the pitcher were sterling silver and the cups were porcelain. Yet the girl had ragged nails and a ring through her left nostril.

"Did Vincent send you to talk to me?"

"No. Tell him if you want," Elaine said.

"Shit, I'm not going to say anything." Kelly laughed. "I saw him last night at the studio. Victor Ramirez. I think he gets off on it." She stirred her coffee. "Are they going to give us the studio master tapes?"

"I don't know. I haven't heard about that."

"They have to. The band is working on the songs, over and over, and in the back of my mind I'm afraid it's for nothing. We need the tapes, Elaine. You're the prosecutor. Tell Vincent Hooper he has to give them to us."

"Kelly, that's really not up to me."

Letting her head drop back on the booth, Kelly closed her eyes. "God, I'm so tired of this. They take more and more and more. First they said they just wanted to know about Miguel. So I said okay. I didn't know Miguel, except that he was Martha's boyfriend. Then they wanted me to look around Rick's office because I was working there. Oh, it wouldn't be much, just take a little peek. And then I have to tell them who Rick talks to, where he goes. It's horrible. But if I say no? What do we have for Miss Dorff behind door number one? Minimum mandatory ten years in prison!"

That wasn't likely to happen, Elaine knew, but she couldn't make promises. She said, "I heard you broke up with the man you've been seeing. The lawyer?"

"One of the breed."

"What does that mean?"

"Oops. I forgot you're one too." Kelly put her fingers over her mouth.

"Did you ever tell him about your arrest?"

"Of course not. He's like totally straight."

"Straight?"

"You know. Thinks he's so fuckin' perfect. No smoking, no bad words. Wears these preppy clothes." She laughed. "Washes out his bottles and peels the labels off before he puts them in the recycling bin. Uses shoe trees. My *grandfather* used shoe trees."

"Not the kind of man to keep grass in his night-stand, I suppose."

"I never saw any."

Elaine nodded. "So if you had told him about your arrest—"

"What could I have said? I'm spying for the DEA? Right. He'd have told Rick, and then Vincent Hooper would have found out and he'd break my neck."

"There's no way—"

"Oh, please. The DEA shoot people. I think about that every time I see his ugly face." Kelly stared at the ashes she tapped off the end of her cigarette. "We need those tapes. He'd keep them just to be the son of a bitch he is."

"Fine, I'll ask agent Hooper about the tapes," Elaine said.

"Swear."

"All right, I swear. Why are they so important to you?"

"Because we're making a demo out of them."

"A demo. I don't know what that is."

"It's for the talent scouts from the record companies. There's this guy from Capitol Records who says he'll come to our concert if he likes our demo. We'll have three songs on it—if we can ever decide which ones." She exhaled. "Martha's into rave. The drummer has a background in salsa. Our new bassist likes thrash metal. And me? Well, I'm more toward alternative, but I like blues."

She picked up her cigarette from the ashtray. The

calluses on her fingertips were smooth, but gave her slender fingers an almost spatulate shape. She saw Elaine looking and held up her hands. The smoke curled as she turned her palms one way, then the other. The muscles and tendons moved in her arms. The nails on the thumb and first two fingers of her right hand were worn down, and the cuticles were ripped.

"Ugly," she said.

"They're strong," Elaine said. "How long have you been playing guitar?"

"Since I was thirteen. I started on my brother's Fender Telecaster. He didn't like it, so he made our mother buy him a new Stratocaster, and he gave me the old one. I begged for a guitar, but no daughter of hers was going to play rock and roll."

Kelly lit another match. When it was burning brightly, she lowered the tip of her left forefinger into the flame till it went out. She studied the burned spot, her eyes going a little crossed. She brushed some soot away and tossed the match into the ashtray.

"My brother had a band in high school, and I liked the drummer. I thought the best way to get his attention was to learn to do what they did. They tolerated me. I was cute. My brother and his friends got drunk and smoked pot, and I practiced. I stayed in my room for hours and hours playing, headphones on so nobody could hear how bad I was. But I kept doing it, and one day I was as good as they were. Better. After that they didn't want me around. The band broke up after the bass player committed suicide. My brother got kicked out of about six private schools—we're from Baltimore. I don't know where he is now."

"Your parents are living?"

"The last I heard. My dad's a doctor, a big deal at Johns Hopkins, but such a shit. He more or less wrote me off. My mother's in Montreal with husband number three or four. She'll send me money when I get completely desperate, as long as I beg and do the daughter routine. They sent me down here to go to school. That didn't work out too well. I got into the club scene and started playing guitar again, mostly to scream my guts out when I felt like screaming. I was in about five different bands and sang backup on a couple of albums that went nowhere. At first Mayhem was myself, a bassist, and a drummer. Then this girl I met at the clubs, Martha Cruz, wanted to join, so I said sure. I was working part-time at Coral Rock, and Rick heard us and wanted to be our manager. He made some changes in our sound. I thought he was out of his mind, but it worked. We've done some gigs, and people like us. So now we're doing a demo."

Elaine said, "And after that you'll get a record contract?"

"Ha! I wish. We could record with one of the companies down here, but Rick wants a deal with a major label. He almost makes me believe it could happen. We wouldn't get rich, necessarily. People think, oh, you got signed. Next stop, MTV. Well, MTV pays the band like five bucks each time they play your song, which sucks unless you're some huge name. And the label takes back every dime they spent on us, right off the top. Publicity, road expenses, promotion—everything. We'll go on tour and all sleep in the same hotel room, bust our buns for a couple of years, then it's over. But you never know. We might take off. I think, God, if it does work out. This band is probably the last one I'll be in as lead guitar that has any chance of making it. I'm twenty-six. For a guitarist, that's getting into my prime, so if it's going to happen, it better be now. I don't expect a lot. A car that runs. My own house. Is that too much to ask for, a place where you can paint the walls any color you want? I could go back to school. Maybe even have kids before I'm too old." She exhaled smoke and crushed out her cigarette.

"Maybe. Maybe. Everybody wants to be a star. Martha especially, and if you ask her she'll tell you, 'I am going to be a star.' She's young, you know? I've been in the business almost ten years, but this is her first real band, and she thinks it's easy. Miguel just bought her a synth, a MIDI board, and a computerized notation system for—God, what was it?—about forty thousand dollars. I nearly freaked."

Elaine asked, "What's he like? Miguel Salazar."

"Scary. Sexy."

"I've seen photos. He's not all that good-looking."

"You don't think he's hot?" Kelly's mouth twisted into a smile. "If you saw him in person, you would." She sat back with her coffee. "I don't like to be around him. Well, I guess that's because I know who he is, right? He's got Martha like this." She made a fist. "Jesus, I'll be glad when this is over. You're going to put him in jail, aren't you?"

"I hope so."

"What about Rick? He's not like Miguel. What are you going to do with Rick?"

"I . . . really can't talk about that," Elaine said. "Let me ask you, as long as we're here. What about that conversation you overheard between Rick and Dan Galindo? They mentioned a deal with Miguel Salazar. Is that what you heard?"

"That's right."

"What led you to assume it involved laundering drug money?"

"Because that's what Dan said. He used those words. Launder. Money. Drugs. Rick's doing a deal with Miguel and doesn't want to get screwed. He wanted Dan to talk to Salazar about it, sort of make sure they all understood the terms."

"Mr. Galindo specifically mentioned 'drug money'?"

"That's what I just told you." She dropped her cup back into its saucer.

"And where did this take place?"

"Outside the studio on a break. I'd already gone out to have a cigarette, and they didn't see me. They passed by, and I could hear them talking. Then they were too far away. I went back inside and pretended I'd been in the ladies room."

"Is there anything else you can tell me about the

conversation? The amount of money involved? How the deal is to be transacted?"

"No. That's all I heard."

Elaine nodded slowly, making no other reaction. She said, "Were you initially told to gather evidence on Dan Galindo? Or did that come later, after you were already involved with him?"

After a second or two, Kelly's face flushed. "They didn't say to *seduce* him. They sent me to his office with a fake traffic ticket. I was supposed to ask him out for a drink or something, then see if he was working with Rick. Okay, we had sex, but I didn't do it because anyone *told* me to."

"You liked him."

"I guess so."

"Were you in love with him?"

"Not really."

"But you slept with him."

The green eyes rolled upward again. "Yes, Elaine. Duh."

"Why did you break off your relationship?"

"Why? Because it was a dead end. I have to work on my career right now. He was a user anyway. He's a guy, what can I tell you? They get you in bed, then they start looking for a way out."

Elaine was silent for a while, occupying the empty space of time by aligning the handle of her cup with the edge of the table. As a witness Kelly Dorff would be flayed alive by a defense lawyer with half a brain.

"I don't quite understand something. You say that

Dan is so straight he won't keep a joint in his house, but he was talking with Rick Robbins about laundering drug money. That doesn't seem to fit."

"Well, you don't have to be into drugs to want to make money off it. I've met a lot of people who would surprise you."

Elaine carefully phrased her next question before asking, "Did anyone—Vincent Hooper or anyone else—ever suggest to you that if you found evidence against Mr. Galindo, the DEA would treat you more favorably?"

Kelly pushed her hair behind her ears. "They never said that."

"But did it occur to you?" Elaine waited for an answer.

"No."

"If Mr. Galindo is involved in money laundering, and we can prove it, he would go to prison. Do you feel that would be appropriate?"

"I don't know."

"Would you testify in court as to what you heard?"

"You said you wouldn't make me testify."

Elaine shook her head. "Our agreement had to do with Rick or Miguel. If you have new evidence about Dan Galindo, that's another matter."

"Well, I'm not going to court."

"You will if I have a subpoena issued," Elaine said.

"You promised I wouldn't have to. I *can't*!"

"I told you and your attorney that you *probably* would not have to testify against Mr. Robbins or Mr.

Salazar. Are you prepared to tell a jury what you heard Mr. Galindo say last night?"

Kelly bit down on her lips, making them disappear for a moment into a thin line. "If I said it didn't happen, would you still call me as a witness?"

"If the conversation did not actually take place, then no. I'd have no reason to put you on the stand," Elaine said.

The unblinking green eyes seemed enormous. "You know Dan, don't you?"

"He was a prosecutor in my office."

"That's not what I *mean*."

"We worked together." Elaine added, "Yes, I know him."

Kelly sat back in the booth, smiling. "Right. I was so dense."

"Excuse me?"

"I've been sitting here trying to remember something that Dan told me, and *voilà*, it finally clicked. Dan said he had a friend, a really great woman friend, at the U.S. attorney's office. She got him a job where he is now. Was that you?"

"Kelly, please. I'm trying to determine the truth here, that's all."

"Ooooh, sneaky, Elaine. What if I told the DEA? What if I told them that you wanted me to change my story to keep your friend Dan out of jail?"

"That is not so!"

Kelly lurched forward, fists on the table. "Then you

better tell them to get off my back. I want out of this. *Now!*" Her face had gone white with fury.

The people at the next table were listening, turning around in their seats.

Elaine whispered, "It isn't up to me!"

"Liar. What are you doing here?" Kelly grabbed her matches and cigarettes and dumped them into her purse and picked up her coat. "Making sure I'm all right. Just a little chat to see if I need anything. Bullshit. You're all users. All of you!"

"Kelly, sit down."

She bumped the table going out, and coffee sloshed into the saucers.

CHAPTER 12

Charlie Dunavoy played piano sometimes at the Northside Club, a little place in a strip of storefronts on the north end of Miami Beach. Strings of lights twinkled in the windows, where posters announced upcoming gigs. A sparse crowd was listening to Charlie and a stand-up bass. By nine the place would be packed with people waiting for the main show. A jazz combo would be playing later. Elaine had read it on the handwritten events calendar. A stack of them lay on the bar.

The bartender said that Charlie's set had just started. Elaine asked her for a vodka tonic with lime.

Charlie was at the piano. The spotlights lit up the white V of his shirt under a dark jacket and shone on the sideman's bald head. The bassist was old and black, and kept his eyes closed behind his glasses. He hummed along with the music, head bobbing, hands moving on the strings. Elaine didn't know the name of the tune, only that she liked it. She sat at the end of the bar, her back to the adjacent empty stool. She wanted no company. Not many single women in here, mostly middle-aged couples and a few stray men. Even sitting alone at the bar, she knew she wouldn't be mistaken for a hooker. She wore very little makeup, she dressed plainly, and didn't do a damn thing to her hair except have it trimmed every month or so. She brushed the sides back, fluffed the top, and ignored the few gray hairs among the light brown ones. With her habit of staring straight back at people when they spoke to her, nobody was ever surprised when she told them what she did. *I'm a federal prosecutor. Boo.*

She listened to the music and had another drink. She tried not to look past the stage at the narrow hallway in the back. The bathrooms were down the hall, a telephone booth between them. She could drop in a quarter, punch the right numbers. Vincent Hooper lived in North Miami, not so far away. He would look at his beeper screen and see the code to call his voice mail. He might come over and have a drink with her.

Elaine sipped through the little plastic straw. If she could finish that one without getting out of her chair, she thought she would be all right. She read silently the different kinds of liqueurs behind the bar. Chambord. Sambuca. Midori.

If he decided to come by, he would tell his wife some lie or other as a matter of courtesy. They had separate bedrooms, and he could do what he wanted as long as she didn't hear about it. Before Elaine and Vincent had become involved, he had explained the situation to her. He would stay married to his wife until their younger daughter finished high school. Until then he wanted a monogamous sexual relationship with a woman he could trust. No games, no pressure, total honesty. If both were in the mood, fine. If one of them wasn't, just say so. He had put it to her this way: *I respect you, Elaine. I think this would be good for both of us. What about it?* Surprising herself, she had told him to give her a few days to think about it. She considered his proposal carefully. They liked each other. Vince Hooper was attractive and intelligent. Now thirty-five, Elaine had been single since her husband's death four years ago. Her job scared off most men, even if she had time for dating. The singles scene was depressing. So she told him yes.

It had sounded reasonable a year ago. Exciting, not tawdry. She had even hoped—still hoped—that it would last. Maybe Kelly Dorff had the low-down. *They get you in bed, then they start looking for a way out.*

The bartender was leaning over the sink washing glasses. Her frizzy blond ponytail bounced against her neck. She smiled at Elaine. "Are you celebrating? I heard you laughing."

"No, I was just thinking about the guy I'm going out with."

"Yeah, I laugh about that all the time." The bartender dried her hands. "Can I get you a refill?"

"Sure. Maybe it'll keep me away from the telephone."

"Did you have a fight?"

"Not really." Picking salt off a pretzel, Elaine watched the bartender measure vodka. Then the bottle clattered back into the rack. Soda bubbled out of the mixer nozzle. "It's tiresome to talk about. What's your name? I'm sorry I've forgotten."

"Terry." She set down the drink. "And you're Elaine. A friend of Charlie's."

"Yes. He and my dad went to law school together. Charlie's a peach, isn't he?"

The stand-up bass player was off on a solo riff now. The notes reverberated deep in the wood, then grew thin as the bass man worked close to the tuning pegs. His mouth twisted into odd shapes. Charlie stood up and clapped his hands in time with the beat. Then he sat back down at the piano, taking over the melody. A man at a front table whistled, and everyone applauded.

"Whoooo!" Terry raised both arms, then went to see what they wanted at the other end of the bar.

When Charlie's set was over, and he had chatted with some friends, Elaine waved at him to come sit with her. He settled down on the next stool, straightening his jacket. "Hey, toots. How's it going?"

She put an arm across his shoulders. "Let me buy you a drink, sailor. I want to talk to you."

"A lady who buys the drinks. I won't say no to

that." He told Terry, "Seven and soda, my love. Make it light."

Elaine said, "I haven't seen you in a while, Charlie."

"That's right. Where have you been?"

"Too busy. How's Alva? Tell her I send a kiss."

"I will do that. You know our daughter Lucy is expecting again?"

"Is she? That's wonderful." Elaine remarked how long it had been since she had seen Charlie's daughter, and how quickly people lose touch these days. Terry brought the drinks. Elaine put down some bills and told her to keep the change. Charlie lifted his glass to hers. "To the most beautiful girl in the joint."

She laughed. "You're a sweetie, aren't you?"

The bass player came over, and Elaine shook his thick, dry hand. Now she could see he was blind in one eye. Charlie told her that George had played with Cab Calloway. George smiled widely, showing gaps in his teeth. *Ooooo, that's a looong time ago. Before you was born, I bet.* Then he waved across the room and said he had to go, his harem awaited. A woman stood up, holding her arms out, shimmying. Another with gray hair was telling her to sit herself down this minute.

"What a nutty place," Charlie said.

Elaine turned to face him. "Charlie, how's Dan? I was thinking of him today."

"Dan's fine."

"Really? He's doing all right?"

"He bitches and moans, but I told him, buddy, if

you were meant to be anyplace else, you'd be there, right?" Charlie laughed, his belly moving. "We don't have the penthouse office at the Sun Trust building. He's bringing in some business, though."

"I wouldn't have suggested that he work with you if I hadn't thought he was a decent sort of guy. How do you tell about people, Charlie? I always considered myself a good judge of character. But maybe not. How do you know?"

"Hell, don't ask me. Just pay attention, I guess."

"I do. I thought I could tell. Dan, for instance. This is funny, Charlie. I had the biggest crush on him a couple of years ago. Don't you dare tell him."

"I won't," he said.

"Thank you. So I paid a lot of attention, and I thought I knew who he was. But if Dan isn't what I thought, then who is?"

Charlie looked at her. "What brings this on?"

"Nothing, I was just using that as an example."

The bass man, George, was heading for the stage. Charlie finished his drink. "Time to go. Why don't you come around to the office, Elaine? We'll all go out to lunch."

"I wish I could get away." She set down her empty glass. "Terry?"

"No, honey, I should have cut you off already."

Elaine shook her head. "How much do I owe you?"

"You already paid."

"Oh. Right. Did I leave you a tip?"

"Yes, you left me a good tip."

Charlie said, "Whoa, you better not drive. I could call you a cab."

"Maybe I'll sit here awhile. I didn't have any dinner. It goes straight to my head."

"You bet it does. Terry, get this girl something to eat. It's on me." He gave Elaine a squeeze. "Don't forget. Come see us."

"Bye, Charlie."

Stepping onto the small stage, Charlie leaned over to hear a request from a woman at a table in front.

Elaine opened her wallet and poked among the coins there. "Terry? Do you have a quarter?"

"Lots of 'em."

She realized what she was doing and put the wallet away. "No. Never mind."

CHAPTER 13

Standing on the edge of the pool at the Lakewood Village Country Club, Dan flipped a quarter in a high, spinning arc. It went in with a *plonk*, and Josh, holding onto his dive mask, jumped in to find it. Dan saw his son wriggling along in his red swim trunks and bright green fins, skinny arms and legs moving as if he were trying to crawl through the water. Josh swung his head around, getting a fix through the mask, and spotted the quarter.

Bribery—the only way to coax Josh underwater. He had clutched the ladder at the shallow end, shivering. His eyes had pleaded through the glass in his face mask. Thirty bucks, top-of-the-line silicone in a small size, pulled so tightly under his nose it made his upper lip stick out. Dan had told him he had to learn how to dive if he wanted to go see the fish. It had taken a buck-fifty to lure him to the four-foot depth.

The water was clean as crystal, from the unblemished turquoise bottom to the decorative mosaics at the edges, where the water lapped over the sides and was routed under the Mexican-tiled deck to a hidden stainless steel machine that filtered out the occasional stray leaf or bird feather. Not many people were out now; the temperature barely nudged seventy. A foursome played cards at an umbrella table. Two teenage girls lay facedown on chaises listening to Y-100 Top 40 on their boombox. A white-haired man with oiled, sun-browned skin turned a page in the Sunday *New York Times*. In the distance lay the undulating green expanse of the Lakewood Estates golf course.

Josh popped up with the quarter in his fist and dog-paddled over to put it in his stack. He grabbed the edge. "Dad! Throw one real far!" Dan spun out a quarter toward the six-foot mark.

Usually on weekends Dan took Josh to see a movie or whatever, but today he wanted him to try out the new mask and flippers. Lisa was still opposed to spearfishing in the Bahamas, but Miguel Salazar's bloody little tale about hunting wild pigs had pushed her toward a long weekend in the Keys.

Lisa, who was playing tennis, had signed Dan in as her guest today. He kept up the membership for her and Josh, part of the divorce settlement. He used to play golf with two guys on his street, none of them anywhere close to par, having no time to devote to the game. He hated the sweaty pounding of tennis and had rarely used the pool, preferring the ocean and the pull of the tides. On weekends, if he wasn't preparing for a trial, he had used the weight room. Through the glass he had watched the step-aerobics class. The women would be there, incredibly fit women, ponytails bobbing, their thong leotards showing mount-me moons of bright pink tights. He had never gone after them. He had been in love with his wife, in those days.

Had he been happy then? His life had been pleasant. One season flowing into the next, distinguished only by the variation in the slant of the sun at the end of a forty-minute commute home or the bill for air conditioning. He had ridden his bicycle along green and tranquil streets. No graffiti, no trash. There had been evening concerts lakeside in the town park. Fireworks on the Fourth of July. The Lakewood Plaza shopping center had a cappuccino shop between the hair salon and Birkenstock. Store clerks smiled. Minivans were filled with Evian and merlot, fresh pasta, prosciutto, raddicchio, a paperback best-seller, instant-starting charcoal, rock salt for the water filter—

The weekends were quiet, not even the racket of lawn mowers—the yard men came and went Monday through Friday. The kids played in the streets. There would be the smell of backyard cookouts, and the sound of football games on television. If a car alarm went off, it was only accidental. The local chapter of Kids in Distress had to go outside Lakewood to find enough constituents.

The nights were starry this far from the city. He had lain in bed listening to crickets. Or to tree frogs in their season. He had heard Lisa's steady breathing. She used to wear a thin cotton nightgown, a white one with narrow straps that he would slowly push off her shoulders.

"Dad!" Josh held up another quarter. Dan showed his empty palms. He put on his mask and flippers and somersaulted into the pool. He angled for the bottom, stayed out of sight behind an air mattress, then shot upward, grabbing Josh around the belly. The boy sputtered and shrieked happily.

Dan told Josh to hang on tight and hold his breath, they were going under. Josh locked his arms around Dan's neck. They cruised along at a depth of about six feet.

The water flowed over Dan's body, cool and clean. Through the mask everything was visible. An arm hanging off a red air mattress, the slow kicks of a chubby girl on a bright yellow boogie board. Light flickered and danced. He missed this place, he realized. He missed the order and purpose of it. How in the name of God had he thrown all this away? He ached for his son. For his family. Lisa. His wife. The thought ran through Dan's mind with startling clarity. He missed his wife.

They broke the surface at the edge, and Dan stood up, Josh still clinging. As water ran off his face mask, the view on the pool deck wavered, then cleared. Dan could see a pair of heavy black sandals, narrow ankles, and golden brown skin. Around one ankle curled a tattoo of leaves and tendrils. A skirt of some silvery gray material hung loosely at the knee, then hugged closer at thighs and hips. A hand with unpainted nails held a cigarette. The cigarette rose, and he followed its progress past a tight, long-sleeved gray top and ropes of black and silver chains.

Dan pushed his face mask to his forehead.

Martha Cruz. She smiled down at him through shiny green oval sunglasses. "Hi. I saw you from the restaurant." Her hair was unbound, a cloud of black around her shoulders. "Nobody can smoke up there." She gestured with the cigarette to the second-floor windows.

"Hey, Josh." Her voice was low. "You met me at Anita's party, remember? I played piano for you guys." Splaying her fingers, Martha Cruz rocked side to side, singing softly, "Where ya gonna go when the sun goes down—"

"Yeah." Josh smiled.

Lifting him by an elbow, Dan deposited Josh on the deck. "He's learning how to dive. Next comes the snorkel, then the tanks, when he's older."

"Too cool." The lenses of her sunglasses sent his tiny, doubled image back to him in green. "I haven't seen you here before."

"Lisa has a membership. I visit."

"Visit your son, I assume."

Dan took off his mask and fins. He placed his palms on the edge and vaulted out of the pool in one move, dripping water. Martha Cruz looked him over and exhaled smoke to one side. Dan pushed his wet hair back with both hands.

"Dad, I'm free-e-e-zing."

"Go get your towel." He turned back around. Martha was still watching him. Her mouth was deep burgundy. There were four earrings in each earlobe.

Dan reached for his own towel, which hung over the back of a chair. The old guy with the Sunday paper was looking at them. Dan dried his face and chest, then hung the towel around his neck.

He said, "You don't strike me as the country club type."

"I'm not. Miguel pretends he is, and he likes me to come along." Her elbow rested in her palm, and the light breeze shifted the smoke. She said, "I got the names and addresses of witnesses, like you asked me to. There are only a couple of people, though, and they're such flakes they might not show up for the trial."

"I don't expect a trial, Martha. The witnesses are primarily to say we have some. Bring the list with you on Wednesday." They had arranged to meet at Dan's office prior to the arraignment at the criminal courts building, where Dan would enter a plea of not guilty on her behalf. Martha didn't even have to be there. It wasn't much of a case, Dan had reported to Rick, who had called to check on things. Hearing that, Rick had tried to weasel out of paying the thousand bucks for legal fees. Not a chance, Dan had told him.

"Don't wear that dress," Dan said, "or jeans either. Do you have anything conservative?"

Martha smiled. "I think I can figure out what to wear." Then she traced the edge of a tile with the toe of her sandal, shifting so that her back was to the clubhouse. "Can I come a little early? I'd like to talk to you about something else."

"All right."

"Great. I'll see you Wednesday," Martha said.

As she turned to go, Dan saw her eyes over the top of the sunglasses. She glanced upward for an instant before walking toward the gate. She moved like liquid, the hem of her skirt swaying. She took a last pull on her cigarette and sent it into a hedge of red hibiscus flowers.

Dan looked toward the high windows in the upper level. A man in a jacket and open-collared shirt stood there watching Martha Cruz. Then the dark eyes with their slightly Asian tilt fixed on Dan.

CHAPTER 14

The hot tub was busted again, so Arlo Pate was on his knees at the little door with his flashlight. He peered into the works. A gasket on the pump this time. Last week it had been the electricity. Miguel Salazar had called him a few minutes ago, said bring your toolbox.

Arlo rose up far enough to tell Martha Cruz that the motor would be back to running in a few minutes. She nodded but didn't say anything. She was pissed, looking icepicks at Leon Davila, who was tapping his drumsticks all over the patio—the wood deck, the wet bar, the vine-covered lattice screens. Miguel had wanted screens so that he and whoever could come out here and get naked and the neighbors wouldn't see. Lately the whoever happened to be Martha.

In a way, Arlo felt the house was his. He had operated the dragline that dug the lakes, had smoothed the ground with a bulldozer, and had laid the foundation.

When Miguel bought the house, he hired Arlo off the construction crew because he could build things. The other reason was, Arlo had broken the arm of a sheetrock worker who had tried to take the cell phone out of Miguel's car.

Right now Miguel was in his bedroom getting on his swimsuit and making some phone calls, like he usually did after a deal went down. He didn't use the phone out here because he wanted to keep Martha out of his business.

Leon tapped his drumsticks on the hanging pots with orchids in them, then across the umbrella table, then along the edge of the hot tub itself, where Martha sat drinking her wine. Steam was rising out of the water. She'd be warm enough in there. It was pretty chilly otherwise, the patio being open to the night sky.

Shining his flashlight around the pump, Arlo found the loose gasket. He lifted a tray in his tool box to get his pipe wrench. He looked at Leon and slapped the wrench into his palm a couple of times, then went in to tighten the nut.

Leon had just come back from delivering some cash to one of Miguel's customers, and now he wanted to be patted on the head for it. He got too close to Martha, and she grabbed for one of his sticks and missed. He laughed at her. Martha called him a name and sank farther into the soap bubbles.

"Don't hide from me, girl. I know what you look like."

"You do not."

"No? Who was that girl up here the other night with a tattoo of a bird on her ass? That wasn't you?"

"Stay away from me, you shit. I'll tell Miguel."

"Go ahead. I'm family."

Arlo kept working. People as stupid as Leon usually had their mistakes pointed out to them one way or another. If Leon hadn't been related to one of Miguel's partners back in Guayaquil, he would have been gone already.

Now Leon was saying that he could feel the vibrations from the moon. He jumped off the edge of the hot tub, his shirt flapping behind him. He tapped his drumsticks against the air, like the moon was a big drumhead. Breathing hard from all the exercise, he fell into a chair. His hair hung over the back. "Martha, you need to loosen up, girl."

"I'm *trying* to. Why don't you leave?"

"Because I'm waiting for you to stand up." Giggling, Leon took a joint out of his shirt pocket and lit it.

Arlo gave the nut another turn, then said, "Leon, if I was you, I'd put that away. Miguel will be back in a minute, and he don't like it around."

Leon sucked in smoke, held it, then said, "That's ironic. You know what that word means, Arlo? Ironic?"

"I don't give a fart, Leon."

"No, that's 'apathy.' " He made one of his high-pitched laughs. "It's ironic that Miguel doesn't like grass around."

"You better shut up," Arlo said, jerking his head toward Martha.

"Like she don't know. She knows. She knows everything. Don't you, Martha? You so smart." Leon sucked on the joint again, smiling at her. "Martha Cruz. Big star."

Steam floated over the hot tub like fog. Martha reached out and grabbed her wineglass. "The band stunk until I got into it. You don't want to hear that, do you?"

Leon wasn't paying attention. He was staring at the sky again, grinning like the idiot he was. Arlo reached inside the door and felt if the nut was tight yet. Almost. He didn't mind working with his hands. He had arrived in Miami with twenty dollars in his pocket. That had been right after Hurricane Andrew had buzzsawed through, the whole county looking like a big fist had come down on it. They needed construction workers. A good time to leave Memphis anyway, after he accidentally killed a guy who jumped him in a bar, but try to explain that to a cop.

When Miguel Salazar didn't have anything for him to do, Arlo worked for Rick Robbins. He was a grip for the bands that came through town. That meant he toted and carried. When he wasn't a grip, he wore a black T-shirt that said Security, and he could keep order at the door. At punk rock concerts he would supervise the mosh pit and kick some skinhead ass, if need be.

Rick also let him drive Mayhem around to gigs and set up the equipment. Arlo didn't give a hairy rat's tit about the others—Leon most of all—but he liked Martha. Arlo had some talent himself, not as much as hers, but some. He used to hang out at a blues bar on Beale Street, where he had once backed up Stevie Ray Vaughan, God rest his soul. They said, *Arlo, you got a job here if you want it.* A memory like that could keep a man going for a long time.

Last night he'd been lying on the roof looking at the stars—they were in a little different position than back home, but they were still the same stars. And as he lay there he was playing a TV show in his mind. What if he was the one behind those shiny red drums, not Leon? What if it was his name going to be in the magazines? Maybe even at the Grammys. Best new band—Mayhem. It griped him to think of Leon up there. Leon was a little roach. Arlo wanted to smack him. His hands itched to do it. He wouldn't hit him with his fists, though. Since Martha had told Arlo a couple of months ago that she liked the way he played drums, he'd been more careful with his hands. If he slammed Leon in the teeth, which he dearly wanted to do, he might cut a knuckle.

Arlo threw the switch, and the water started bubbling and rolling in the hot tub. He closed the little door and wiped his hands on a rag. He said, "How's that, Martha?"

"Ahhhhh, you're wonderful, Arlo."

Leon was drinking Miguel's liquor now, still waiting for him. He took his drink to the table, making up a new song. "*Soy el poeta. La voz del aire, del sol, del cielo.*" He banged out a rhythm on the top with his sticks. "I am the voice of the universe—"

"Shut up!" Martha Cruz yelled. "Leon, please!"

"You want those sticks down your throat, Leon?"

Leon banged harder, the sticks turning into blurs. "Listen to me, girl. Take you to my world. *A mi mundo, al fondo de mi alma—*"

"Stop it! Arlo, make him stop."

Arlo walked over and took the sticks away and snapped them. "My cat could play drums better than you. You're stoned half the time and can't keep the beat. Martha and Kelly have to cover your ass. You better get straight before the concert, man."

Leon sat on the edge of the hot tub. "You like to cover my ass, Martha?"

With a splash Martha stood up. Arlo turned his head, but not before he got a good glimpse of her in the lights coming up through the water. Didn't have a stitch on. Her breasts were slick, and the soap was running down her stomach, between her legs.

He saw her arm reach for a towel.

"Arlo's right. You're a stoner. The band would be better without you in it. I wish you'd go back to Ecuador. I don't know why Miguel lets you stay here."

Leon smiled in her face. "At least I don't have to fuck him, do I?"

Arlo grabbed the little greaseball around the neck.

"*¡Quítelo!* Arlo, let him go."

Miguel Salazar was standing in the doorway. He

had one of his heavy silk robes on. Arlo wondered how long he'd been there. He gave Leon a shake and let him go.

Martha stomped over to Miguel, leaving shiny footprints across the wood deck. She was crying. "I can't take this anymore. He's ruining the band. We're never going to get a record contract. Never! *¡No puedo suportarlo más!*" She threw her glass. It hit the faucet on the hot tub and shattered. Her towel fell halfway off. She grabbed it around herself and ran inside. Miguel turned to watch her go.

Arlo cursed under his breath. Now he would have to filter the water. It would be a bitch finding every last piece of glass.

When Miguel turned back toward Leon, there was a cold flash in his eyes. Then it was gone. Leon started talking in Spanish, and Arlo gathered that Leon had delivered whatever it was he had to drop off.

Arlo wanted to take Leon over to that vacant lot behind one of those rock mounds and straighten him out. Arlo would use his work boots. He started thinking of where exactly to kick Leon, not to ruin Leon's hands either, because they needed him for the band.

Miguel said a few words, like Leon had made a good point. Then he shook the ice cubes in his glass and said he needed another drink. He smiled to include Arlo. "And for you?"

"No, I'd better go. The pump's working now."

Leon said, "Yeah. Miguel and I have stuff to talk

about." He sat on the wooden bench by the hot tub, which was all lit up, the water bubbling.

Arlo looked down at his hands. The big knuckles. The cobra tattoo on one hand, a Harley insignia on the other. The reddish hairs. Maybe putting just one in Leon's gut wouldn't do any damage. He shook his head and picked up his toolbox. "See you in the morning, Miguel."

"No, stay awhile. Have a drink with us."

Leon flipped his greaser hair out of his eyes and stared at Arlo. Arlo said, "Yeah, okay." He put his toolbox on the table.

Miguel opened and shut the little refrigerator under the bar. He filled three glasses with ice and poured in some liquor. Usually Miguel made some small talk. Leon was too ticked off to speak, and Arlo couldn't think of anything to say. He heard the motor under the hot tub. He felt a cold breeze drift through the vines. The moon went in and out of some clouds.

"Leon, come get your drink."

He stood up, a black outline in front of the hot tub.

Miguel reached into his robe, pulled out a pistol with a long barrel, and fired it twice. Two flashes of light. Two quick pops.

Arlo jerked from the surprise of it, then watched Leon cough, eyes wide open. Miguel still held the pistol pointed straight at him. A little black one, a .22 with a silencer.

Miguel shot him again, and Leon fell over backward. After a second or two, Arlo walked over to look down into the water. Turning red now, the steam still rising, Leon rolling around in there like meat in a soup pot. "Dang."

He looked back at Miguel, who was pouring Leon's drink out. Miguel couldn't see behind him. Couldn't see Martha standing way back in the darkened room. Arlo made a tiny nod. She opened the door. The sliver of light widened for a second, then got narrower till it was gone. He figured she was smart enough to keep this to herself.

CHAPTER 15

The arraignment in *State of Florida* v. *Martha Cruz* was scheduled for Wednesday. Dan dropped by the prosecutor's office first thing Tuesday morning and knocked on her door.

"Hi, Ruthie. Got a minute?"

"Sure, babe, come on in." He and Ruthie Martin knew each other, having met on other cases. "What's up?"

"Martha Cruz," he said. "Arraignment tomorrow."

Ruthie found the Cruz file in one of the boxes on the floor. "Here it is. What was this one about, Dan? Oh, yes. Your client slugged the Miami Beach cop. What do you want?"

"What are you offering?"

"This is contingent on the officer's approval, of course." Ruthie scanned the arrest affidavit. "Jim Purdy. Oops. Well, I could probably talk him into probation if your client agreed to counseling. You might even get a withhold of adjudication. How about it?" She took off her glasses and whirled them by one stem.

Plea bargaining. Most of Dan's cases went that way—he and an overworked prosecutor trying to cut a deal. For the most part, his clients were ordinary folks who through stupidity, bad temper, or bad luck got themselves into trouble. They rarely had much money. The Martha Cruz case fell outside the usual pattern, however. Mentally adding up the $1,000 that Rick would pay him, plus another $4,000—the value of one forty-six-foot, fully equipped Bertram sportfisher for a week—then dividing by the time he expected to spend on this case—two hours—he had arrived at a pretty damned good hourly rate. The two hours included the five minutes he had spent yesterday on a call to Miami Beach.

Dan said, "Ordinarily I'd say sure, Ruthie, that sounds fine, but I think you've got a little problem here. Your cop. He's retiring."

"So?"

"Going back to the old hometown—Evanston, Illinois." Dan drummed a rhythm on the edge of her desk.

Ruthie Martin sighed, a hand on her hip. "Tell me you're lying."

"I called the Miami Beach Police Department to see if he'd talk to me—sometimes they do. Nope. He's gone, as of next Monday. Check it out if you want."

She tossed the file onto her desk. "He can fly down for the trial. He'd come back. Get out of all that snow? You bet he would."

"Are you telling me that your office would authorize a high-season, short-notice, round-trip ticket to Miami, plus hotel and meals for two days—"

"What two days? This is a half-day trial, max."

"You haven't seen my list of witnesses yet."

"Forget the counseling, then. Plead nolo contendere and take a withhold."

Dan shook his head. "Can't do it, Ruthie. The girl is a talented young singer, right on the verge of a major record contract, a real sweet kid. Any kind of legal problem at this point could ruin her career. I'm representing Martha as a favor to her manager, a good friend of mine. The situation just got a little out of hand after Officer Purdy roughed up one of her fans. She's sorry—sincerely sorry."

A smile started to work through. "How much of this is bullshit?"

"Ruthie. You've got better things to do."

"I never liked Purdy anyway," she said.

In the lobby downstairs Dan called Martha Cruz at the Salazar house in Lakewood. She was rehearsing at the studio. He left a message for her to call him, hung up, then looked in the case file for the number of Salazar's company in Miami. A woman with a Spanish accent answered. *Señor* Salazar was in conference. "Tell him Daniel Galindo called. The matter we discussed has concluded satisfactorily. Let me know when to pick up my payment. He'll know what that means. Thanks."

The last call was to Coral Rock Productions. Rick Robbins was out. Dan left a message with the receptionist. "Tell Rick I just scored a bull's-eye on that case he gave me. It's time to pay up."

Dan picked up his mail from Alva Dunavoy's desk, where a fifties doo-wop tune was playing on the radio. He could see Alva at the open front door, bitching to Charlie about the flowers that had been stolen out of the planters—again. Dan heard Charlie asking why she had to have flowers at all, and Alva retorting that they gave the office some class. Charlie's bass voice boomed out, "My God, Alva, put in some plastic plants. Nobody would steal those, and you don't have to water the damn things."

Smiling a little, Dan shook his head. He would miss these people. Charlie had taken in an unknown lawyer without a single client to bring with him. Dan had opened his door that first Monday to the smell of lemon wax. Alva had polished the old furniture in the spare office till it gleamed and put a potted plant on his credenza. Dan got right to work on the cases Charlie had given him, most of them routine criminal or family matters. Charlie had laughed and slapped him on the back. *You and me, Dan, we're simple swabbies on the great ship Jurisprudence.*

Dan had done all right in this office, but it was time to move on.

He took the *Business Review* off Alva's desk and flipped to the classified section as he went to find some coffee. The pot in the tiny kitchen was empty, so he made some more. Waiting for it to drizzle through, he leaned against the counter to read the ads for professional employment. Hialeah wanted a city attorney, $45,000. Quite a few ads for personal injury lawyers. *Coral Gables area. Associate litigator wanted. Must be able to successfully try personal injury and employment discrimination cases. Salary 40–70K depending on experience.* Not criminal law, but a courtroom was a courtroom. He circled that one.

He turned a page, reading the ads for offices to rent. *Fort Lauderdale. Trial and/or criminal lawyer wanted to share space, secretarial services incl., walk to courthouse, $1,000/mo.* Dan read it again. Fort Lauderdale. Twenty-five miles due north. Closer to Josh and Lisa. It would mean starting over. Losing his clients here, finding new ones in Broward County. A thousand a month. Possible.

Dan scanned the list for Miami. *Space avail in established criminal law firm with elegant offices in bank bldg, walk to courthouse. Conf room, library, etc. $2,000/mo.* Perfect—but not yet.

He laughed at the next one—a way to avoid rent altogether. A law office on Brickell Avenue offered a "business identity" for $80. He could interview clients in the living room of his apartment.

Charlie came in and took down a mug. "What's so funny?"

Dan folded the paper. "Just reading about the latest city commission meeting."

"Hey, I meant to tell you, but I didn't see you yesterday. I ran into Elaine McHale at the club last weekend. She's not doing too well."

"What do you mean? Is she sick?"

"I don't know. I couldn't make much sense of what she was saying. She was drinking. She sounded depressed as hell." Charlie filled his mug. "Elaine's a great gal. A shame to see her that way." He poked the spoon at the caked sugar in the bowl. "She asked about you. Maybe you should give her a call."

"I will. Definitely."

Taking his coffee to his desk, Dan dialed her number from memory. They had worked together on dozens of cases during the six years he had been employed at the U.S. attorney's office. Elaine had always been so steady, so assured. Even after her husband, Mack, had died— what was it?—four years ago, she hadn't lost her equilibrium. Henry McHale had been a lieutenant with Metro-Dade. He had died at the scene of a bank robbery, protecting one of the hostages with his own body. A hero. Elaine had received a letter from the White House. She had not remarried, and she lived alone. Her solitude must have become too much to bear.

The ringing at the other end switched over to her voice mail. Dan smiled into the phone. "This is one of your many admirers. Where are you, in court? How about lunch? You name the place, my treat. Call me at the office—and if you don't know who this is, shame on you."

* * *

Watching Kelly Dorff walk out of the restaurant last week, Elaine McHale had experienced a quick surge of panic. She had gone against John Paxton's advice not to talk to a confidential informant, and that same C.I. had threatened to tell the DEA about their meeting. Elaine had calmly finished her coffee. She decided to talk it over with Vincent Hooper.

He came to her office on Tuesday.

Vince looked at the ceiling, rubbing his fingers through his beard. "Elaine, Elaine."

"I had to find out for myself where Kelly was coming from with this story of hers about Dan Galindo. I'm the one who'll have to put her on the stand."

"And I'm waiting for Rick Robbins to hook me up with Salazar. This operation is balanced right on that one point, and the slightest thing could tip it over."

"Okay. You're right. Did Kelly contact you, by the way?"

"Not about you, no."

"I told her I'd ask you about the master tapes from the studio," Elaine said. "The band needs them to make a demo for a New York talent scout."

"I know," Vince said. "Rick Robbins was whining about it over the weekend. Here's what I told him. If this meeting with Salazar goes as planned, he can have the tapes."

"I feel sorry for that girl."

"Kelly? Give me a break. People put themselves where they are, Elaine. Feeling sorry won't save her, and it sure as hell won't help you prosecute Miguel Salazar."

"Vince."

He held up his hands. "All right. You're the last person I want to preach at."

"How much longer are you going to need her?"

"Hell, I don't know," he said. "Till it's over. I wish I could say thanks and good-bye, have a nice life, see you on the cover of *Rolling Stone*."

"I don't want to put her on the stand," Elaine said.

"You might have to."

"Kelly Dorff will make a lousy witness. She's desperate not to testify because she thinks her career would be over. Based on what I saw last Friday, a good defense lawyer would have her crying in two minutes, how the DEA—specifically agent Hooper—threatened her if she didn't —"

"Oh, good God almighty. What was I going to do, beat her with a rubber hose? Throw her in a dungeon? Where do people get these ideas?"

"She was talking about Luis Barrios again."

"Really? Why am I not surprised? Now, there's a nifty reason not to use her as a C.I. on this operation. Did anybody figure that out? No. I go to Ecuador, come back, and there she is. And then I find Dan Galindo at the studio."

"I think she was lying about him," Elaine said.

"Oh, you do? Rick Robbins tells us he's involved, Kelly Dorff tells us the same thing, and that isn't enough for you?"

"I think Kelly Dorff had a motive to lie."

"Which is?"

"She wanted to give you some scrap as her ticket out. And second, she's intensely angry at Dan. She told me her father wrote her off. Her brother got what he wanted, and she was ignored. She trusted her last boyfriend enough to carry a kilo of smack for him, and he lets her take the fall. Then Dan comes along. He's kind, he's smart, he's good-looking. A lawyer, no less. Of course she falls for him. When he broke it off, she felt betrayed—again—and she wanted to strike back."

"Wait. She told me she broke it off with *him*, not the other way around."

"Trust me, Vince. No."

Vince was silent for a moment. "All right. I can buy that, but you've still got Rick Robbins. He says Galindo is involved."

After a second or two, Elaine rolled her eyes to the ceiling and shrugged.

He smiled at her, his cheek propped on a fist.

Elaine loved him when he looked at her that way. The feeling was so real she could imagine wrapping herself up in it. She could almost forget what else went along with loving Vincent Hooper. Waiting. Pretending the other half of his life didn't exist.

"I haven't talked to John Paxton yet," she said.

"About what?"

"Meeting Kelly. He told me not to. Well, he said he advised against it."

They both knew what she was asking.

Vince said, "I don't think you should worry about John."

"You're sure?"

"Why bring up a non-issue? He's such a stickler for the rules he'd see problems where there aren't any." Vince came around Elaine's desk to kiss her on top of the head. "I have to go, sweetheart." Then he kissed her on the lips.

"I like that," she said. "Do it again."

"Oh, now you want me back, since I promised not to rat on you."

She grabbed the lapels of his jacket and pulled him back down for another kiss. "Too bad for me. I always want you."

CHAPTER 16

Martha Cruz told Dan to meet her at the marina in Coconut Grove. He arrived just after six o'clock, having first changed his suit for khaki pants and well-worn canvas deck shoes. The marina was a sprawling facility behind Miami City Hall, and docks fanned out into the water. This time of year every slip was taken, and dozens of sailboats and cruisers were moored just offshore. The old wooden docks where Raul Galindo used to keep his fishing boat had been torn out years ago, replaced with concrete.

Coming from the parking lot, Dan saw a black-haired girl sitting on a bench along the seawall. She wore green sunglasses. Her face turned toward him, and in one quick motion she rose to her feet.

"Hi." She lightly kissed his cheek, a gesture more formal than affectionate. "I was about to wonder if you were coming." Her black hair was a riot of curls around her face and down her back.

"To see the boat that's going to take me to the Bahamas, believe me, I'll be here. Just don't tell me Miguel changed his mind."

Martha reached into the pocket of her jeans and withdrew a set of keys, which swung from one finger, jingling softly. Dan reached out, but the keys disappeared into her hand. "Come on." She crossed the walkway and unlocked the gate.

They walked along the dock, passing people in swimsuits and shorts going the other way. Without much daylight left, boats were coming back in, tying up. The *Basilón* was in a slip near the end. Forty-six feet of boat, close to a million dollars' worth of fiberglass, stainless steel, electronic gear, and living quarters, with two big diesel engines to push it all through the water at a thirty-knot cruising speed. Tinted windows, long foredeck.

Dan stepped onto the gunwale, then down to the cockpit. The boat barely dipped under his weight. He ran his hand up the smooth metal ladder that led to the bridge.

"I think you're in love."

"Oh, yeah. Absolutely." Dan examined the bait-prep station on the bulkhead. "You say Miguel never takes the boat out?"

"Hardly ever." Martha jumped aboard, landing lightly in her sneakers, steadying herself on Dan's shoulder. "He lets his friends use it, but he never does. I think he gets seasick."

"What a shame."

Martha put her sunglasses away in a small purse,

then unlocked the salon and turned on the lights. Dan went inside. The interior was done in dark blue and teak. Built-in sofas and cabinets. Bar, TV, VCR. Steps led to the galley, then a hall to a master stateroom, head, and guest bunks in the bow. He took a quick look around, Martha pointing things out to him.

On the way back through the galley, she said, "How did you make the state attorney dismiss my case?"

"If I told you, you wouldn't need me next time."

"Miguel thinks you paid off the police."

Dan shook his head and laughed, letting her go first up the steps to the salon.

"Whatever you did, thanks." Her manner was subdued tonight, as if she were so fatigued from anxiety that good news couldn't touch it. He gave her a quick squeeze around the shoulders.

They went back outside. She locked the salon door, then suddenly turned to him with an open-mouthed smile, a sudden burst of energy.

"You want to take the boat out?"

"Now?"

"I can show you how to run it," she said. "We could go for a ride if we don't stay out too long. The band has rehearsal tonight." She grabbed the ladder to the bridge and took a step up. "Okay?"

"Why not?"

Under her sweater she wore a short top that exposed a few inches of bare skin and three silver rings in her navel. A chain went through the rings and dropped below the waistband of her low-slung jeans. She turned to climb the ladder. The seat of her jeans had worn to threads in a couple of places, only bare skin underneath.

Martha stood at the captain's seat and unlocked the helm. "If Miguel happens to ask—just in case—tell him that you picked up the keys from Rick, okay?"

"Why?"

She pushed back the helm cover. "Well . . . Miguel gets jealous over nothing. He almost didn't let me hire you."

"He doesn't know you're here?"

"Not really. He knows you're borrowing the boat. We have to be careful, that's all. See that switch? You have to flip that first."

"Martha, what are you getting me into?"

"Nothing. Go untie the ropes."

"It's called casting off," Dan said.

"Okay, let's cast off."

"After we start the engines."

"Whatever."

At no-wake speed they maneuvered out of the marina, going around the mangrove island that shielded the harbor from the bay. The setting sun had turned the clouds pink and purple. Martha let Dan have the wheel, then sat back in the other chair with her sneakers propped on the helm.

Dan pushed forward on the throttle as they got into deeper water. The boat surged ahead, water hissing past the sides. Martha spoke louder to be heard. "You like it?"

"Are you kidding? I love it." Steering due south, Dan planned to make a long loop. He pushed the speed up to twenty knots, twenty-five. The water was calm, and the boat seemed to lift over it. On Sunday he would take Josh out. And Lisa, if he could talk her into it. She would see this boat and want to go to Cat Cay herself.

Martha's hair was whirling around her face. Her brows drew together, making a crease in the smooth skin between them. She said, "I suppose you think I'm a slut for being with Miguel."

"No. You have your reasons."

"We get along all right," she said. "He's very sexual and romantic, you know? I like that. Up to a point. He doesn't want to let me go, but he's going to have to. Soon as we finish that demo, I'm out of here. If it doesn't happen, I'll kill myself."

If her mood had been less serious, Dan might have smiled. "Come on, Martha. Your career doesn't depend on one demo tape."

"It does. In this business? If you don't get that one break, it's over."

"You're only twenty-one years old, for God's sake."

She pulled her sweater tightly around herself and hugged her knees. "I could be dead next week too."

"No. You'll make it. You're very talented."

"This is true. I can hear things other people can't. In my mind, you know? It's like . . . seeing colors, and most people are color-blind." She smiled at Dan and pushed her hair away from her face. "I've been like that since I was a baby. When I was two years old, my dad split, and my mom had no money, and so she, my sister, and me lived in a shelter. Somebody gave me this toy xylophone. All the notes were different colors. One octave, eight colors. You could sing a song and I could play it back to you. We had to move after a while, and they said I couldn't take the xylophone, and I cried and cried. I can't tell you what my dad looked like, or where we lived back then, but I can still hear that xylophone. I can see it, like it's right here. When I was about six, my mom joined some evangelical church in Hialeah. They had a keyboard, and I found that thing, and wow, they couldn't pull me off it. They were, like, Hey, would you stop already? The pastor said for them to give me lessons for free. Then of course they wanted me to play for services, this really stupid-ass music, so I stopped going."

Martha scooted down a bit to stay out of the wind. The temperature was falling as the light faded. She said, "I never finished high school. I got pregnant and dropped out. My mom made me have the baby, then somebody adopted it. I never went back to school. I'm smart, but I can't read very well. Isn't that a horrible thing to admit? It's true. I can read music, though. I taught myself. I'm a better musician than Kelly. It's funny to realize that about people you used to think were so amazing. Music is all I do. It's like my obsession. I would do anything before I'd give that up. I would die first. I mean that sincerely. If you told me I couldn't sing anymore, that I would have to stop playing music, I would die. I told Miguel that. He understood, you know? He said he'd help me, and he did, so I have this, like, loyalty to some extent. But lately—like in the last few days—I've been thinking about leaving. I think about that a lot."

"You could leave," Dan said. "Rick and Sandy would let you live with them. Or stay with Kelly."

She was silent, hugging her knees.

Dan asked, "Is Miguel violent? Does he hit you?"

She gave her head a quick shake. "Don't worry about it. I wouldn't stay if I thought he would hurt me. He's in love with me. He'd do anything for me, is what he said. He yells when he's mad, but he's never hit me." She pressed her full lips tightly together. "I just— It's complicated."

"What are you waiting for, the concert to be over?" Dan asked.

"The demo tape, the concert. Yes. If I left now—" With a sudden groaning exhalation she dropped her forehead to her knees. After a second she raised her face, laughing. "I might show up at your door some night. Help! Help! Would you let me in?"

"What's going on, Martha?"

"Would you?"

"Yes, if you were in trouble. Of course. But if you want to leave him, then leave."

"No, I don't want to. Not really. Things are just, like, *tense* right now, that's all. A teeny bit tense."

Dan watched her for a moment, then said, "Last time we talked, you had something on your mind. What was it about? Miguel?"

She kept her eyes on the water rushing toward them. "No. The demo tape. Who owns it? Say we finish the demo, but the studio won't let us have it. It's still ours, isn't it? We did the work. We wrote the songs."

"Why wouldn't they let you have it?"

"I don't know. Like . . . they didn't get paid."

"Is that going to be a problem?"

"It's an example, okay?"

"Well, I'm not up on the standard practices in studio recording, but my guess is, the studio doesn't have to release anything they haven't been paid for. Talk to Rick if you're concerned about it. He's your manager." Dan added, "I'm not much good at giving legal advice when clients don't give me all the facts."

Martha stood up and leaned on the helm. "We lost our drummer. Did Rick tell you?"

"I haven't talked to Rick." Dan turned the wheel sharply, seeing what the boat would do. Steady. No wallowing. The horizon seemed to tilt. Dan made a tight circle, then came out of it heading north. "What happened to the drummer?"

"Leon went back to Ecuador, but we've got another drummer already, Arlo Pate. The tall red-haired man? He was at the studio the night you came."

"How's Rick taking this?"

"He's okay with it. Arlo's better than Leon. I think so, anyway. Kelly disagrees, but she and I disagree about a lot of things. Arlo has to work on the songs. That's why I have to get back tonight."

"Why did Leon quit?"

Martha shrugged. "Miguel told him to. They were—They're like cousins or something. Leon was living at the house, but Miguel didn't like him, so he told him to get out."

"All the way back to Ecuador?"

"Well, Leon never cared that much about the band." Martha grabbed Dan's arm. "Listen, we're having a party Friday night on South Beach, in a penthouse suite on Ocean Drive. You're invited. Miguel's paying for it, naturally, but Rick has invited all kinds of people. Please say you'll come."

"Well . . . I might drop in."

"You have to be there. The band's going to play—our first time with the new guys. You don't want to come because of Kelly?" Martha hugged his arm closer, and he could feel her breast. "She won't care. I'll talk to her."

"No, no, it's not that. I told my son I'd take him out on Friday." Dan took his arm away and turned on the running lights. "The concert. I'll be at the concert, count on it."

That sent Martha spinning into another mood. "If we make it to the concert. We have to. Yes!" She threw her head back. "The man from Capitol Records will love us. What a band! You're amazing! Sign here, Ms. Cruz. Please." She suddenly swung out over the edge of the bridge, hanging onto the tower ladder.

"Be careful!"

Martha only laughed, bending backward into an arch, her sweater blowing open, her hair whipping like a dark flag. Dan could hear her singing but couldn't make out the words. He glanced ahead of them to check for other boats, then yelled, "I hope you like swimming in the ocean."

Holding on by one hand, she balanced on the edge of the bridge. She shouted back, "I know why you left the U.S. attorney's office. You wouldn't tell me, but I found out."

"What did you find out?"

"That you lost a case against a drug dealer, and they wanted to fire you, so you quit."

"Not exactly, but close. Who told you that?"

"Someone. I know a lot about you."

"Is that right?"

"Like you wear silk boxers to bed, but you always take them off in the middle of the night."

"No offense, Martha, but what I wear—or do—in bed is none of your business."

Her laughter came clearly over the steady growl of the engines. "Maybe I'll find out for myself." Her arms were over her head, and the silver chain through her navel rings bounced slightly on her taut, tanned abdomen.

He felt the heat build in his groin. "Are you trying to get me in trouble?"

"With who? Miguel?"

"He might hang me up like that sailfish he caught."

She laughed. "I don't see Miguel out here, do you?"

Dan slid his hands over the ship's wheel and took a slow breath. He could cut the engines and drop the anchor. Take her below. Explore the staterooms. See where that chain went. He said, "You're awfully young."

"Miguel is forty-one, and he doesn't think so. How old are you?"

"Thirty-five next week."

"Yeah, that's so old." Balancing on the edge, she stepped toward the bow, then dropped out of sight. She reappeared on the foredeck, whirling around, arms extended. The boat hit a trough and sent up a spray. She screamed, delighted, and grabbed the railing.

"Hey! Don't do that! Martha!" He took the engines out of gear.

For a while the boat glided forward on its own momentum. Martha Cruz stayed on the foredeck, dancing. The boat was rising and falling on the swells. The sky had turned colorless, a few stars coming out. Over the low pulse of the engines, Dan heard her singing one of her songs. "Hey, yeah, touch me, be with me. We're okay. We're all right now, doin' so fine, baby, yeah, yeah, yeah."

Dan said under his breath, "Don't. Don't. You will regret it."

She sat down suddenly on the deck and hit it with both fists. Then again. Her hair fell around her. Water slapped against the hull. A speedboat angled by, heading in to port before the light was gone completely.

He called out, "Martha?"

She raised her face, as blank and empty as the sky. She said, "It's late. I have to get back."

CHAPTER 17

The band picked a hot blues number, "Goin' Down," for the last song in the set. Last song, toughest one too. Might as well go for it, Rick thought, standing at the edge of the crowd, chewing his thumbnail.

The band had been nervous as cats all week, Martha pushing them hard, Kelly screaming at Martha, the guys fucking up every other song. But tonight they were pulling it all together. By God, they were. They were playing to a couple hundred people jammed into a South Beach penthouse, the place all lit up with neon, the music screaming off the turquoise and pink walls.

"Come on, baby. Come on," Rick murmured to himself, watching Scott Irwin. His solo was coming up. "Right on the beat. Come on."

Going into the bridge, Scott reached out to tap an effects pedal with the toe of his high-top sneaker. Kelly was singing, her face red, spittle flying out, working her head around the mike as if her mouth were a pivot. Scott hit the pedal again. Waited for the drum. Did his four bars of fast fretwork. Then back into the blues beat.

Rick thrust a fist into the air. "Yes!"

Now Kelly was jumping up and down with her guitar. Martha grabbed the microphone over her keyboard with one hand, and Scott leaned over to sing into his. Arlo Pate just pounded the drums, sweat pouring down his face, scraggly red hair bouncing under a bandanna. He had a big gut and big arms; he could have bench-pressed a cow. Rick had felt his heart seize up when Arlo told him that Leon had gone back to Ecuador. It didn't make sense. A guy didn't just walk away from a band on the verge of making it. He was afraid that Arlo had taken Leon to the Everglades to play with the alligators and land crabs.

People were dancing where there was room for it. A bunch of them had spilled outside onto the terrace.

Miguel had wanted to throw this party in his backyard, but Rick had said no way would anybody drive forty miles to the Broward County suburbs for an unknown band, didn't matter how much free booze you gave them. It just wasn't hip. Rick had told him, What you do is, you rent a penthouse in an Art Deco hotel on Ocean Drive. You get a caterer to lay out stuff like goat cheese, thin-sliced raw tuna, and curried black bean dip. The bartenders are very buff, preferably models. Buy a dozen cases of pretty good champagne, invite the pivotal people in the club scene, the local music critics, a few literary types, a couple of drag queens, and whatever B-list rock musician might be in town that weekend. Put out the rumor that Madonna might drop by. Then stand back.

Martha had set up her tape machine in the other room, recording it all. Tomorrow they would pick it apart, see what they needed to fix. Rick had never seen her so frantic. He told her to chill, that these people wouldn't make or break the band, but she had barely looked up from her cables and amps. Next week the band would do some final bass guitar overdubs and patch up the vocal tracks a bit, if they had time. If they got into the goddamn studio.

Rick felt queasy with dread. He had told the manager of the studio, Victor Ramirez, that he could get him a deal with Miguel, but so far, Miguel hadn't responded. Ramirez wanted an answer and he was starting to be a prick about it. He'd said, *No deal, no demo tape.* Rick needed to get Miguel alone, find out what was going on.

He stood on tiptoe and looked around one of the drag queens, who was dressed like Courtney Love. Miguel was over there with some of his buddies, the silk-jacket-and-Rolex crowd from South America. Rick put a fist to his sternum and pressed hard. Was it the speakers making his bones shake, or was he having a coronary?

The band was getting near the end of the song now. Scott Irwin shuffled across the floor toward Kelly. They sawed the air with the necks of their guitars. Her hair hung over her face. She hit the reverb and leaned back into the final chord. Martha slammed her hands onto the keys, and that was that.

The people applauded and cheered and whistled. Rick wondered if they had liked it. Most of them were either drunk or stoned. Aside from the few important people who had showed up, they were various hangers-on, party people, and out-of-town asswipes. One guy saying he knew the president of MCA. Another who owned a gallery in SoHo. Experts in how to wear black and look cool. Maybe they were waiting to see if anybody jumped up on the bar and started stripping.

Rick went over and gave each of the musicians a hug. Except for Arlo Pate. Rick said, "Good job, Arlo."

"Yeah. Thanks." He mopped his face with a towel and reached for a long-neck beer, which he chugged in three seconds flat.

An arm went around Rick's waist. Sandy had come up behind him.

"What'd you think, cookie?"

She said, "I'm ready to get on back home. This is the most phony-baloney bunch I ever did see." Sandy had teased her hair and put on a tight, fringed miniskirt and a sequined cowboy shirt, making people snicker behind her back. Rick knew she got a charge out of it, and if he'd had the guts he would have worn his Elvis costume from last Halloween.

He said, "No, what'd you think of the *band*?"

She looked up at him—long black lashes and shiny

blue eye shadow. The corners of her eyes crinkled when she smiled. "Honey, I think you got yourself a winner."

"It's ours, baby. You and me." He kissed her forehead. "Go find us a drink. I need to talk to Miguel."

Kelly signed a few autographs and had her picture taken with people she didn't know, then asked Martha if she could use Miguel's telephone. Kelly took the phone out onto the terrace, found a more or less quiet spot, and dialed Elaine McHale's office number, waiting for the voice mail to pick up. Nobody would be at the U.S. attorney's office at midnight, but Kelly didn't want to talk to a real person, who would start asking questions.

Leaning on the railing on the sixth floor, Kelly stared out at the black ocean, no way to tell sea from sky, except for the tiny dots of light—boats, way out there. Below her, cars moved slowly by on Ocean Drive. People filled the sidewalks, looking funny from this angle.

Elaine McHale's voice said to leave a message. Kelly cleared her throat, raw from so much singing. "Hi. This is Kelly Dorff. I'm sorry for the way I acted at the restaurant. I was like totally freaked. I'm really sorry. I already called Vincent and took back what I said about Dan. And listen. I didn't tell him about you and Dan being friends and everything, okay?" She exhaled. "I guess that's it. Oh. Don't forget about the demo tapes. You promised. Bye."

Kelly disconnected, then stared at the phone for a moment. "Okay, you bastard." She punched in Vincent Hooper's number, not expecting him to answer. He never did. There was never even a message on the other end, only a beep. "This is Kelly. I need to talk to you. Call me at my apartment before ten o'clock tomorrow morning. After that I won't be there. You'd better do it."

More people started coming out to the terrace with their drinks, laughing and talking. Kelly retreated behind a potted tree with a braided trunk. She dialed Dan Galindo's number at home. She counted four rings. Then his answering machine came on.

"Dan? If you're there, pick up." She waited. "You're there, aren't you? Or maybe you have company. Hey, chick. He's a dangerous man. Be careful." She laughed. "Or maybe you're really out. Well, what I wanted to tell you— Here I am on the sixth floor of a fabulous penthouse on Ocean Drive—" Kelly crooked her arm over her eyes, moved the phone away from her mouth to take a few breaths, then said, "The party went really great, in case you're interested. What I called about was . . . I'm really sorry for freaking out on you. I left some stuff at your house. Maybe I could come get it sometime. Or you could bring it to me. I'll be staying with Martha for a while."

A long beep came from the other end of the line.

Kelly clicked the off button and let her head fall on her arm. After a while she squinted to find the redial button in the dark. She poked around and finally heard the tones again. Then his message. She wiped under her nose with the hem of her T-shirt.

"It's me again." She felt tears burning her eyes. The line was silent. "I have to go back in. They want us to do another number, I think. Leave me a message or something. And . . . I hope you're happy. No lie, okay?"

By the time Rick got to him through the crowd, Miguel Salazar was telling one of the suckups that he himself would pay for publicity—spots on radio, ads in the *Miami Herald*—if the man would book Mayhem into his club in Coconut Grove the night before the concert at the Abyss, three weekends away. The important thing, he told him, was to make sure that the A&R scout from Capitol Records, and the others who might be at the Abyss, all believed that the band was popular in Miami.

The man's hair was gelled to stand straight up, and his glasses were long black rectangles. "Three *weeks*? Oh, please. If you'd called me before Christmas, then maybe. But look. We're not the right venue for a rock band. Miami likes dance music, you know? The town where disco never died. It's the demographics. Half Latin, twenty percent black. Dance music. Cutting-edge rock and roll just *limps* along. Oh sure, the clubs on South Beach, but it's so derivative. Miami has only two presumptive rock stations, and those are so into, like, pop rock and altie you could just *gag*."

"How much do you think to get a single on the radio?" Miguel asked.

Martha, standing next to him, rolled her eyes. "Miguel, forget it."

"Oh, she's right," the man said. "You can't get on a P-1 station. That's like the Holy Grail. They only do national hits. You can't even *pay* to get on, and if you did, it wouldn't affect the national market, would it? Drop in the *bucket*. There's a local music show on Sundays, but like, is anybody listening?"

He came in closer to Miguel and reached out to pull Rick over, fingers like spiders crawling around his wrist. "Rick, my friend, come here. Can I offer an irreverent prediction? You're gonna restructure this band sooner or later."

"You think so?"

"Oh, yeah. Martha is way too much for these guys. Mayhem. Oh, God. Excuse me, but is that juvenile or what? She'd get further on her own with a backup band."

"What should we call it?" Miguel asked.

"I'd call it simply 'Cruz.' It's ethnic, but not too. Can you see the headline in *Billboard*? 'New band on Cruz control.' Subhead—'Martha Cruz goes platinum.' What do you think? Perfect?"

"I like it," Miguel said.

Rick said, "Hey, Miguel. I need to talk to you."

Kneeling on the wood floor, hiding behind the drums, Kelly wiped off her guitar while Arlo and Scott started packing everything away. She shined the chrome tuning pegs and worked the cloth down the strings.

It was a Fender Jaguar made in 1969, worth about $2,000. The old hippie who had sold her the Jag thought he was ripping her off for the four-fifty she'd paid him. He said that Jimi Hendrix had played it, then passed it on to Carlos Santana. A total lie, but she liked the sound of it and the color—Lake Placid blue—and the curves of the body, and she liked to imagine that his stories were really true.

She noticed that her arms were shaking. It was partly muscle fatigue. The rest was . . . cold, stone fear. Knowing she had been at the furthest edge tonight, playing as well as she could, and it wasn't good enough. Her hands had felt stiff, and she couldn't concentrate. In her solo on "Let It Ride," she had screwed up for a bar and a half. Martha had covered her. Scott got a little confused, but Arlo didn't miss a beat. Rick had looked scared for a second, but nobody else had noticed.

She saw a pair of blurry canvas high-tops. She dried her eyes with the cloth. Scott asked her what was wrong. "I'm okay." She stood up.

He grabbed her arm before she tripped. "Kelly, what's the matter with you?"

"I have to get out of here." She gulped in a breath, feeling like she might scream.

Sandy Robbins put her arm around her. "C'mon, honey. We gon' find ourselves a glass of nice cool water. Maybe just lie down for a sec. Thank you, Scott. She's okay. She's just fine. Aren't you, hon?"

"I wanted to play my music, that's all. That's all I wanted." Kelly let Sandy walk her down the narrow hall away from the penthouse living room. "Oh, God. I'm so sorry. Sandy, I'm sorry."

"You hush. Not a thing to be sorry for."

"There is, there is."

Voices behind them were curious, asking if she was sick, or what. Sandy yelled, "Y'all leave her alone. She's all right. Where's Rick?"

There was a bedroom down the hall. It had a picture of Marilyn Monroe, a white chenille bedspread, and a little table shaped like a flying saucer. Sandy made Kelly lie down, then got her a glass of water out of the bathroom and a wet washcloth. Told her to sip the water. Sandy wiped off her face. Kelly felt so heavy she couldn't move. After a while she stopped crying.

"Are you all right now, hon?" The sequins twinkled on Sandy's cowgirl shirt. There were gold lassos on the pockets, and the buttons were mother-of-pearl.

"You're very nice, Sandy."

"Oh, well. We girls have to look out for each other." Sandy wagged a finger. "You gonna start bawlin' again?" Her face softened. "Anything you wanta talk about, Kelly? Man trouble? I think I know who."

"No. I'm okay now." Kelly closed her eyes. "I'll take care of it."

Out on the terrace, Miguel told Rick to go find his telephone. Martha had it, he thought. Rick got it from her, then came back out. Miguel lit a cigar and talked with some of his friends while Rick dialed the number that Victor Ramirez had given him. Victor came on the line.

Rick told him who he was, and that someone wanted to talk to him. He tapped Miguel on the shoulder. "Hey. Can you possibly do this now?"

In Spanish Miguel told the other guys to excuse him for a minute. He took the telephone, walked a little farther down the terrace, and put an elbow on the railing.

"Victor? This is Miguel, how are you? . . . Yes, the band is sounding great. Rick says you're doing a good job for him at the studio. We should talk about it sometime. Maybe lunch, what do you say? . . . Monday is better . . . I'll call you that morning and let you know where. . . . Not yet. First let's get to know each other, okay? Then maybe we'll do business. . . . Good, I'll see you then." He hung up and handed the phone to Rick.

Sweat was running under Rick's arms and down his back. He forced a laugh. "Finally. For this you should give me a break on what I owe you."

Miguel eyed Rick over the glowing end of his cigar, then walked back to his buddies. A bimbo in a tight minidress glanced past Miguel's shoulder for a second, then started laughing at whatever it was he said to her.

Rick gripped the railing, stared over the side, and wondered if six floors were far enough to fall.

CHAPTER 18

On Sunday morning Elaine McHale sat cross-legged on the floor of her living room, going through stacks of personal papers, filling garbage bags with trash. Last night she had noticed how much junk had accumulated in her bedroom closet. She had pulled unworn clothes off hangers and out of dresser drawers, thrown out faded sheets and threadbare towels, then attacked the guest room closet and the bookshelves in the living room. She had worked until two o'clock in the morning and was awake at dawn. Now the living room was strewn with papers, and six black plastic bags were stacked behind the privacy fence on the front porch.

Sometimes she and Vince Hooper would read the Sunday paper and have breakfast together, but he would usually call the night before to tell her he was coming. He hadn't called, and to her surprise, she hadn't minded so much. She had scrubbed her face, but her hair was still uncombed. She had on an old Miami police T-shirt, running shorts, and the red socks she had worn to bed. The radio was tuned to a classical music station. The solitude was delicious.

One of her two cats lay in a patch of sunshine, toes splayed, yawning so widely his tongue lolled out. Elaine patted his tummy, then reached for another cardboard box. Inside were folders of notes from law school. Christmas cards in a rubber band that broke when she touched it. A glass doorknob from her grandmother's house. A flamingo swizzle stick. Labels from bottles of wine. Old bank statements for Henry and Elaine McHale. Then undated photographs with people whose names she couldn't remember. All these she tossed away. She found an announcement of Mack's graduation from the police academy and set that aside to send to his parents in Ohio. They already had his citations for bravery, posthumously given.

The Mozart violin concerto on the radio ended, followed by an ad for Cadillac. She aimed the remote and turned down the volume, then took another sip of tea. Mango-strawberry, which she hadn't tried before.

The next box contained loose photographs that she had never found time to put into an album. She flipped through the photos. Nothing she wanted, but she couldn't just throw them out. Could she? The Siamese cat was playing in the trash bag. She pulled the cat out and tossed in the photographs by the handful.

A cool breeze came in through the open door to the

tiny backyard, and the sunlight shifted into patterns of leaves. A wind chime tinkled softly. The people in the apartment next door were having breakfast on their patio. Elaine stood up to dump an entire box of old bank statements and tax returns and receipts into the bag. Some fluttered to the floor. She scraped them together, hurled them in, then jerked the top of the bag into a knot.

Leaning back against the weight, she carried the bag outside and dumped it with the others. She turned to go inside. Then someone called her name.

Dan Galindo was coming up the walkway to her porch, veering around an elephant-ear plant that had grown past the flower bed. "This is lucky. I wasn't sure I remembered which apartment was yours."

"Dan? What are you doing here?"

He held up a bag from the deli around the corner. "Surprise."

"Bagels?"

"Six assorted, still warm, plus three flavors of cream cheese. I got your message the other night, and said, gee, it's been months since I've seen that woman. Let me go say hello." He came onto the porch. "Hey, sexy red socks you've got on."

"You should have called." Elaine quickly finger-combed her hair. "Three flavors of cream cheese? How cruel."

"That's for turning me down for lunch." He held out his arms. "Don't I get a hug?" Before she could speak, her nose was pressing into his collarbone through a striped crew neck sweater. He kissed her cheek, then looked at the bags on the porch. "You're not moving out, are you?"

"No, just cleaning my closets." At the door the Siamese cat yowled softly, staring at them with round blue eyes. Elaine reached over and pulled the door shut. "Where are you going, dressed like that? On a boat? Make me jealous, Dan."

He glanced down at his khaki shorts and well-worn canvas deck shoes. "I borrowed a really slick forty-six-foot Bertram from a client—the client's boyfriend, more accurately. I'm going to take Josh out, maybe go around Key Biscayne and back. He's a little afraid of the ocean, and I want to get him over it, because the big plan is— We're going to Cat Cay. That's just north of Eleuthera."

She smiled. "Such an adventure."

"I'll tell you about it." He handed the bag to Elaine. "How about some coffee to go with these? Orange juice?"

She took the bag reluctantly. It had occurred to her with a sudden stab of regret that she shouldn't be talking to him at all. Worse, she couldn't tell him why: The DEA suspected he was involved with Miguel Salazar.

"Dan . . . I'd invite you in, but I'm just about to get dressed. I'm expecting company any minute now."

He came closer, having to look down at her. His eyes searched her face. "How are you doing? I mean, generally speaking, are you all right?"

"Of course. Why?"

"Charlie Dunavoy told me he saw you the other night."

"Charlie. Yes, at the Northside."

"He said you seemed a little depressed."

"Depressed? Me?"

"He said he hated to see you in such a bad way."

She laughed. "What?"

"You were too smashed to drive yourself home."

There was a silence. Elaine said, "I had a few drinks. Big deal."

"On a Thursday night?"

"Excuse me? I don't see you in months, then you show up asking me questions."

"You know I didn't mean it that way," he said, gently chastising.

There were some dead leaves on the ivy that wound through the wooden slats in the privacy fence. She picked them off, one by one. "Sorry. I was up till all hours last night going through all the stuff in my closets. It accumulates so fast you feel buried. Some of it's been in boxes for years—" Dan was still looking at her. He used to look at witnesses that way in the courtroom. Concerned. Expectant. Brown eyes wide open, eyebrows slightly raised. Not accusing, just waiting for the witness to say too much. She smiled and tucked the leaves into one of the trash bags. "Well. Thank you for the bagels. Tell Charlie I'm fine. Not to worry."

She could tell Dan wasn't satisfied with that. If she

were more duplicitous, and if he weren't an old friend, she would bring him into her kitchen, slice a bagel, pour the coffee. *Tell me, Dan, why you and your former wife were having drinks at the home of the chief money launderer for the Guayaquil cartel.*

He asked, "How are things downtown?"

"You know. Same old, same old."

"Are you dating anybody?"

"No. Not really." She smiled at him. "What about you?"

"Me either."

"Wait a minute. Somebody told me you were going with a rock guitarist. Now where did I hear that?"

"Well, I *was* dating a rock guitarist. Yeah, I know. Bad idea. We split up." Dan leaned against the stucco wall with his hands in his pockets. "Listen, don't mention this to Charlie, but I'm looking for a job closer to Lakewood Village, maybe something in Fort Lauderdale."

"Why?"

"Well . . . it's closer to Josh. And Lisa. I've been thinking of making another go at it—if she'll have me."

"That's great," Elaine said. "I guess."

"You guess?"

"No, it is. Definitely."

He nodded. "Lisa's a terrific person. She's attractive, smart. A great mom. I've dated since the divorce—not a lot, but enough to know that it's depressing, what's out there these days. She and I split up a year ago, and now I can't explain why. I took a nose dive after the

Barrios case and never recovered. Oh, well. That's history. I'd like to see if I can rewind the tape. Get it right this time. I'm hoping for that." Dan smiled as if it were he who had revealed too much.

"Be careful," Elaine said. "Statistics prove that a second marriage between the same people doesn't usually work out any better than the first one did."

He said, "You've done a study."

"Oh, yes. I always read *Cosmo* in the grocery store checkout line." She smiled when he did, then said, "Well. I have to go now."

He reached for her hand. "I'm going to call you more often."

"No need." She backed away. "Thank you. And stay out of trouble."

At the sidewalk he waved good-bye, car keys in his hand. When he was out of sight, Elaine leaned against the fence and thanked all manner of deities that Vincent Hooper was not waiting inside with his ear at the door. He would tell her that Dan Galindo was a manipulator who expected that half a dozen bagels and a hug would buy him information about Operation Manatee from a former pal at the U.S. attorney's office.

In his car, parked along the street under a banyan tree, Dan sat staring through the windshield at the shady entrance to Elaine's apartment. He had last seen her in October, a chance meeting on the street downtown, leading to a shot of espresso outside a Cuban diner and a slow walk back to the federal building, where they had parted company at the revolving glass door. Even so, he decided that he still knew Elaine McHale well enough to rely on his instincts. She had been hiding something.

He considered briefly the presence of another person—a man—in her house, then discarded the idea. No woman would wear a stained T-shirt and red socks with a man around—unless they had been married for years. Was her house in such a state she would be embarrassed for anyone to see it? Were there empty liquor bottles sitting around? An X-rated movie on the video? Dan was not reassured about her state of mind, but if she didn't want to talk about it, there was nothing he could do.

He started the engine. As he reached the end of the block, a late-model sedan pulled along the curb on the other side of the street and the door opened. A man got out. At the stop sign, Dan put on his turn signal and glanced automatically at the rearview mirror. The man seemed to be going up the walkway to Elaine's apartment.

Dan stared across the intersection. He waited for a bus to go by. Then a bicycle. He glanced in the mirror again, then made a fast U-turn and went back the way he had come. Driving slowly, his hand at his face as if to scratch his temple, Dan looked through the passenger window at Elaine's front porch. The man was waiting by the door, his profile to the street. A second later the door opened. He went inside. A dark-haired man with a beard. Black windbreaker, heavy shoulders. Five-ten, mid-forties, probably Hispanic. Dan made another U-turn.

At the intersection he studied the man's car. Dark blue Chevy Caprice. No bumper stickers. Regular state of Florida license plate. No blue light on the dash, no extra radio antenna. But an undercover cop car, sure as hell.

As Dan turned toward the expressway, heading north, he knew he had seen the man before. He tried to grab it, but the memory skittered out of reach.

CHAPTER 19

Vincent Hooper had seen the white Acura coupe going the other way when he parked at the end of Elaine's street. As it passed he noted the license plate, making sure he wasn't hallucinating.

Dan Galindo.

He didn't think Galindo had recognized him. It was possible but not likely. When Elaine opened the door, he went inside and waited to see what she knew.

She kissed him, then said, "This is a surprise."

"I was on a stakeout all night and couldn't call. How about some coffee?" He hung his windbreaker over the back of a chair, put his cellular phone on the table, then took off his pistol and holster. He noticed a deli bag. He unrolled the top and looked inside. Bagels.

"We heard from Salazar," he said. "The meeting's on."

"Congratulations." Elaine was fixing coffee. "What did he say?"

"Let's meet on Monday. He's going to let me know where. He's being cagey, wants to sniff me out first." Vincent took a serrated knife out of the block and put a bagel on the counter to slice it.

"Dan Galindo brought those," Elaine said. "He just left. I gather you didn't see him."

Vincent dropped the bagel back into the bag.

She laughed. "They aren't poisoned."

"What was Galindo doing here?"

"Well, obviously he was attempting to bribe a government official." Elaine finished slicing the bagel, then put the halves in the toaster. "Look. Strawberry cream cheese. Maybe I should've said yes."

"Funny, Elaine."

"All right. He came by to say hello. I made some excuse about having no time to visit, we chitchatted on the porch for five minutes, and he left."

"Really? He shows up the morning after I speak with Miguel Salazar. What a coincidence."

"Good Lord." She thrust a coffee mug at him.

He laughed. "Dan Galindo would have to be caught in flagrante delicto before you'd believe he'd so much as jaywalked. Listen to this. You know we got photos of him and his former wife at Salazar's house having drinks. Last Tuesday we intercepted a call he made to Salazar, alluding to some business they had satisfactorily completed—I think that's how he described it—and he wanted to be paid. Then Martha Cruz called Galindo and left a message about picking up 'keys.' What could that be, Elaine? Keys. Makes you wonder.

On Wednesday he and Martha Cruz got on Salazar's boat at the marina in Coconut Grove. Nobody knows where they went in it."

She was staring at him, and the color had gone out of her face. Vincent kept his voice quiet. "But he brings you bagels on Sunday morning. For no reason, just to say hello. What a sweet fellow."

"This is crazy," she said.

"You tell me, Elaine. What do you think he's doing?"

She shook her head.

Then he watched her put the toasted bagel on a plate and smear cream cheese on it. "You're going to eat that?"

"Yes, Agent Hooper. It's fresh. I'm hungry. And there is no principle that would be subverted by eating one damned bagel." She raised her eyebrows at him.

"I hope you enjoy it," he said. When she turned to tear off a paper towel, Vincent swatted her on the back of her running shorts. "Let's go sit down. I'm about to fall over."

Generally her place was fairly neat, but today the living room was strewn with boxes and loose papers. "What's this, spring cleaning?"

"Excavation," she said, moving a box off the sofa. "Clearing out the debris that's accumulated over the past ten or twelve years. Some I'll keep, most of it just takes up space. I've been at it all night."

"Don't save so much junk, you won't have to go through this," he said.

Vince sank into the sofa and closed his eyes, exhausted to his bones. He stretched his feet out on the coffee table, the only corner of it not stacked with papers. Before dawn he had been lying on his stomach on a Little Havana rooftop with a pair of night-vision binoculars watching for a drug shipment that never came.

Elaine sat beside him. Kissed his cheek and combed her fingers though his hair. Asked him about the meeting with Salazar, and he told her what he knew.

The DEA had already lined up certain people who could verify to Miguel Salazar that Victor Ramirez was who he said: a freelancer out of Puerto Rico, handled heroin for the nightclub trade, very discreet. Vince could act more like a doper than the dopers. The trick was to adopt the target's mannerisms and style of dress, make him feel he was talking to his kind of guy. Depending on the situation, Vincent might wear a hooded sweatshirt and gold chains or an Armani suit and a $15,000 Patek Phillipe wristwatch. The DEA had a safe full of jewelry seized in drug busts. For Miguel Salazar he would do an upscale suburban—a golf shirt, designer jeans, and a gold link bracelet. He wouldn't be wired. Right now they were only at the hand-holding stage.

If Salazar was interested, he would propose another meeting. The special agent-in-charge of the DEA's Miami office would then frantically beg the Justice Department to release the $500,000 cash they had been told about several weeks ago, and which Justice had promised in writing to release. There would be arguments, whining, and threats. Justice might approve the money, but Vincent wouldn't get all of it. He would have a flash roll of maybe a hundred K and tell Salazar the rest was coming. If Salazar took the bait, they would nail his ass.

Elaine had the plate in her lap. She took another bite of bagel. Crunched into it, then licked pink cream cheese off her thumb. Strawberry. Vincent had spent an extra half hour bullshitting with the Miami narcotics unit this morning, killing time. What if he'd come straight here instead? He and Galindo could have had a few words. But then the deal with Salazar would be off.

Elaine McHale was a tough prosecutor, one reason Vincent had been drawn to her. He had seen her destroy defense attorneys and make witnesses do a one-eighty on the stand. Her blind credulity about Daniel Galindo surprised him. It could be a problem if she ever had to prosecute him. Vince wanted to grab the bagel out of her hand and pitch it through the open door into the backyard.

He shifted on the sofa and stroked his fingers through her hair. "Put that plate on the coffee table, Elaine, and come here."

Smiling a little, she leaned over and dropped plate and bagel on a pile of old newspapers. He was tired, but not that tired. He toed his shoes off, stretched out on the sofa, and watched Elaine cross her arms and pull her T-shirt over her head. She had small breasts. Pretty. He drew her down and kissed one, then the other. She took his face and ruffled through his beard with her nose. "Make love to me, Vincent."

He could smell the cream cheese. Strawberry cream cheese. Jesus Christ. He shifted, making a little more room, and unzipped his pants.

Awhile later his eyes drifted open. He might have dropped off to sleep. He heard the toilet flush. Saw one of the cats curled up by the back door, staring at him. Then he noticed the clock on the VCR. "Holy mother of—" He sat up quickly and put his briefs on.

Elaine came out of the bathroom. "What's the matter?"

"Kelly Dorff. I have to call her before ten o'clock. She's moving to Salazar's house, staying with Martha Cruz for a while. She said I'd better call her, whatever that means. You wouldn't know, would you?" Vincent zipped his trousers.

"No. I haven't talked to her since last week," Elaine said. "What a sad, mixed-up girl she is."

"Oh, please. People put themselves where they are. Nobody's responsible for fucking up their own lives, are they?" He reached into his hip pocket for the small notebook he kept there, then held out his hand. "Bring me my phone, will you?"

She looked at him for a second, then went into the kitchen to get his cellular telephone. He'd have used her line, but it might show up on caller-ID. He dialed the number at Kelly's place. She lived in a condo her father owned near Hollywood Beach. He checked his watch. 9:52. She answered on the sixth ring, just as he was about to hang up.

"This is Hooper," he said.

Kelly Dorff talked; he listened.

She sounded out of breath, which meant that she was either scared or lying, or both. Elaine mouthed the words *What's going on?*, and he waved for her to be quiet. He wondered what he'd been thinking, making this call with her standing there. He went into her bedroom and shut the door.

He said, "Kelly, this is bullshit. You know it, I know it. . . . Don't fuck around with me. . . . Yeah, that's extremely amusing. . . . Here's my counter-proposal. Pay attention. You keep your fucking mouth shut, I won't let Salazar's friends find out who set him up. Okay? They're not nice guys, sweetheart. . . . No. That's it. Good-bye."

He hit the disconnect button and cursed under his breath. He looked at his watch. No time to send somebody to pick her up. She must have dropped the phone and scooted out the door. By now she was on her way to Lakewood Village.

He came out to the living room, glanced at Elaine, then went back to the kitchen. He put his phone down next to his holster. He heard footsteps. She was going to ask him, so he told her.

"Kelly Dorff just informed me that she was going to expose the so-called Luis Barrios cover-up if we don't drop her as a C.I. and give the band the master tapes from the studio. She's going to call the *Miami Herald* and the TV stations. She says she has a tape recording of the raid. She's got my voice on it. The sound of my gun blowing away Luis Barrios in cold blood. What do you think about that, Elaine?"

"My God."

"All bogus, of course, but it makes a hell of a story."

Elaine let out a breath. "Kelly has mentioned Barrios to me a couple of times. She was there."

"I *know* she was there!" He slammed his palm against the wall. "That's what I have been telling everyone. She shouldn't be anywhere near this fucking operation. What did she tell you? Agent Vincent Hooper shot Luis Barrios in the back while he was on his knees praying the rosary, and the rest of them—DEA, City of Miami cops, and Florida Department of Law Enforcement— they covered it up. They all lied. But I know the truth, by God, because *I* was there. I recorded the whole thing on a hidden microphone."

Elaine followed him back down the hall. She said, "Tell me about Barrios. I read the reports. You never wanted to talk about it."

Vincent sat on the edge of the sofa to put his shoes on. He looked up at Elaine, then asked, "Did Dan Galindo come over here with that on his mind?"

The surprise on Elaine's face looked real. "I told you why he came."

"Oh, right. He brought you some bagels. I thought you hadn't seen this joker in months. What did you talk about?"

"Nothing. He asked me how I was. He told me he split up with Kelly, and he's going back to his wife—"

"What did you tell him about Kelly?"

"Nothing! Dammit, Vince. Stop this."

If he had not known her, if he had not been trained to observe such things, he might have missed it. She wasn't leveling with him. That was more true than not, the people he dealt with, but with Elaine he had counted on some basic honesty. Or maybe he was the one not thinking straight, after thirty hours without sleep. He couldn't go like he used to.

Elaine went to the back door and shut it, then turned around. "What about Luis Barrios? Could anyone interpret the events to say that you were too quick to do what you did? Could your credibility as a witness be attacked in the Salazar case? I want to be certain that we're not vulnerable."

"Is that really what you want to know, Elaine?"

She said quietly, "Maybe I want some reassurance. And maybe it's personal. There is so much of you that's hidden from me. Our lives only meet in court, or at the U.S. attorney's office. Or here, in my apartment."

"Is this a complaint?"

"No. Just tell me about Barrios. Was he armed? Kelly says he wasn't."

"Yes, Elaine. He was armed. He was most certainly armed. He had a Tec-9 converted to automatic fire. Kelly wasn't in the fucking room, so how the hell can she open her mouth? They started shooting at us. A Miami cop was hit in the throat. He died, and two of our guys were shot up pretty bad. We got three of them, including Barrios, and I haven't lost one second of sleep over it. Jesus, why do I feel like I'm on trial here? There was a DEA inquiry. A Metro-Dade police inquiry. I was put on an automatic suspension with pay till the special agent-in-charge got the ruling: justifiable self-defense. We had a warrant. We were going to bust a drug buy. Two hundred kilos of cocaine, a house on the water in Coconut Grove. They were having some kind of party that we didn't know about beforehand. Kelly Dorff's band was there, and I think the owner of the house—he played guitar in a rock band in Mexico—fancied himself a musician, so they were letting him sit in. We couldn't cancel the raid. It had been planned for days. Our agent was inside, and he was wired. If we didn't get him out, he would be killed. But those other people were there too. Luis Barrios was among them. A surprise to me. I heard he'd flown to Quito after his case was dismissed. Maybe he did, but he was sure as hell back in town. We got the signal and came in. We screamed for everybody to get down, but the damned music was so loud. The place went nuts. Gunfire and smoke everywhere. Barrios ran for the back door with his weapon. I went after him. I told him to freeze. He didn't, and I shot him. End of story. If Danny boy had done his job, we wouldn't be having this conversation, would we?"

Elaine was looking at him strangely, and he couldn't read it.

He looked back at her, not able to tell—and maybe it

was his fatigue—if she was hiding something. He didn't want to think that. She had never lied to him that he knew of. He was with her because they had some honesty going on. Some loyalty. To imagine it any different had some consequences he didn't care to think about.

She asked, "What are you going to do about Kelly?"

"I don't know yet. Give her the studio tapes for Mayhem, probably. It's no big deal. I've been using them to get Rick Robbins in the right frame of mind, and it looks like we're okay there, so maybe I'll let them have the tapes. I am mightily pissed off, however. I hate it when a C.I. threatens me. I get truly perturbed."

"Why does she say she has a tape of the Barrios raid? Where would it come from?"

"They were recording that night. That's right. Had their little reel-to-reels going." Vincent made circles with his extended forefingers. "As I say, the target thought he was some kind of musician, and he wanted a recording of himself. Yes, there was a tape. We listened to it. There was nothing on it. Well, gunfire and a lot of yelling."

"Where is it now?"

"In a property room somewhere. Destroyed, lost, I don't know. All the targets of the raid pleaded guilty—we got them with their pants down—so the tape wasn't an issue. If Kelly Dorff says she has it, she's lying. But it is still a bother."

"Because this might get back to Salazar and scare him off?"

"No, Jesus, I hadn't even thought of that." Vincent sat down heavily in her armchair. "No, because it would give the boys in D.C. a reason to ship me off to Kansas or some damn place. Doesn't matter if it's true or not, it's bad publicity. People believe what the media tells them. Never mind that I was cleared. Here we go again. The suits getting tired of Vincent Hooper's big mouth, so they find him a nice desk job. You don't like it, retire. Yeah, why not? I'm forty-four years old. I've put in my time. I could collect a pension. I'm not a rich man, Elaine. What have I got? A pension. A pension and my reputation. I'm not going out like this. I will not do it."

She came over and sat on the arm of the chair, put her arms around him. "You could resign. You could do something else."

"What?" He stood up and smoothed his hair back into place. "What would I do?"

"You've mentioned jobs with security companies." She looked up at him.

"I've got to go. I need to get to the office before I go home."

"Stay awhile." She held onto his hand.

"No, I've got some reports to finish." Laughing, he headed toward the kitchen. "God, I love this job."

She followed. "I wish you would quit. What I said to you before, Vince— You're right. It was a complaint. You come when you like, you leave when you like—"

He picked up his holster off the table. "You never bring me flowers. What's a girl to think?"

"Dammit, don't trivialize this!" she shouted.

Weariness pressed down on him. "What do you want me to do?"

"I want to be able to walk into a restaurant with you. To take your hand in public. Something that simple. That's what I want."

He noticed the pattern in her wallpaper. Little tulips. He ran his belt through his holster, then rebuckled it. He dropped his pistol in and pressed down the safety strap. "We'll talk about it."

"You bet."

"We will." He looked at her, then cupped her cheek with his palm. "We will." She held his hand tightly and kissed it. Curled his fingers around hers and pressed them to her face. Her skin felt feverish and damp, and her eyes were closed. After a while, he said, "Elaine, I have to go."

CHAPTER 20

At the security gate outside Heron Hills the guard was standing by his shack. Dan Galindo showed him his driver's license.

"I'm here to pick up my son at Lisa Galindo's house. She said she'd call and let you know."

The guard checked off his name, then told him to wait a moment. He went inside and came back with a camera. "We're starting a new procedure with our frequent visitors, such as yourself. This is digital. We scan the photo into our computer, then we can bring it up on the monitor. You want to look this way, please?"

"Hold it." Dan held up a hand, fingers spread. "I don't want my picture in your computer."

The guard looked back at the other cars in line. The brim of his hat cast a shadow over his gold-framed glasses. He said to Dan, "Sir, we're trying to save everyone some time here."

"I said no."

"Suit yourself." He went over to his computer and tapped on the keyboard.

Dan said, "Tell me something. Do these crime-fighting efforts pay off?"

"Well, it makes the residents feel more secure. People can't just come up here and drive around looking for a house to burglarize."

"Right. Let them stay in Miami. Do it in their own neighborhoods."

The guard shifted his eyes toward Dan, then ripped the entry pass out of the printer and handed it through the window. "Have a pleasant day."

The gate arm went up, and Dan went through it.

Two minutes later, he was parking behind Lisa's minivan. A neighbor smiled brightly from the adjoining yard. He couldn't remember her name, but he waved back. She was weeding a bed of caladiums. He spotted Josh shooting hoops in the woman's driveway with two other boys. They had one of those bright plastic, kid-sized basketball goals on wheels to roll back into the garage at night. Dan cupped his hands at his mouth. "Hey, Shaquille O'Neal!"

Josh stopped running so suddenly he staggered in his big shoes. "Dad! I gotta finish this game."

Dan pointed at the house. "I'm talking to your mom."

He rang the doorbell, then went inside. The sliding glass doors beyond the dining area were open, and he could see straight through to the small backyard, the wood fence around it, and swing set under the shade tree. The roof overhang kept the barbecue grill out of the weather. Music came from farther back in the house. Hootie and the Blowfish. He walked down the hall leading to the bedrooms.

Lisa's cocker spaniel came out of the master bedroom to see who was there. The dog yipped once, ran back in, then out again.

"Lisa, it's me." Dan could smell paint. The furniture in the master bedroom was shoved to one side, plastic drop cloths thrown over it, and Lisa, in jeans and long-sleeved shirt, was pushing a paint roller up the wall, changing pale blue to creamy white. Strands of blond hair had fallen from her ponytail.

Lisa turned to dip the roller into the pan and noticed him standing at the door. "Early again. Gee. You used to run half an hour late. I'm amazed." Her voice echoed on the bare walls. Even the curtains were gone, and the carpet had been torn out.

"What's all this for?" he asked.

"I'm redecorating. I'd have someone come in and do it, but I don't have money to spend like that." She lifted the roller and resumed her path up the wall, around the window that faced the street. "Josh is next door, I think. I put his bag by the front door. Be sure he uses his sunscreen." The dog sniffed at the paint. "Poppy, out. Go on."

The cocker spaniel flopped down in a corner with its chin on its paws, ears to either side, its eyes rolling from Lisa, then to Dan, and back again.

Dan lifted a corner of the tarp covering the bed. She hadn't changed the mattress. He said, "How would you like to go out with Josh and me in the boat? We could dock it over on Key Biscayne and have lunch at the Rusty Pelican." Two days ago, arranging to pick up Josh, Dan had described Miguel Salazar's boat to her in detail—the engines, the electronics, the galley and staterooms. He had not mentioned that Martha Cruz had been aboard, an irrelevancy that would only be misconstrued.

Lisa's roller made a sticky, crackling noise in the wet paint. "I'm a little busy right now."

"Do it later. I'll help you clean up," Dan said. "Josh would like to have you along. So would I."

"You?"

"Sure."

She looked at him steadily. "Why?"

He shrugged. "I've missed you."

"Really." She lowered the roller to the pan. "What is that supposed to mean?"

"I think I'm asking you for a date."

Her mouth opened slightly, then her eyes went to the ceiling. "Oh, my God."

"Come on. It would be fun."

"I'm sure it would." Putting some energy into it, she pressed out the extra paint, and the pan screeched on the bare concrete. "Are you still dating that lovely girl with the nose ring?"

"No. That's over. Lisa, it was nothing."

"A tattooed rock singer. My God. I would love to know what you saw in her."

"She was there. It's not worth talking about. Come with Josh and me. It's a beautiful day, too good to waste inside."

Lisa glanced at him. "I'm meeting someone at the club at two o'clock. We're playing tennis."

Dan felt a little twist in the pit of his stomach. "Who? Am I allowed to ask?"

"You don't know him." She erased another section of blue. "He's a lawyer. You'd think I'd learn, wouldn't you? He's a senior partner in a firm in Boca Raton. I met him when I went up to visit Mom and Dad."

"Is it serious?"

"What, as if I were ill?" She laughed and submerged the roller in the pan again. "I do date. I lead a normal life. But I think this guy just wants to get into my knickers."

"Who could blame him?" Dan picked a smudge of dried paint off the marble windowsill. "Right after we bought this place, we christened it by making love in every room—even the closets, remember?"

Lisa stared at the opposite wall. "Don't do this. Please."

"I think of you with somebody else—Josh coming home to some creep sitting on my sofa, watching my TV, sleeping with my wife—"

"I'm not—"

"I know," he said sharply. "I know you're not. But you were my wife for nine years, and it's a habit, thinking of you that way. Ever since I left, something's been missing. A chunk right out of my middle." He drew a circle. "Right here. That's what it feels like."

"Sentimental you." She smiled a little, her profile to him. Her skin was still perfect and a dimple played at the corner of her mouth.

He said, "A friend of mine in Fort Lauderdale says there's an opening for a criminal lawyer in his firm. I'm going to redo my résumé and take it up there. What do you think?"

"Why ask me?"

"Because I want your opinion."

"Fine. Do what you want. It's your life."

"Busting my chops, Lisa?"

"You deserve it."

He took the handle of the paint roller and leaned it against the wall. "We could do things differently this time," he said.

"We? Excuse me? Look, Dan. I'm getting along just fine. I forced myself not to think about you, or our marriage, or what you did, and I'm over it."

"Are you really?" He bent his head to kiss her. She let him do it, opening her mouth to him. Then he murmured into her ear, "Lisa, I want to come back."

"Oh, you do." She pulled away, resting her hands on his chest. "You should hear yourself. *I want*. It's always about what Dan wants. Like that damned boat. It doesn't matter what I say, you're going to make the decisions."

He nearly laughed. "Is this starting to be an issue with you?"

She made a small noise of impatience with her tongue. "No. It illustrates what I'm trying to tell you, which is: Nothing has changed. When you were doing that trafficking case two years ago, I said, Dan, please let it go. It doesn't matter. The man is a criminal. But you said, Oh, no, Lisa. I have a duty as a lawyer to seek justice. Well, fine, if you were trying to save some innocent person from death row, but you turned a guilty man free. Tell me where the justice is. You didn't do it for justice. You did it for pride, like a medal to wear on your chest. Look how noble Daniel Galindo is. You wanted that more than anything."

He took a breath. "I didn't know you saw it that way."

"It's taken me a long time to sort out my feelings." Lisa slid her hand up his cheek. "I'm not angry."

"Oh, honey." Dan closed his eyes and held onto her hand, not letting go. "Sometimes I wake up in the middle of the night wondering how I managed to screw things up so badly."

"Well. At least you finally sound sorry."

"Of course I am."

She pulled her fingers out of his grasp. "Go on. Go for a ride in that million-dollar boat and have yourself a good time. Take Josh to the Bahamas for a week in it, you and Josh and your macho speargun, pretending you aren't thirty-five, and when you figure out there's a little more to life than that, then you come tell me how much you've missed me."

Her blue eyes glistened with sudden tears, and she laughed self-consciously. "I've missed you too. Wild, huh? I have an investment in this relationship, and I don't want to lose it all. So yes, send out your résumé. Get a job you can be proud of. Do something with your life."

She picked up the paint roller and attacked the pan, and ivory paint sloshed onto the floor.

From the passenger seat Josh said, "Are you mad?" After a second, he said, "Dad?"

"What?" Dan loosened his grip on the steering wheel and looked back at his son. "No, buddy, I'm not mad." He ruffled Josh's hair. "You ready to go on that boat?"

"Maximum. I told Evan next door about it. He wanted to go, but his mom said no."

"Is it okay, just the two of us?"

"Yeah. It's fun." Josh smiled. The glasses made him look wise. "I'm making a card for you on my computer, but you can't see it till your birthday. Can you come get it?"

"Sure I will."

At the guard shack at the entrance to the Isles of Lakewood, Miguel Salazar's subdivision of the Village, Dan gave his name and ID, tapped idly on the steering wheel while they took down his license tag number and made a phone call.

Josh was peeling the wrapper off a low-fat granola bar. Lisa had packed two of them in his bag, along with an apple, some carrots, and a bottle of filtered water. He rose up in the seat to see out the window. "This is the way to Anita's house."

Dan said, "We're going by for just a minute. I have to drop some things off."

After Kelly Dorff left her message on his answering machine, he had packed her things for her, the clothes she had left at his house, along with some CD's and stray earrings, a comb, a bottle of shampoo. At least he could do that much for her. He had put a note inside the box. Regrets, no hard feelings. Good luck with the band.

As he parked in the circular driveway, he noticed a monstrous black Harley-Davidson leaning on its kickstand in front of the triple garage. A red-haired man built like a pro wrestler was shining the spokes. Arlo Pate—the band's new drummer. With his eyes fixed on Dan, he slowly stood up and tossed the rag back and forth in his hands.

Dan opened his trunk and took out the box. "I'm here to see Kelly Dorff."

"Kelly's busy."

"Can you give this to her?"

"Martha said for you to take it out back."

Going through the house, following the short Indian woman with braids, Dan thought he heard the wail of a guitar, muffled and slow. He remembered that Martha had a rehearsal studio on the property, and he imagined that Kelly Dorff was out there behind the soundproof walls, avoiding him.

White curtains billowed at the open back doors. Through the windows Dan could see the green lawn stretching down to the lake and the line of royal palms along its shore. The red and yellow sail of a beached catamaran luffed in the wind. Dan walked under a trellis thick with deep pink bougainvillea, then onto the terrace. He squinted. Sunlight reflected off the pool, creating a nimbus around a table where Miguel Salazar sat reading the paper.

When he saw Dan and Josh, he lowered the newspaper but didn't get up. His white terry cloth robe was open, revealing a turquoise Speedo and a darkly tanned, hairy chest. His bare feet were propped in another chair.

He smiled briefly at Josh, then raised his black eyes to Dan. "Good morning." The greeting was quizzical.

"Some clothes of Kelly's," Dan said. "She's staying here now, I understand?"

"Yes. Martha's guest." He didn't sound happy about it. Recovering his manners, he extended an arm. "Please, sit down. Have some orange juice." Over Salazar's head fluttered the scalloped edges of a white umbrella. He sat in its shade. There was a tray with pastries, napkins, and an insulated silver pitcher.

Josh spotted Salazar's niece and sped off to tell her where he was going today. Several people were splashing around in the pool, and a yellow boom box at the far end played a salsa tune, all brass and popping drumbeats.

Dan put the box beside his chair and poured himself a glass of juice. "The man out front cleaning his motorcycle said to give the box to Martha."

"She's swimming. I think she saw you." Salazar pointed out the other people on the terrace. Relatives from Ecuador—an uncle and his wife, their daughter-in-law, her baby in a playpen. Salazar's sister paddled on an air mattress. In the middle of the pool a woman's slender arms steadily rose and fell as she knifed through the water, coming closer.

"I thank you again for helping her in the court."

"And thank you for the boat," Dan said.

"Did you take the boy fishing already?"

"We're going out this afternoon. Maybe we'll do some fishing. He says okay, Dad, but I'm not putting any worms on hooks."

Salazar smiled. "When will you go to the Bahamas?" His hand hovered over the tray of pastries, then selected a small roll crusted with almonds.

"Well . . . I'm not sure. I still have to work that out with Lisa."

That brought a soft laugh. The pockmarked skin drew up along Salazar's high cheekbones and narrowed his black eyes to slits. "No, my friend. You want to go? Go. You say to Lisa, I'm going to the Bahamas with my son. Oh, you don't like it? Too bad." He bit the pastry in half, then gestured toward Dan. "Never beg a woman. It's weak. You must stay in control. If you let women tell you what to do, they don't respect you."

"I'll try to keep that in mind, Miguel."

As they talked, their attention moved to the ladder where Martha would emerge from the pool. Dan saw the top of her head, then her hands curling around the shiny chrome, then the water was pouring off her body. The one-piece swimsuit was the same color as her golden-brown skin, giving the impression that she wore nothing at all, and the fabric of the suit was so thin Dan could see the dark rose color at the point of each perfectly rounded breast. Her body was hard and sleek. She glanced at the table where Dan and Salazar sat, then bent over to pick up a ribbon from a lounge chair. The swimsuit barely covered her backside. There was a tattoo of a bird on one buttock. Dan let his eyes wander down her legs to the leafy tattoo around her left ankle, then up again as she wrung out her heavy hair and tied it into a ponytail. Her earrings sparkled against her neck.

Aware suddenly that he was staring, he turned back around. Salazar was looking at him. Dan smiled. "She's a beautiful girl."

"Thank you," Salazar said, as if his possession of this woman entitled him to the compliment.

With a towel over one shoulder, Martha put on her shiny green sunglasses and came to say hello. Salazar held out an arm. She bent to give him a fast peck on the cheek, but his hand tightened and pulled her back down. He murmured something in her ear, then let her go.

Glancing at Dan, she wrapped the towel around herself and knotted it on one hip. "What's in the box, Kelly's stuff?"

"Dan is the delivery man today," Salazar said. He gripped the handle of the silver pitcher and poured her some juice. "Sit down with us. Have a sweet."

"I just ate, Miguel, I'm not hungry."

"Sit down."

Dan hadn't touched his juice. He had brought the box, and now he could leave. But he wanted to stick around for a few minutes and see what was going on. He stood up and held a chair for Martha so that she and Salazar were on opposite sides of the table, his own chair between them.

"Thanks." She smiled at him and sat down. Her shoulders glittered with drops of water. She smelled faintly of chlorine.

Dan said, "Kelly told me she'd be staying here with you. Just curious—why did she decide to do that?"

Salazar laughed. "Because she wants to make sure Martha doesn't take over the band."

"That's not true, Miguel. My equipment is here. We're working on the songs. Arlo is here too, so it's easier." She said to Dan, "At the party last night, Kelly messed up big-time, and I'm sure people noticed. She really needs to work on her timing. I don't know what we're going to do if she wigs out like that at the concert."

Salazar leaned back in his chair and knitted his

fingers over his stomach. His gold bracelet glittered on his wrist. "Someone told us that Martha would do better on her own with a backup band. We can call it 'Cruz.' What do you think, Dan?"

"I don't have an opinion. It's up to the band." He looked at Martha. "What do you think?"

"Well, I don't want to change anything now. It's two weeks till the concert." Martha was getting bold—possibly because her lawyer was sitting with her, Dan thought. She added, "Anyway, it's Kelly's band. She started it."

Salazar smiled patiently at her. "What did the people tell you last night, Martica? You're the best one. The star."

Martha raised her arms to adjust her ponytail, and her breasts lifted. "Kelly's a better songwriter."

"I can't understand her lyrics. She doesn't sing, she screams."

"She has a lot to say, Miguel. You should try listening."

"What does she say? This is such a bad country, such a terrible place. She should go to Ecuador. When I was ten years old, my father took us to the city because there was no work in the mountains. In Guayaquil we lived in a house with a dirt floor. The police beat my father, and he went deaf. Then my mother died with her seventh baby, and we had to pick garbage to live. So I know what's terrible and what isn't. Kelly should go there." Salazar said to Dan, "Martha forgets how she lived before I met her."

Martha made no response. She kept her sunglasses pointed toward the lake. A drop of water slid down her neck out of her hair.

Dan looked back at Salazar. "Martha's going to do all right. I wouldn't worry about her one bit."

"Yes, Miguel. This time next year, I'll be on a national tour. We'll be famous. Kelly and me and Scott and Arlo."

"You can see her on *Saturday Night Live*," Dan said.

Salazar sat up in his chair, smiling across the table at her. "What will I see? A fat cowboy playing the drums. Kelly Dorff in rags like a beggar, and Scott, the punk with his blue hair, like a *maricón*! And you—Martha Cruz with her *culo* hanging out of her pants."

"If you don't like it, complain to Rick."

Salazar slapped her, a loud crack. Her glasses went flying off. Martha made a single, sharp intake of breath and held her cheek.

The people at the other end of the pool stopped their conversations for a second, then turned their backs.

Dan realized he was standing. He looked down at Salazar. The black eyes were deadly. Dan took a breath. "What the hell did you do that for?"

"I think you should leave."

"Yeah?" He took another breath. His head swam with fear. "Martha, I'll take you out of here right now. Go get whatever you need and I'll wait."

Salazar stood up. The white robe hung open, and his muscled belly glistened with suntan oil. "She doesn't go anywhere with you."

"If she wants to leave, I'll take her. If that causes you a problem, tough."

Salazar smiled. "Not a problem for me. For you, I think."

"Don't!" Martha's shrill voice pierced the air between them. She grabbed Miguel's arm. "Leave right now, Dan."

He stared at her.

"I want to stay. Okay? Just go." The mark of Miguel Salazar's hand flamed on her cheek, and her eyes pleaded. "Miguel's right. This isn't your business. Please go."

"Are you sure?"

"Yes. I want to stay here."

Salazar said, "You have the keys to my boat?"

"At my apartment. I'll drop them in the mail today. Then you can drive the boat up your *culo*."

Quick as a snake, Salazar's hands shot out and closed on the front of Dan's sweater. "I think I'm going to kill you." He laughed as if somebody had suggested he held the winning lottery numbers.

"Miguel, stop it!" Martha dug her fingers into his fists. "His son is over there playing. Let go!"

Josh. It was thinking of Josh that kept Dan from wrestling Salazar into the pool, where he knew he would have the advantage. Keep him under till he ran out of breath and choked. Then leave him on the deck gagging.

Salazar shoved him away. "Go on. Take your boy and get out."

CHAPTER 21

Under a bright sun, the big sportfisher flew across the water, twin diesels roaring. Dan stood at the wheel, and Josh sat to his left in the mate's seat. The bay was alive with pleasure craft, sailboarders, speedboats, and multicolored sails tilting in the wind.

Dan had decided that his manhood did not depend on mailing back the keys immediately. Josh had expected a boat ride; he could have one. They had already made a complete circuit of Key Biscayne, then had raced up the Atlantic side of Miami Beach, about five miles out, the boat crashing into the swells and throwing up a spray, leaving a half mile of wake behind it. Now they were coming back south through the intracoastal, just cruising. As they passed under the causeways that connected the mainland to Miami Beach, Josh clambered down the ladder to the cockpit and waved at the fishermen dangling lines in the water. Dan had told him the truth of the situation, more or less: The man who owned the boat needed it back sooner than expected. But they would take a trip together, count on it. He smiled and laughed and hid his anger. He wanted to pull the drain cock and scuttle the miserable boat. He was angry at himself as well. He had goaded Salazar, like sticking pins in a rattlesnake, and Salazar had taken it out on Martha.

Gradually the open blue sky and the task of steering the boat calmed his churning frustration. By the time they reached the marina and the Bertram backed obediently into its slip, the sun was a fading memory on the horizon and the fuel tanks were sucking air. Dan drove Josh back to Lakewood Village. Lisa barely spoke. Exhausted, dispirited, Dan headed home.

As his car rose higher on the tangle of roads that made up the Golden Glades interchange, Dan could see the lights of Miami spread out to the south and west, and over to the east, where the land stopped, a line of darkness indicated the ocean. Beyond that, over the curve of the Atlantic, lay the Bahamas.

He would collect the thousand dollars that Rick owed him for taking Martha Cruz's case. That and a MasterCard would get him and Josh to Cat Cay for a week. Rick would send the demo tape to the A&R guy from Capitol, who would come to the concert, love it, sign the band, and Martha would be on her way to New York. *Adiós*, Miguel.

Dan passed over 151st Street, then 125th Street to North Miami, then 119th. He was bearing down on 103rd when a face jumped into his memory. He jerked

the wheel right, cut across three lanes, exited the interstate, then got back on. At 125th Street he headed for
North Miami. He had to find Manatee Studios.

Maybe it was thinking of the demo tape that
had jogged his memory. Quick as a strobe light, off
and on, he had seen a dark-haired man with a beard. If
he could find the studio—it would be open, they
were always open at night—he might remember who
it was.

It took him almost half an hour to find the studio.
Sodium-vapor crime lights cast their yellowish glare
onto the empty parking lot. Dan recognized a dump-
ster, then a weedy pile of wooden pallets. His headlights picked up a sign: MANATEE STUDIOS. He turned
off the engine and looked through the glass door.

It came to Dan slowly. He had seen the man twice.
Once here, a couple of weeks ago, then again this
morning outside Elaine McHale's apartment. Her guest
was the same man he had glimpsed in the studio's
dimly lighted control room. Not the engineer, the
other one. Looking for Rick, Dan had opened the control room door. The man had remained absolutely
still, as if any motion would give him away. For a split
second their eyes had met, then the engineer stood up,
casually blocking Dan's view. And Rick had taken
Dan back out and closed the door.

If it was the same man, then why would a record
producer visit a federal prosecutor? Dan wiped his
sweating palms on the thighs of his shorts. He knew
he could be wrong about this. Dead wrong.

* * *

Standing in a pool of light on his ex-brother-in-law's front porch he heard Rick yelling *okay, okay*. Then a pause, like he was looking through the peephole. Then the click of the door opening.

Rick was belting his plaid bathrobe. "What is this? Don't you call first?"

"I didn't think you'd be in bed," Dan said quietly. "Is Sandy asleep?"

"No, she's waiting for me, ready to boogie, if you get my drift." Rick's hair was standing up, and he smelled of cologne. "Dan, you look like shit. What's going on, man?"

Dan heard a creak and glanced toward the stairs. He called out, "Sandy? It's only me. Dan. I need to talk with Rick for a minute. Don't bother getting up." He grasped Rick's arm and drew him toward the den, a small TV room off the main living area, which glittered, even in the semidarkness, with mirrors and polished tile.

"What the—"

"Be quiet and listen."

He was halfway through telling Rick what he had seen when the door swung open. Sandy stood there in a sleep shirt, arms crossed, hair tousled. "You boys mind tellin' me what the hell is goin' on?"

"Go on back to bed, pumpkin."

When Rick tried to turn her around, she slapped his hand away. "Don't you do that. I asked a question. This is my damn house too, by God."

"It's nothing, baby—"

"Rick, I mean it!" She looked from one of them to the other. Rick breathing too fast. Dan frozen. She clenched her shirt over her heart. "Oh, my God. Did somebody die? Is Josh okay?"

Dan said, "Josh is fine. I'm sorry to have disturbed you so late, Sandy. I had to ask Rick some personal questions—personal to me, I mean."

"You were bangin' on the door like an ax murderer was after you."

"I wasn't sure if you were awake."

"Why didn't you call?"

"Well, I don't have a car phone, and I was nearby."

She looked at him hard. "You're lyin' to me, mister."

Rick said, "Jesus! This is between me and Dan. Okay? Man to man? Now would you get back upstairs?" There was sweat on his upper lip.

"No."

Dan put a hand on Rick's arm. "I'll give you a call in the morning."

"Aaah, shit." Rick sank down on his chair, hands dangling between his knees. His bald spot shone in the light from the reading lamp. He raised his head and looked at Dan. "Tell her. There won't be any peace and quiet around here tonight if we don't."

After a second Dan said, "Sandy, I didn't use a telephone because I was concerned that your lines might be tapped. It's possible—not certain—that a man I saw by chance on the street this morning, who appeared to be an undercover police officer, may also be the man I saw in the control booth at Manatee Studios. Rick told me his name is Victor Ramirez. I just realized this on the way back from taking Josh home, or I would have come sooner. I was asking Rick what he knows about Ramirez."

"Oh, my God. Rick—"

"It's okay," he said, reaching out to squeeze her hand.

"What have you done?"

"Nothing. I swear." Rick cleared his throat. "I met Victor Ramirez about two months ago. He gave me some references, and I checked them out. The man is a record producer. The engineer, Willy Silva, is the real deal. Their equipment was exactly what we needed to do the recording for Mayhem. They had Mesa-Boogie Mark III amps, a dynamite console, DAT tapes, computer backup. How many studios you know have computer backup?"

Dan said, "But if Ramirez and Silva are so good, why are they in that rathole of a building in North Miami?"

"Why not? In recording, you don't pay high rent. You don't need to impress anybody. All you need is the hardware, and they've got it. Victor is an investor. He has a couple of nightclubs in Puerto Rico, one in Atlantic City—"

Dan let out a slow breath, and Sandy glanced at him as if reading his thoughts.

Rick said, "Come *on*, guys. He's legit. Being in

the entertainment field, Victor wants his own label. People do it all the time. He wants to start his label here, not so much competition as New York. So Victor comes to Coral Rock one day. We have lunch. He says he heard about the band, heard they were hot, and he wants to record them and distribute the CD's. I say, no thanks, we're going for a deal with a major label. And he goes, okay, that's cool. Let us do your demo. If the band gets signed, we can work a deal with Capitol or Atlantic or whatever, or at the very least get some good publicity. I go, no, this demo has to be done right. I mean, *perfect* quality. We need super-experienced people. He says no problem, talk to our engineer. And I did. I talked to Willy Silva. I checked his credentials. I listened to some of his mixes, and they blew me away."

Rick laughed, "Dan, undercover cops do not go to this much trouble. It would've cost— Jesus, the equipment alone! Cops don't have recording equipment like that around."

"They could rent it," Dan said. "But I doubt Ramirez is with North Miami or Metro-Dade. I'm thinking he's a federal agent, and his credentials are forged, or else he tells a damned good story."

Sandy stifled a gasp with her fingertips. Dan glanced at her, then said, "I'll tell you where I saw Ramirez— the man who could be Ramirez. Going into the apartment of a friend of mine, an assistant U.S. attorney. That's federal, Rick. FBI, DEA, Customs— It could be that Manatee Studios is a front. A sting operation, but I don't know what they're after."

For a second Rick sat there as if somebody had dipped him in concrete. Finally he said, "What . . . does this mean, exactly?"

Dan said, "Did Ramirez tell you he owns the building?"

"No. He just rents space there, a couple of the studio rooms, including the one we're using for the demo tape."

Dan tapped his fingers on his knees. "Is it possible there are any deals going down on the premises? You notice people coming and going who might not belong there?"

"Deals?"

"Drug deals, Rick. Narcotics? Cocaine? Are you with me?"

"I—I don't— It's possible, I guess."

Sandy was staring at Rick, not saying anything.

Rick said, "No. Uh-uh. Wait a minute, now. I'm trying to think. We've got the IRS off our back. I keep my nose clean. If Victor is DEA—let's say he is, for the hell of it—why would he look at me? I didn't do anything. I mean, I don't hang out with drug dealers. I don't involve myself with that. It's suicide."

Dan didn't like that answer. He closed in. "Who do you know, Rick? Who do you know that the feds would be interested in?"

"I know tons of people. And yeah, some of them are shady, but it's not something we chat about over cocktails, you understand? It doesn't come up."

"Which of them are involved with Manatee Studios?" Dan waited, then said, "Only the band, right?"

"Mayhem? Oh, no way. I know these people," Rick said. "Right, Sandy? They do music, that's all. Okay, they might smoke a little dope, but *deal*?" He laughed.

"I heard today," Dan said, "that Leon Davila went back to Ecuador. Do you have any information on that?"

"He didn't say anything to me. I don't care, I didn't like him. And they put Arlo Pate in there so fast, it didn't matter. See, Dan, artists are notoriously unreliable. Like our bassist. He split for Atlanta. They get better offers, they go."

"What about the new bassist?"

"Scott Irwin. He was interning with me before I met Ramirez. He's a student at the local broadcasting college. And Kelly Dorff? You know her better than I do, so you answer that one. Arlo Pate— He's a strange dude, but I can't see the feds after him. Martha? Never. She's too smart to fall into that life. All she wants is a record contract."

Dan said, "What about Miguel Salazar?"

"Oh, no. No way. He's fine."

"You think so? I was over at his place in Lakewood this morning. Martha said something he disagreed with, and he hit her."

"He hit Martha?" Rick sucked in a breath. "Oh, man. Is she okay?"

"Sure, except she won't leave the SOB."

"Well, no. She can't. We talked about it. First the

concert, then she'll be okay. Man, I knew she was having problems, but— He hit her?"

"Salazar gives me the creeps, Rick. I think he may be the one they're looking at."

Sandy reached out a hand, grabbing Rick's arm. "Darlin'?"

Rick ignored her. "Salazar's got a company in Miami, and he bankrolls the band. If he's doing something else in his spare time, I don't know about it. Dan, I think you're making too much out of this." Rick finally looked down at Sandy, who was tapping his arm. "What?"

Sandy stood up on her knees. "Last night when Kelly was so upset, crying and all? Before you came in to see about her, she was going on and on, and I didn't pay much attention, but she said she had been arrested with a kilo of heroin, and how it started everything. Did she ever tell you about that?" She looked from Rick to Dan.

"*Heroin?*" Rick threw himself back in his chair, arms dangling over the sides. "Oh, what next? Take me now, God."

"I didn't know either," Dan said. "She never said anything about it. When was this? Was the case dismissed for some reason?"

"I didn't ask her, she was bawlin' so hard. I got her calmed down, then she didn't say another word."

"What did she mean, 'It started everything'?"

"Hon, I don't know any more'n you do, but we could ask her."

"Rick, did you ever see Kelly with any dopers?

Don't tell me you don't know who they are," he said. "In this business you know."

"When she was with her prior band, Black Mango, their manager was connected." Rick stared at the ceiling. "Out of Philadelphia, I think. He was arrested in that raid down in Coconut Grove. That was when that other guy, the one from Ecuador, shot it out with the cops. Who was that? You know, the one you lost your job over."

"Luis Barrios."

"Right. Black Mango's manager was arrested along with a bunch of other people in that raid, then convicted of big-time cocaine trafficking. I knew Kelly at the time, and I'd met Martha and Leon, who were also in the band, but I wasn't their manager till later."

Rick sat up. "Wait a minute. We might be getting our shorts twisted up for nothing. You asked me if Kelly could be dealing? No way. She used to do coke on a fairly regular basis, but not lately. I haven't seen it, and I've had every opportunity to see it, believe me."

Smiling now, Rick smoothed his hair. "You don't know it was Ramirez you saw. You saw some guy with a beard, about the same age, same build." He stood up, and Dan followed him with his eyes. "Right? Is that what you saw? Is that what you got me out of bed to tell me?"

Dan said, "I could be wrong. As I say, I only caught a glimpse of the man."

"Oh, jeez—" Rick buried his face in his hands for a second, then threw them into the air. He grabbed Dan and kissed his cheek. "Dan, I love you, but you're full of shit. Now get out of here, will you?" He waggled his fingers at Sandy, motioning her to get up. "Beddy-bye."

"Rick." There was an edge to Dan's voice.

"What?"

"I'm going to give you some advice, okay? Legal advice. Right here in front of your wife, so you can't tell me later that I didn't warn you. You're not playing straight with me. We both know it. Whatever is going on with you, you'd better tell me now—as your lawyer—because later on it could be too late." Dan was speaking slowly, each word like the ringing of a low, muffled bell. "Do not screw around with the feds. If you do, they will send you to prison for the rest of your life on principle."

Rick made a little laugh, looking at Dan, then at Sandy. He said to her, "I think he's going mental on us. He sees a guy, and all of a sudden I'm dealing coke."

"I'm trying to help you, dammit."

Rick pointed his finger at Dan. "I'm sorry I ever asked you to take Martha's case. I was doing you a favor, pal, because my sister asked me to. I shoulda got some ambulance chaser down on the Boulevard, wouldn't think he was God's gift to the fuckin' American justice system."

Dan pressed the heels of his hands together to keep from shoving Rick into the wall. "Okay. Fine. Tell you what. The U.S. marshals show up, call somebody else. I've had it with you."

"I haven't done anything!"

A low wail came from over by the chair, where Sandy still sat on the footstool. "Rick?" She was shaking. "Please don't do this."

Dan put his hands on his hips. "Tell her about Salazar's loan."

"Oh, for the love of God."

"Tell her."

"I borrowed money from Miguel Salazar. So what! If that makes me a goddamn criminal—if that makes me connected to whatever the hell he's doing, and I don't know *what* the guy's doing—then I plead guilty."

Sandy stared up at him. "How much?"

"A hundred thousand."

"Why, Rick?"

He only shook his head.

"Why?"

"Because . . . you wanted a new car and the furniture—"

"You're blaming *me*, you son of a bitch?"

"—and I couldn't get it for you. The business was off this year. I didn't want you to know how far off. And I didn't want . . . to lose you." Rick's voice was shaking. He was on the edge and going over. "I'll pay him back. He's being good about it. I gotta get this demo done. Then we'll have the concert. It's gonna be okay. I promise you, it will."

"Dammit, Rick!" She threw herself at him, and he stumbled backward. "What have you *done*? I knew it. I *knew* it!" She was screaming now, hitting him.

Rick had his hands up. "Stop it! Sandy!" He moved away, grabbed a pillow off the sofa, and hit her with it. She came in low and punched him in his belly. Rick sat down hard on the sofa, his robe falling off one shoulder. Dan pulled her off him. She screamed once more, then silence fell. Rick patted down his hair with a shaking hand. He wiped some blood off his nose with the belt of his robe, then got up and retied it.

She sat down in a chair and closed her eyes. "How much am I supposed to take, Lord?"

"Sandy?"

"I can't stand it anymore. I'm out of here."

"Don't leave me, pumpkin."

"I damn sure will. I'm going back to Georgia. You're making me old real fast."

"No. You're the most beautiful woman in the world." He got down on his knees. "Please, Sandy. I'll pay him back, as soon as the band gets a contract—"

"Soon as the pope sprouts horns."

"I'm begging you. Please, baby. Give me another chance. Don't leave."

"You said that last time too, and I stayed, and now look!"

"I love you so much. Oh, God. Please don't leave me. I wouldn't have a reason to go on. I'd kill myself, I swear. Sandy, you're all I live for. Don't go. Please. Please don't."

His face was buried in her lap, muffling his words. His shoulders shook. Tentatively at first, Sandy touched the back of his head, the wisps of hair curling between her fingers. "You dumb-ass little peckerhead."

Dan said quietly that he would let himself out.

A kilo of heroin. A kilo. Not a few grams but 2.2 pounds of the stuff. Dan knew the penalty in federal court. Ten years minimum mandatory. Kelly Dorff had been arrested—but not convicted. And she had never mentioned it.

Dan stopped for gas and stared at the pump until he remembered that he had already heard it click off a couple of minutes ago. He got back on the interstate, heading south. He overshot the exit to Biscayne Boulevard and kept going past downtown, finally getting off near Coral Gables.

He drove past Elaine McHale's building, a quiet street with a park on the other side. There was a light on. Her car was there, a small Ford sedan. Driving past again, he checked all the other cars, not finding a dark blue Chevy Caprice among them.

Cursing, barely moving his lips, he parked and walked up the sidewalk to her porch. The bags of trash were gone. Light leaked from around mini-blinds at the window. He leaned on the buzzer. Nothing. Pressed it again. Put his ear to the crack. Not a sound.

He slammed his fist on the door, then walked back to his car. As he drove away, he realized how stupid he'd been, coming here. She wasn't a friend, she was a federal prosecutor. He breathed deeply to quell the shakes.

CHAPTER 22

The dense banyan tree outside Dan's apartment cast such a shadow that Dan had asked the landlord to install a sensor on the porch light. It went on at sunset, off at dawn. It had failed to work a few times, so Dan was not particularly surprised when he found his front entrance dark. It was an old building; something was always breaking.

He came in, closed the door, and flipped the switch on the wall. The lamp did not come on. He assumed the bulb had burned out. He could barely see his way inside. A gray rectangle marked the front windows, and the shapes of furniture—sofa, chair, a curve of lamp shade—were barely visible. There was a glint of light on the TV screen. The place occupied by the aquarium was dark and oddly silent without the usual watery bubble of the aerator.

Power failure, he thought. Then noticed a soft blue glow reflected on the wall toward the kitchen—the digital clock on the microwave. In the same instant he saw the tiny amber screen on his stereo: 11:08.

And then a soft tick, a shift.

He froze. It was completely dark where he stood. Nothing short of night-vision lenses could see him. He stood motionless, listening.

Another tick, an odd noise he could not place. Not from outside. Not next door or overhead. Someone else was here in his apartment.

He thought of going quickly back outside, but he had already turned the dead bolt, and he was several steps away from the door. If he moved, he would give away his position.

It had to be a kid from the neighborhood, someone as scared as he was, scoping out the electronic equipment. There wasn't much Dan valued except for his dive equipment, worth several thousand dollars—tanks, regulators, spearguns, underwater camera. He kept it in a corner of the living room near the hall.

Dan didn't breathe, didn't move. He heard the shush of tires on the street. The distant overhead grumble of a jet. Faint voices through the walls.

Then the soft tick again. And another. Dan tilted his ear toward the sound. It came from the area near his aquarium. He let out his breath. It was the fish, his blue neon gobys. They were opening their mouths at the surface. He usually fed them when he got home. The little guys were hungry.

He felt foolish. He had imagined Miguel Salazar waiting to grab him and stick a knife through his ribs.

The power was off because a circuit breaker had flipped. That had happened before. He decided to turn on the lights in the kitchen and take a look at the breaker panel. Dan started carefully across the living room, hands in front of him, when he wondered why, if the circuit breaker had flipped, the stereo lights were on. The aquarium was off, and they were plugged into the same outlet.

He stepped in water. He could hear the splash under his rubber-soled shoe. Then his foot shoved something across the wood floor. He bent down, groping for a second before his fingers closed around a thin metallic cylinder. A speargun, his short one with the two-foot barrel. The heavy rubber tubing was loose, hanging free. The nylon cord had played out. The spear was gone; the thing had been fired.

A wave of heat swept over his body, then icy sweat. He let the gun down again quietly, carefully. Eyes adjusted now to the darkness, he could see the outline of the doorway to the kitchen. He stood up and felt his way, then fumbled for the light switch on the wall.

The blaze of fluorescent tubes overhead half blinded him. He waited, hearing nothing, then looked around the corner. Past the armchair he could see into the living room. An overturned lamp. The metal stand for his aquarium on its side, the glass smashed. Water, sand, seaweed. Bits of bright blue—his dead fish. A piece of white coral shaped like fingers. In the next instant he recalled there had been no coral in the tank. He walked around his chair, able to see it now. Not coral. A hand, outflung. A sleeve, blue denim. Long blond hair.

He ran across the room and dropped beside her. His knee skidded on the bloody floor. He felt a sharp jab of pain.

"Kelly!" He pulled her upright. Her head lolled back, then fell forward. He felt the wetness on his hands. Her white T-shirt was soaked with blood. A line of it was drying on her cheek, running from her mouth. The light glimmered in her half-closed eyes.

The homicide detective sat across the kitchen table from Dan, writing in a small spiral notebook.

Dan had given him her name. Had told him who she was. Where she was living. Had lived. Dan suggested that he contact Martha Cruz and Rick Robbins. Dan explained that Rick was the manager for Kelly's band, Mayhem, and Martha was her best friend. Gonzalez wrote down their numbers.

Slumped in his chair, Dan leaned his head against the wall. He had washed his arms and legs. There was a bandage around his knee. The paramedics had pulled out a piece of broken glass from the aquarium. The police had wanted his clothes, and he had changed into jeans and a sweatshirt. There were still smears of blood on the telephone. Dialing 911, he had known it was too late to save her. The spear had gone completely through, entering just under the sternum, nicking her spine on its way out. The medical examiner had just left. Dan had not seen the examination of the body, but he had watched the gurney wheeled out the front door. In front of the building, crime scene tape ran from streetlight to tree to a series of folding wooden barricades, outlining a twenty-foot-wide corridor from the street to Dan's front porch, keeping back the few onlookers about at this hour. The backyard was similarly cordoned off. Crime-scene techs were now taking more photographs and dusting for prints.

Dan noticed the clock on the microwave: 2:36. He had to concentrate to remember that it was A.M.

The homicide detective was asking him how he had met the deceased. Dan told him that she had come to his office to ask advice about a traffic ticket. They had started dating. That had been six weeks ago, something like that.

A card lay on the table. Jesus A. Gonzalez, Detective Sergeant, Homicide Division. Gonzalez looked fairly hip for a cop. He had thinning gray hair, longer in back, and a small diamond in his left earlobe. He found it interesting that Dan was a lawyer.

"*Eres cubano?*"

"No, my grandfather was Cuban. He came over in 1940. A fisherman."

"I see the fish tank in there. You collect fish? They're pretty, those blue ones. What are they called?"

"Neon gobys."

A second detective, a younger man, was leaning casually against the sink, arms crossed. A badge hung on the pocket of his sports coat.

Gonzalez asked, "When did you split up with Miss Dorff?"

"A couple of weeks ago, I guess."

"Why'd she come over tonight?"

"I don't know. I haven't spoken to her since we broke up."

"Was there any degree of rancor, let's say, between you and Ms. Dorff?"

"Rancor? No. She wasn't happy that we broke up, but she didn't hold a grudge. I got a call from her Saturday wishing me well, in fact."

"You just said you haven't spoken to her."

"She left a message on the machine."

"I see. And you haven't seen her since you broke up?"

"No, I saw her at the studio a couple of days after that. This morning I took some things of hers to her. She's staying—she was staying with Martha Cruz. I didn't see her, but I heard her playing her guitar. They had rehearsal tonight. I don't know what time they finished. Ask Martha."

"I will. Did Kelly have any enemies that you know of?"

"Not that I know of."

"It would be helpful," Gonzalez said, "if you could give us the names of anybody who, you know, might want to do this young lady in. Could you help us with that?"

"Sure." Dan closed his eyes momentarily. Saw the speargun on the floor where he had dropped it. The nylon cord that went through Kelly's body. The spear had a barbed steel point, and the police had pulled it out of the wall behind the aquarium.

Gonzalez was saying, "Nobody broke in here tonight, did they? I'm thinking maybe the house was broken into, Miss Dorff comes along, sees the intruder—"

Dan shook his head. "The doors were locked. I didn't see any broken windows."

"Did she have a key?"

"No. Oh, wait. I keep a spare key under the back steps for emergencies. She knew where it was. It's possible she used it to get in."

Gonzalez looked at the other detective, who unfolded his arms and went outside to take a look. He said to Dan, "You want a glass of water? Mind if I have one?"

"The glasses are over the sink." Dan propped his forehead in his hand. He heard the refrigerator door open. The gurgle of water. Water had been ticking out of the aerator tubes, the last few drops. Kelly had bled to death. If Dan had arrived ten minutes earlier, he could have caught the son of a bitch. Around eleven o'clock the neighbor next door had heard a scream, then a crash. She had ignored it. Had gone back to her television.

Adjusting the knee of his trousers, Gonzalez sat down again. "Where were you coming from when you got home?"

"My former brother-in-law's house in Pompano Beach. Rick Robbins."

"The manager for Kelly's band. And you left his house when?"

"Let's see. Got there about nine-thirty, left around ten o'clock."

"And before that?"

Dan blinked and rubbed his eyes. The kitchen seemed too bright. "I took my son home. He lives with his mother, my former wife, in Lakewood Village. That's up in Broward County."

"I know where Lakewood is," Gonzalez said. "Nice area. Your former wife is . . . Mr. Robbins's sister? Do I have that right?"

"Yes. Her name is Lisa Galindo. Do you want the address?"

"I'll get it from you later if I need it. And you left her house at what time?"

"Around seven-thirty." Dan glanced up. The other detective was coming in the back door.

"No key," he said, "but the M.E. found a loose house key in the pocket of her jeans."

Dan said, "I just remembered that when I came in the door knob was locked but the dead bolt was open. The same key fits both. Kelly would lock both of them when she'd come over."

The detective said, "So?"

"So someone followed her in, then left by turning the thumb lock in the knob."

"Which proves what?"

"I don't know. She let someone in."

"We'll get to that," Gonzalez said. His tone told the

younger man to butt out. He looked back at Dan. "Mind if I ask how long you've been divorced?"

"Since last August."

"You and your ex get along okay?"

"Fine. We're trying to work things out. We might get back together."

Gonzalez nodded. "Good luck. I'm divorced too. Last year. My ex is always giving me shit about the women I date." He laughed and propped his ankle on his knee. "I'm going with this young chick, right? My ex hits the ceiling, and I'm not even married to her anymore. Did your ex know Kelly?"

"I think they met, probably through Rick."

"They got along all right?"

"They *met*. They didn't know each other," Dan said impatiently. "Are we done? I'd like to take a shower."

"Almost." Gonzalez glanced down at his notes. "What was the nature of your visit with Mr. Robbins?"

"A legal matter. I'm his attorney."

"What was this about?"

"I'm sorry, it's confidential."

"I assume it had to do with the band. He's the manager, correct?"

"It's confidential, Sergeant."

"Okay." Gonzalez rolled his pen between his flattened palms. "Help me figure this out. You leave your ex-wife's house at seven-thirty. You arrive at Mr. Robbins's house in Pompano Beach, just north of Fort Lauderdale, at nine-thirty. That's a half-hour trip, that time of night. I wonder if you can help me pinpoint exactly where you were during that extra hour and a half."

Dan remembered suddenly that he had been driving up and down the interstate, then around a warehouse district in North Miami, looking for Manatee Studios, trying to find the man with the beard. "It's not relevant where I was at that time. Kelly died at eleven."

"Mr. Galindo, let me decide what's relevant. I like all the squares filled in. I'm funny that way."

Dan felt the first rush of anger, fueled by awareness of his own stupidity. He'd walked right into this. A Miami homicide detective was interrogating him. Daniel Galindo was a suspect in a murder. Of course he was. The ex-boyfriend. Dan had told his clients again and again: Don't talk to the police. Whatever you tell them, they'll think the worst. Give your name, your address, and then call a lawyer.

"Mr. Galindo?"

But he *was* a lawyer. There would be reporters crawling all over this case at dawn, and the last thing he wanted to hear on the news was, *Police say that Miami lawyer and former assistant U.S. attorney Daniel Galindo refuses to comment on the mysterious death of his former lover, rock singer Kelly Dorff, whose body was found last night in his apartment.*

Dan crossed his arms. "Between eight and nine o'clock I made another stop which had to do with Mr. Robbins—and which I am not prepared to discuss—and after that I drove to his house in Pompano Beach, arriving, as I said, about nine-thirty. I left around ten, arrived home, unlocked the door, came inside, and found Ms. Dorff dead in my living room."

"You arrived here at eleven."

"Eleven-oh-eight."

"And you didn't see Kelly Dorff earlier tonight? Didn't speak to her by phone?"

"No."

"You came home and found her body."

"That's what I just said. Eight minutes—more or less—after my neighbor heard a woman's scream and the crash of my aquarium going over. Are we finished now?"

"Bear with me. You leave the Robbins place around ten o'clock. Ms. Dorff is killed around eleven, you arrive at 11:08, according to you."

"According to the clock on the stereo," Dan said.

"Right. Pompano to Miami is . . . what? Thirty miles? And it took you an hour and eight minutes. On the interstate." Gonzalez was waiting. "Can you explain that? Clear it up for me?"

The underarms of Dan's shirt were soaked, and he could feel sweat tickling down his spine. "Yes. I was at a friend's house. I went by to discuss some business."

"You just now remembered this?"

"That's correct."

"Who's the friend? I'd like to call him—or her."

Dan shook his head. "I've answered enough questions. I'm going to make a phone call."

"Who are you calling?"

"My lawyer."

"You need a lawyer? Come on. You?" Gonzalez put the notebook aside. "Listen. Wouldn't it be simpler if you just told me what happened?"

"I did." Dan walked past him out of the kitchen and through the living room, not looking at the blood or the remains of his aquarium. Two officers in dark blue uniforms watched him. He could hear Gonzalez calling his name. In his bedroom, there was an answering machine built into the telephone. Dan noticed for the first time the green light that indicated two messages.

Standing at the door, Gonzalez pointed. "Don't touch that." A uniformed officer walked over, not sure what was going on. Gonzalez came in and pressed the button with the end of his pen.

A beep. Then Lisa's voice, annoyed. "Dan? I hope you're on your way. You said you'd have Joshua home by seven-thirty."

Silence. Another beep. Then Kelly's husky voice.

"Hi. It's me. I saw you when you came to Miguel's today. I should've come out, but I was scared to. Stupid, huh? Thanks for the clothes and stuff. And for the note. Dan, I need to talk to you tonight. We've got rehearsal, then I'll come over. It's important. Please don't be busy. See ya."

Gonzalez hit the replay button. "Hi. It's me. . . ."

In his mind Dan saw Kelly's narrow face, the thin lips. He could see her speaking, tossing her hair out of her eyes.

"I'm going to take a wild guess and say that the first

one is your ex. And the other one is Kelly Dorff." With his handkerchief over his hand, Gonzalez opened the lid and took out the tape. "Your neighbor told me she recently heard some fighting in here. Yelling, screaming, profanity, some loud thumps. You saw her in the yard the next day, and she asked you about it. You apologized. Said it wouldn't happen again because Ms. Dorff wasn't coming back. You remember that?"

"Get out. I have a call to make."

"We're going to discuss this at the station."

"Not unless you place me under arrest, and you don't have a warrant. You don't even have probable cause to get a warrant."

Gonzalez smiled at him. "Based on what we have already, I don't foresee a problem."

Dan kept his voice under control. "I can't kick you out of a crime scene, but I'm going to call my lawyer. Then I'm leaving."

Charlie Dunavoy arrived fifteen minutes later, rumpled and gruff, telling the cops he wanted them out by noon and Dan's keys returned to his office. Dan hung his suit bag in the back of the Cadillac.

As they pulled out of the parking lot past the police cars and a crime-scene van, Dan could see Detective Gonzalez watching from the front porch.

"Good God. Charlie, I talked to the bastard. I don't believe it. I sat right there and answered his questions. I knew better and I still did it."

"Oh, we'll get it all sorted out." Charlie turned left toward Biscayne Boulevard. "Lawyers are the worst. We think we can explain it all away. We're smart. And what will the Florida Bar say if we don't offer an explanation? What will our clients say?"

The boulevard was dark and quiet, only a few cars in either direction.

"They think I killed her! It's inconceivable. Why am I sweating like this?"

"You're sweating because you feel guilty. You feel guilty because we all do when somebody we care about suffers. It's human nature. You're thinking, Oh, if I hadn't ended our affair, this wouldn't have happened to her. Right? Yeah. Two-bit psychology."

"I should call Rick. He can't hear about this on the news."

"We get to my place, we'll talk about what to do."

"It's late."

"I'm wide awake as a hooty owl myself. Alva's up waiting for us. She said she'd put some coffee on."

"I'll tell you everything I know, Charlie. It's going to take awhile."

Kelly's face appeared in Dan's mind again, and he felt his throat tighten, then ache.

CHAPTER 23

The murder of Kelly Dorff sent a tremor through the Operation Manatee task force. The U.S. attorney's office, the federal agencies involved, and local law enforcement assumed that someone had found out who she was: a confidential informant. Expecting that the targets of the investigation would start running for cover, the FBI wanted them arrested immediately. The DEA argued for a delay. When the targets continued in their normal routines, it was agreed that U.S. marshals would conduct their sweep as scheduled, after the DEA had arrested Miguel Salazar over the weekend.

The initial meeting between Salazar and agent Vincent Hooper, posing as Victor Ramirez, had resulted in Salazar's proposing another. He would meet Ramirez again on Sunday, this time to do business. Ramirez would bring $500,000 in cash; Salazar would deliver an equal amount in credits in a foreign bank, less his customary fee of ten percent. Salazar would handle the transaction in person. His usual courier, Leon Davila, had returned to Ecuador. At least that was the story. None of the contacts in Ecuador had seen him.

With attention focused elsewhere, the investigation into Kelly Dorff's murder had been left solely to the Miami police. Elaine McHale had read the newspapers. She knew that the police suspected Dan Galindo, assuming a quarrel between former lovers. She did not know who else might be on the list of suspects; nor did she know why Kelly had gone to see Dan that night. She was curious how the DEA had responded.

DEA agent Scott Irwin appeared as a witness before the grand jury on Tuesday afternoon, one of the final sessions for Operation Manatee. Elaine decided to ask him.

The grand jury—actually two dozen separate panels, meeting on various days—convened on the ninth floor of the federal building. The nondescript gray lobby was strewn with newspapers and empty coffee containers so late in the afternoon. Coming out of one of the jury rooms, Elaine saw Irwin chatting with undercover police officers, all of them wearing ties and dark sports coats. She had to look carefully to pick out Irwin, the one with curly dark blond hair. The wig looked real. His blue punk-rocker hair was completely out of sight.

She nodded toward the other officers, then said, "Agent Irwin, I'd like to talk to you for a minute."

They went into a conference room off the lobby, a small one facing west.

Elaine tilted the blinds, and stripes of light angled across the gray walls and carpet. Irwin said nothing. They were so good at this, she thought. The blank stare. Neither hostile nor friendly. Waiting but not anxious about it. She felt like she was looking at a screen saver on a computer monitor.

She leaned on the edge of the table. "I want to find out what happened to Kelly Dorff. She and I talked on several occasions, and I got to know her. Whatever is in the *Miami Herald* is not, obviously, the whole story. I wonder if you could fill me in."

Irwin said, "You should talk to the police."

"Yes, but here you are," she said, "and I'd rather have the DEA's view of it. Yours in particular. You were rehearsing with her in Martha's studio at Salazar's house the night she died."

"That's correct."

"And she left around ten o'clock?"

"Yes."

"Well, what happened?"

He took a small breath, as she had seen him do before answering a question for the grand jury. "We rehearsed until shortly before ten. Kelly had already mentioned meeting Dan Galindo that night. Martha Cruz didn't want her to go. She was anxious to keep working. We were in the middle of a song when Kelly unplugged her guitar and said she was leaving."

"And then what?"

"She and Martha had an argument about it. Martha said that Arlo and I needed more work to learn the parts before the concert. Kelly said we had all worked for ten hours already, and everyone was tired. She accused Martha of wanting to change the focus of the band—the same argument they've had for weeks. Then Kelly walked out."

"Did the rest of you continue working?"

"No. Martha wanted to, but I told her I was too tired. I had hoped to follow Kelly, but by the time I got outside, her car was already gone. I drove by Galindo's apartment at ten forty-two. If she left at ten, that was plenty of time to get there. The lights were off, and I didn't see either his or Kelly's car, so I assumed they had met somewhere else. Then I continued to a previously scheduled meeting with Agent Hooper."

"Did Salazar know where Kelly was going?"

"He knew. He asked her why she wanted to speak to Galindo. She wouldn't say."

"Did you know why?"

"No. I teased her about it. I asked if she and Galindo were getting it on again, but she wouldn't discuss it."

Elaine idly noticed how the strips of light through the blinds formed a jagged Z where they bent at the corner of the wall, then again at the floor. "Is it possible that Salazar suspected she was working for us?"

"It's possible. Having seen the man up close, I can tell you he's very smart and very suspicious. The first meeting between him and Vince Hooper almost didn't take place." Agent Irwin leaned on the edge of the desk, clasping his hands loosely in front of him. The bars of light curved around his jacket, tie, and white shirt. "If Salazar had suspected she was a C.I., he wouldn't necessarily have connected her with Victor Ramirez, however. The meeting Sunday is still on. That indicates that he doesn't suspect it's a sting."

"Where was Salazar during the rehearsal?"

"In and out. When Martha and Kelly started arguing, Salazar left the rehearsal room and didn't come back in. A few minutes later, when I was leaving, I checked the garage. There were several cars in and around it, but I didn't see Salazar's car. I went back in and on some pretext asked the maid where Salazar had gone. *No sé, señor.* She didn't know. But the next day he told the police he was home all night playing cards with his sister. She backs him up."

"Do the police know that Salazar's alibi may be false?"

For the first time Elaine could see a blip on the computer screen. Then it was gone. Irwin said, "I'm not certain whether that information has been conveyed to them or not."

She couldn't help smiling. "You're not certain. Well, did you yourself convey that information to the police?"

"No. I did not."

"Why didn't you?"

"I was not asked to comment on Salazar's alibi or lack thereof, Ms. McHale."

"Information directly related to a homicide investigation, and you didn't think it was worth bringing up?"

"We're staying out of it."

"I see. So that the police won't inadvertently disrupt the meeting between Hooper and Salazar on Sunday."

"Correct."

"Even if in the meantime Daniel Galindo is arrested for murder."

The agent had a smile that wasn't quite there. Look at it straight on, and it disappears. "If he's innocent, Ms. McHale—and I sincerely doubt that—then he has nothing to worry about. Does he?"

A small laugh escaped her. "You people are unbelievable."

Irwin stood up from the edge of the table. "I'm sorry about Kelly Dorff. You shouldn't feel bad, though, not personally. She hung out with dopers. Cops arrested her for helping transport heroin. Nobody put her there but herself."

"Yes. Exactly what Vincent Hooper said."

"If we're finished," Irwin said, "I have to be somewhere."

She nodded. "Go ahead."

He walked over and opened the door, the light sliding down the surface. "One more thing, if I may? Let Hooper attend to his job. If you want to fuck him, that's your business, but try to wait till this operation is over."

The door closed behind him, and for several minutes Elaine was too stunned to move from the room.

* * *

John Paxton, the lead prosecutor on the task force and Elaine's boss, had scheduled a meeting with the U.S. attorney at five o'clock. They wanted to go over details of the statement that would be read to the press next Wednesday morning.

After crackdowns in the early 1990s on the massive flow of cocaine entering the United States through Miami, the drug lords began to route it through Mexico. When border surveillance tightened in the Southwest, shipments into South Florida resumed. In 1995 it was common for Customs to come across 500 kilos hidden in cargo containers or false compartments in ships or airplanes. Soon the seizures became 1,000 kilos, then 3,000. The indictments and arrests in Operation Manatee would tell the public that the authorities were fully responding to the situation.

The press conference would be televised at noon. The United States attorney for the Southern District of Florida would be at the podium. Agents from the FBI and DEA and local law enforcement would stand behind him. Two Florida congressmen would be on his right. John Paxton would be to his left, and then Paxton's chief assistant, Elaine McHale.

Elaine waited for Paxton in his office until his meeting was over. He was not surprised to find her there; they often dropped in on each other.

She told him about her conversation with DEA agent Scott Irwin.

Paxton, who had tented his fingers halfway through

her recitation, began tapping them slowly on his chin, then lowered his hands to the desk. "Well. What do you suggest?"

"I think it depends on what the Miami police are doing. Where are they in the investigation? Do they have any leads besides Dan? Do they seriously want to arrest him?"

"They plan to do it tomorrow morning," Paxton said. "He hasn't been told."

"Tomorrow?"

"Crack of dawn. He's with his former wife in Lakewood Village, so the arrest will be made up there. That's the information I get from the state attorney's office. The homicide detective on the case is pretty sure he has the evidence. Galindo couldn't supply an alibi. He has a motive. His fingerprints are on the murder weapon, a speargun, which he certainly knows how to operate." The springs in Paxton's chair squeaked slightly when he leaned back. He said, "Maybe it was an accident that Dan doesn't want to own up to. I'd be willing to believe that."

Elaine shook her head. "That isn't the *point*. The police should be told that Miguel Salazar is lying about his alibi. Do we stand around and watch an innocent man charged with murder?"

"I admire your concern, Elaine. It's noble, it's fair-minded. But stay out of it. I have to agree with the DEA on this one."

She stood up and paced to the window. "Look. We simply tell the state attorney's office to hold off till after Monday. Dan isn't going anywhere. The police can check out Salazar, then they can make a decision."

Paxton said, "The DEA isn't going to allow that. They don't want anything to jostle this case. They've got full bladders and no potty break till next week. Don't expect Scott Irwin to go willingly, in any event. We could discuss it with Hooper, but at this point I can't see him getting involved."

"I could go to the police myself," Elaine said.

"Oh, Jesus. Then what? The press would start poking their noses up our skirts. It's bad enough having a former prosecutor suspected of murder, aside from the fact that he might be part of a money-laundering conspiracy."

"Kelly Dorff completely recanted that allegation," Elaine said. "She told the DEA that she had made it up to get back at Dan for breaking up with her."

"You are so eager to prove him innocent, aren't you?"

"No, but I question the way this is being handled." She had raised her voice. She exhaled, then said, "Look. If we have exculpatory evidence, and we do *not* come forward, what would the press say about that? Oh, we could try to cover the fact that we knew about it but did nothing. Save ourselves from embarrassment. We're good at that. Or maybe we could wait until Salazar is taken into custody. We can ask him where he was when Kelly Dorff died. How forthcoming is he going to be? Dan Galindo will have been arrested for murder by then. Is Salazar going to say, 'Oh, no. Let him out. *I* did it'?"

Paxton asked, "Did he do it?"

"With a speargun? I doubt it. If Salazar were going to get rid of her, why do it in Dan's house? He could just as easily—more easily—have taken her a mile or two west and dumped her in the Everglades. But the point remains, John. We're withholding evidence from the police."

Paxton's attention seemed focused on his desk, on the twelve-sided white plastic calendar that he turned one way, then the other, exposing June, then August, then March. "When was the last time you saw Dan Galindo?"

She frowned, not understanding what he was getting at. Paxton flipped the calendar around again. September. July. Then raised his eyes. "When did you last have a conversation, in person, with Dan Galindo? It's a simple question, Elaine."

"He came by my house last Sunday morning. We talked for a few minutes outside on the porch. He came by to say hello. I didn't expect him. I told him I was busy, and he left."

Paxton was still looking at her.

She said, "Why did you ask me that?"

Pushing aside the calendar, Paxton said, "I didn't want to have this conversation with you, Elaine. You've been my right hand on Manatee. I've relied on you, and you've come through. But I have lost confidence in your ability to appear impartial. I want you off the task force. Now. Immediately."

It was as though the floor tilted. Elaine automatically reached out to touch the back of a chair.

"I think you're stuck on this issue of Dan Galindo. I don't get it. But be that as it may—"

"John, that is absolutely ridiculous!"

"What really ices the cake," he went on, "is that you went against my instructions not to speak to a witness. You remember that discussion? I told you not to speak to Kelly Dorff. But you went right ahead—"

"In no way did you expressly forbid me to—"

"Expressly? Don't tell me you didn't understand. You went right ahead and had a chat with a confidential informant for the DEA, without their knowledge, causing me to wonder whether that discussion had anything to do—" Paxton raised his voice, preventing her from speaking. "Anything to do with this."

Shifting some papers on his desk, he picked one sheet out of the stack. "This. It's a transcript of a call made from Miguel Salazar's telephone last Friday night. It came to me today, part of the usual pack of transcripts from DEA-intercepted telephone calls. You might recognize this one."

He put on his glasses. "It says, in part, 'Hi. This is Kelly Dorff. . . . I called Vincent and took back what I said about Dan. And listen. I didn't tell him about you and Dan being friends and everything, okay? . . . Don't forget about the demo tapes. You promised.' "

With the last word Paxton glanced up at Elaine. Waited for her to speak.

"I never told Kelly to do that, John. She was driven by her own guilt. She was sorry for lying."

"She may well have been. But assume that this transcript found its way, as it probably will, into the hands of a defense lawyer. 'It's obvious, ladies and gentlemen of the jury, that this confidential informant is a liar, and the government knows it. Elaine McHale *promised* to obtain the studio tapes for Kelly's rock and roll band if Kelly Dorff would take back what she said about her former boyfriend, Dan Galindo.' "

Elaine could only stand mutely while John Paxton continued his tirade. "Forget that. What is worse, *by far*, is that you chose to go behind my back. Nor did you tell me about this telephone call from Kelly Dorff. I find out in a *transcript*. And I am left wondering, because *no one* has filled me in here, exactly *what* you said to her, that was *so sensitive* she couldn't tell the DEA about it. Why are you smiling? I don't think you're in a position right now to find anything amusing, Elaine."

"I don't. I was reminded of all the times I've argued inferences to a jury. Giving them the prosecutorial slant. Then the defense gets up and does its thing, and the jury has got to wonder if we're even talking about the same case."

Paxton slowly took off his glasses and laid them on his desk. "Don't you know what I'm trying to tell you?"

"Yes. I am sorry, John."

He rubbed the back of his neck. "I refuse to believe you were trying to help someone escape prosecution, but other people might. Other people *do*, in fact."

"Who said that to you?"

He shook his head. "I'm not able to share that information."

"The DEA? Can I assume that much?"

"Don't push, Elaine." Paxton dropped into his chair. "I want you to take a week off. Tell people in the office your mother is sick, or you're having a root canal."

"And watch the press conference on TV," she said. "We don't want to embarrass anyone."

He shot her a look. "When you get back, tell me what you want to work on. Anything but Manatee."

"Never mind that I've done most of the work on it for the past six months."

"Elaine—" He held up a finger, a request for acceptance.

She leaned on extended arms on the back of the chair, then lifted her head. "Fine. I'll have the files in your office by Friday afternoon, memos attached."

"Thank you." She was at the door when he said, "And, Elaine? You're close to the line. Don't go over it. Do not contact Dan Galindo before tomorrow morning. Do not talk to the Miami police about Miguel Salazar. Am I being *absolutely* clear on that?"

She nodded and went out.

In her own office, Elaine left the light off and stood by the windows. The sun was nearly down, just a few vague strips of light across the buildings and rush-hour streets. She felt utterly spent. Ashamed, though it would be hard to say precisely why. She thought that she would probably go home and get deservedly drunk.

Kelly Dorff did not have to be dead. Since hearing the news, Elaine had wondered what might have happened if she'd taken Kelly off the case. Let her go, which was what Kelly had wanted. Elaine could have said, Thanks for your help, but go now. I don't need you to testify. Go on. Sing. Play your guitar.

It would have to be a good one, Elaine thought. Enough booze not to see Kelly Dorff sitting across the table at the restaurant, pouring cream into heavy mugs as if they were the finest porcelain. Pushing her long hair back behind her ears. Those surprisingly ugly, incredibly strong hands. Kelly had put a burning match out with her callused fingertips. She had been dismissive of her chances for success, but she had wanted it all the same. *My last chance*, Kelly had said. *If I don't do it this time, it's all over.*

Enough booze so she wouldn't get up early in the morning. She didn't want to stumble out of bed, turn on the radio, and hear Dan Galindo's name on the morning news.

CHAPTER 24

Dan spent Monday night at Charlie's house, then asked Lisa if he could use her guest room for a couple of days. He needed to get out of Miami. Away from his apartment. He arranged for a thorough cleaning, someone to replace the area rug and scrub the floors. Until then Dan didn't want to see the place.

Rick drove over to Lakewood to talk. He and Dan went out in the backyard and had a couple of beers while Lisa cleared away the dinner dishes.

Dan said, "You talked her into letting me stay here, didn't you?"

"Yeah, well." Rick stared at the bottle in his hand. "What's gonna happen to you?"

"I don't know yet."

"The cops gonna arrest you for this?"

"Probably. I haven't told Lisa."

"Oh, jeez. Tell me what I can do."

"Take care of her and Josh, if I can't."

"No problem."

They sat for a while in silence.

Dan said, "I know they can't make a case, so I'm not too worried. Oh, to hell with it. How's Martha taking Kelly's death? I haven't talked to her."

"Martha says get a new guitarist. This is true. Cold-blooded little bitch, isn't she?" Rick finished his beer, then belched softly and set the bottle on the patio. "The others are ready to fold."

"How about you?"

He laughed softly. "I'm gonna be at the studio starting tomorrow night, checking out lead guitarists. I got a few guys lined up. No girls. Maybe one of them could wear a blond wig. Sing in falsetto." Rick sobbed suddenly, then clamped his teeth together. He took a breath. "Oh, Jesus. That poor kid. Everything's coming apart, Dan."

Dan heard the screen slide back. Lisa's shadow fell onto the patio. "Dan? Josh is ready for bed. Can you come say good night?"

"Be there in two minutes."

The screen slid shut.

Rick got up. "I should go."

"Wait." Dan said quietly, "Sunday night the band was rehearsing at Salazar's house. What time did they quit?"

"I wasn't there," Rick said, "but Martha told me Kelly cut out for your place about ten o'clock, and when she didn't come back to Salazar's that night, Martha figured she'd stayed over."

"Does she know why Kelly wanted to talk to me?"

"She says she doesn't. Those girls were pretty close, though. It's hard to believe Kelly wouldn't tell her."

"Who else knew where she was going?"

"They all did. Kelly was antsy to finish early, and Martha wanted to keep working. They'd been at it since noon. She and Kelly got into an argument, then Kelly put away her guitar and said she was leaving, and they could keep playing without her."

"Did they?"

"No, they packed it in."

"Where did they go?"

Rick leaned over to pick up his beer bottles, and they clanked together. "Arlo and Martha stayed at the house. Miguel was upstairs with the family. Scott split when Kelly did. Martha doesn't know where he went."

"He wouldn't have a reason to go after Kelly, would he?"

"I can't figure it. They got along okay. He says he has a girlfriend."

Dan said, "I guess the cops checked out where he was?"

"No doubt. They even asked me where I was. I'm thinking one of your local crackheads noticed her going in, followed her, got scared. Maybe that was it."

"Maybe."

Rick tapped Dan on the chest with a bottle. "Hey. Sandy and I were talking. We're getting you a new aquarium."

"You don't have to do that."

"Marine Mart. I called them already. Whatever you want—up to a point. Don't go crazy."

Josh kept his room neat, everything in its place. Plastic storage crates full of colorful games and toys were stacked along one wall. The curtains matched the bedspreads. He had bunk beds for when his friends slept over. A small fish tank bubbled under his window. There was no television, but he had a new computer and color printer. No modem. Lisa didn't want him hooked to the Internet until he was older.

When Dan knocked lightly at the open door, Josh, in his pajamas, stood up from his desk with an envelope in his hands. The lamp reflected in his glasses when he tilted his head up to look at his father.

"What you got there, bud?"

"Your card."

"My birthday's not till tomorrow."

"This is in case you aren't here tomorrow," Josh said. "I asked Mom and she doesn't know yet."

"Well, that's true. I might not be here." Dan squatted beside him. "May I see the card?"

"I made it on my computer." Josh glanced down at the envelope. "I'll do it over if you want me to. This one's not very good."

"What do you mean? It looks great." Dan sat cross-legged on the carpet, and Josh stood next to him, looking over his shoulder, waiting for the verdict.

The yellow envelope said DAD on the front in red 3-D letters that slanted from small to large. "Very nice." Dan took out the card. On shiny white paper Josh had printed a cartoon boat and blue waves. Two tiny figures, hand-drawn, stood in the stern with fishing poles. In the upper right was a smiling yellow sun. Inside was printed, "To my dad. Your the best. Happy birthday. From your son, Joshua D. Galindo."

Dan felt his eyes burning. He said quietly, "It's stupendous."

"Mom said I misspelled 'your.' It should have an 'e' on the end." Josh pointed at the word.

"That's all right. I bet she liked it, though."

"She said I should do it over, but I didn't have any more paper like that."

"No. This one is fine." Dan kissed Josh, then pulled him onto his lap. "Did your mother explain to you why my name was on TV?"

"She said because somebody died at your house. She wouldn't let me watch TV, though. My friend Taylor at school told me a woman got murdered by a spear. What happened?"

"It was a friend of mine who came to visit, and I wasn't home yet. Someone—we don't know who yet—killed her, Josh. The police will find him. He won't hurt anyone else."

Josh looked at Dan steadily through his glasses. "Was she, like, stabbed and cut in pieces? That's what Taylor said."

"No, son. She was shot with a speargun. One of mine." Dan added, "I threw the rest of them out."

"Did you see her dead?"

"Yes, but she looked very peaceful, like she was asleep."

"Are you sad?"

"Sure. She was my friend." Dan squeezed Josh's shoulder. "Her name was Kelly. She played guitar and sang in a rock and roll band."

"No way."

"It's true. She even had tattoos and a nose ring. You never met her, but I showed her your picture. She said you looked like a great kid, a junior stud. Her exact words." Josh laughed, and Dan ruffled his hair and stood up. " 'Night, son. Thanks for the card. Why don't you write a poem to go with it?"

"A poem?" Josh rolled his eyes back into his head and pretended to gag.

"A story, then. A story about you and me going fishing."

"That would take a long time, a story," he said.

"We've got time."

Lisa made up the sofa bed in the guest room. Unfolded a fresh sheet and flipped it to settle onto the mattress. Neat corners, tucked tightly. Held a pillow under her chin, slid it into the pillowcase. Turning to take a blanket from the shelf in the closet, she noticed Dan at the door.

He took the blanket away and dropped it on the bed. He put his arms around her. The small lamp made the room seem intimate and safe. He exhaled heavily and held her more closely.

"I need you, Lisa."

She moved her hands on his back, up the tight muscles along his spine. Her breasts were soft and warm. "I didn't think I'd ever hear you say that."

"Let's go to bed." When she went still for a moment, Dan said, "I won't touch you if you don't want me to."

Lisa raised her head, and her pale gold hair fell back from her face, a ripple of silk. She smiled slowly, the corners of her mouth curling into her smooth cheeks. "I do want you to." She put her lips next to his and whispered, "I'm glad you're back."

He lay in the darkness listening to the night sounds and watching the digital numbers on the clock radio tick off the minutes: 11:56.

The room still smelled like paint. The carpet would be installed next week, Lisa had told him. A low shag, very plush, an ivory color to match the walls. Karastan, on sale for $42.95 per yard, installed.

The sheets were new. The top sheet was folded down to Dan's waist so he could cool off. They had that crisp, just-out-of-the-package smell. A set, together with pillow shams and a duvet, all of which Lisa had put on the bed for the occasion. She had laughed, refusing to tell him how much. But the bedroom would be fabulous.

Lisa's cocker spaniel, Poppy, was down on his mat, awake, panting softly, guarding the house from intruders. Dan had walked him earlier, trying to find on Heron Way a place where a dog could do his thing, finally letting him go in the backyard. Poppy had been to the groomer today, and he had a ribbon in his hair. Useless mutt.

Lisa shifted. Sighed. Rubbed his upper arm. "Dan, it's all right."

"I guess I'm tired," he said. "And my knee still hurts where I cut it." He found her hand. "I don't mean to be making excuses." He brought her hand to his lips and kissed each knuckle.

She said, "I was thinking."

Dan turned her palm over and laid it against his cheek. "What were you thinking?"

"Miguel Salazar's boat. I think it's for the best that you gave it back."

"Damn. I forgot to mail him the keys."

Lisa said, "Not getting that boat means that you have to put some serious thought into what you want to do. For instance, why the Bahamas? Why does it have to be just you and Josh? Maybe we should all go." She propped herself on an elbow. She was naked, and the moonlight through the open window flooded across her skin, turning it silvery blue.

He closed his eyes and turned to her, and put an arm around her waist.

She said, "We could find a resort. Something for all of us. White sandy beach, calypso band, sunset cruises. Doesn't that sound romantic? Golf and tennis. Josh could find kids to play with, and we—" She kissed him lightly, quickly. "We could get to know each other again. I want you to think about it. Okay?"

"I don't know."

"Dan—" She shook his shoulder. "It would be good for us. I mean, if you're serious about wanting to try again. That's what you said. I mean, you are serious, aren't you?"

"Of course. I've just got some things on my mind right now."

"Oh."

"Yes. Oh."

She lay flat and looked at the ceiling. "Is it going to be all right with the police?"

"I'll be arrested. I don't know when. I have a friend at the state attorney's office who said the police sent the paperwork over."

"Oh, my God. Why didn't you tell me?"

"I was trying to decide how."

"What does this *mean*?"

"It means I'm going to jail, Lisa. There's no bond for murder. My law practice will probably be ruined. I won't see you or Josh except on visiting day. Jesus. What does it mean?"

"All right. You don't need to snap at me."

"Sorry." He reached for her, and she put her head on his chest.

"What about a lawyer?" she said. "Charlie Dunavoy is your friend, but is he good enough?"

"I'd have to hire someone else."

For a while there was silence in the room. He heard her take a breath. "Dan, I can't sell the house. I can't."

"No. I never suggested that," he said. He rubbed her back. Her skin was like satin.

"Even a mortgage— There just isn't that much equity left. There was the roof, then the back patio— Oh, Dan. I'm sorry. I feel so awful for even bringing it up." She rolled off him and stared up at the ceiling.

"Lisa, it's okay."

"Maybe my parents would help. Do you want me to ask them?"

Dan laughed. "I can hear your father now. 'Lisa, you just divorced the man.' "

She pressed her hands to her forehead, arms like pale inverted V's in the dim light. "This is unreal. I can't believe this is happening."

"Tomorrow I'll have Charlie call and ask what's going on. If they're going to arrest me, I want to get it over with."

"Would they come here?"

"Possibly. Or I could turn myself in." Dan looked at her. "Should I go back to Miami?"

She shook her head. "You don't have to do that."

"I will. Maybe it would be better."

"No, don't." Lisa was quiet awhile. "All right. Maybe it would be better. What if they came and Josh was here?"

Dan sighed. "I'll go in the morning."

"I wish—Oh, God. I don't know what to do," she said.

"Don't worry," he said. "It's going to be all right."

He turned on his side, and before he closed his eyes he noticed the clock on the nightstand: 12:07.

Lisa said, "Why are you laughing?"

"It's Wednesday. My birthday. So this is what thirty-five feels like."

CHAPTER 25

"I asked for the C shift," Gonzalez said. "Eleven p.m. to nine in the morning. That's a good shift for Homicide. You'd think that most people are murdered on the C shift, in the dark of night, the wee hours, so to speak. Not so. Most of them are on B shift, three in the afternoon to one a.m. That's when you've got people coming home from work, they're tired, they're cranky. Kids after school stabbing each other. Fights outside nightclubs, a large portion of your convenience store holdups, plus you got your drunk-driving vehicular homicides, and most of your robberies and rapes that go bad. I don't like the A shift either. Seven to five is a zoo. Phones ringing, people running in and out. Of course, in Miami there are homicides around the clock, so whatever shift you're on, you always have something to keep you busy."

Detective Gonzalez escorted Elaine to his desk and pulled out a chair for her.

The Homicide unit was on the fifth floor of the building, and Elaine got a good view out the window before she sat down. The city was a grid of lights under a black sky. On the perfectly flat land, the long ribbon of the interstate rose and dipped over cross streets on its way north into Broward County and beyond.

Elaine had already explained over the telephone her connection to Kelly Dorff, and had told Detective Gonzalez that she might have information relevant to her death.

She explained how she knew Dan Galindo. She began to explain the delicacy of the situation—the DEA, the FBI, the—

"I don't care," he said. "I do homicide cases. I want to find out who killed her. Anything else is a secondary consideration. You want a soda?"

"No, thanks."

Jesus Gonzalez put his ankle on his opposite knee, pulled up his sock, and adjusted the hem of his trousers. He was a nice-looking man, forty or so, going gray already. A diamond in one ear. He spoke English without an accent. He said, "Okay. Talk to me."

"I have a question first," Elaine said. "The news reports said that Kelly died around eleven o'clock. Is that correct?"

"Ten fifty-nine, close enough to eleven. The lady next door was in bed watching TV when she heard a woman screaming, then a crash. The crash was the aquarium going over. Galindo kept a ten-gallon saltwater tank in his apartment, and we found Ms. Dorff's body next to it. Some of the cuts were from glass, but it was the spear that killed her." He touched a point a few inches above his waist. "Went in here, came out the back. We found it in the wall. I didn't know spearguns could do that. So the neighbor goes back to watching the news. She didn't call 911 because she'd heard a fight over there a couple of weeks ago, and she thought they were at it again."

"Did she hear any other voices besides the scream?"

"No. Dan Galindo told me that he arrived home at eight minutes past eleven. We show his call to 911 coming in at 11:12, four minutes later. He was agitated but under control. We found his blood on the floor— he had a cut on his knee. His fingerprints were on the speargun. Only his. He says he stepped on it in the dark and picked it up."

Gonzalez stretched his arms up, then locked them behind his neck. His tie was loose, and the collar of his long-sleeved pale yellow shirt was open. "What else? We have the tape out of his answering machine. He went to see Kelly in Lakewood Village that same morning. She'd moved up there to stay with her friend, Martha Cruz. The girls were in the same band together. On the tape Kelly says she didn't come out to speak to Galindo because she was afraid to. But he left her a note, and I guess it alleviated whatever fears she had because in the tape she says thank you very much, and can I come by tonight after rehearsal, it's really important. I asked Martha Cruz about the note, and she says it got tossed, so we don't know what Galindo wrote, but she says Kelly placed the call to him around four o'clock in the afternoon. Let's see. Time. Okay, Galindo left his wife's place—ex-wife—at seven-thirty that night, after spending the day with his son. She confirms that. Galindo was at his brother-in-law's house from nine-thirty to ten. Check. He refused to tell me where he was between seven-thirty and nine-thirty. It doesn't take two hours to get from Lakewood to Pompano Beach. And it doesn't take an hour and eight minutes to get from Pompano Beach to his apartment."

Leaning back in his chair, Gonzalez tipped until the front legs came off the floor. "So what I assume is that he came home around eight, eight-fifteen, heard the message, and took off for his brother-in-law's place. They had some kind of a discussion he won't tell me about. Attorney-client privilege. Whatever went on, he came back home, found Kelly, they argued, and he shot her. He forgot to erase the message."

Gonzalez kept his chair balanced by one finger on the edge of his desk. "We're arresting him for first-degree murder. I personally think it's more like second, even manslaughter. He's a decent guy. He and Kelly had fights before, and he's now back with his wife. Maybe Kelly was causing problems for him. I think a jury would give him a break." Gonzalez glanced at Elaine. "That's my story. Now tell me yours. What've you got?"

"Two reasons he didn't kill her."

"Let's hear them."

Elaine put an elbow on the desk and rested her head in her open palm. "The fish are one reason. You said the aquarium was knocked over. Do you know what he had in there?"

"I remember little blue fish on the floor."

"Blue neon gobys. Dan caught them himself."

Gonzalez took his finger off the edge of the desk, then caught his slight forward momentum. "You're saying he wouldn't have put his fish in danger by shooting a speargun in that direction. It's a thought. But let's say Kelly ran into the tank trying to get away. Or maybe he shot her because she pulled it over. What's your other reason?"

"An alibi. He wasn't there."

"That might work. Alibis are very helpful."

She smiled. "At 10:47 the night Kelly Dorff died, Dan Galindo was ringing my doorbell. I didn't answer the door, and I suppose he thought I wasn't at home. My living room lights were off. I was in bed going over files for the next day. When I heard the doorbell I looked at my clock, which is accurate to the minute, and then I went to see who was there. The porch light was on. I could see him clearly through the viewer in the door. Mr. Galindo rang the bell once more, then he left. He was there for no more than fifteen seconds, but I saw him clearly."

The detective continued to rock slightly on the rear legs of his chair. Elaine sat up straighter in her own and said, "I wouldn't invent this story to protect him. I haven't spoken to Dan since Kelly's death."

"I believe you."

Taking a deep breath, Elaine was surprised to find herself shaking with relief.

Gonzalez said, "I might wonder about it, except for one thing. Galindo mentioned going by a friend's house just before he got home. He didn't say who, whether it was male, female, or what. Then he refused to answer any more questions, so I couldn't clear it up. Was that you? The friend?"

"Apparently so," she said.

"Where do you live?"

"Coral Gables, near the University."

"And he was at your house at 10:47."

"Yes."

"He says he got home at 11:08."

"Twenty-one minutes," she said.

"No way he could make it from your house to his house by 10:59."

"I wouldn't think so," Elaine said.

The front legs of Gonzalez's chair came down heavily on the floor.

"What are you going to do?"

"Call the Broward Sheriff's Office. They're serving the warrant for us. Can I ask you to sign a formal statement?"

"Of course. Do you anticipate any problems in cancelling the arrest?"

Gonzalez flipped through his Rolodex. "Nah. It's

just paperwork." He punched in a number on his phone. "Blue neon gobys. I think you're right. After Kelly's body was taken out, Galindo picked up every one of those damn fish and flushed them." Gonzalez shook his head. "Burial at sea. Scooped them right out of all that glass and blood, wrapped them in tissues, then stood over the toilet and watched them go down. One by one. Well. He should've answered my next question. We wouldn't be going through all this at four o'clock in the morning, would we?"

CHAPTER 26

The next morning, one of Dan's clients, a man charged with possession of stolen property, said he had heard about Dan's troubles on the news. He expressed sympathy. "Watch out they say you did it. The po-lice accuse folks all the time of shit they ain't did."

The client signed a contract for representation and gave Dan $1,000 in jumbled bills out of a paper bag before he left. Dan counted it out on Alva's desk. Her radio was playing a Doris Day song. *Que será, será, whatever will be, will be . . .*

"This is going to sound odd," Dan said, "but that client may be innocent."

"Is this a problem for you?" Alva licked the flap of an envelope and sealed it shut.

"Absolutely. When a client is guilty—and most of them are—you give it your best shot, and if a jury convicts them, you don't feel too bad. But when they're innocent, you have the burden of knowing that you'd better not screw up, or they could go to jail for something they didn't do."

When the phone rang, she frowned at it. Her brows were penciled on. "It's been doing this all day."

"I'm sorry," he said.

She picked it up. "Law offices of Dunavoy and Galindo. . . . No, he's not in. . . . He won't be in and I'm not taking messages, so don't call back." She slammed down the telephone so hard her bracelets jangled.

Dan said, "Tell me that wasn't a client."

"Another reporter," she said. "He was with *Inside Edition*."

"Oh, Jesus."

"You want to answer it next time?"

He raised his hands and retreated to his office. *Entertainment Tonight* had already run the story, losing no time. Rock singer found murdered inside ex-lover's apartment. They even had a video clip of one of Kelly's performances with her previous band, Black Mango. Dan had not seen it himself. He had not watched television all week.

The odd thing was, the police had not shown up. The tension was making him jumpy. He kept looking out the window, expecting to see Detective Jesus A. Gonzalez with two uniformed officers and a set of handcuffs. Charlie had called Gonzalez, who would say only that the case was still under investigation. Dan's contact at the state attorney's office had been baffled.

Dan let the blinds fall back into place. Alva Dunavoy had come in with a chilled can of chocolate liquid supplement for the geriatric crowd. She levered up the tab on the can with a long orange fingernail. The nail polish matched her tight jersey blouse, through which her bosom pointed dangerously at him, daring him to object.

"Drink this," she commanded. "It's nearly three o'clock. If you don't have something, you'll faint."

"I have never fainted in my life, Alva. Stop mothering me."

"That's a lousy attitude," she said. "Some people happen to give a damn."

It was her way of apologizing for her bad mood earlier. Dan took the can from her. "Well, I guess I am a little hungry. Thanks."

After she was gone, Dan poured the chocolate drink into a potted plant, sorry to have to do it. He'd had no appetite since Sunday night. He was feeling hollowed out and fragile, but he doubted he would die of starvation. After finishing some phone calls, Dan put a disk in his computer, searching the *Supreme Court Reporter* for opinions on involuntary confessions, but it was hard to concentrate. The text on the screen would disappear, and he would be back in his apartment four nights ago, pulling Kelly Dorff upright, not accepting that she was gone even as her blood, still warm, flowed onto his hands.

Dan blinked, then pressed his fingertips momentarily against his eyes. He turned off his computer and leaned back in his chair.

There was something screwy about this case, and

the sudden silence from the police was only part of it. They must have found some other lead. Dan did not believe that Kelly had been murdered by an opportunistic thief who had seen her use a spare key to get into his apartment.

Heroin. He had thought of her arrest several times—the one she hadn't told him about. She couldn't have simply forgotten; a conviction would have sent her to prison for ten years.

Another image had flickered in his mind—that of the bearded man he had seen last Sunday morning outside Elaine McHale's house. Elaine, a federal prosecutor. Not the same man, Rick had assured him, as the person Dan had glimpsed so briefly at Manatee Studios. A resemblance, nothing more. Déjà vu, a trick of light, an odd transference of memory.

Dan swiveled his chair until he was looking squarely at his telephone. He dialed a number, said who he was, and asked for Elaine McHale. He waited. Waited some more.

Another female voice picked up. "Mr. Galindo? This is Ms. McHale's assistant. I'm sorry, she's out of town for a family emergency."

"Is she all right?"

"Oh, yes. She'll be back a week from Monday."

"Well, if she calls in, have her get in touch with me, will you? Thanks."

Dan hung up.

A sound of knuckles on wood interrupted his

thoughts, and he swung his chair toward the door. "Come in."

Charlie Dunavoy, just back from a hearing in probate court, sat down and asked how he was doing.

Dan told him he had managed to get some sleep last night. "The apartment looks great. The cleaners moved the furniture around, and with the new rug I hardly recognized the place. Rick and Sandy got me a new aquarium. I guess I'm doing all right."

"You come on over and stay with Alva and me, if you need to."

"I appreciate that."

"Glad to do it. But listen. I want you to talk to one of your buddies about your present situation. It's been too long for me, Dan. Too long. I handled a first-degree murder trial in, oh, 1965, I think it was—a high school math teacher who allegedly stabbed his wife for going out with the coach. Did I tell you about that one?"

Dan replied that he had. "You were pretty proud of getting an acquittal."

Charlie's veiny hands were planted on his knees, and his belly hung over his trousers. "Well, I like to talk about it because it was the only damn murder trial I've ever done, but I'll tell you, it was rough—the worry, do I know what the hell I'm doing, am I going to send this man to the electric chair, and so forth. I'd taken the case because the defendant knew my brother, and the family had no money, and they trusted me. I'd done some criminal cases—robberies, thefts, things like that—so I wasn't a complete boob, but I was a kid, younger than you, and when you're that age you think you're smart. After it was over, I went into the men's room and puked. I told myself no more of that. I'd not be living up to my professional oath to take your case, Dan, if it turns into one. You find yourself a tiger, not an old dog like me. You young guys are more up on the law than I am. But if you need help with the fees, you say so. I mean it." He held up his hands. "Nope. Don't argue with me."

"All right. Thanks." Dan had already spoken to a friend of his, a top criminal lawyer who would jump in if necessary. Then he said, "Charlie, I've been thinking about finding a job closer to Lakewood Village, probably in a large firm, where I could have some financial stability while I work my way up to a partnership. Lisa and I—well, we're thinking of trying again, and Josh needs me around. I want you to know how much I appreciate what you've done for me. You took me in when I was going down for the count, and you didn't even know me."

"Oh, Elaine twisted my arm." Charlie smiled, not wanting to be a bad sport about it. "I hope it's not the money. I've made a decent living in a general practice. You're not doing too bad, you know, and it's getting better."

"No, I need to get out of Miami. It drives me crazy. People are at each other's throats, nobody shuts up. The congestion, the noise, crime, trash—"

"I was born here too," Charlie said. "My father came

down in the Depression, rode a boxcar, just a kid, practically. He swore he'd never see another snowflake as long as he lived, and he didn't. Oh, I know Miami's not what it was, Lord a'mighty. It's a big city now. A lot of my friends moved away, and I was tempted to go with them, but I couldn't leave. Maybe I'm an egocentric old so-and-so, but I feel useful here. I wouldn't be, in Coral Springs or Boca Raton. They don't need me. They've got enough lawyers, a lot sharper than Charlie Dunavoy." With a sigh that turned into a little grunt when he pushed himself out of his chair, he said, "No, I understand, young guy like you, wants to make a place for himself in the world. I understand."

Dan's phone buzzed—the intercom line. He glanced at it, then said, "Not that young. I turned thirty-five yesterday."

Charlie ran his thumbs up under his suspenders. "I was there once myself. Damned good age. Forty is better, though. You'll see."

Dan picked up the phone to see what Alva wanted. Her voice was low, nearly a whisper. "There's a girl out here to see you, Dan. I told her you're not taking any visitors, but she says you know her. Martha Cruz?"

"Yes, she's here to pick up some keys."

Standing at the entrance door, looking out at the street, Martha might have been a statue. Only the slight movement of her torso above a wide, silver-studded belt marked her breathing. Smoke drifted around her hair, which waved down her back in glossy curls. Her wine-colored dress held tightly to her arms, fell over her hips, and with a beaded fringe touched the tops of slouched black leather boots. The toe of one boot held the door open. A jacket, carelessly tossed onto the waiting room sofa, lay halfway on the floor.

Perhaps from a small noise behind her, she sensed someone was there and turned around. Dan had never seen her face so pale. Her eyes looked bruised and shadowed, and even her full, rich mouth seemed to have faded.

"Come on in," Dan said.

Martha sent the cigarette past the front steps, then picked up her jacket and a fabric purse, which she slung over one shoulder. Her skirt swished around the tops of her boots as she followed him into his office. He closed the door and gestured to the client chair facing his desk.

She remained standing, scowling at him sideways, as if sidling up cautiously to whatever she had to say. "Did you do it?" Her voice cracked, then grew stronger. "I can tell if somebody is lying. My people are into *santería*, and it's in my blood. I can tell." She seemed ready to leap. Leap out the door, leap at Dan, he couldn't tell.

Halfway into his chair, he paused. "No. I came home and found her, Martha."

Martha Cruz pressed her lips together, staring at him for a few seconds longer. Her dark eyes seemed to bulge, and her brows were drawn in like a fist. "You knew Kelly was coming over. She called you."

"She left a message, which I didn't hear until the police played it at my apartment."

With a shudder Martha crossed her arms and dug her fingers in. "I was wondering, you know? I didn't think you *did*, but people can fool you sometimes."

"Would you like to sit down?"

After a second she nodded. She hung her bag over a corner of the chair, sat down, and crossed her legs. The fringe on the hem of her skirt swung with the steady movement of her boot, and the beads tapped on the leather. "Kelly's funeral is Saturday in Baltimore. Are you going?"

Dan shook his head. He opened a drawer for the ring that held the keys to Salazar's sportfisher and the gate to the marina.

"Me either," Martha said. "Nobody's going. We have to work. She'll just have her mom and her dad and her brother. They'll probably put her in a cardboard coffin. Do you know what that asshole father of hers asked me? Where's Kelly's guitar? He wanted to sell it to pay for the funeral. Bastard. I hung up on him. We're going to send flowers, lots and lots of them. Miguel says order whatever I want, so that place is going to look like a flower garden, believe me. The guy at the funeral home is going to take pictures, I'll show you. We made up a little box to put with her. It's got guitar picks and a cassette of the band. Kelly and I made the tape at the party on South Beach. It came out all right. What Kelly would hate, more than anything, is if the band died too. We have to go on. Rick's finding a new guitarist—I hope. He knows more people than I do. The concert at the Abyss is in two weekends. It's all on me now. I'm the main singer. But we'll be all right. If we can get through the concert, we'll be okay. We're doing the final mix over the weekend, then we have to get the demo tape to Joel Friedman by next Monday. That's the man from Capitol, and Rick promised him the demo. It won't have Kelly on it, that's the only thing, so we have to dub in the new guy, as soon as we have one. Rick's at the studio now, doing auditions."

Martha, who had been staring into her lap, raised her eyes. "I don't mean to disrupt your schedule. I can't stay long. You know how Miguel is."

"Are you going to get in trouble for being here?"

"No way." She waved a slender, silver-ringed hand. "He's at work. He doesn't even know you called me."

"Don't take this so lightly," Dan said. "The man hit you."

"Well, that was the last time." She laughed. "As soon as we get a record contract, I'm gone, no matter whether he hits me or he doesn't. I can't believe you said that stuff to him. My God. That took guts."

"It wasn't smart," Dan said. "I think I provoked him. Free advice, Martha. Leave him now. Go stay with Rick." He heard the beaded fringe on her skirt tap-tap-tapping on her boots.

"That's sweet of you. Being worried about me like that." She made a quick shrug and rose from her chair. "I'll think about it after the concert."

He walked her back to the entrance to the law office.

Dan said, "Martha, why did Kelly come to my apartment?"

"I really don't know."

"No clue? Rick says you and Kelly were close, that you talked to each other."

"Yes, but mostly on stuff about the band." As they reached the waiting room, Martha slowly smiled. A warm glow had come back into her face, a rosy tint under the olive tones. In a low voice she said, "I found out something about you. I told you I would."

Dan was not in the mood for this. He said, "You're a resourceful girl, Martha."

"Remember on the terrace at Miguel's? You didn't want to tell me why you weren't a prosecutor anymore, but I found out."

"And I hope the search provided several days of amusement for you."

"More like ten minutes." Martha put on her short black jacket and shook her heavy curls free of the collar. "I asked Rick. And Kelly told me some things. I wouldn't have done what you did myself—because look at the way it turned out."

"Not only resourceful," he said. "Pragmatic. Or let's say, a keen sense of ethics, *ex post facto*."

She didn't care to venture into that terrain. "Whatever." She whirled out the door, leaving Dan with his thoughts.

Luis Barrios. The doper who got away, thanks to one young federal prosecutor's notion of right and wrong. Dan had taken a stand; he had fallen off. The point he'd been trying to hang onto was a narrow, windy precipice, and in the end it hadn't mattered, as Lisa had said. Let it go.

Walking back into his room, he was stopped by Alva's honk.

"Daaa-a-an. Phone."

He backed up a step and asked her who it was.

"It's not a reporter. He says he's a client, but he wouldn't give his name. Says he needs to talk to you."

"I'll take it in my office."

The voice made him nearly drop the receiver.

"This is Salazar. Why was Martha in your office just now?"

Dan went to the window and pulled down a slat in the mini-blinds. "Where are you?"

"I saw her leave your office. Don't play with me. Why was she there?"

"She came for the keys to your boat. What did you think?"

"I tell you this one time only. If you touch her, I will kill you. This is a promise."

The line went dead.

Going to hang up the phone, he saw the key ring still on the desk.

The criminal court building was on the Miami River under an expressway, an eight-story square gray edifice where most of Dan's legal practice took place—not the white-collar criminals and major drug traffickers found in federal court, but a clientele consisting for the most part of unlucky, usually poor, and sometimes violent men.

In the clerk's office Dan showed his bar card at the line for lawyers and court personnel. He wanted to see records for Kelly Dorff, any case within the last two years. He did not have her Social Security number, but he knew her birthdate. The clerk tapped at the computer and said there were two entries. Miami Beach, possession of marijuana, withhold of adjudication. Then eight months ago an arrest in Miami for possession of heroin.

He asked about disposition of the latter case. None. It was still on hold. He asked who had represented Ms. Dorff. The public defender.

Dan walked across the street and past the jail to the Public Defender's Office. It was swarming with people, most of them black or Hispanic, most of them poor. The receptionist sat behind thick glass. He asked her if George Everett was available.

He and George had worked together a few times representing codefendants on the same cases. George was a Miami native, a law-review editor at Yale who had turned down offers from big firms in Boston and New York. He had planned to work a couple of years as a public defender before going back up north, but here it was eight years later, and he was still kicking prosecutorial butts in his hometown.

George was between clients and could afford a few

minutes to speak to Dan. He had heard about the murder of the girl in Dan's apartment, and whatever he could do, ask.

"It's about the same girl, George." Dan explained that Kelly Dorff had been represented by someone in the P.D.'s office. The case, however, had never been prosecuted. "What happened to it? People arrested with a kilo of heroin don't just walk away. There's got to be something else going on."

"Ordinarily, I couldn't talk about this, you understand," said George after a moment's reflection, "but the girl is dead— correct?—and you do seem to have a legitimate interest."

"No shit," Dan said.

George looked at the computer. A lawyer by the name of Lori Rosen had handled the case. Lori Rosen had left the office a month ago—gone to Washington, in fact—but the file was still around somewhere.

"Let's see what we can find in storage," George added.

"You're sure this isn't a bother?"

"No, you got my curiosity aroused now."

Dan accompanied George to the storage room, and five minutes later George pulled it out of a box on one of the dozens of rows of shelves. He blew off some metaphorical dust and opened it up.

A thin file. George read through it briefly, then looked at Dan. "On hold per agreement with the U.S. attorney's office. Let's see . . . There's a note. 'Case not to be prosecuted pending full cooperation with Justice Department, per AUSA Elaine McHale.'"

Dan took this in slowly.

George said, "Kelly Dorff was a snitch for the feds, my man."

CHAPTER 27

Miami rush-hour traffic was usually bad; today it was insane. Dan cursed other drivers. They flipped him off. He cursed himself for not having a car phone. It took him almost an hour to reach the exit for North Miami.

He found the warehouse complex ten minutes later, screeched into the entrance, and gunned his engine along the road leading to the back, where Manatee Studios was located. In the graying light of dusk he saw Rick Robbins's yellow Mustang. He parked beside it and went inside, walking straight down the hallway past the office.

A man stuck his head out. "Hey, who are you?"

"It's okay. I'm looking for Rick Robbins."

"He's in a closed session. Hey, you can't—"

Dan heard another door opening behind him in the hall, glanced around, and saw a man with a dark beard and a windbreaker. The man shouted, "Stop where you are!"

He ran.

The sound of a rock guitar whanged through the hall from the studio behind the last door. Dan sped toward it. Behind him came the pounding of footsteps. Dan reached for the doorknob, but the man caught up. He grabbed Dan around the waist, and they both careened into a door on the opposite side of the hall. It fell open and they staggered inside. Teenage musicians screamed and scattered. A drum set went over, crashing in a cascade of thumps and cymbals. The man threw Dan to the shag-carpeted floor and put a knee in his spine.

Dan craned his head around and found himself looking into the barrel of a 9mm pistol. He stared up into the man's eyes and he knew. He hadn't seen him up close in two years, but he knew who it was. Vincent Hooper, DEA.

"Get off me, goddammit."

"Shut up!" Hooper ordered the kids to get out. They did, leaving their instruments behind them.

Pointing the pistol at Dan, Hooper went over and kicked the door shut. The vibrations shook the slabs of gray foam rubber soundproofing.

"Hands flat on the wall, feet out and spread. Do it! Now!"

Enraged, Dan stood up. "Get out of my way, Hooper. You have no right to tell me to do a damn thing."

Hooper reholstered his pistol under his windbreaker. Dan moved back, his arms automatically moving up to protect his face. Hooper slammed a fist into his stomach. "There's my right, asshole." When Dan gagged and dropped to the floor, Hooper came down close and clenched his fingers in Dan's hair. "What are you doing here?"

"None of your fucking business." He found himself suddenly flying toward the wall, which was covered with ugly purple shag carpeting. Overhead, fluorescent bulbs buzzed and flickered.

The door opened and a woman with short auburn hair burst in. She saw Hooper with his fist drawn back. "Vince! That's not a good idea."

Hooper gave Dan one more shove. He asked her, "What are they doing across the hall?"

"Still going through guitarists. They didn't hear anything." The woman looked down at Dan. "Now what do we do?"

Ribs aching, Dan struggled to his knees. "Unless you're making an arrest for a specific crime, I'm walking out of here."

Hooper lifted Dan by his lapels. "I could have your ass right now on any number of charges—"

"Name one."

"Interfering with an investigation. Battery on a federal agent."

"Bullshit. I came in here looking for my client and you attacked me."

Hooper threw Dan into a chair, which tipped, then

came back down on its legs. "Sit there with your mouth shut or I will break your fucking jaw." He pointed at Dan long enough to make sure he got the message, then went over to speak to the other agent. Their voices were quiet. The woman went out.

Hooper turned another chair around and faced Dan. "We're going to sit here for a minute. My colleague went to make a phone call. We want to find out what to do with you. I asked a question, so answer it. What are you doing here?"

"Kiss my ass," Dan said.

Hooper laughed. "Still the same pathetic jerkoff you always were, Galindo. I should have taken you out two years ago."

"You finally got Luis Barrios," Dan said.

"Not on purpose. I didn't know he'd be there. We got lucky. *I* got lucky. He drew a Tec-9 on me and I blew him away. God watches out for the good guys."

Dan knew that Vincent Hooper was looking for an excuse to get his hands on him again, so he sat quietly, trembling more from anger than fear. Hooper was even bigger now across the chest than he had been, and there was some gray in his beard, but he had lost none of the thuggish physicality. His thighs, straddling the chair, were tight with muscle. His scarred fists rested lightly on the chair back, ready to reach for him. Hooper would probably enjoy fracturing his jaw more than shooting him.

A flame leaped from Hooper's lighter and he drew deeply on his cigarette, then clicked the lighter shut and slid it back into his shirt pocket. "I shouldn't complain. A major doper is gone, and you ended up in a rat-hole law office down on Biscayne Boulevard. Common street criminals for clients. A washed-up old fart for a partner. Now you're a murder suspect. No, I can't complain."

Dan leaned back casually in the chair, just out of arm's reach. "Kelly Dorff was your confidential informant."

Hooper exhaled smoke. "Is that why you killed her?"

"Who was she spying on? Rick? Me?"

"I told you to shut up."

Smoke drifted upward to the acoustical tiles in the ceiling, which had been painted black. Cold air and drops of condensation came out of a hole half clogged with filthy yellow insulation. The metal vent was missing. Dan could hear a rock guitar going across the hall. Start, stop. Start again.

The female agent came back in and whispered into Hooper's ear. Hooper nodded, then said to Dan, "We're going to sit here for a little while longer. Fifteen minutes. I don't want to hear you whining about false imprisonment. I don't want to hear anything out of you. Got that?"

Dan tensed, ready to duck away from a fist. "Where is my client? What are you doing with him?"

"Nothing. He's having a good time picking out a new lead guitarist. Rock and roll."

* * *

A half hour later there was a knock at the door. The woman agent brought John Paxton in. Paxton was not happy. Under his thick gray brows, his eyes snapped with fury. He glanced down at Dan, then told the agents to leave, both of them.

As soon as they had gone, Dan exploded out of his chair. "You're all going to be in deep shit for this, John. I want to see my client. Now."

"If you walk through that door, we'll arrest Rick Robbins immediately." The tone was sharp enough to make Dan look around. "I told Hooper to keep you in here till I arrived. If there's any fault, it's mine. Give me a few minutes, Dan. You need to understand what's going on."

John Paxton told him that a federal task force called Operation Manatee had been gathering evidence against members of the Guayaquil cartel living in South Florida. They had imported and distributed an average of 1,000 kilos of cocaine per year for the past six years, which at approximately $18,000 to $20,000 per kilo—Miami wholesale prices—came to around $115,000,000.

Miguel Salazar was the man who turned the proceeds into spendable cash. He used several methods, most often bank manipulations and wire transfers. These were difficult to trace. Salazar also ran money through legitimate businesses. One in particular the DEA had been watching—Coral Rock Productions. By creating false reports of ticket sales and expenses, Salazar had sent over $3,000,000 through this company—with the knowledge and assistance of its owner, Richard Robbins.

The grand jury had issued a sealed indictment against Richard Robbins, based in large part on evidence supplied by Kelly Dorff. The problem for the government, Paxton explained, was that evidence against Salazar was not as solid as against other members of the cartel. The DEA had arranged a meeting between Salazar and agent Vincent Hooper, posing as Victor Ramirez, the man whose company, Manatee Studios, was recording Rick Robbins's band. Ramirez wanted Salazar to launder a half million dollars for him. If Salazar took the money, the DEA would have him. The meeting could not be rescheduled. The arrests would go down next week.

Hooper had not known why Dan was here, but when he saw Dan rushing toward the studio, he had to stop him.

"Here's my offer for you," Paxton said. "Your client helps us out, we won't send him away. Otherwise, he's looking at a minimum mandatory of twenty years plus a fine of two million. Based on the business this cartel has done, he could get so much time, he'd die owing us years. In any event, he forfeits the business, his real estate, and his personal property. Everything. I want him to testify to the grand jury early next week, before we announce the indictments and send the marshals out."

Dan realized that the music across the hall had stopped awhile ago. He doubted that Rick had left.

Hooper would see to that. Rick might have head-phones on, listening to the guitar played back with the bass, drums, and keyboard tracks. Not a clue that his world was about to end.

"Are there any questions?" Paxton said.

"I need to discuss it with Rick."

"Of course. Take the weekend. I hope to see you both in my office at eight o'clock Monday morning. We'll debrief him in the afternoon, and he can go before the grand jury the next day. And tell him I expect the meeting with Salazar to proceed as planned."

"Rick has no control over what Salazar decides to do."

"Just don't let us find out he warned him. That would be very bad for your client." Paxton added, "And tell him to be careful. Most of these dopers are businessmen. Profit, loss. They try not to use violence. I don't think it bothers Salazar. He was married awhile back. He caught his wife cheating on him. He made her watch him castrate the guy, then he shot her."

Dan blew out a breath as if he'd been holding it too long.

Guitar music filtered in from the studio. Loud. Not the same player, someone else this time. A heavy, rocking blues beat. "What about the demo?" Dan looked back at Paxton, who didn't know what he was talking about. "The band is recording tracks for a demo tape, a sample of their music to send to the labels. Someone is coming from New York next week and wants a copy before he attends their concert. The band members aren't targets of your investigation. Let them have the demo."

"Well, that's up to the DEA. It's their studio," Paxton said.

"Listen to me, John. If you want Rick, work with him on this. He lives for the band. If all their effort comes to nothing, I'm not sure he wouldn't shoot himself."

"All right. I'll talk to Vince Hooper."

"No. You *tell* the son of a bitch."

"Here's what we'll do," Paxton said. "If this meeting with Salazar goes off without a hitch, your client can have the tapes. I remind you, however. He's not going to keep the company. If he makes any money on this band, it will be forfeited."

"If he pleads guilty," Dan said, keeping a hold on his temper. "If. I'm not promising you a damn thing at this point."

A slight smile twisted the lines in Paxton's face. "Combative as ever." He uncrossed his legs and stood up. "We haven't talked to each other in a while, have we? I'm sorry it's under these circumstances, but it's good to see you again."

He offered his hand, and after a second or two, Dan took it. At the door, Paxton said, "I'm glad to hear you're off the hook with that other matter. I never thought you should have been charged."

Dan looked at him. "What do you mean, off the hook?"

"For Ms. Dorff. They quashed the arrest warrant. You hadn't heard? A friend of mine at the state attorney's office told me. The police say you had an alibi."

"Who?"

Paxton let out a laugh. "Someone who swears you were elsewhere at the time of death, obviously. I don't know who."

It took Dan a few seconds. At the time of death, he had been knocking on Elaine McHale's door. For some reason she hadn't told Paxton. Dan could see that Paxton was curious, but he shook his head as if he had no idea.

Dan said, "I'd like to talk to my client."

CHAPTER 28

Dan told Rick that they had a matter to discuss and that Rick had to come with him. Now. It might have been his grim expression that kept Rick from putting up much of an argument. Rick told the sound engineer to close down for the evening, he'd see him tomorrow. There were some lank-haired guitarists sitting around. Rick had a fast conversation with a tattooed bald guy while Dan paced by the door.

In the hall, Rick said, "He's the one I'm gonna pick for the band. He played with Ozzy Osbourne. Would you slow down? What the hell is the matter with you?"

"Just keep walking."

It was dark outside and getting cold. Dan headed around the corner out of view of anyone inside. A security light on the roof filtered through the tree overhanging the parking lot. Rick was so impatient his shoulders were jerking. He said, "Okay. What?"

Dan told him.

Halfway through, Rick squinted his eyes as if he'd walked into a sandstorm. "U.S. attorney's office," he said, moistening his lips. "Okay. Be there Monday. We do the overdubs on Saturday, the final mix on Sunday— There's time."

"Rick—"

"Did you hear that new guy? Bobby. He's fantastic." Rick laughed. "He's not as pretty as Kelly Dorff, but we're gonna feature Martha now. We'll be okay. She can carry it."

"Listen to me!" Dan grabbed him by the front of his tweed jacket. "They won't let it be okay. You are going to be indicted under the drug trafficking and conspiracy statute. They want to seize everything you own—your business, your house, cars, bank accounts. They want you to give them Salazar, and they'll burn you if you don't do it. If you plead not guilty and go to trial, and you lose, you would spend a minimum of twenty years in prison."

Rick stared up at him. "What?"

Quietly Dan said, "You're in trouble, Rick."

"Drug trafficking? No. No way. I didn't do that, Dan. I would never do that."

"Anyone who helps a drug cartel can be held liable for everything the cartel has done. That's the law. If the cartel has received more than ten million dollars—and this one has earned closer to a hundred million—a person who renders assistance will receive a sentence of mandatory life in prison. If Paxton has the evidence he says he does, and they can prove it, they've got you in the cross-hairs. If you don't co-operate, they'll tag you for the entire conspiracy." Dan took a breath. "But we're going to discuss this calmly, then we'll decide the best course of action."

Even in the dim glow from the security light, Dan could see the sheen of sweat on Rick's forehead. "I didn't know Victor was DEA. He offered me free use of the studio, if I'd put him in touch with Salazar. That's all he wanted. Just to set up a deal with Miguel. And I did, trying to help him out. That's all. Was that such a crime that now they want my blood?"

"That is not all, Rick."

"Maybe they faked the evidence."

"No."

"They have the capacity to doctor evidence," Rick said. "The federal government has access to all kinds of advanced technology."

"They don't, Rick. They don't do that. It would be stupid. They tapped Salazar's phones and they have you on tape discussing his business. They have your bank records showing that you profited from Salazar's activities."

"Victor *lied* to me! How can they get away with that?"

"Of course he lied. What did you think? That you could ask him, 'Are you a narc? No crossing your fingers, now. Be honest.' And he says, 'Why, no, I'm not a narc.' 'Well, all right, then.' Is that what you thought?"

"It was entrapment," Rick said. "They suckered me into this."

"Maybe. We'll talk about it," Dan said. "I'll get your

side of it and we'll see. We might argue entrapment if the DEA led you into a crime that you weren't predisposed to commit. That the only reason you went sliding down the chute to hell was that the DEA greased it and gave you a push."

"That's exactly how it was!"

Dan said quietly, "But you were already involved with Miguel Salazar before you met Victor."

"I didn't mean to do this!"

"Great argument. 'Your honor, I didn't mean to do it.'"

Rick took a breath. When he spoke his tongue was so dry it clicked in his mouth. "What I told you the other night at my house about Victor Ramirez was the truth, I swear. The guy was so damned convincing. Victor—whatever the hell his name is—said he owned some nightclubs and wanted his own record label. He also told me—which, okay, I didn't tell you about—that he had half a million in cash he wanted to make disappear, and he heard that Miguel Salazar could help him out. I didn't want to get into that, so I told him no way. Then he offered me a deal on the studio. I had to do a high-quality demo tape, and I didn't want Miguel involved any further than he already was. He has his way, he'll make the band sound like Abba. Jesus Christ, Dan, I swear to you, I got sucked into this. First Miguel, then the DEA. Oh, Jesus, I'm gonna pass out. I might as well die right here."

"Calm down, Rick."

"Oh, God. Sandy. Oh, what am I gonna tell her?"

Rick put a hand flat on his chest. "What about the demo? Did you ask him?"

"Yes. You can have the demo if you cooperate with them, but forget the demo, Rick. It's over."

"How can it be *over*? The concert is a week from Saturday!"

"I'm a little more concerned right now with keeping you out of prison."

"They can't do this," Rick said. "I'm not a criminal, not like Miguel. I'll happily give them Miguel. I'll testify, whatever. But why do they have to take everything I've got?"

"Because they can. Because they want to make a point."

"I want you to get me off. I don't care what it costs, if I have to owe you for the rest of my life."

"There's a saying, Rick. 'You can beat the rap, but you can't beat the ride.' You know what that means?"

He laughed without a trace of humor. "I'm not gonna like this, am I?"

"It means, we can go to trial. We might win. But the minute they indict you, the public is going to believe you're guilty. Your business is going to head for the basement. Maybe you can pull it out, maybe not. The jury might acquit you—you could beat the rap. But hang on tight, Rick. You're not going to beat the ride."

"Oh, my God."

"We're going to my office," Dan said. "You're going to tell me everything that happened between you and Miguel Salazar. How you got involved, what you did, what he did. I need to find a defense for you, Rick. Forget the damned band."

"I want to see Sandy," Rick said. "She's up at Coral Rock. I have to talk to her."

"Not now."

"I want to talk to my wife!"

"No. You're the client, I'm the lawyer. If she's angry enough, Sandy could testify as to what you told me. I can't allow that."

"She wouldn't," Rick said, "but if she did, I don't care. It's my decision, right? I'm the client?"

"You're an idiot."

Rick said hoarsely, "Sandy would be better off if I had an accident, you know that? I have life insurance."

"No. It's never better that way." Dan put his arm across Rick's shoulders and steered him back across the parking lot to their cars.

"It's a tough business," Rick said. "You can be rich one day, poor the next, then rich again. I was okay, then I made some bad decisions. Had some bad luck. Gigs fell through. I spent tons of money on promotion and nobody showed up. Usually I'd make it back on the next concert, but about a year ago I got in real deep. Sandy and I had been having troubles, so I said, baby, let's go to Paris. We got back, I bought her a car. She was happy, I was happy. We threw some great parties. Everybody was there. I heard Kelly's band that season and knew I had to represent them. I gave

Kelly a job part-time at Coral Rock. Leon Davila, their drummer, introduced me to Miguel Salazar, who said he'd make me a loan. It wasn't a hundred grand all at once, it came in dribs and drabs. I didn't tell Sandy, naturally, because she would have raised hell.

"Did I know what Miguel was? Yeah, probably. Leon was such a cokehead, always hanging with guys I knew were dopers. They like the entertainment industry. If you're on the outside, it looks glamorous and exciting. Miguel wanted to be inside. Did I care what else he was doing? Not really. That was his business. Then it became mine. You know, these things always start off so small. He was pushing me to pay him back, but I didn't have the cash. He said okay, let me produce one of the shows, I'll take my money out of that. Yes, I knew he was going to run money through the ticket sales, but after it was over, we'd be square. But we weren't. The Palm Beach winter festival was rained out, and I hadn't bought insurance. It never rains in the winter, right? He lent me thirty grand to cover office expenses. Now I see he kept me on the hook like that, reeling it in, little by little. Early on I had a choice, but I didn't see it coming. No. I saw it. It was easier not to care.

"There was a point when I wanted out. I was scared he'd get busted, scared I'd go down with him. After he did what I know had to be close to a million bucks through that huge rave concert at the Orange Bowl last summer, I said it's definitely over. No more or I'm going to the cops. He and Leon Davila took me in Leon's Jeep out on Alligator Alley into the Everglades. I knew I was going to die. They made me kneel down. I was crying. Jesus, I wet my pants even. Begging him. I could see the sawgrass against the blue sky, and hear the damned mosquitoes, and feel the muck going through the knees of my pants, and I remember the regret. So sorry that I'd never see any of that again, and how little I'd valued a damn mosquito, you know? I thought of Sandy, and my last thought was, man, is she going to be mad at me. Miguel put his pistol to the back of my head and pulled the trigger. It wasn't loaded. He said, 'You see how easy I could do it? You see?'

"After that I didn't say anything else. I denied it was even happening. You take that attitude, all your problems go away.

"Miguel's big interest was the band, which by then had changed names from Black Mango to Mayhem. That was Kelly's choice. Miguel didn't like it, but Martha did, and he's crazy about Martha. The way I heard it from Kelly, Miguel and Martha took one look at each other and bells went off. His money, her talent. She doesn't know about his other life. She thinks he made all his money shipping videos and CD's to South America. What Miguel wants is to make Martha a star. He said if I got Martha a contract, he'd consider my debt to him paid in full. My desire to get the band signed was also a desire to get rid of Miguel.

"I guess the DEA was already on to him. They used Kelly Dorff. Now I know she had no choice, so I'm not going to think bad of her. I know how it is. I can't throw stones. Whoever killed her, I blame the government. But I can't make excuses, either. Not for her, not for myself. It's over."

Rick spoke for almost an hour. The last of the employees had already gone, and the office was quiet. They were alone, the three of them, Rick behind his desk, Sandy and Dan in chairs facing him. When he finished, he smiled slightly and straightened the edges of papers stacked next to his computer monitor.

"Sandy, I don't expect you to stay after this, and I'll make sure you don't leave here with nothing. I've got stuff put away nobody knows about—not a lot, but enough to set you up in a new life back in Georgia, wherever you want. Dan can make the arrangements for that, if he's not too squeamish about lying to the U.S. government, who wants everything but the caps on my teeth. Dan, you can say no if you want to, but I'd appreciate it if you'd help Sandy out."

He finally looked across the room at his wife, who only stared back at him. "I won't sit here and say I'm sorry, pumpkin, even though God knows I'll be sorry for a long time. Now Dan and I have to decide what to do, take their offer or put my fate in the hands of a jury. Whatever happens—and maybe I'll go to prison for the rest of my life—I'll be all right as long as I can remember that you loved me. Those years with you were the best. You made me so happy."

After a moment Sandy turned her head toward Dan and wiped her cheeks with her fingers. Her hands were shaking. She spoke in a whisper. "Dan? I think Rick and I need to be alone right now."

CHAPTER 29

A cold front was coming through; the temperature would drop to the mid-forties by morning. The palm fronds rattled, and the wind chime on the back porch played its patternless five-note tune. The stars were icy pinpoints. Elaine sat in a white chair made of two curves of mesh with spindly legs that rested unevenly on the paving stones. The chair rocked when she pulled her legs up and crossed her arms, tucking her hands inside the sleeves of her sweater. She could hear Vincent in the kitchen making drinks. She had asked for brandy.

Vincent brought the drinks out and set them on a metal table between her chair and the one that matched it. Still standing, he lit a cigarette, hand cupped around the flame, cheeks going hollow for a second. The lighter clicked shut, and the smell of fluid vanished in a gust of air. The backyard was small, enclosed with a woven wood fence choked with ivy.

It hadn't rained lately, and the plants were turning brown and brittle.

"Go ahead and ask me, Vince. I can tell you're itching to get it off your mind."

He picked up his drink. "I know why, Elaine. You believe he's innocent."

"Yes, perhaps my clock was wrong."

"*Perhaps*," he said, mocking her tone, "you saw what you wanted to see."

Elaine freed her hands from the sleeves of her sweater and took a sip of brandy.

Vince said, "You could have discussed it with me first."

"I wonder what advice you would have given." She balanced the brandy snifter on her knees. "How did Scott Irwin find out? You didn't say."

"He was curious why Galindo hadn't been picked up, so he asked."

"And then came running to you."

"It wasn't like that," he said.

"Batman and Robin."

He looked at her as he brought the cigarette to his mouth.

She laughed. "You know what Scott told me? That if I wanted to . . . to fuck you, I ought to wait till after this operation is over. I mean, *what*? You're the one who's married, not me. Maybe I'm sapping your strength, Vince. Delilah with her scissors, mucking around in the boys' tree house."

The wind chime swung and tinkled. Elaine swallowed half her brandy. It burned her throat.

"What was Galindo doing here?"

"I do not know."

They were circling now, ready to close in.

"Was he here, Elaine?"

"No, I gave him an alibi because Miguel Salazar paid me. Or maybe I'm fucking Dan Galindo too."

With his back to the house, Vince's face was in shadow. The orange end of the cigarette rose, then fell. "That morning I showed up unexpectedly, he had been here. It bothered me. I kept wondering, thinking about it. How long had he been here? Five minutes? Two hours? All night? It went through my mind."

"Oh, for God's sake."

"No, let me finish. I can accept five minutes. I believe it. But it never used to occur to me to wonder." Vince spoke softly. He always did when they came out in the backyard. Training. In case someone had an ear pressed to the fence.

"I trusted you absolutely. That's why we got together. Fidelity. Honesty. Honesty above everything else. Now we're into these games. I hear about things going on I didn't know about. You met Kelly Dorff, and you told me only because she threatened you. Then you asked me not to say anything to Paxton about it. Maybe nothing's going on. That's probably the case. But I don't like having to convince myself of that every time we're together."

"Honesty. Oh, let's hear it for honesty." Elaine lifted

her brandy glass. "John asked me, 'Elaine, when was the last time you saw Dan Galindo?' The way he said it, I could tell that he already knew the answer—last Sunday morning, right outside my front door. John wanted to see if I'd lie. How did he know, Vince? Let's see how honest you can be."

Vince looked at her, but she couldn't see past the surface. "I don't know why John was asking you that. I didn't tell him."

"Gee, I wonder who did? Robin? Did you two guys discuss it together? Honesty, Vince."

"Of course we did," Vince said sharply. His voice dropped once more to just above a murmur. "We talk about whatever might affect this case."

"I suppose that means he told you he spoke to John? Well?"

"I won't play these games with you, Elaine."

"What a suspicious, cynical, bitter man you are. It makes me tired."

He flicked his cigarette into the darkness. "I think I'd better go."

"Yes. Why don't you?"

So this is how it ends, she thought. Like cutting off a dead limb. Maybe later there would be the rush of blood, but for now, there was no sensation at all.

Vincent paused beside the chair. "Be seeing you."

"Probably not," she said.

"No. Probably not." He reached down and patted her cheek. "Take care of yourself."

CHAPTER 30

When Arlo Pate went to Miguel's study to tell him that Rick Robbins was on his way with the new guitarist, the door was half open. Arlo crossed his arms over his chest and came a few steps closer. He was wearing tan lace-up boots with heavy rubber soles, but he made no noise on the marble floor.

Miguel was talking on the phone. Arlo leaned closer to the door. Spanish. He had picked up some of it on the construction site, enough to order a snack from the roach coach or understand a joke. He didn't usually eavesdrop on Miguel, but with everything going on lately, he wanted to figure out where he stood.

Ice cubes dropped into a glass. There was a bar in the study with smoky mirrors and a gold sink. Arlo had installed it himself.

"... el Domingo, sí. ... No hablamos de eso por teléfono, Victor. ¿Me entiendes?"

He was talking to Victor Ramirez, the guy who ran

the studio. Arlo wondered what that was about. A meeting on Sunday. Don't talk about it on the phone.

"*Que me llames por la mañana, okay? . . . Bueno. Nos vemos.*"

He hung up. Arlo backed off a few paces, then walked back stomping his boots before he knocked on the door. Miguel turned around from the bar, putting his glass in the sink.

"Rick is here with the guitarist."

"Good. What do you think of him, Arlo?"

"I haven't seen him. The guard shack called. Martha sent me to get you."

Miguel turned off the light in his study and closed the door. Following him down the stairs that circled to the main floor, Arlo could see both of them reflected in the big windows looking out over the lake. One guy had everything, and the other was an ugly redneck whose chances were just about to run dry.

Rick had told everybody in the band he wouldn't hold it against them if they quit. He had cried. Broke down and cried, talking about Kelly. He had told them nobody could replace her, but she wouldn't have wanted them to give up. They decided to check out the guitarist, then decide what to do.

For a little while Arlo had thought things would work out. Not that he'd get rich and famous, but that he'd be able to say he did more with his life than mow lawns and fix toilets. Lying up on the roof at night, he would make up scenes, like riding his Harley home to Memphis, going into a music store, and finding the

Mayhem CD in the racks. He'd pick it up, turn it over. Run his thumb over the shrink wrap and hear it crinkle. Read the list of songs, look at his own face right there with Kelly and Martha and Scott. Somebody would notice what he was holding and say, *Hey, that's Mayhem. They kick it, man.* Now, with Kelly gone, Arlo wondered if he would ever have that CD in his hands.

They went out the kitchen door, then past the tennis court to the guest cottage. To please Martha, Arlo had ripped out the carpeting and blocked up the windows, making a rehearsal room out there where she could play and not bother the household.

Coming closer, following the little lights along the walkway, Arlo could hear guitar music right through the walls. A chill skidded down his chest and landed in his gut. He could swear it was Kelly in there. What if it was? What if she wasn't really dead, but some other girl was dead who looked like her? And the real Kelly was in there like always, leaning way back on the high notes, tossing her hair out of her eyes. Those skinny arms in the white tank top, that blue Fender Jag screaming.

Miguel opened the door.

It was the Jag, but it wasn't Kelly. It was some dude about thirty-five, looked like he had TB. He was playing Kelly's guitar. The others stood around listening. Rick smiling like he'd found the Lord. Scott dancing, his blue hair swinging over his forehead. Martha with her arms crossed. Arlo couldn't tell what she thought, but that was Martha.

The guitarist kept playing till Rick went over and signaled him to stop. Rick glanced their way, then said, "This is Bobby Doyle."

The guitarist said, "Hey." He took the lit cigarette out of the strings at the neck of the guitar, where he'd wedged it. Tattoos went from his wrists all the way up under the sleeves of his black T-shirt. He was totally bald, with a stripe of blond beard under his lower lip and about six earrings. His left hand hung over the top edge of the guitar like a dead fish.

Miguel said, "He sounds like Kelly Dorff."

"That's the point," Rick said. "He's perfect."

"Sorry about Kelly, man," the guitarist said. "She was fine. I heard her up in Lauderdale at the Edge jamming with the Lunachicks. She had vibe."

Nobody said a word. Arlo guessed they were all thinking about Kelly Dorff in their own ways. He was. Miguel had said that her boyfriend, Dan Galindo, had done it, according to the newspapers. Nobody had seen him do it, but Miguel was sure he had. Last night, not being able to sleep, Arlo had thought about what he would do if he could get Galindo alone. He would probably bury him next to Leon, out past the vacant lot under one of those piles of rock near the lake. If Galindo went to court, he wouldn't be convicted. The judge would throw out his confession. The lawyers would make the jury think the DNA didn't match, or whatever. Arlo had gone to sleep making up scenes of how he would torture the guy before he buried him.

The guitarist, Bobby Doyle, took another drag on

his cigarette and stuck it back in the strings. "Rick gave me the board mixes of the band yesterday, plus Kelly Dorff's tracks. I was up all night working with the songs. I've got a reputation for being able to duplicate particular styles. I've gotten some studio work as a result. I've done Jimi Hendrix, Eric Clapton, B. B. King, Stevie Ray Vaughan—"

"Stevie Ray," Arlo said. "He's my man."

"Dead now. Yeah. Stevie." The guitarist hit an effects pedal and his fingers moved over the strings, and Stevie Ray's "Cold Shot" came out. After a few bars the music slid into Kurt Cobain, then Peter Buck.

Scott said, "Amazing."

Rick said, "Just sound like Kelly Dorff for the concert, Bobby."

Miguel stared at the guitarist. He walked closer. "You smell like you been smoking funny stuff."

Bobby smiled. His eyes were half-closed. "Rick? Who's this joker?"

Rick was sweating through his shirt. "Be polite, Bobby. This is the person who's paying your salary."

Miguel's black eyes bugged out a little. He said to Rick, "Why are you doing Kelly's songs at the concert?"

"Because the guy from Capitol Records expects to hear basically what he heard when I played him the tape in New York. He liked Martha's part in it. He'll hear her at the concert, but for the demo we have to stick with what we've got."

"I want more of Martha's songs."

Bobby Doyle said, "Hey. It's not your band, dude."

Miguel spun around and yelled, "Get out!"

Martha screamed, "Miguel, you can't do that!"

Arlo went over next to Miguel and turned his back on the rest of them. He wanted to smack Miguel a couple of times, make him calm down. He barely moved his lips, saying, "I'll take care of it. Don't worry. Bobby gets out of line, I'll take him out back and explain things."

For a second Miguel held onto the doorknob, then he said to Martha, "*Hablamos después*." The door slammed behind him. Arlo didn't plan on explaining anything to Bobby. Rick dropped into a chair and put his face in his hands. "I'm gonna die. I am gonna drop dead. Please, God. Please."

Arlo stood over his chair. "Is he playing in the band with us?"

Blinking, Rick looked up. "If you like him. What do you say? Martha?"

"Sure."

"Arlo? Scott?"

They all agreed to let Bobby Doyle in. Bobby Doyle said, "Cool."

They rehearsed for a couple of hours. Getting into the music again, Arlo felt better. He could close his eyes, Kelly would be in the room. In Bobby Doyle's hands her guitar was singing her songs. Kelly would be happy if she could've known a part of her was still making music.

They took a break. Martha wanted to work for a while, so the guys put on their jackets and went out in the backyard with two six-packs. Arlo cut the terrace lights off. He and Scott dragged some chairs to the lake. They all sat down, and Bobby Doyle rolled a joint.

They talked about the rehearsal for a while, then talked about the concert. Bobby got up and moved his chair. He said, "I'm deaf in my left ear. The other one will go too if I don't wear earplugs."

They drank some beer, then Bobby told Scott it didn't sound like he'd been playing bass too long, but that was all right because basically the Mayhem songs were pretty simple. There was a little blue tattoo in the shape of an infinity sign next to Bobby's mouth, and in the starlight it gave him a crooked smile. The top of his shaved head shone. He rolled another joint and lit up. "Hey. What's the story with Martha's boyfriend? Is he Colombian?"

"From Ecuador, I think," Scott said.

Bobby laughed. "No, man. Is he a drug dealer?"

Scott said, "I don't think so."

"He looks like one."

Arlo said, "You shouldn't say that, man."

"What do you guys know about that dude that runs the studio? Victor."

Arlo and Scott looked at each other. Scott said, "Yeah, he's doing our demo tape. What do you mean?" He gave the joint back to Bobby Doyle.

Bobby held his breath. It took him awhile to answer. "I think Victor is a cop."

"Whoa," Scott said. "Why do you think that?"

"I don't know, man. I'm getting these vibes all over. I'm sharing this with you because I'm in the band now. That's why I asked you about Miguel. Call it my narc radar."

Arlo looked at Scott. "Miguel doesn't deal drugs. I know that for a fact. But you think Victor could be a narc?"

"I don't know any narcs that run recording studios. If he is, there's nothing we can do. Leave it be."

"Yeah." Bobby nodded. "Don't carry anything in there, though. That's my advice at this point. We ought to tell Martha and Rick."

"And Miguel," Arlo said.

"No," Scott said. "Don't tell anybody. They'd ask Victor what's up, then we wouldn't get the demo tape. We'd be screwed. I say we wait till after the concert, like Bobby said. Okay?"

Arlo thought about it. "What do you think, Bobby?"

"Sounds reasonable. Leave it be."

Scott opened another beer. "Where are you from, Bobby?"

"Chicago. I was born there, but I've been all over."

"Rick said you played with Ozzy Osbourne."

The glowing orange dot passed over to Bobby again. They waited for him to exhale. He said, "No. I auditioned with Ozzy in 1986 to play for his tour. I was green, but they gave me the gig. You want to hear a total screw-up? I got drunk the night before the first rehearsal and slept through it. They fired me. I said to myself, Oh, so what? I don't need this shit. Like you justify it in your own mind that you didn't really want to do it, you know? Play backup for a washed-up rocker. That was my mind-set at that stage of my existence. Yeah. But Ozzy is cool, man. He's all right."

"But you did come close to making it," Scott said.

"Close? I was a guitar tech for Aerosmith and Metallica, man. Year and a half on the road."

"No shit. Whoa."

"Deluxe tour buses. Plenty to eat. We could have anything we wanted. The best grass, the best beer. Any girl we wanted. Three at a time if we wanted. But it gets boring. That's hard for you to conceive of at this point in your careers, but after a while it gets to be a drag. Looking for that perfect high. Looking for that woman who won't let you down."

Bobby Doyle faked holding his guitar, and when he sang it sounded like a file on sheet metal. "Don't let me down, mama. Don't let me down, pretty mama, 'cause here I am, girl, standin' at the edge of heaven, waitin' for your sweet, sweet touch to save me—" He strummed in the air. "Bah-dah-dah-da-da-daaah." Then he took the joint from Arlo. "Wow. We're retro tonight, folks. Didn't mean to sound so . . . Nirvana." He fell off his chair giggling.

Arlo let out some smoke. "You just made that up right now?"

"Yeah. My voice is shot."

"I like it," Arlo said. "What was that chick died of heroin in the sixties?"

"Janis Joplin?" He laughed. "Great. I sound like Janis on smack."

They opened another beer each.

Bobby Doyle said, "You know what I like about Mayhem? The music is about unseen forces that want to control the human spirit. They hold the place in modern mythology that used to be occupied by the Devil. They foster an impulse to destroy. That's what my songs are about—how people respond to annihilation of the spirit in an age when violence is more acceptable and social constraints have loosened."

Arlo nodded.

"I don't know," Scott said. "Martha Cruz has her own ideas."

"Yeah." Bobby Doyle made a little smile. "She'll learn. Nobody does it alone, man. I used to think so. Then I mellowed. I'm older now, I'm just happy to have a job."

"How old are you?" Scott asked.

"Guess."

"Thirty-eight?"

"Thirty-one. I only look ancient."

Arlo fell asleep on the roof in a flat spot so he wouldn't roll off. Voices woke him up. He opened his eyes and pushed down the top of the sleeping bag. Martha's voice, popping mad. Then Miguel, yelling back at her. This time of year, in winter, people would leave the windows open to get some air, opposite what it was up north. Sometimes they forgot that other people could hear.

Arlo was in his socks. Carefully picking his way over the barrel tiles so he wouldn't crack them, he made his way down the slope, stepping over a vent pipe, bracing himself on a chimney. From forty feet up, he had a view of the surrounding land—two or three huge houses already built and another under construction, with a lake all the way around, except where the access road came in. There was the big dragline that Arlo had worked on. In the darkness the water looked black, and the mounds of white rock were like jagged gray hills.

Arlo finally stopped on the side of the house outside Miguel's bedroom. There was a little balcony down there, and light was coming through the doors. He could barely make out his watch. Two-thirty in the morning.

They were yelling in Spanish. Miguel told her to shut up a couple of times. Their words would be clear, then get muffled, as though they were pacing around in the room, coming nearer to the windows, then going away.

Shivering in the cold air, Arlo peered over the edge of the roof. He heard a couple of sharp cracks. Martha cried out. Told him to stop it. Miguel shouted at her. Something about the keys. Where were the keys? Arlo shifted his weight. Miguel had smacked her around before, but this was getting to be too much. Martha had a mouth on her, and she could be stupid what she said, but still. He leaned out farther, holding onto the chimney. The door banged open, hitting the wall. Martha came out onto the balcony, and Arlo ducked back. She ran down the stairs barefoot, wearing nothing but a short red satin nightie. The balcony had a stone staircase going down the side of the house to a flower garden and a little fountain. Miguel was right behind her, just his black trousers on. He and Martha disappeared past some hedges. There was the sound of snapping twigs. Martha yelped once. Then silence.

It was pretty dark out there, no moon or anything. Arlo waited. The fuzziness he'd had in his head when he woke was gone now. He was worried what might be going on. He looked down at the balcony, wondering if he could hang off the edge of the roof and drop without breaking his leg. Then he saw them coming across the flower garden, Miguel dragging Martha along by her elbow. The front of her nightie was ripped, and her hair was hanging in her face.

Arlo didn't wait for them to come back to the house and go inside. He knew that if he stayed by the balcony and listened, he would hear them making love like wild animals. On all fours he went up the steep incline of the roof, then over the highest point of it, able to see his way in the starlight pouring down. He pulled his sleeping bag over his head, but he doubted he'd get much sleep the rest of the night.

CHAPTER 31

Elaine was on her second vodka and tonic, listening to Charlie Dunavoy play "Sophisticated Lady," when she heard someone pull out the stool beside her. Fridays were busy. She couldn't expect solitude. She turned her eyes, prepared to give someone a dismissive glance.

It was Dan Galindo. "Well," she said.

"Hi, Elaine." He gave her a peck on the cheek, then told the bartender to bring him a draft.

"Is this a coincidence?" she asked.

"Not really. Charlie called and said why didn't I come over." Dan propped the heel of his sneaker on a rung of the bar stool. "It's been a long time since I've heard Charlie play. He's pretty good." A button-down collar showed above the neck of his blue pullover sweater. He smiled at the bartender when she set down his beer.

"Terry, don't take money from this man. Wednesday was his birthday, and I'm buying him a drink."

"Happy birthday," the bartender said.

Dan looked at Elaine. "How'd you know that?"

She shrugged. "We went out for a beer when you turned thirty, sort of a bitch-and-moan party because I lost a big jury trial the same day."

"Has it been that long?"

She touched her vodka tonic to his glass. "We'll do it again when you're forty."

Dan took a swallow of beer, then said, "Charlie told me forty would be better. I hope he's right."

"Well, don't ask me, I'm certainly not there yet." Elaine reached for a pretzel, then scooted the bowl toward Dan. "I hear you're looking for another job."

"It's time," he said. "Charlie's about to retire. I'm thinking Fort Lauderdale."

"Oh, yes. Your ex lives up that way." Elaine picked salt off a pretzel. The band swung into "Satin Doll," and she turned her head toward the stage. A few couples got up to dance. Charlie and his bass player were accompanied by a young saxophonist, a student at the school of the arts downtown. She watched his cheeks fill, watched him lean back with his horn. A sweet sound.

"I came to say thank you," Dan said. "If it weren't for you, I'd be in jail right now. When I knocked on your door that night, I thought you weren't home."

"I couldn't let you in." She smiled. "No, Dan. I

didn't have company. I just couldn't talk to you. Why were you there?"

Dan came a little closer to be heard over the music. "I wanted to ask who the hell that bearded guy was outside your house last Sunday morning. He looked just like Victor Ramirez."

Still watching the saxophonist, Elaine said, "I figured it was something like that. Don't ask me about the case, Dan."

"Are you still on it? When I called your office, they said you were out of town on a family emergency, but here you sit. Did Paxton find out what you did for me?"

"Oh, it wasn't just that."

"Well, what was it?"

Poking the lime slice down into her drink, she shook her head.

"Okay." Dan settled back on his stool, and his hands kept the rhythm of the music. The sleeves of his sweater were pushed up. He had long arms and angular, graceful hands. The skin was deep golden—many hours on the water, she assumed.

He said, "What do you know about Kelly's death? The police won't tell me anything. Are there any leads?"

"Not that I know of." She glanced at him. "The police don't keep in touch."

"Why did Kelly come to see me that night?"

"I have no idea."

Dan's shoulder was lightly touching hers. "She

wanted to tell me something, Elaine. I wish I knew what it was. I'm asking you because I know that you were involved with bringing her in as a confidential informant, and I have to assume that you knew her pretty well, and that you must have talked to her."

Elaine reached for another pretzel, nibbled it halfway down, then said, "We didn't talk very often. I can tell you this. A couple of nights before she died, she left a message at my office. She was sorry for having lied about you. You see, she had told the DEA you were involved in money laundering with Miguel Salazar—" Dan dropped his hands on the bar and exhaled, and Elaine said, "I never believed that. She called me to apologize. I think she was going to see you for the same reason. When you ended your relationship with her, she was devastated—maybe that's too strong a word. She was angry, and she wanted to hurt you."

Dan took a moment to think about it. "If she was angry, I suppose she had a reason. I let her think we had something when we didn't. She had her clothes in my bedroom and makeup in the bathroom, and I was ashamed to be seen with her. I look back now, and that's how it was. I made excuses not to introduce her to my friends. My son never saw her. I knew we had no future, and I kept sleeping with her. Pretty sad."

"Easy to say all that, looking back," Elaine said, "but I think you're too hard on yourself."

The bartender came over to check on the level of

their drinks. Elaine said to bring her another. Dan's beer was only halfway down. He shook his head.

"The last time I saw her," Elaine said, "she told me about her life, her childhood. How she got into music. Her dreams. I want to grieve, Dan. I want to cry, but I feel just . . . numb. I feel responsible somehow, you know? Not legally, but—"

He nodded.

For a while they listened to the music. Charlie waved at them from behind the keyboard. Lights played on his white hair, and the old bass man's hands moved up and down the strings. Then the saxophonist came in—a rich, breathy melody.

"Vincent Hooper doesn't deserve you, Elaine."

The words surprised her, they were spoken so simply and earnestly. From anyone else they would have sounded insincere. "Don't talk about what people deserve, Dan. That's funny, though. I'm the one sleeping with a married man, and he's the one who isn't good enough."

"You should leave him."

"Think so?"

"Don't waste a minute."

She saw them both in the dim, glass-sparkled surface of the mirror. Dan's profile, his hair neatly parted to one side. Large brown eyes, slightly downturned at the corners, which she had always thought rather affecting. Juries invariably trusted him.

"Well, it's already over, Vince and I."

"When?"

"Last night. I thought I'd celebrate." Dan glanced at her vodka tonic. "This is only my third. I might even stop with this, who knows?" She set it down on the bar. His eyes were on her, that patient, wordless gaze. "Part of the reason I split up with Vince, believe it or not, was you. He wasn't sure what's going on with you and me. I told him the truth—nothing—but you kept popping up. With a man like Hooper, you're either on his side or you aren't. If you're part of the team, he would die for you. But if there's any doubt, he slams the door." She touched Dan's shoulder and gave it a little push for emphasis. "Bagels. That's what did it. You showed up on Sunday morning with a half dozen fresh bagels. What an underhanded tactic that was."

"Don't expect me to apologize, seeing how it worked out."

She picked up her drink, then put it down again. "Dan, what are you doing, leaving Miami? If you go anywhere else, you'll throw away every one of your clients. Okay, you want to go back to your wife and son, but make the commute for a while. Charlie says you're starting to build a good practice."

"Wow. I'd forgotten how bossy you can be." Dan leaned on an elbow, cheek in his palm. "Why did you send me to Charlie?"

"Because he needed someone younger and decent and competent to help him out. Because I like both of you. Dan, why am I talking to you? We're supposed to be shooting at each other."

He sipped his beer. "I spoke to John Paxton today. Dropped by the office to clear up some details on a possible plea bargain for Rick Robbins—which I guess we can't talk about—"

"No, we can't."

"Anyway, Paxton asked me about Luis Barrios. I don't know why he brought it up, I guess it still bugs him. He asked me if I'd do the same thing again."

"What'd you tell him?"

"That I didn't know. I've given it a lot of thought lately too. Luis Barrios. Dead but he keeps on coming. I can't get rid of him." Dan turned to face her. "What was your advice back then, Elaine?"

"Mine? You never asked for an opinion."

He laughed. "That sounds like me. I knew everything. After I got my ass kicked, you helped me fend off the criticism, but I never asked what you thought. Maybe I wanted to see my name in the paper. 'Young prosecutor upholds ideals of truth and justice.' Maybe that's why I did it."

Elaine saw that he wanted to know. More than anything, he had to know—as if her opinion would have been listened to then, or if given now, two years later, would make any difference.

She said slowly, "I think—knowing you—that you did it because you believed it was right."

"But was it right?"

"It may not have been *wise*, Dan, but . . . yes. It was right. Very right. That was about the most foolish—but the bravest—thing I've ever seen from a lawyer." He gave her a wondering look. She retreated by laughing and sliding off her bar stool, tugging him by the wrist. "Okay, that's enough. Come with me."

"Where are we going?"

She pushed through the crowd on the dance floor. "Come along quietly. Charlie!" She pointed at Dan as she dragged him toward the band. "Guess who has a birthday this week."

Dan pulled backward. "Elaine, for God's sake."

He put a hand over his face when the band went into a jazz version of "Happy Birthday." Terry, the bartender, made a loud whistle through her teeth. The people jammed into the bar sang along, ragged and off-key.

CHAPTER 32

Seeing who was on duty at the guard shack, Dan banged his head lightly a few times on hands curled over the top of the steering wheel. When the car ahead had gone through, Dan drifted forward. He held his driver's license out the window.

The guard glanced at the list of names on his clipboard. "You're here to see Lisa Galindo, right? Your name isn't on here."

"She must have forgotten to call you."

"Apparently so. I'll see if she's home." He stepped back inside to use the telephone.

Dan's arm hung outside the car, and he tapped a rhythm on the door. Headlamps shone in his rearview. He had driven up last night; Rick had asked him to. He and Lisa had spoken for over an hour. At the end Dan had given her one piece of good news—the police had dropped him as a suspect.

The guard hung up and came out to say there was no answer. "I let it ring seven times."

"She took our son to Boca Raton. I guess she's not back yet. Well, look. I'm spending the weekend. I'll be moving in next week, in fact. She gave me a key."

"Oh? Congratulations."

"Thanks. But she didn't give me the spare gate opener."

The guard was shaking his head. "If it was up to me, I'd let you in."

"Who's going to know, for Pete's sake?"

"Nope. Can't do it. I'll call her again in a while and see if it's okay for you to come in. Meanwhile, there's a McDonald's in the shopping center you could wait at." He pointed with his pen at the turnaround. "Would you clear the road, sir?"

Cursing silently, Dan took a fast left around the guard shack. His headlights swept across the flower beds, and his tires skidded on the herringboned bricks. He parked a half mile away in the lot outside the country club. Parking was not allowed on the grass that edged the streets of Lakewood Village. Cars would be towed. Dan walked back toward Heron Hills as if he were out for a stroll.

There was no way in except past the guard shack—unless a person swam the moats or vaulted over the walls at the entrance. The landscaped, white stucco walls were six feet high and about twenty feet long, with the name of the subdivision cut into the concrete. Dan timed it so that he got near the entrance just at a break in traffic. He jogged to the wall, put a toe in the O of Heron, grabbed the top, and went over, landing lightly behind some bushes. He brushed the dirt off his jeans, pushed the branches aside, and cut behind someone's yard. He looked over his shoulder. The guard was checking the ID of some other poor bastard.

It took Dan two minutes to walk to the house. He let himself in with his key and flipped on the light in the foyer. Immediately the cocker spaniel started its racket, coming across the living room, ears flopping.

"Shut up!"

The dog whined and slunk off to hide behind one of the sofas. There were two, both upholstered in white, facing each other across a glass-topped table.

Dan went to the kitchen to look for the gate opener. He opened and shut drawers. It wasn't sitting out on the counter or the table in the breakfast nook. He checked Lisa's bedroom. The dresser, nightstand, desk. She had cleared out one side of the walk-in closet for him. In his car—which he would retrieve as soon as he found the damned gate opener—were most of his shirts, ties, and suits. He thought he could bring boxes up each time he came. The furniture could stay in Miami. She already had everything she needed, and better quality than his.

Passing Josh's room, he noticed the glow coming from the fish tank, heard the aerator bubbling softly. He went inside and watched the goldfish and guppies for a minute. Dan had bought a new aquarium for himself, thanks to Rick and Sandy, a twenty-gallon beauty with two hundred dollars' worth of angel fish—which he should not have done since he would only have to dismantle the thing and transport it all the way up here to Lakewood, but oh, well. Turning to leave, he noticed the white envelope on Josh's desk, the word DAD in Superman-style letters. Dan had left it there Wednesday morning, not meaning to. He read it again as he went back to the living room. *To my dad. Your the best. Love, your son, Joshua D. Galindo.*

Dan read it again and smiled. *Your the best.* He slid the card into the envelope.

The house was quiet. The dog sat by the sliding glass doors, looking out. There was the dark glass, then the terrace splashed with light from inside. Dan walked toward the doors, his own reflection coming closer. The gas barbecue grill was out there under a zip-up cover. Dan had bought it for $749 on sale at Home Depot, a top-of-the-line model. They'd had cookouts with the neighbors. He didn't think it had been used since he left. He wondered if Bob and Meredith had gone back to Ohio yet, and then remembered he hadn't even liked Bob.

Lisa would be here any minute. She had taken Josh to his grandparents' house for the weekend, although Dan had told her he would be spending most of the time with Rick, getting his side of things, trying to decide what to say to John Paxton in the meeting on Monday.

She had cried. Angry tears. She had said it didn't

surprise her, really. *Look at the kind of people Rick hangs out with—rock musicians and God knows what. Like that girl you dated. And Sandy! I knew what she was the first time I saw her. Look at that new BMW. That diamond on her finger. Flaunting it at family dinners. Daddy and Rick hardly speak to each other now. What am I going to tell them? And Josh! Oh, my God.*

The dog's head swiveled toward the front door, then its claws were scrabbling on the tiles. It barked at nothing for a while, then, satisfied that the intruder had gone away, it came back to watch Dan.

Dan saw the gate opener on the console table in the foyer. He had walked right past it on his way in. The table was glass on long, slender legs, with a beveled mirror above it and a pale blue rug on the floor. The style in Lakewood Village went toward glass tables, tile floors, light wood, cool colors. Potted plants to bring the outdoors in. Magazines in a neat row on the coffee table. Lisa had done a good job decorating the house. Josh knew not to leave his toys in the living room, and to straighten the fringe on the rug if his shoe scuffed across it. She preferred him to come in by the kitchen.

The cocker spaniel was sitting at Dan's feet, panting softly. He knelt to pet its long, silky ears. "Hey, Poppy." Hearing its name, the dog looked around at him. "I'm going to leave now. Be good."

In one of the kitchen drawers Dan had seen a pad of lined note paper. He found a pen beside it. He wrote, *Dear Lisa, I waited for you awhile, but what I have to say is brief and there would be no point in our arguing over it. I have decided to stay in Miami. I had hoped we could start over, but I don't think it would work out. I'm sorry. Call me if you want. I'll be home tonight.*

He hesitated over how to close it. Love, Dan? Regards? Sincerely? He wrote, *All the best, Dan.*

A postscript: *Please let Josh make birthday cards on his computer the way he wants to, without pointing out his spelling errors (unless he asks you). He was embarrassed to give me my card. I thought it was great the way it was.*

He left the note on the counter, put the key and gate opener on the note, and turned off the lights.

CHAPTER 33

Dan parked as close as he could to his apartment and opened the trunk. A garment bag of suits over one arm, he unlocked his front door. The new aquarium filled the living room with its soft light. Dan hit the switch for the lamp as he passed it, then made three more trips back and forth from car to bedroom. He was dropping his suitcase near the closet when he noticed the light blinking on his answering machine.

He stood by the small table under the window and pushed the button, not surprised by the shrill voice that came out of it.

This is Lisa. I can't believe you. I was just at my parents' house, and I told them— Oh, my God. Oh . . . damn you. Stay in Miami. And don't think you're going to take Josh to the Bahamas! This is the most—

Dan hit the button to erase the message. As the tape spun backward, a noise came from the hall outside his bedroom door. A footstep. A squeak of wood.

He turned slowly around.

A person was there in the doorway, a figure in black jeans, black sweater. He tensed at the same instant he recognized her. Martha Cruz was the first to speak, pointing vaguely toward the living room. "The front door was open."

Relief flooded through him so strongly he felt dizzy. He dragged in a breath. "What are you doing here?"

Her eyes seemed enormous. "I have to talk to you."

"I didn't see your car."

"I left it around the corner," she said. "I came straight from rehearsal at the studio."

"Afraid someone will come looking for you?"

"Miguel? He can look all he wants, I'm not going back to him." When she came farther into the room, Dan could see by the one light on his dresser that there was a discoloration on her cheekbone, which he had first thought was a shadow.

"Come here, let me see your face." She lowered her head, but Dan took her chin and lifted her hair out of the way. There was an ugly purple bruise at the corner of her left eye. "Son of a bitch," he murmured.

"Last night he lost his temper when I told him I left the boat keys at your office. He thinks I did it on purpose, which I did not."

"They're on my key ring." Dan took it out of his pocket. The silver ring with Salazar's keys on it swung with the others. "I meant to mail them yesterday. I'll give them to a courier on Monday." He tossed the key ring onto his dresser, keeping himself calm in front of her, wanting to ram the keys down Salazar's throat. In the mirror he could see Martha fluffing her hair over the bruise. All hidden now.

Dan glanced in the direction of the front door. "I'd better lock up."

"He doesn't know I came here." Martha followed Dan to the living room, then stood on the porch while he closed his car. He motioned her back inside and locked the front door of his apartment, putting on the chain for good measure.

"I was about to make some tea," he said.

"I'll have some too. Thanks."

In the kitchen she sat sideways in a chair and tossed a small shoulder bag onto the table. Dan put on the kettle and took two mugs from the cabinet over the sink. "Martha, we'll have to decide where to put you. It wouldn't be a good idea for you to stay here tonight, given the circumstances. What if I call Rick and Sandy?" He turned to see what she thought.

Her dark hair shadowed her eyes. "Rick's in trouble, isn't he?"

Dan hesitated. "What do you mean?"

"Is he going to jail?"

"Jail?" Dan leaned back against the counter and crossed his arms.

Martha said, "Our new guitarist, Bobby Doyle, told me that you came to the studio on Thursday and made Rick go with you. And yesterday at Miguel's house, Rick was totally freaked and he wouldn't tell me anything. I think it's because of Victor Ramirez. He's a narc."

"Who told you that?"

"It's true."

"Just answer the question, Martha."

She took awhile with it. "Tonight Arlo Pate said that Bobby Doyle has this narc radar. Bobby is such a stoner, Arlo wasn't sure, but he's worried because he heard Miguel talking on the phone yesterday to Victor about meeting him on Sunday. Arlo doesn't know what it's about, but he thought he should tell me."

Standing at the counter, Dan could feel his control over Rick's case, so tenuously grasped, beginning to slip from his fingers as if they were greased. He asked quietly, "Is Miguel aware of what Bobby Doyle thinks?"

She shook her head. "Bobby and Scott and Arlo all agreed not to tell him because the concert is so close, and if Miguel found out—"

Dan said, "Martha, what's going on here?" The kettle behind him started to tick on the stove.

"Bobby is right about Victor. He works for the DEA. Kelly told me about two months ago. She said they made her spy on Rick. She didn't want to, but Victor made her do it. Victor isn't his real name, it's Vincent Hooper. Kelly said they were trying to get Miguel, and they were going to use Rick to do it—"

At the sound of a car door slamming, Martha got up and walked to the open archway, looking toward the living room.

"It's nothing," Dan said. "Come back and sit down."

She took a breath, a ragged inhalation, then looked around at him. "Did you know about Kelly? You don't act surprised."

"I found out recently," he said.

"How?"

"Never mind that. What about Rick?"

Martha returned to her chair. "I was Kelly's best friend, and she needed to tell someone. They arrested her for possession of heroin last summer. When she started dating you, she wanted to tell you everything—her arrest, the DEA, Miguel, Rick—but I said no, are you crazy? I hadn't met you then, but I knew you were Rick's lawyer, so I told her, Kelly, if you tell him, he'll go straight to Rick, and then Miguel will find out. It would be awful. So she didn't say anything, and neither did I. We just waited for the demo tape to be done and waited for the concert. She couldn't stand it. She started making mistakes in the songs, she was so scared, but they wanted more and more information on Rick. And they kept after her and after her."

"Hold it," Dan said. "Let me get this straight. You told Kelly to keep her mouth shut because you wanted a record contract?"

"That wasn't the reason!"

"You didn't let Kelly tell me because you didn't want to screw up your relationship with Miguel. He was paying for the band, wasn't he? Keep that money coming in, never mind what happens to your manager."

She stared back at him with her mouth half open, but an answer didn't occur to her. She let out a breath. "Are they going to put Rick in jail?"

"They might," Dan said. He thought of the meeting that he and Rick would attend on Monday morning at the U.S. attorney's office. Dan would be pitching a defense of threats and extortion. He had hoped it would buy some time, perhaps even persuade John Paxton to reconsider seizing all of Rick's assets. If Salazar got wind of who Victor was and canceled the meeting, the DEA might blame Rick. But now it appeared that the DEA's cover could be blown by the pot-fuddled observations of one rock guitarist. And Martha Cruz had known for two months and had said nothing.

A low whistle came from the teakettle, increasing steadily in pitch and volume. Dan turned off the stove. He heard Martha's whispery, tear-clogged voice. "I was so scared."

"You were selfish."

She swung her head up, glaring at him. He could see the bruise beside her eye. "Right! Selfish. I'm a selfish slut for sleeping with Miguel Salazar. Think what you like, I don't care. He said he'd help me, and I let him. He knew what I wanted. My music. That's all I've ever wanted. It's all I've got. I have my voice, my hands—" She held them up, slender and strong, rings on most of the fingers, short nails painted dark red. "That's what I have. It's all Kelly had. No fancy college, no money. Can you possibly understand that? Mr. Lawyer?"

She dropped her hands back in her lap. "Kelly and I decided not to do anything that might hurt the band. We'd think about the demo, we'd get the songs going for the concert, and that was all. After we got signed, everything would be all right. That's what we thought. Then it started getting worse, and then it was too late."

She was crying silently. No sobs, just tears running slowly down her cheeks. "When Kelly told me Rick should be our manager, I said *what*? He's never had a band that made it. We need somebody good. Kelly told me shut up, you don't know everything." Martha laughed, then cleared her throat. "He kept us together. When we lost Bill-E, our bass player, then Leon, our drummer, Rick wouldn't let us give up. Then Kelly." Her voice was tight. "Rick said, Martha, you can't give up now. So he found me a new guitar player. I know we're not going to get the demo from Victor——there's no way—but it doesn't matter. Mr. Friedman from Capitol Records, you can come to the concert or not, and if you don't sign us, too bad for you. Somebody will. But without Rick— I don't know the business. What would happen to me? Maybe that's selfish, but like I said, think what you want to."

A tear wobbled on the point of her chin, a speck of light. She dug her chin into the shoulder of her sweater. "What's going to happen to him?"

"I'm not sure yet, Martha, but don't expect him to be managing the band." Dan tore a sheet off the roll of towels over the sink. "The government wants to seize everything he's got, and he'll be lucky to stay out of prison. We're trying to work a deal with the prosecutors. I can't tell you any more than that."

She blew her nose. Her eyes were puffy and red. "I know a way to help Rick. Maybe. That's why I came over here."

Dan looked down at her. "What do you mean?"

"It was Kelly's idea. You asked me why she wanted to see you that night. I said I didn't know, but I do know. She wanted you to help her get away from Victor."

Martha fell silent. She stood up and walked toward the living room, stopping just beyond the opening. Dan heard footsteps along the walkway in front of the building.

"Is the door locked?" she said.

"Yes. Don't worry." His heart raced.

They stood without moving. A door slammed upstairs. Martha let out a breath. "I guess I'm just nervous."

"Tell me about Kelly," Dan said.

Martha turned around and said, "She had this tape recording of Victor shooting somebody in cold blood. She was going to the *Miami Herald* with it if they didn't leave her alone. That's what she wanted to tell you about."

Dan stared at her. "What tape?"

"Last summer she was at a party in the Grove, this big house on the water, and the owner was a drug dealer—which she didn't know. She said that on the tape you hear this party, and the band, and then you hear all this shooting and yelling. It was the police coming in. The police and the DEA. She was there. She told me about it. She said it was horrible. People died, like right *there*. She saw Victor running after some guy. On the tape you can hear voices, like, Halt! Drop your gun! It's in Spanish, and it's definitely Victor. Then the other man says okay, okay, don't shoot. Then you hear *bam, bam, bam!* And Kelly said, Martha, if I tell Victor I have this, he'll stop bothering me. So now I'm thinking maybe we could use it to help Rick. Right? The DEA would drop the charges. They'd have to."

"Hold it." Dan held up a hand. Her words had tumbled out so fast he couldn't grasp the meaning. "Whose party was this?"

"I don't *know* whose party. Some guy she knew. He wanted her to bring the band over so he could play with them. She had this band back then called Black Mango. Okay? So the DEA was going to arrest this guy, is what she said, but she didn't know that. They came in and shot this *other* guy. I mean, Victor shot him. The first guy, the one who lived there, was recording the band, and when the police came in, the tapes were going."

"Kelly had a tape recording of a DEA raid?"

"Yes." Martha let out a breath. "That's what I'm trying to tell you." She turned her head toward the living room again.

"Martha—"

"Shhh!" Her palm rose to keep him quiet.

Dan followed her around the corner. He saw her walk quickly toward the window, the leather soles of her boots tapping softly on the wood floor. Only the one lamp was on, and the aquarium light. The curtains were drawn. Nothing was out of place in the apartment, and no unusual sounds came from outside, yet Dan felt a tremor in the muscles of his chest, as if Martha's fear—and she was trembling with it, visibly shaking—had set up a similar vibration in his own body. "What did you hear?"

"A car. I know the sound of Miguel's car." She was breathing fast. "Look out the window."

Dan put a knee on the sofa and opened the curtain a crack. He dropped it slowly back into place. "Good thing I locked the door," he said quietly.

Martha spun around as if looking for somewhere to hide.

"I won't let him in. He'll ask if you're here, and I'll say no. Your car is down the street. He'll go away." Dan's voice came out calmly, but when he heard the footsteps on the porch he involuntarily tensed.

She ran toward his bedroom as the first knock came.

He expected her to hide herself in the closet, but she reappeared a moment later carrying his key chain, fumbling at the mechanism that would release the fob from the ring. "What are you doing?"

Martha whispered, "I wasn't here. Come to the marina. We can talk on the boat. He'd never find us." She slid the keys to the Bertram off the ring from the others, then tossed Dan his own keys. He grabbed for them, caught them against his sweater. Martha hurled herself across the living room, caught the corner at the kitchen, and disappeared. He ran in that direction in time to see the back door close.

The knock came again at the front.

Dan looked into the darkness of the backyard, seeing in the weak light of a street lamp on the corner the pale outlines of rusty furniture the tenants of the building infrequently used. A line of trash cans stood along the chain-link fence. Then to his right, at the edge of the property, he saw the hibiscus bushes swaying. They thickly covered the low concrete wall on that side. A dog began to bark next door.

Dan wondered about going inside. He could pretend not to be home. But it might be wiser, under the circumstances, to go over the wall. He was on the point of making the decision when Arlo Pate stepped around the corner and into the light.

CHAPTER 34

Miguel Salazar stood in the middle of Dan's living room, pivoting slowly.

Arlo Pate's left arm circled Dan's neck. The big man's denim vest smelled like sweat and engine oil. Dan strained to keep his eyes on Salazar. "I don't know where she is. I was taking out some trash and didn't hear you at the door."

Salazar walked into the kitchen. Came back with two mugs.

"I'm expecting company from upstairs," Dan said. "My neighbor is a very nervous woman. She's going to see you guys and call the police." He pushed at the hairy wrist under his chin. "Let go, I can't breathe."

The mugs dropped to the floor. Thud. Thud. The handle snapped off one of them, and the mug rolled. Salazar kicked it aside with one low-cut woven leather shoe. His hair was untied tonight, falling forward slightly as he bent to look at Dan. "Where is she?"

"I told you, I haven't seen her!"

Salazar's black eyes shifted back and forth, white showing beneath the irises. "At the studio she went for a break and didn't come back. Rick doesn't know where she is. I'm worried what might happen to her, you know? Miami. On the streets alone."

"She didn't come here."

Salazar glanced toward the bedroom, straightened, and went down the hall. Arlo let Dan stand up, but kept a hand on his shoulder, the meaty fingers digging in, the forearm bristling with red hairs.

"Kelly died in here, didn't she?"

Dan looked at him.

The hand on Dan's shoulder increased its pressure. He thought his collarbone might crack. Arlo said, "I've decided what I'm gonna do to the guy that killed her. I'm going to pull his guts out through his asshole, real slow. Make him watch."

Dan heard the shower curtain rings slide across the rod. Heard a closet door open, then shut.

"Arlo, I didn't kill Kelly."

He let Dan go long enough to grab him again by the upper arms. Dan was over six feet tall, but he had to look up to see into Arlo's face. Sun-bleached brows were a pale ledge over eyes the color of faded denim. The sun had turned his skin dark red. His short nose had a bend to it, the result of a fist or a beer bottle. Pushing thirty. Dumb as a stump.

"I found her body, Arlo. That's all I did. The police

know I was somewhere else when she died. I have a witness."

The faded brows drew together. "Miguel says you did it."

"Miguel is the guy who beats up your friends. I saw him hit Martha across the face. What does he do when no one's watching? You let that happen to her?" In the depths of those blue eyes flickered a glimmer of light.

Dan heard the slow, hollow sound of heels on a wood floor. Arlo Pate released him. Salazar came back out. He lifted his hand, thumb and forefinger set slightly apart. He showed Dan what he had. Silver glinted in the space. An earring.

"I found this on the floor in your bedroom. Where is she?"

Dan felt sweat around his hairline. "I think that was Kelly's. She told me she lost an earring. That must be the one."

Salazar looked at it. Frowned. "No. I bought these for Martha."

"She must have lent them to Kelly." Dan's voice was husky, his mouth was dry as dust. What had make him think he could handle this? He should have gone over the wall with Martha.

Arlo Pate's hand fell on Dan's shoulder, and he bent his neck to ease the pain.

Salazar said, "I don't like when things go on behind my back."

"I can appreciate that," Dan said, "but I haven't seen Martha since Thursday."

"Yes. She came to your office. You told me she came for the keys to my boat, but she didn't have them when I asked her where they were."

"She accidentally left them on my desk," Dan said. "I mailed them yesterday."

"I love that woman. I love her."

Dan nodded and pushed at Arlo Pate's fingers.

"It bothers me when I don't know where she is."

"I'm sure she feels the same way, Miguel."

Salazar dropped the earring into the breast pocket of his jacket and came out with a pistol. He stepped back and extended his arm. The pistol was a small black one, a silenced .22. "She was here. Where did she go?"

From raw animal fear, without thinking Dan dropped and ducked sideways. The sudden movement broke Arlo Pate's grip on his shoulder. He saw a flash, heard a pop like a single hand clap. As he ran for the door, he saw Salazar turning, tracking him with the pistol. Saw Arlo Pate's arm knock it out of the way. And behind them the shattered aquarium poured sea water and fish, a silvery tide that gushed to the floor.

The taxi driver who dropped Dan off in Coral Gables asked if he was all right. Dan said he was fine, gave him a twenty, and told him to wait.

He rang the doorbell on Elaine McHale's front porch. Leaned on it. After a minute the curtain fluttered, then he heard the dead bolt click open.

"Dan?"

He waved for the cabbie to take off, and went inside.

"My God, what's the matter? You're sweating."

"I had to jog a mile or so before I found a taxi." He laughed, still out of breath, but from nerves, not exhaustion. "You like boats, Elaine? How would you like to go out on the water tonight?"

"I must be out of my mind," Elaine said, clenching the wheel of her car with both hands. Her back barely touched the seat. "No, you're out of yours. Dan, you shouldn't talk to me. I'm the prosecution."

"The prosecution fired you off the case, Elaine."

She glanced at him. The street lights slid over her face. "I was not *fired*."

Dan smiled at her. "Neither was I, after I lost the Barrios case. They didn't fire me, they just transferred me where I couldn't embarrass anyone."

"Even if that were true, do you think I would switch loyalties so easily?"

"No," he said. "It means you're a person of integrity, and I could use someone like that right now."

Her eyes moved to the rearview mirror. "How do you know Miguel Salazar isn't at the marina waiting for you?"

"The man isn't clairvoyant." Dan looked behind them, then said, "Kelly never told me she was at that party where Luis Barrios was shot. It's too bizarre to be real."

"She was there. She couldn't tell you about it be-cause she would be talking about the DEA, and she was afraid of going to prison. Vincent Hooper was outraged when he found out she had been made an informant against Rick Robbins. He even yelled at me, although at the time I didn't know the connection. Vince was right; it was risky to have her on the case. But the so-called Barrios tape doesn't exist."

Elaine took a right into Coconut Grove, going south from the highway onto a quieter, tree-lined street. It would dead-end at the bay. "Vince and I discussed it. And the reason we discussed it is because Kelly Dorff brought it up. Vince was at my house when he returned her phone call. He told me that she claimed to have a tape of his shooting Luis Barrios after Barrios threw down his weapon. Vince was angry about it, of course, but not because it was *true*. He said he didn't like to be threatened by C.I.'s. Dan, the story about the raid was in the *Herald*. Didn't you read it?"

"Yes. They didn't mention Hooper, though, except to say he was there. A few witnesses at the scene claimed that the DEA shot without provocation, but it was all tidied up by a board of inquiry." Dan looked at her. "Martha says Kelly's band was recording that night. Is that true or not?"

Elaine lifted her hands from the wheel a moment, a quick gesture of acquiescence. "There was a tape recorder at the scene, but there was nothing on it but noise."

"Where is the tape now?"

"Vince said it's probably been destroyed." She glanced to her right, then rolled her eyes. "Yes, it must have been a cover-up."

Dan turned in his seat. "It doesn't even make you wonder? Not the least bit curious? What if Kelly did have a copy of the tape? Maybe someone there had a portable tape player going. What then? John Paxton, your esteemed boss, the man who presumably has something to say about your future, is going to stand in front of the TV cameras on Wednesday with the United States attorney and a bevy of high-kicking federal agents, and the first question from the press is going to be, 'Is it true that the lead DEA agent on Operation Manatee committed murder?'"

Elaine shifted gears, not looking at him.

"Will you go to Paxton and say, 'John, you know, I had a chance to check this out for you, but by golly, I just didn't think there was anything to it.' I guess if you want to see the office sandbagged, you could do that, but you're supposedly the person with loyalties."

"I wish you'd shut up," she said unconvincingly. "You're a scumbag defense lawyer."

"This is true," he said. "I am working for my client—who, if truth be known, did not go willingly into money laundering. Miguel Salazar took him out to the Everglades one sunny afternoon and put a pistol to the back of his head. This is true, Elaine. No, Rick can't prove it, but Paxton himself told me what Salazar did to his wife and her lover. Ah. I see you've heard that story. You're right, I'm working for Rick

Robbins. And yes. If this tape proves what I think it does, then I, in my scumbag way, will probably take John Paxton aside and say, Here's the deal: The government drops charges against my client, and I won't take this to the *Miami Herald*. You and the DEA special agent-in-charge talk it over, let me know."

Dan tugged Elaine's right hand off the steering wheel. "I don't mean to treat this lightly. I'm roaring on adrenaline right now. I'm sorry about you and Hooper. Not sorry for Hooper, because he is truly a vicious bastard, but sorry to bring you into this. I wish I didn't have to, but I don't know who else to ask."

She pulled her hand away. "You want to even the score, don't you?"

"You mean, I'm out to rub Hooper's nose in it? Do you mind?"

"I thought you had more class," she said.

"Well, I've been beaten up and shot at. Hooper and Salazar both hate my guts. And I'm pretty sure that one of them set me up with the police."

Elaine looked around at him. "Why do you say that?"

Dan pointed. "Take a left."

At midnight on a Saturday, the marina was still busy enough not to look deserted, although the parking lot had emptied out. There were spaces near the entrance to Pier Six. Elaine stopped under a tree, where the light did not reach them.

Dan took a breath.

"You think she's on the boat?" Elaine asked.

"I hope so. And I hope she's alone."

Elaine looked out both passenger windows.

Dan opened the door. "Thanks for bringing me. There's a phone on the boat, and I'll call you at home in an hour."

"Wait." She took her keys, and her fingers were visibly trembling. "I'll go with you."

"No."

"Yes." Elaine gave him a look and got out of the car. "I want to speak to Martha Cruz myself." She grabbed her purse and green fleece jacket.

They walked casually along the covered, lighted sidewalk that curved around the water until they reached the gate to Pier Six. Her eyes darted around, aware of everyone. Dan touched the turquoise-painted bars. There was no way around or over.

Elaine said, "Wait here."

A minute later she came back with the dockmaster. He flipped through a heavy key ring, then unlocked the gate. She thanked him and, with a firm grip on Dan's arm, pulled him inside. "I showed him my badge."

"Is that legal?"

"Shut up, Dan."

The dock was well lighted, fifty yards long. As they hurried toward the end, the sound of low conversation or music came from a few of the motorboats, sportfishers, and sailboats in the slips on both sides. The *Basilón* was where Dan had left it a week ago, mooring lines still neatly cleated off and taut. There were no lights coming from inside.

"Nice boat," Elaine said. Her fingers were clamped on his arm.

"Forty-six feet," he said. "Two 740-horse diesel engines. Sonar, radar, a depth finder. You could catch a sperm whale with those outriggers."

She looked at him. "Are we going on board or not?"

Dan loosened her grip, then walked along the side of the boat and leaned over the water to tap on the salon window. He waited, then tapped again.

He saw the curtain move, Martha's face at the glass. Then her head, with its mane of black curls, poked out of the salon door. "Hey, you made it," she said.

CHAPTER 35

Before starting the engines, Dan noticed the fuel level. Last weekend, taking Josh out, he had run the tanks nearly dry. The nearest marina with diesel fuel was five miles away on Key Biscayne, and it was now closed. At slow speed he steered south, then moored the boat a hundred yards offshore in shallow water. It was as far as he dared go at night. There were others in the area; no one would notice the Bertram.

He let the anchor go and cleated the line at the bow. With no wind the bay was calm, and the boat barely rocked in the diminished wake of a speedboat farther out. He went inside. Martha Cruz had made coffee, and now she and Elaine sat on opposite sides of the salon, their mugs in their laps. Martha had resented Dan's bringing a federal prosecutor, but Elaine showed no sign of tension. She was good with witnesses, Dan recalled. He sat down in an armchair equidistant between the women.

In greater detail Martha repeated the story she had told Dan earlier. Her hands shook when she lit her cigarette, and from time to time she would get up and look out the open salon door.

She said, "This is what Kelly told me. The house where it happened was owned by some guy from Mexico, and he had a bunch of people over that night. Kelly was there with her bassist, Bill-E, and another guy who played drums. The owner was a guitarist, and he had turned one of the rooms into a studio. He had money, so he had some pretty good equipment. They were in there jamming while the party was going on. About ten o'clock they hear this big crash, then some yelling and screaming. Guns go off. They stop playing and open the door. Then there are gunshots and smoke and cops are yelling 'Federal agents! Get down! Get on the floor!'

"Kelly threw away a couple of joints she had in her pockets and crouched down behind an amp. She could see into the hall, a big open area, and people were diving behind the furniture to get out of the way. Then some guy, a friend of the owner, comes tearing down the hall with a gun. Not a regular gun, an Uzi or something. Right behind him was a man in a jacket that said DEA. They went onto the enclosed back porch right next to where Kelly was. She couldn't see them, but she heard the DEA agent say, 'Drop it, Luis!' He's screaming in Spanish to drop the gun or he'd blow him away. And the other guy, Luis, goes, *'No me mates*. Don't kill me.' But the agent calls him a *comemierda*, and he shoots him anyway! You hear three loud bangs on the tape. Then a couple more agents go out there, and one says, 'What did you do, man?' And the first agent laughs. "What does it look like?' At the same time, cops are coming into the studio telling Kelly and the bassist to lie on the floor. She thought they were going to die. The DEA agents ripped out the reel-to-reel that was still going, and they took it with them."

Dan glanced at Elaine McHale, who was still listening to Martha Cruz with perfect composure. He knew that she had to be horrified. Had to know where this story was going: If it was true, her former lover had committed murder not once but twice—Luis Barrios and Kelly Dorff.

Martha continued. "A few months ago Kelly met that same agent. His name was Vincent Hooper. She almost didn't recognize him because he had grown a beard. She nearly fainted. This was the same guy. The same. She was afraid to say anything, and nobody would believe her anyway. One day she told me about it. I told her not to do anything, just be quiet and wait for it to be over. After they arrested Miguel, it would be okay. We couldn't tell Rick because then Miguel would know. He might kill her, or Rick, or all of us. But she was getting pushed by the DEA too, and she was afraid of Agent Hooper. Then Kelly thought of a way out. She remembered the DAT tape. The house had a studio with a reel-to-reel and also a digital-analog tape used for backup.

"Kelly went to see the owner's wife. He was put in jail, but his wife still had his equipment waiting for when he gets out, just the way he left it. The DEA got the reel-to-reel, but not the DAT tape. If you don't know sound engineering, you'd miss it. The owner's wife let Kelly have the DAT tape, then Kelly called up Vincent Hooper and told him she wouldn't snitch for him anymore. I told her she had to. She couldn't even play anymore—"

Martha Cruz stopped speaking, but her body and face were tensed as if for the next words. She stared ahead of her. The smoke from her cigarette curled into two strands, intertwined, that drifted toward the open door.

Dan glanced at Elaine. She made a small shake of her head. Wait.

After a moment Martha's lips moved. She left them parted as if she had seen a vision that stunned her. She spoke again. "Kelly was so scared she couldn't concentrate on the music. I said . . . make them leave you alone. You have to. If you don't, I'll push you out of the band, I swear. I could have, even if it was her band. Miguel didn't want to put any more money into it as long as she was in control. I don't know if . . . her death was my fault. I couldn't stand that. Maybe I shouldn't have told her to call Vincent Hooper, but the band had to finish the demo. The concert is only next weekend, and Friedman is coming from New York, and I had to do *something*."

As if waking, Martha Cruz looked down at her cigarette, then leaned over to crush it out in her empty coffee cup. She crossed her arms tightly over her chest.

Through the salon door Dan could see that the boat had slowly revolved on its pivot of anchor line, its stern swinging more to the south with the tide. There were no lights out there, only darkness.

He heard Elaine get up and looked back to see her going over to the sofa. She sat on the edge, hands in her lap. "Martha . . . where is the tape?"

"I talked to you because Dan said to, but I'm not going to let you have the tape."

"Where is it?"

Martha's eyes moved to Dan. "It's in my studio."

"No." He exhaled. "Your studio or the DEA's?"

"Mine."

Dan made a pained smile in Elaine's direction. "Martha's studio is at Salazar's house."

Elaine said, "Well, can't she go get it?"

Martha pushed back her hair, exposing the left side of her face. Elaine winced. "Miguel did this to me last night. He said . . . if he ever caught me with Dan Galindo again, he would kill me. Then at the studio today—Manatee Studios—we got into an argument. He took me to his car and raped me in the backseat. He's done it before, and usually I do what he tells me after that. But this time I sneaked out during a break and I didn't come back." She was crying. "I didn't know, when I left the house today, that I wouldn't be back. I'd have brought you the tape if I'd known, but I can't get it now!"

Elaine put a hand on her shoulder.

Dan said, "No. You won't go back there."

Martha looked at him. "You have to go."

"Dan? Why should Dan go?"

"Because he's the only one," Martha said. "I trust him. It wouldn't be hard. I have my key to the studio—"

"Wait a minute," Dan said.

Martha came across the salon and looked down at him as he sat in the armchair. "There's no fence, only some bushes. Nobody ever goes over there. They keep the dogs inside—"

"Absolutely not," Elaine said.

"It wouldn't be hard. He just unlocks the door, takes it off the shelf, and leaves."

The two women argued over Dan's head. Elaine said, "Martha, did you ever personally listen to this tape?"

Martha hesitated. "Well, no, but Kelly told me what was on it."

"Then how do you know she wasn't making it up?"

"Make that up? I saw the tape! She gave it to me to keep for her."

Dan said, "Wait. This is simple. Martha, just tell one of the maids to bring it to you."

"Right. Find one who isn't loyal to Miguel. They tell him everything."

Elaine said, "I need to check this out. I can make a few calls on Monday."

Dan said, "Monday is too late, Elaine. Rick and I have to meet Paxton on Monday and give him an answer."

"I'll ask for an extension."

"You do that. And tell him all about Agent Hooper while you're at it."

Elaine gave him a sharp look and went over to the door. She put a hand on the frame and stared out.

Dan said, "I refuse to send Rick onto Salazar's property. We can't send Arlo. Bobby Doyle is a pothead. How about the other guy, the bassist? What about him?"

Martha said, "No. You're the only one."

"Why?"

"Scott can't do it. He'd ask me why. He's always asking questions. What would I tell him? What if he messed up? He doesn't care about Rick. I trust you."

"He cares about the band, though. You're in it. Tell him the truth. Miguel beat you up."

At the door Elaine had turned back around. "No. Not Scott Irwin."

"Why not?" It took Dan about two seconds to get it. "He's DEA, isn't he?"

Martha screamed, *"What!"* She spun around and kicked the nearest thing, the built-in cabinet holding the television and stereo. "He's a *narc*? I could kill him. What about the concert? Oh, no. Another bass player. Rick is going to shit. How could this *happen*?"

Dan turned her around. "Hey. Calm down. Tomorrow Miguel is going to meet Vincent Hooper. The DEA is going to offer him a suitcase with money in it. Hooper will be wired, and cameras will be going. If Salazar agrees to the deal, the DEA will arrest him on the spot. Then you can go back to the house. I'll go with you."

Martha looked up at him, then nodded. "Okay. That would work."

"Good. So tonight I want you to call Miguel—"

"No!"

"Tell him you went to a hotel, not to worry, and you'll be home tomorrow night. We don't want him too nervous to miss the meeting."

Elaine was shaking her head. "A hotel? And who is she with, Dan? You're obviously not home. If he has caller-ID and she calls from the boat—"

"You're right." Dan dropped his hands by his sides. "We'll just have to hope the meeting goes as planned."

Martha said, "It will. When it comes to business, Miguel doesn't let anything bother him. It's just his personal life that's so screwed."

There were two staterooms below. Elaine said she and Martha would share the one with two bunks, and Dan could have the master stateroom. He said he preferred to sleep on the sofa, not in Miguel Salazar's bed.

They found something to eat in the cabinets: crackers, soup, and canned tuna. Around two in the morning Martha went off to sleep, leaving Dan and Elaine with the mess. "Let Miguel clean it up," Dan told her. "It makes me sick, being on this damned boat. Sick to think I wanted to put Josh on it. I hate breathing the air in here."

Elaine turned around from the sink, a soapy dish in her hands. "Then go outside and cool off."

Dan went on deck to make sure the anchor rope was

secure and the running lights were on. The sky was clear and starry black. Light fell through the salon door and windows and shone on the water, where it wobbled slowly on the surface.

Dan thought about what Martha had told them. It seemed incredible. He had no doubt, however, that Vincent Hooper could have shot an unarmed man, particularly if that same man was a murdering doper who had slipped away from him the year before—Hooper's way of handing down some belated, but well deserved, justice.

Making his way aft along the port side, Dan heard Elaine call to him from the tower. He climbed the ladder and they sat on the narrow seat up there under the white canvas top, twenty feet above the water. She had brought two mugs of hot tea.

"What are you thinking?" Dan asked.

Elaine turned up the collar of her jacket. "I was thinking of Vince." Then she glanced at Dan, smiling a little. "How sad this would be if it's true."

"You can't believe it."

"I guess I don't want to." She sipped her tea. The steam rose from the insulated plastic mug.

Dan propped his feet on the stainless steel railing in front of them. "Don't tell me you're sorry you and he broke up."

"No. I can't say that. But . . . a person can't just . . . pretend it never happened." She was looking at Dan. "You think he murdered Luis Barrios, don't you? Would that make you happier if he did?"

"I wouldn't be surprised, but I can't say it would make me happy," Dan said. Elaine's intelligent face was open without being naive. A light breeze ruffled her short hair. He asked, "What about Vince Hooper and Kelly?"

"Well, I know he pushed her hard. He believed he had to. It occurred to me that Kelly could have invented this story. She was there, of course, so she has her own version of the events. Let's say she turned them around so convincingly, even in her own mind, that she believed it that way. Then she made Martha believe it."

Dan took her hand. "Oh, Elaine. That's not what I'm talking about. You can't even conceive of it, can you? He's not a nice guy."

Her eyes widened slightly. "You mean . . . that Vince murdered Kelly Dorff? No. He couldn't have. He was with Scott Irwin."

"According to whom?"

"Scott told me."

Dan remembered him: Scott, the phony bass player. Blue hair shaved halfway up one side of his head. "He wouldn't cover for Vince, would he?"

"Good Lord, no. I think Miguel Salazar did it. If Kelly were gone, Martha Cruz would be the star of the show. You heard her tonight. Salazar is obsessed with her. He could have killed Kelly and tried to frame you for it. He told the police he was home playing cards with his sister when Kelly died. But Scott Irwin told me that Salazar left the house before Kelly did, knowing where she was going."

Elaine shrugged. "In any event, we'll find out more tomorrow, once we have the tape. If it exists."

Dan put down his tea. He faced her and said, "You need to believe Hooper didn't do it. You're still in love with that SOB. Aren't you?"

"Oh, come on. If I can't immediately accept Kelly Dorff's story, it's not personal. Since you seem to be concerned, my motivation is simply to find out how far the U.S. attorney's office could be drawn into this."

"Never let your emotions run away with you."

She looked at him straight on. "I don't usually. Except with Vince. I know what you're thinking. Maybe you're right. Poor Elaine, running out of control."

"That's not what I meant," he said.

"I'm sorry. I know you didn't."

Dan said, "Tell me something. I need a woman's perspective here. Why would a smart girl like Martha put up with Salazar? For the band? Is she that ambitious?"

Elaine held her mug with both hands and took a sip. "Okay. This is what I think. Kelly once told me that Salazar was 'hot.' That he's scary and sexy. That appeals to some women, like it or not, at least in the fantasy stage. Sex and danger. The fantasy doesn't last, of course, but by the time they realize what they've gotten themselves into, it's too late. I think Martha went into it thinking she would use him. She stayed because he excited her. Then she couldn't get out."

Sex and danger. Dan thought of Vincent Hooper, wondering if that had caught Elaine's attention. He said, "Martha's pretty sexy herself. Before he shot at me tonight, Salazar said he loved her. Or whatever he thinks is love. She must've driven him wild."

Elaine raised her brows. "You find her attractive?"

"Not really."

"Yes, you do."

"Well . . . in theory. I mean, I wouldn't consider, in real terms, sleeping with a girl like that, but in an abstract sort of way she's attractive, I suppose."

Elaine laughed. Her face, usually so serious, glowed with amusement. She trailed off with a sigh, hiccuped a giggle, then started again. Then she said, "You're too much."

"Sexy and dangerous Daniel Galindo."

"Well—" She put down her mug and leaned over laughing, then wiped her eyes on the sleeve of her jacket. Looked at him and bit her lower lip.

He smiled at her. "Thank you, Elaine."

"I'm sorry, it's just . . . this whole night has been crazy." She let out a breath, then frowned. "Why are you looking at me like that?"

"It just hit me. All these years I've known you, I never told you how pretty you are."

"Oh, please." She darted a glance toward the heavens. Her lashes cast a faint shadow across her cheek.

Dan leaned over and kissed her. Then put his arm

around her and did it again. The fleecy jacket was soft and warm.

She drew back. "Oh, my God."

He looked at her. "That's so reassuring."

"No, I didn't mean that. I meant . . . No, you're very attractive, Dan. I've always thought so. And . . . I like being with you, but please. After a total disaster with a married man, I can't do that anymore. I won't."

"Elaine—" He took her hand. "I'm not going back to Lisa."

"You said you were."

"Well . . . I'm not." He kissed her knuckles.

"You're sure?"

"Positive. She's just not the kind of woman who would drag me onto a dance floor in a crowded bar and embarrass me by asking the band to play 'Happy Birthday.'"

"I see. And that's what you want?"

He stood and pulled her up off the seat. She didn't object. Dan kissed her forehead, then moved his nose slowly through her hair, taking in the clean, fresh scent of it. He felt the blood surge through his body so fast it took his breath. That useless pounding with Lisa. Trying to make something that wasn't.

He kissed each corner of Elaine's mouth, then nudged her lips apart and slid his tongue inside. She welcomed him eagerly and moved her hands down his back to pull his hips tightly against her. No, he decided, there wouldn't be any problem here.

CHAPTER 36

Setting up Manatee Studios, the DEA had built a new control room, the original too cramped to hold the sophisticated recording equipment Rick Robbins had demanded. He had wanted top quality for the Mayhem demo tape. The DEA had eaten the cost.

Now, at two-thirty on Sunday afternoon, Vincent Hooper stood in the middle of a space quickly being reduced to bare concrete and two-by-fours. The sound engineer and his men were loading the equipment on dollies to take back to wherever they had rented it from. Vincent would have to write up a report on all this. How much money spent, and the result of the expenditures. The result, in this case, being nothing. Not precisely zero, because they had netted Rick Robbins. Thinking about Robbins, with his fruitflavored Tums, his nervous laughter, and his rumpled tweed jacket, Vincent preferred a perfect zero.

At 11:54, a few minutes early, he had arrived at

Venezia, a trendy hangout for the pasta-and-merlot crowd on Las Olas Avenue in downtown Fort Lauderdale. Vincent had dressed in his Victor Ramirez outfit of silk jacket, pleated slacks, and gold jewelry. His briefcase contained $200,000 in cash, with the rest of it—supposedly—in the trunk of a Porsche Turbo-Carrera behind the restaurant. He had a body mike. There were six DEA agents and four Broward County deputies ready to make an arrest.

At 12:45 Vincent called Rick Robbins from his portable telephone. Robbins said he didn't know what had gone wrong, but he'd call him, he'd find out. Vincent calmly said no, he would handle it himself.

The maid at the Salazar house told him, *Lo siento, el señor Salazar está fuera del país.* Out of the country. Where? *No se, señor.* He had slipped through their fingers.

"Vince, what about the tapes?"

It took a second for the question to work through. Vincent looked around. The engineer, Willy Silva, was holding a cardboard box filled with reels and cassettes and plastic cases.

"What about them?" Vincent asked.

"These are the tracks that the band cut over the last few weeks. I've got some mixes as well, and the final demo tape. I finished it last night." Willy took out a cassette in a clear plastic box. "I don't mean to brag, but considering that I had to do overdubs on a new bassist, new drummer, *and* a new lead guitar, this is a great-sounding tape."

Vincent took the cassette from him, turned it over. It was labeled *Mayhem Demo, Manatee Studios, W. Silva, Sound Engineer.* The cassette was dark gray in color and oddly sized. "It's smaller than usual."

"It's a digital tape," Willy said. His hand was poised to take it back. "What are you going to do with it?"

"I can't let you keep it. We might need it for evidence. All of these tapes will have to remain in our property room until the U.S. attorney's office tells us what to do with them." Vincent nodded toward the boxes stacked in the corner. "Put it over there for now."

Willy Silva made an expression like Vincent had told him to leave his newborn son in the snow. "Well . . . let me make a copy," he said.

"Sorry. Tell you what. You get in touch with me in a couple of months, I'll have an answer. Don't worry, it won't get lost."

"You ought to make a copy for yourself, Vince. This demo might be valuable someday."

"Not my thing, Willy."

Two DEA agents were up on ladders taking out wiring and speakers. Vincent lit a cigarette and watched.

Last night he had called Elaine. She hadn't answered. Or hadn't wanted to answer. He was going to tell her . . . something. He wasn't sure what. He had believed, truly, that Elaine understood what kind of a life he had. The things he had to do because there was no one else to do them. He didn't feel betrayed, just disappointed. He had thought she was stronger than that.

Vincent noticed one of the agents point toward the door and laugh. The other whistled.

Scott Irwin stood there grinning. He extended his arms and made a little curtsy, then waved the men quiet. He had shaved his head. The blue hair was gone, and so were the ragged jeans and T-shirt. He came over to speak to Vincent.

"Cute," Vincent said.

"Like it? I look like Bobby Doyle. Give me a cigarette." He drew one out of Vincent's pack and borrowed his lighter. "Tough luck about Salazar," he said. "The SAC have anything to say about it?"

"The usual. He's catching it from the Feebies. Told you so, that kind of thing."

Scott Irwin thumbed the lighter and drew in smoke. He exhaled, then looked at Vincent. "What are you going to do?"

Meaning, what will you do if you get transferred to a desk job. Vincent didn't know what he would do. He had run out of ideas. He knew he ought to leave. Go to the office, start on his reports. He was tired. Standing and talking to this kid made him feel old. Vince Hooper had been chasing Pablo Escobar over the rooftops of Cali when Irwin was still at the academy.

"Do? We've got two dozen dopers to pick up, and that's starting tonight."

"I thought Wednesday."

"No. I talked to John Paxton. He says let's do it. Salazar didn't make the meeting, so he's probably on to us. That means the others could start taking off. Salazar might still be around, though. We'll drop by his house tonight and see if he's home." Vincent looked at Scott Irwin's head again and laughed. "Jesus. We were all getting used to the punk haircut. I assume the concert is over."

"Mayhem won't be there. The band is over, as of last night, and I'll tell you about that in a second. Where's Willy Silva? I'd like to get the demo tape, or a copy of it. My life as a rocker."

"The tape's over there in one of those boxes." Vincent tilted his head toward the stack of them. "Willy wanted it too. I told him we needed it for evidence, but go ahead and make a copy for yourself. Not for general release."

"Thanks."

Scott Irwin watched the men loading the mixing board onto a dolly. "Martha Cruz is gone. Vanished. I can't find Dan Galindo either."

Vincent drew on his cigarette and said nothing. Scott had a way of drawing stories out. Making them into a TV action drama. "Just cut to the chase, will you?"

"Last night during a break Martha went to the ladies' room and didn't come back. Salazar was here and he started asking, Where's Martha? Nobody knew. So he left and took Arlo Pate with him. I decided to follow. I lost them, but they'd been heading south, so on a hunch I went by Dan Galindo's place. His car was out front, and so was Salazar's. A few minutes later, Salazar and Arlo come out, they take off. I had two

choices, see where they went or check out the apartment. I went inside. The back door was unlocked.
Galindo wasn't there. I saw water and fish all over the
floor. The glass in his fish tank was broken. His clothes
were all over the bedroom, thrown into boxes. Looks
like he had to leave in a hurry."

"With Martha?"

"That's my guess. When I saw Martha yesterday, I
noticed she had a bruise on her face. She took me aside
and said that Salazar had beaten her up the night
before, and she wasn't going back to him. I'd say she
went to Galindo's house. Before she left the studio, she
told me that Bobby Doyle thinks Victor Ramirez is a
narc. I said, 'Yeah, he told me the same thing, but
don't let Miguel know.' And she said she wouldn't,
that she never told Miguel anything she did."

Scott turned his back on the room and flicked ashes
onto the bare concrete. "Martha said that something
was about to go down, and Rick was going to be
arrested. I said, 'No way. Martha, what're we gonna
do?' She said not to worry because she had a way to
save the band. I pressed her to tell me more about it,
but she wouldn't."

Scott Irwin's voice had dropped to barely a murmur, which Vincent had to strain to hear over the
wrenching metal noises from the control room. They
were ripping out an aluminum stud to get to the
wiring under the floor.

"I called Rick this morning. I said, 'Rick, what's
going on? Martha split. What about the band?' He

said, 'Sorry, man, Mayhem is history.' He said it was too bad and so forth and so on, thank you, good-bye. I said, 'Rick, where's Martha?' He told me not to worry about it, she was fine. Then he hung up."

Vincent looked at him. "Any ideas?"

The dolly and mixing board moved toward the door. The wheels squeaked, and the sound echoed on the bare walls.

"I thought of the tape that Kelly told you about."

Vincent could feel the weight of it coming down on him again. "Scott, there is no tape. I told you that."

Scott dropped his cigarette on the floor and stepped on it. Black leather shoes with heavy soles. "Okay, Vince."

Vincent said, "Looks like Salazar is after Galindo. Might save me the trouble. I was thinking Galindo might have tipped Salazar off. Now I'm not sure."

"No, it was Bobby Doyle's narc radar that picked you up, Hooper."

"Really? How come it didn't pick you up?"

"Because when Bobby passed around the joint, I inhaled."

"Very funny."

The debris was piling up on the floor now. The agents came down off the ladders and started rolling the wires onto a spool.

CHAPTER 37

Elaine waited for Dan to say something as he stood looking at the remains of his aquarium. It must have been a nice tank. The sides and back were still there, so that it looked like a stage set. A humming noise came from a small black box, uselessly blowing air through a clear plastic tube. Jagged pieces of glass attached at the corners hung downward, and sea grasses were draped over the front, washed forward by escaping water. The dead eyes of small striped fish stared up at the ceiling.

Dan turned off the aerator, then squatted on one heel, picking up the dead fish by their tails and placing them in a bowl. He got up and carried the bowl into the bathroom. Elaine heard the repeated sound of the toilet flushing.

They had driven to Dan's place so he could change into black pants and a navy blue sweater. He would be walking onto Salazar's property after dark, and in case anyone was home, they would be less likely to see him unlocking the door to Martha Cruz's rehearsal room if he blended into the shadows.

A telephone call that afternoon had determined that he and Martha could not simply drive in and retrieve the tape in broad daylight. Salazar might be there. Elaine had called John Paxton to ask if the DEA had taken him into custody. Paxton replied that Salazar had not shown up at the meeting with Victor Ramirez. "The DEA is pissed off. They know someone warned him, but they're not sure who. By the way, have you heard from Dan Galindo in the past twenty-four hours?"

"No, John, I haven't. What's going on?"

"He seems to have disappeared with Martha Cruz. The DEA can't find either of them. Vince Hooper wants to ask him some questions."

Elaine told him she would call Agent Hooper the minute she heard from Dan, although she couldn't imagine why he would call her. Then she asked, "Where is Miguel Salazar?"

"The staff at his house say he's gone back to Ecuador, but they could be lying."

Lies. Feeling sick, Elaine had hung up the phone, then wiped her sweaty palm on the thigh of her jeans. Now her job was on the line. If they didn't get the Barrios tape, she would be fired, and that would be the least of it. She could also be criminally prosecuted for assisting in a burglary.

Elaine looked at her watch: 6:15 P.M. It would be dark in another hour. Leaning over the sofa, she looked through the crack in the curtains. Dan had already moved his car around the corner, and Martha had taken hers; she would leave it in a parking lot near Elaine's house.

Water was running in the bathroom sink.

"Dan? We should go."

He came out drying his hands. "I'm getting bullet-proof glass in my next aquarium," he said.

At Elaine's house Martha Cruz spread a map of Broward County on the kitchen table and showed Elaine the route. Dan would have Martha's electronic gate opener, allowing them to get through the security gates at Lakewood Estates and the Isles of Lakewood.

Dan looked down at the map, hands on his hips. Elaine traced with her finger the access road into the Isles of Lakewood. It was a narrow road, more like a causeway a few hundred yards long, water on each side, ending in a free-form piece of land in the center of a lake. The road made a loop, with room for no more than a half dozen estate-sized homes. Salazar's was one of them. She remembered how isolated it had seemed as she looked across from the surveillance house. She recalled the soaring red-tile roof, the tennis court and pool, two-acre lawn sloping down to a small white sandy beach, the luffing sail of a beached cata-maran, the children running happily on the back ter-race. To the south a separate guest quarters had been converted into a studio for Martha Cruz.

"It's a narrow road," Elaine observed. "Where can we park?"

"Go around the loop," Martha said, tracing the road with her finger. "Let us off at a vacant lot about here, then we'll go straight to the studio—"

"We?" Dan shook his head.

Still leaning on her elbows, Martha looked up, her brow furrowing. Her black hair was twisted into a braid, and she had removed all her jewelry. "I'm going with you."

"Rick is my client; I'll handle it. I don't want you along. It's potentially dangerous."

"Miguel's not even home."

Elaine asked, "What about Arlo Pate?"

Dan said, "I'll take along a steak to throw at him. This won't take more than five minutes. I've seen the house. You and Martha park down the street at the vacant lot. I'll walk back, get in the car, and we'll leave."

"How will you know which is the right tape?" Martha sat back in her chair with her arms crossed. "Kelly didn't write 'DEA raid' on it. There are dozens of tapes, and I'm the only one who knows where it is. Even if I tell you, you might pick up the wrong one, and we're not going back."

Cocky bitch, Elaine thought.

Dan's face was tight with anger. Or fear perhaps. He knew what this involved. Martha had no idea. Even so, she had a point.

"Dan, she's right."

He was looking at Martha Cruz. "If Miguel is at

home, we're taking off. Understand? The tape isn't worth our lives, and I don't care what's on it."

"He isn't home," she insisted. "While you and Elaine were gone I called the house and made sure—"

"Oh, my God. Caller-ID," Elaine said.

"I used a *pay phone*, Elaine. Look, I'm not stupid. Believe me, I know what Miguel is. I saw him shoot Leon Davila."

They both looked at her.

"It was on the second-floor terrace. Miguel shot Leon in the chest three times, and he fell into the hot tub. Miguel doesn't know I saw. I'd gotten out of the tub, but I came back to see what Leon had to say. He had been on an errand for Miguel, delivering some cash. Arlo was up there fixing the plumbing, and he saw it too. I never asked, but I'm pretty sure that Arlo buried Leon's body out where they're widening the lake. Arlo used to work over there on the dragline."

"Why did Miguel shoot Leon?" Dan asked.

"Well, basically, aside from the fact that Leon was a cokehead and becoming undependable, he saw me naked and he was bragging about it. That tells you how coked out he was. I was surprised when Miguel shot him. I thought he'd just send him back to Ecuador. Maybe—now that I think of it—Miguel did it because of what I said about Leon. That he was ruining the band, and we'd never get a record contract with him in it—which was totally true."

Dan was staring at her. "Leon died because of what you said?"

She made a small laugh. "It's too bad what happened to Leon, but it wasn't my fault."

"No, you didn't shoot Leon. You expected Miguel to take care of it. Hadn't you already proved to yourself how much he would do for you? He turned his guest house into a studio, bought you a new keyboard. Paid everybody in the band. Gave you a car, jewelry, clothes. No, let me finish. What did you want most, Martha? You wanted to be the star. When it came to a choice between your best friend and your career, hey, too bad for Kelly Dorff."

"That's a lie! I never told him to get rid of Kelly!" Martha was on her feet now, fists clenched at her sides.

"I'm sure you didn't say to him, 'Miguel, kill Kelly for me.' What was it you said? I remember that last Sunday morning we were on the terrace of Miguel's house. I'd brought over a box of Kelly's things. Miguel didn't seem happy to have her as a guest. Then you said, in his presence, that you were afraid that Kelly would ruin the concert. That you wished she weren't in the band. How many other times had you said that to Miguel? And last Sunday were you holding back more than usual because I was there?"

Martha laughed, a single short peal of astonishment. "You think I wanted her *dead*?"

"You still needed her for the concert, but Miguel couldn't wait. Lucky thing that Rick came through with a new guitarist."

She rushed at him, screaming. Dan deflected her fists,

spun her around, and held her around the middle. Her flailing legs kicked over a kitchen chair.

Elaine moved quickly out of the way. "Martha! Stop it!"

She went limp, crying. "He didn't do it. He was upstairs with his sister." Dan let her go, and Martha stumbled back into a chair.

Elaine said, "No, Scott Irwin saw Miguel leave shortly before Kelly. And he knew where she was headed, correct? He could have arrived first, waited for her to let herself in using the spare key, then shot her with Dan's speargun. He hated Dan. Why not try to frame him for Kelly's murder?"

"Kelly was my best friend." Martha took the tissue that Elaine gave her, but kept her head bowed. The braid had come half undone, and her hair hung over her face. After a minute she looked up at Dan. "Are you still going to help me?"

"Let's get this straight," Dan said. "I'm going to get the tape, but I'm not doing it for you, Martha. It's for Rick. If you indirectly benefit, great. But I don't care."

Elaine put a hand on Martha's shoulder. "I'm going to talk to Dan for a minute. We'll be right back." She pulled on his wrist. In her bedroom, she closed the door and leaned on it. "I've never seen such a perfect match. That girl's as ruthless as Salazar." She opened the nightstand by the double bed. "I want you to take this." She handed him a .38 Smith & Wesson revolver in a brown leather belt holster.

"You want me to shoot Martha with it?"

"Be serious." Elaine flipped out the cylinder, unloaded the six bullets, then closed the gun and pulled the trigger. "Don't take it out unless you mean to shoot. Hold it with both hands, arms extended. Squeeze slowly—"

"I didn't know you were such a tough broad," Dan said. "Thanks, but if they catch me for an armed burglary, I'd be in real trouble."

"Yes, and if Salazar is at home, he'll kill you, and you can avoid jail completely."

"Give me the gun." He dropped it into the holster, then put it back into her nightstand.

She threw her arms around his neck. "Please, Dan. I know you want to help your client, but don't risk yourself for him. For me either. What I've done has been my choice, and I'll live with it."

He held her tightly. "I'll be careful."

Driving into Lakewood Estates, Elaine could see the buildings of the country club to the right beyond a landscaped parking lot, then an empty expanse of black, marked here and there with the vague shapes of sand traps. The guard shack was dead ahead, occupying an island that divided the road. Another two miles would bring them to the Isles of Lakewood. Martha sat in the front seat, Dan in the back. Martha kept a gate opener in her car, and she had brought it with her. As they neared the guard shack she pressed the button. Elaine slowed. Martha's thumb went up and down, pressing without result. The striped arm did not move. "Dammit! Oh, my God! They've changed the access code again!"

Elaine said quickly, "I have my badge."

"No." Dan's hand gripped her shoulder. "Just go through and tell the guard you took the wrong turn."

They came back out and parked at the country club. Martha said, "I'm sorry."

Elaine exhaled. "Now what?"

"We can walk in," Martha said.

"Dan, you've been to Salazar's house. What do you think?"

"It's risky," he said. "We might get around this guard gate, but the approach to the next one is narrow, with the lake on both sides. They might notice us."

Martha said, "We have to try!"

"There's no way in," Elaine said.

Elaine drove slowly along an unpaved road west of Lakewood Village. To their left was a swamp being drained for more houses. On the east side, a wide canal guarded the Isles of Lakewood, most of the home sites still vacant. Martha looked for landmarks. The overcast sky hid the sliver of moon.

Turning her headlights off, Elaine parked behind a weedy hill of dirt pushed to the side when the road had been bulldozed. Martha said nobody ever came out here, except for kids smoking pot. Construction debris was scattered around—five-gallon paint cans, old lumber, some twisted rebars. Crickets chirred in the weeds.

Dan explained that when the road was finished,

a long mound of earth would run alongside to keep motorists from seeing into the residential areas. Nothing had been planted yet; it was only weeds, bare rock, and black Everglades muck, which had dried to powdery dust.

The three of them climbed to the top of the hill, Dan catching Elaine by an arm when she nearly slipped backward on the loose ground. Across the lake, some hundred yards distant, the Isles of Lakewood spread out ahead of them, most of the home sites still undeveloped. A light shone weakly from a construction shack, a temporary metal building. There were some fuel tanks for the dragline, which sat idle, a sleeping brontosaurus with a huge steel bucket Elaine could have driven her car into. Farther away, past the vacant lots and over the trees, were the roofs of the houses already built. Martha pointed out Miguel Salazar's. There were one or two lights in the upper windows; nothing could be seen below that.

"My studio is on this side," Martha said. "The door faces the house, but there are trees between, so nobody could possibly see us. The dogs stay in the garage at night."

At Dan's direction, Elaine had driven to the nearest grocery store. He had purchased a styrofoam cooler, black plastic bags to cover its whiteness, two dark-colored towels, and an airtight container for the tape. Dan and Martha would float their clothing across and get dressed again on the other side.

Martha Cruz bounded down the slope and sat on a

rock to take off her boots, then her black jeans and sweater. She wore nothing underneath. She tossed her clothes into the cooler, then raised her arms over her head and moved as if she were dancing.

Elaine shivered, more from nerves than the cold. Dan turned back to look at her. He was a silhouette in the faint light from the construction shack. "We'll be back in ten minutes."

On the roof Arlo Pate stared south into the darkness. He could see the tops of trees, then the white, weedy ground of the vacant lot, and beyond that, a couple hundred yards away at the edge of the lake, was the boom of the dragline. About five minutes ago he had noticed headlights moving on the dirt road. Then they had gone out.

Usually it was high school kids smoking grass or making out or doing what he was doing, which was having a couple of beers, but this was Sunday night. In Lakewood Village they didn't usually party on a school night.

He would have forgotten it and opened another beer, but he had seen silhouettes on top of the hill. He couldn't tell how many. Two or three. Whoever it was, they came on down the slope.

It was when he saw someone go into the water that he stood up and kept watching. Swimming in this weather, sixty degrees. They had to be stoned or crazy. Or they wanted something. If they came this way, he should probably mention it to Miguel.

CHAPTER 38

Martha Cruz shrieked getting into the water, and Dan told her to be quiet. She rubbed her bare arms briskly, then submerged to her shoulders. Pushing the cooler out ahead, Dan stroked smoothly and silently into the lake. Martha dog-paddled behind him.

The rocky ground angled sharply and vanished into the gloom. The steel teeth of the dragline bucket had left deep gouge marks about two feet apart along the shore, as if a monster cat had clawed the earth. When he had lived in Lakewood, Dan used to hear in the distance the great clank and rattle of the machines as they chewed their way around a new subdivision, hoisting tons of pulverized rock from the ground, creating a lake here and higher ground there.

Reaching shore, Dan avoided the light from the construction shed and walked into the shadow of the dragline, a rock-scarred, red and white machine sitting on rusty steel tracks as high as his head. He dried off quickly, then helped Martha out of the water. He turned his back to give her some privacy, although it was too dark to see much. Across the lake he looked for Elaine but could see only the long, jagged hill a hundred yards away.

When Martha was dressed, she said urgently, "Let's go."

Dan pulled her back. "Hold it. I'm going first. When I see that it's okay, I'll flash my penlight two times." He picked his way by starlight through the darkness. He knew that past the construction zone was a vacant lot, then the Salazar property, marked by a line of hedge. They would come at the house from the side. Lake and pool to the right, street to the left. Find an open spot in the hedge, walk fifty yards to the guest house. Martha had the key. She would open the door while he stood guard. She would find the Barrios tape, lock the door, and then they would return by the same route.

Stopping at a pile of branches and old lumber, Dan turned and signaled. Martha ran across the open ground and stopped beside him, her breath light and quick. He went ahead to a tree, then she followed. At Salazar's property line, they crouched for a moment behind the hedge. Dan said, "Wait here." Martha nodded.

He stepped onto the lawn and saw Miguel Salazar with his hands braced on the terrace railing. Dan moved back quickly and dropped. "Stay down. It's Miguel."

"What? He's not supposed to be—"

"He's on the terrace. Let's get out of here."

"He'll go back inside," she whispered.

Dan pointed. "Right back the way you came. Now."

"No, let's wait."

Crouching, he dragged her by the arm.

Martha looked back over her shoulder toward the house. "What about the tape?"

"Forget the damned tape." Dan tightened his grip. At the same moment he heard heavy footsteps thudding from the right. "Get across the lake!" He shoved Martha and she took off.

Arlo Pate crashed out of the underbrush with a flashlight. Dan sent his shoulder into Pate's stomach, and the big man rocked back a step. The beam of the flashlight traced a wild arc through the branches overhead. Dan led him away from the lake, knowing he could run faster, hoping that Martha would be across by the time he hit the water himself. He passed some palm trees made green and pink by small landscaping lights, then heard the thud of a bullet hitting one of them.

Dan dove behind a low wall enclosing a flower garden and flattened himself in its shadow. Starlight revealed the silvery splash of water in a fountain. He heard low murmured voices then the shuffle of leaves. When the flashlight beam swept over the hedges where he lay, he leaped up and ran toward the lake, stumbling over a fallen palm frond in the dark, then scrambling up again. He saw the boom of the dragline and headed for it.

Arlo Pate yelled, "This way!"

Dan glanced around and saw Pate fifty yards behind. He broke into the open and picked up his speed. The light from the construction shed was on him now. The ground spurted up just ahead to his left, and he heard the whine of a ricochet. Pulling his sweater over his head, he ran for the dragline. In its shadow the lake was perfectly black, and he could get quickly out of pistol range.

He threw himself at the water. In that brief second of arc he filled his lungs then submerged. The cold hit his bare chest like a slap. He would zigzag under the surface, coming up for air each time in an unexpected spot, then go down again, moving steadily toward the opposite shore.

Nothing was visible, but Dan could gauge his depth by the variation in pressure on his ears. He stayed level at about four feet. He came up for air and dived again. When he surfaced the second time, a bullet pocked the water a few inches from his head. He dropped under.

As his arms moved in unison forward and around, he closed his eyes and let his body relax. Counted slowly. Willed his heart rate to drop. He realized suddenly that he had forgotten to notice his direction. He let himself sink toward the bottom. The slope would tell him which way to go. His lungs were already burning, desperate for air.

He put his feet on a rock. Strangely, the rock seemed to be vibrating. Through his eyelids he saw a flicker of light and looked up to see a steadily brightening glow as if dawn had arrived. At the same moment he heard the deep growl of an engine. He popped to the surface and pulled in a breath.

The dragline was rolling forward on its enormous tracks, spotlights pointed at Dan. He heard a squeal of metal and tilted his head back, looking upward. The bucket was rising, swinging out behind him. For an instant of incomprehension Dan could only stare at it. Then the cables let go and the thing fell as if in slow motion, tons of steel. Dan inverted and kicked for the bottom. He could feel the rush of water and pressure as the bucket swung past him horizontally, as if he were a small fish and a maniacal giant were trying to grab him in a net. He swam blindly, disoriented. The clank and roar were muffled, and he could tell which way was up only by the light playing over the surface.

If he came up Salazar could pick him off easily. As fear and a pounding heart burned away oxygen, Dan clamped his jaw shut. Curling up, losing his strength, he felt the water break past his mouth. He thought of Josh. And of Elaine waiting terrified on the opposite shore, unable to help him. He would rather have died in the ocean, where the water was clean and free. Not in this ugly, dark water with a bottom of unyielding rock covered by ooze.

Above him, the lights swung across the surface of the water, and the awful clank and groan went on.

Then he felt himself moving forward, rolling like a leaf in a rain gutter. A metal floor seemed to rise up beneath him. The air hit his face and he breathed, coughing and choking.

Dan slid down the immense metal bucket, grit and rock under his bare back. He saw the black sky above him, links of chain a foot across, three of them connected to a heavy cable. The bucket was being winched upward, water pouring through the holes and slits in the metal. He looked through one of them and saw the lights of Lakewood Village. Scrambling the ten feet or so to the other side, he could see moonlight glinting on the windshield of Elaine McHale's car. She was lost in the shadows.

The bucket swung closer to land. It was too late to jump out now. Dan saw Miguel Salazar fifty feet below, both hands on the gun, holding it steady. Dan saw a flash, heard a bullet ping off the bucket. Another one hit the chain, making sparks. The silencer hardly mattered over the shriek of the engine and slamming of the gears.

He looked down again and saw a slender figure in black standing beside the construction shed—Martha Cruz. She cupped her hands at her mouth and yelled. Salazar turned. The pistol dropped to his side and his left arm moved, a gesture of frustration. They were screaming at each other.

Dan crawled up the floor of the bucket, which had shifted to a less perilous incline. The mouth of it faced the dragline, and the steel teeth glinted in the spotlights. He reached the edge and looked down.

Salazar was pointing at the bucket. Martha shook her head vehemently, braid swinging. Then Salazar raised the pistol, aiming straight at her. Martha's hands went out, placating, begging.

Dan screamed, "No!"

At the same instant, cables squealing, the bucket dropped under him. He grabbed for the edge and held on. The descent was fast, but just before he slammed into the ground, the bucket slowed. With a reverberating crash of metal the back end hit first, then the front. The breath was knocked from his lungs.

He pushed up on shaking arms.

When his mind grasped what he was seeing between two of the steel teeth, he staggered backward and fell against the side. Miguel Salazar lay face up, trapped under the bucket. The edge had caught him mid-torso, and his chest, arms, and head were exposed. The teeth supported the front edge just enough not to have crushed him instantly. The front of his white shirt was bright red. Horror gleaming in his eyes, Salazar pushed at the massive weight. Blood streamed from his mouth and nose.

Then he went limp, and his head hit the ground. The engine of the dragline stopped roaring, and Dan could hear a last hiss of air from Salazar's chest.

Martha Cruz screamed into the silence.

Arlo Pate slid down the ladder from the cab and ran toward her, his heavy boots kicking up bits of rock. Before Dan could shout to warn her, Pate had picked

Martha up like a child. He was patting her back, and she buried her face in his denim jacket.

It took Dan a few seconds to stand. Holding onto the edge of the bucket, he managed not to stumble. He could hear Arlo Pate's heavy sobs, like the starter of a truck engine that wouldn't quite catch. Dan inched over to the pair of them. Pate looked over Martha's head at Dan.

"Sorry, man. When I saw Miguel aim at Martha, I figured out you were on her side." Still holding Martha on his shoulder, he pulled off his bandanna and wiped his face. "I feel bad. I let him hurt her before. I feel real bad."

Elaine's frantic voice came from across the water. Dan walked to the shoreline and cupped his hands at his mouth. "Salazar is dead. We're all right." Looking around, Dan spotted his sweater and went to put it on. His slacks were still dripping, and his socks squished in his shoes. His body was shivering from the cold.

Arlo Pate gently lowered Martha to her feet. She ran over and grabbed Dan by the arm. "Let's go get the tape now." There were twigs in her tangled hair, and her face was dirty and tear-streaked.

He knew she would go for the tape whatever he said. "All right, fine." Avoiding the front of the bucket, Dan told Arlo he ought to lift it off Miguel's body, then cut the spotlights. They would call the police from the house.

Arlo caught Dan's sleeve. "Are they going to arrest me?"

Dan stopped walking. All of them would be questioned. It would take the rest of the night. He would have to explain why he and Martha had come here, what they were after, and why. He said, "They won't arrest you. Here's what happened. We came for Martha's keyboard. We swam in because she's afraid of Miguel. Miguel saw us, tried to kill us, and you saved our lives. Okay?"

"Sure."

Dan slapped Arlo on one shoulder, then walked to the water's edge. "Elaine! I'll be right back."

He could see a movement onshore. "You said that last time!"

CHAPTER 39

In her studio Martha opened a cabinet and rummaged through a box while Dan stood by the open door. He combed his fingers through his hair, picking out bits of gravel. Under his sweater his skin burned from abrasions.

Martha was saying, "I hope the police don't take all of this. Seize it or whatever. I don't have receipts, but it's mine. Miguel bought it for me." She told Dan how hard it would be to replace the keyboard, which was a Korg Trinity worth almost $5,000. Plus the rest of it: computer backup, mixing board, microphones, speakers, amps, headphones—

"You know what?" Dan said. "I don't give a damn."

Martha's eyes came up from the box. "What's your problem?"

If she had been within range he might have slapped her. "My problem. Well, after nearly drowning, getting shot at, then seeing a man crushed like a roach, I just can't get too worked up over how hard it would be to replace your fucking *keyboard*!"

She stared at him a moment then went back to the tapes.

"What do you think? Did Miguel kill Kelly for you?"

The only reply was the clicking of plastic.

"Your best friend, remember her? The girl who paid the price for your ambition."

Martha held up a tape then sent it toward Dan, an easy toss. He caught it in one hand, a gray cassette inside a clear plastic case. The label said PARTY.

When she spoke, her voice trembled. "That's what we came for. I've already cried over Kelly. Now Miguel is dead. You may think I never loved him, but you're wrong." She pushed past Dan. "I'm going to get some things from my room."

They walked in silence up the herringboned brick path to the terrace, their way lit by small lamps making pools of light. Martha loosened her braid, and by the time they had crossed the terrace and were inside the living room, she was fluffing her hair into its usual dark cloud of curls. Dan watched her, both fascinated and repulsed, not able to decide if he admired or hated Martha Cruz.

"It's so quiet in here." Her voice seemed to echo on the marble floors and high windows. "Everyone left for Guayaquil, that's what Arlo said. Miguel would have been gone tomorrow." Martha trotted up the stairs.

"Don't be long," Dan said. "I want Arlo to drive me around to Elaine's car so I can give her the tape before the police get here."

Martha turned around on the stairs to look at him. "Give it to Elaine? She works with the DEA."

"No, she's a federal prosecutor," Dan said, "and I trust her."

Martha came down the stairs. "They want to put Rick in jail."

"Rick is my client. I'll handle this."

"Well, he's my manager. Don't be stupid."

"And don't you be such a bitch."

Before he could think, Martha had snatched the cassette away. "This is mine, you know."

Dan grabbed her wrist and peeled her fingers off the cassette. He gave her a little shove toward the stairs. "Hurry up. I don't want to hear your mouth again."

A loud knock on the front door made them both look in that direction. The knock changed into deep thuds.

At the same time a voice shouted, "Open up! Federal officers!" The door flew back and armed men came through it, a dozen or more. The letters DEA were printed like an insignia on the upper left of their dark zippered jackets. Martha jumped back and screamed.

One of them shouted at her, "Where is Miguel Salazar?"

Vincent Hooper spotted Dan and came across the living room, gun extended in both hands. "Get down on the floor, hands behind your head."

Others ran up the stairs or deeper into the house.

"I said, get down!" Hooper's gun pointed straight at Dan's chest.

Before Dan could reply, Martha dashed in front of him, grabbed the tape, and ran toward the terrace. Another agent followed her. He had a shaved head, but Dan recognized him—Scott Irwin.

He could see what was happening. Using the arrest of Miguel Salazar as a cover, they had come in for the Barrios tape.

Turning to look behind her, Martha's eyes widened and she stumbled to a stop. "Scott! You son of a bitch!" She kicked him in the shins with her boot. When Hooper's attention went for an instant to his partner, Dan elbowed him in the side of his head. Martha ran onto the terrace, and Irwin pursued her. Dan followed. He heard the gunshot behind him, saw bits of glass from the door blow onto the terrace and fall like rain into the swimming pool. He skidded over the bits of glass and ran toward the railing. He planted his hands then vaulted over it, landing in the thick grass and rolling.

Irwin was just ahead, and farther out, Martha Cruz. They disappeared into the trees. As Dan raced over the lawn he glanced back and saw Hooper swinging a leg over the railing. Dan had the advantage; he knew where Martha was going.

He broke through the hedge and ran across the vacant lot praying not to fall on the uneven ground. Ahead he could hear thuds and snapping twigs. Then Martha screamed. Dan saw the dragline, its colors barely visible in the dim light from the shed. The boom soared over it and the massive bucket lay on the ground draped with lengths of chain. At the rear of the dragline, directly behind the twin steel tracks, Scott Irwin had caught up to Martha Cruz. He grabbed her by the hair and swung her to the ground. He reached down to rip something from her hands, and she curled around it.

Irwin did not notice Dan speeding toward the front of the bucket. A pistol lay on the ground beside Miguel Salazar. Dan found it in the darkness, picked it up, and came around the back of the dragline in the dark. Irwin was bent over Martha. "Give me the fucking tape!" He punched her in the ribs.

From just behind him Dan screamed, "I've got a gun! Get away from her." He shouted across the water, "Elaine! Call the cops!" If she answered, he didn't hear it. Irwin seemed frozen in position, his weight on one knee. Martha was curled up, half hidden by his body.

Irwin slowly turned his head. Dan stepped into the light and came around so that Irwin could see him. Both men were breathing heavily. He yelled again, "Let her go! Do it or I'll *shoot*." He heard his voice crack. The barrel of the pistol was three feet from Irwin's temple. Dan could see the end of the silencer jerking.

"You're going to shoot me in the head?" Irwin spoke calmly. "Have you ever killed a man, Galindo?"

"Martha, give him the tape."

"No! Shoot him!"

"Give him the damned tape!"

Martha was sobbing. Irwin still held her by the hair. "If you pull that trigger you'll be sent away for murder."

Dan's muscles were jumping. "I won't kill you. I'll put one in your ass. Now let her *go*."

As if to comply, Scott Irwin moved back slightly. Then his right hand reached into his open jacket and a gun barrel glinted in the light. He put the gun under Martha's jaw. She screamed and kicked. Irwin jerked on her hair to shut her up.

Dan yelled, "You want the tape, take it!"

"Drop the gun or I'll blow her fucking head off!"

Footsteps were coming closer. A heavy tread. Dan prayed for Arlo Pate.

Vincent Hooper sped into the clearing. Dan heard his intake of breath as he came to a dead stop. The light was in his eyes. In a crouch he swung his pistol toward Irwin, then toward Dan. The barrel of his pistol swung around again, then back. He shouted, "Irwin!"

"I'm here! Galindo has a gun on me. Take him down!"

Dan screamed, "You want the tape, you can have it. Martha, give it to him!"

Hooper was circling sideways, shifting his position to see them all. "What've you got there, Galindo? A .22? Not much of a weapon. You could miss. I'd blow you apart before you squeezed off a second round."

"Martha! For God's sake give him the tape!"

She awkwardly threw the cassette toward Vincent Hooper. The timing was off. The cassette clattered to the ground in the space between them, and the tape fell out of its case.

With his gun still pointing at Dan, Vincent Hooper looked over at what she had thrown. "What is this?"

"It's Barrios!" Irwin screamed, "Galindo! Drop it or I'll blow the bitch away!"

Hooper's head turned toward Scott Irwin, a momentary flicker of confusion. In that instant Dan knew that only one of these agents had come for the tape. Then the memory of two facts burst into Dan's mind with such force that he nearly staggered. His spare key had been found in Kelly Dorff's pocket. The neighbor had heard a scream from inside the apartment.

"Irwin!" His voice ripped into the darkness. "You shot Kelly Dorff with my speargun! It was you!"

"He's flipping out, Vince. Shoot him!"

"Listen to me!" Dan circled slowly left, keeping Scott Irwin between himself and Hooper. "Kelly had my spare key in her pocket when she died. The doors were locked. Whoever killed her went out the front and turned the thumb lock, but he couldn't turn the dead bolt."

Hooper leveled his 9mm pistol at Dan's heart. "Last chance, Galindo!"

Dan forced his words through a throat clenched with fear. "She opened the door to somebody she trusted. I know this because the neighbor heard a scream from inside the apartment. A scream, then the crash of my aquarium. The killer didn't force his way in. He had time to pick up a speargun, maybe asking her, Hey, what's this? When he aimed at her, she knew what he'd come for. She screamed. She pulled the tank over when she fell."

"Shut him up, he's crazy!"

Dan glanced at Irwin, then at Hooper, who was moving closer, closing the gap. "Who would Kelly have opened the door to? Not Miguel Salazar. And not you. She was scared to death of the DEA. Who, then? Her friend in the band. The same guy who left Salazar's house a few minutes after she did that night. Scott Irwin knew where she was going."

Dan's hands were shaking so hard he had to hold the gun with both of them.

Irwin turned his head to follow Dan as he circled slowly. Shadows shifted on the ground.

Hooper's voice was low and calm. "Lower the pistol. Nobody's going to get hurt here. I'm not going to shoot you if you lower the gun."

"Oh, Jesus," Dan choked out. He dropped the gun by his side, expecting a bullet to tear into his chest.

"Now talk to me."

"Vince, what the hell—"

"Be quiet," he said to Irwin. His dark eyes were still on Dan. "Talk to me."

"I thought you might have done it, Hooper. You had a reason—to keep Kelly quiet about Luis Barrios. She claimed you shot him in cold blood. But I don't think you killed Kelly, and I don't believe you sent

Scott to do it. That would be gutless. You're a son of a bitch, Hooper, but you're not a coward. Right now your buddy has a pistol to that girl's head. Did you happen to notice that? Are you going to let him shoot an unarmed civilian?"

"Vince, for God's sake! Take him out. He's a scumbag. He works for the dopers."

"Did you know that Scott Irwin murdered Kelly?" Dan was talking faster. "I don't think he told you. Elaine McHale says he claimed to have an alibi. He was supposedly with you. Did you cover for him? You'd lie for a member of your team, but I don't think you'd lie to protect a killer."

Irwin was pivoting on his knee toward Dan. The barrel of his gun swung around. There were two flashes of light almost simultaneously and two loud shots. Irwin's went wild. He sank to his knees and awkwardly crumpled.

Martha Cruz scrambled out of the way.

Holstering his gun, Vincent Hooper shouted at Dan as he ran. "You! Stay back!" He dropped beside Irwin and pulled open his jacket. "Oh, my God."

From the darkness came the voices of the other agents who had heard the noise. Flashlights danced in the trees. Hooper yelled for somebody to call air rescue.

Irwin was gasping, "Why . . . did you—"

"Because he was unarmed!" Hooper stripped off his own jacket and holster, then a black pullover, which he pressed against Irwin's side.

One of the agents threw Dan to the ground and put a foot on the back of his neck. "I didn't shoot him!" Dan yelled.

"Shut up!"

Through the legs of the dozen men milling around, Dan raised his head far enough to see. One of the agents discovered Salazar's body, and flashlights were trained on it. A familiar pair of blue jeans and sneakers hurried through the group, paused, then a moment later came toward Dan. By twisting his head around he could see Elaine McHale. She told the man to let him up. Elaine steadied Dan by grabbing his arm.

"I drove around by the entrance and showed my badge to get in. Are you all right?" She looked at him intently. Dan said that he was, then pulled her out of earshot of the men and told her what had just happened.

Her eyes slowly closed, then opened. She glanced over her shoulder at Vincent Hooper then walked over to stand behind him. Dan followed a few steps behind.

Hooper had Irwin's head in his lap now. "Hey, you're going to make it. Don't give up on me. Come on, Scott."

The younger agent's chest was working up and down.

Elaine sat on one heel. "Scott? Can you see me? This is Elaine McHale."

His eyes moved toward her.

"Did you kill Kelly Dorff?"

Hooper looked fiercely at Elaine, this woman who by that question had placed herself on the other side.

"Yes." The word was a whisper.

"Oh, my God," Hooper groaned. "He said he needed an alibi for missing a meeting with a Miami narcotics cop."

Elaine glanced at him, then leaned closer to Irwin. "Did you ever tell Agent Hooper what you did?"

"No."

"Leave him alone, Elaine."

Irwin could barely mouth the words. "She was going to damage . . . the agency, and blow the operation. I had to."

Hooper looked around and screamed, "Where the hell are the paramedics?"

Scott Irwin weakly grabbed Hooper's arm to get his attention. "Vince . . . I wanted . . . Galindo. Like you . . . and Barrios. You shot him. Dirty doper. They all are."

"No. No. Barrios had a gun. I told you."

"But . . . he threw it down first. Kelly said . . . it's on the tape." Irwin was breathing faster. "Oh, God, it hurts. Vince—"

"Take it easy, Scott. Okay. Don't talk anymore. Hang on, buddy, you're going to be all right."

A helicopter was coming in fast now, a Broward County sheriff's copter, its spotlight playing over the ground, catching the lake, then the boom of the drag-line. The light settled on the people standing around Scott Irwin. He was pinned in a wash of blinding white.

Dan felt the downdraft. His hair whipped in the wind, and the agents' jackets fluttered. Dust rose up, and dried weeds and trash swept across the ground. Then the chopper settled a distance away, and two paramedics jumped out with their equipment.

Scott Irwin was still looking up. The dust was in his eyes, but he wasn't blinking. Dan moved aside for the paramedics. He noticed Elaine speaking with Vincent Hooper, her hand on his forearm. Their words were inaudible in the whine from the chopper. It was still running, ready to take off. Then Elaine walked back to Dan.

Her short hair was tousled. "I told Vince we're leaving. They can get in touch with you later. Where's the tape?"

"Martha tossed it to Hooper. He didn't pick it up. I don't know where it is now."

She looked at Dan directly. "I have to turn it in to the U.S. attorney."

Dan said, "Sorry, Elaine. It's for Rick."

"As a federal officer, I'm demanding that tape."

"I don't have it."

She exhaled and looked around. "Well, where is it?"

"Martha might have picked it up. She was here a minute ago." Dan walked past the crowd to get a better view. Martha Cruz was nowhere in sight.

CHAPTER 40

From the driver's seat Elaine looked over at Dan. He could see her face clearly by the lights of the interstate and oncoming traffic.

"I'm fine," he said.

"Your forehead is bruised," she said.

"I have bruises all over, which you can check out later if you like." He caressed her cheek. The amber glow made Elaine's eyes appear huge. "Thank you for getting me out of there."

She grabbed his hand. "I have never been so frightened, watching you in that bucket. Expecting it to tip, and I'd see you fall. Knowing that Miguel Salazar was waiting. And then Scott!"

Dan asked, "What did you say to Hooper about our reason for going to Salazar's house?"

"The truth—that Martha wanted to give you the Barrios tape. Vince never believed it existed. He wants very badly to hear it."

"I'm sure."

Elaine glanced over at Dan. "Understand something. Vince believed, truly he did, that Luis Barrios shot first. Now he wonders if he could have imagined Barrios shooting at him. There was so much noise and confusion, and he has to admit that he hated the man." She put a hand on Dan's arm. "If I talk about Vince, it isn't to excuse him."

Dan saw the green interstate signs counting down the streets, heading toward the center of Miami. "You're saying that if Hooper killed Luis Barrios, it was an accident? Or his mind slipped? I don't think so. Not Hooper. You should've seen the amount of control he had tonight. Irwin's screaming, I nearly pass out, and Vincent Hooper is rock steady." Dan laughed in disbelief. "He blew away his own partner. He shot him. No hesitation. If it weren't for Hooper, I'd be dead."

Elaine held Dan's hand. "I suppose he appreciates the irony of that as well as you do."

Dan asked, "Why did Scott Irwin do it? He said Kelly would have blown the operation. That's no reason to commit murder."

"No, he probably did it for Vince."

Dan looked at her.

"Oh, it wasn't what you're thinking. Scott was devoted to Vince. Many of the younger agents admire him, but Scott took everything Vince said so seriously. 'We're the last line of defense, the only ones with any guts,' that sort of thing. Scott believed that Kelly Dorff would have destroyed Vincent Hooper and that meant the destruction of everything noble and brave. I'm certain that Scott would have given anything to be like Vince."

For a long moment Elaine seemed lost in her thoughts. Then she said, "Someday Vince is going to realize that he helped shape Scott Irwin into what he was. He'll carry that guilt with him as long as he lives."

"I'm glad to know the guy has a heart," Dan said. "What is your office going to do with Rick Robbins?"

"I really can't say. I'm not on the case anymore."

"Well, give me an opinion, then. An agent on the case murdered the confidential informant and tried to kill the defense attorney. The man you wanted Rick Robbins to testify against is now dead. How can Rick possibly be prosecuted? What jury would convict him?"

"Dan, I can't discuss it."

"Okay." He pointed at her car phone. "May I use that?"

"Why?"

"To order a pizza." When Elaine looked around, Dan said, "I want to call my client. It just occurred to me—and I should have thought of it sooner—that the raid on Salazar's place wasn't to get the Barrios tape—that was Scott Irwin's agenda. The DEA wanted Salazar. This tells me there's a sweep going on tonight, and Rick may be on the list." Dan waited for a response from Elaine.

"I don't know," she said honestly.

"Then I need to find Rick. He has to stay out of sight

until after I talk to John Paxton tomorrow and persuade him not to prosecute. So may I use your phone?"

She waved for him to go ahead.

Dan dialed Rick's home number. Sandy answered.

"Sandy, this is Dan. Let me talk to Rick." He listened for a while, then said good-bye and disconnected. He put the telephone back in its holder.

"What was that?" Elaine asked.

"The man refuses to give up. Rick's wife says that he's taking Joel Friedman to dinner tonight, trying to sweet-talk him into giving Martha Cruz a special audition." Dan said, "Friedman's a talent scout with Capitol Records. Do you mind driving by Miami Beach? They're at the Delano."

Elaine stared at him. "You're going into the Delano like that? Your pants are still wet and your sweater is torn."

"It's a very hip place, the Delano. You don't have to go in. Find a place to double-park. I'll only be a minute."

She was still looking at him. "When you say that, I don't believe you."

The hotel was on Ocean Drive, backing up to the Atlantic. Dan pointed at the valet parking entrance, which swept up under a portico surrounded by high hedges. The valet took a look at Elaine's Ford sedan, then at Dan and hesitated taking the keys.

She showed him her badge.

The lobby was bare except for avant-garde pieces

of furniture placed here and there, red or purple uphostered things on skinny black metal legs. The floors were wood, the ceilings high, and wide doors at the far end opened on the Atlantic. Long, gauzy white panels floated in the breeze coming through the building.

Dan walked straight back through the lobby, then through a lounge area with dimly lit niches separated by more curtains. The people looked up from their wine or their cocktails, staring as Dan and Elaine passed. A maître d' put himself in their path.

"Sir, may I help you?"

Elaine held up her badge, and the man melted away.

The bar opened to a dining area. Rick was not there. Dan kept walking through the wide-open doors. The terrace was under a white canvas canopy, the tables were draped in white, and the waiters wore white jackets. The back garden of the Delano, with its topiary and long, shallow swimming pool, extended toward the ocean, stopping at a white picket fence. The narrow grounds were dotted with people out strolling and carrying drinks.

Elaine saw them before Dan did, and pointed. There in a vine-covered niche to one side sat three persons. One man he did not recognize. The other man was Rick Robbins. The third person, in a long, slim black dress and her hair in a black cloud, was Martha Cruz. She was smoking a cigarette.

For a moment Dan stopped, putting the image into focus. Martha Cruz and Rick Robbins. Two hours ago she had been covered with dirt, sobbing for the DEA not to kill her.

"That's Martha," Elaine said, astonished. "How did she get here?"

"She's a resourceful girl," Dan said. He went quickly down the steps from the terrace then followed the path running alongside the pool.

Arlo Pate stepped in front of him. He had been leaning against a palm tree several yards away from the group, and Dan had not noticed him.

Dan said, "I need to talk to Rick."

"Sorry, man. Martha and I just got here, and she needs to talk to Mr. Friedman."

"Arlo, let me have a couple minutes with Rick, then I'll leave."

"Yeah, well, you have to wait." He put his hand out, and the heavy fingers lightly touched Dan's chest.

At the same moment Rick glanced around. He stared at Dan, then spoke to the man next to him. Rick stood up. Martha Cruz remained in her chair. Her lips were deep red, and silver sparkled against her long neck. She put her cigarette to her lips, then turned back to her companion.

Elaine touched Dan's shoulder. "I'm going to sit over here while you speak with your client." She walked toward the terrace.

Dan said to Arlo, "Could Rick and I have a minute?"

"Yeah, sure."

Rick had his hand on Dan's elbow, taking him farther

toward the rear fence. Dan could hear the pounding of the ocean behind it. "What the hell is going on?"

Rick was grinning. "Hey, what a surprise. Where'd you come from? I mean, Martha told me about your run-in out at Miguel's house. Must've been pretty hairy for a while, right? Listen, that guy over there? That's Joel Friedman, and he's talking to Martha about a contract. We got him, Dan."

Dan was staring at Martha Cruz. She was leaning on her arms on the small table, laughing at something Friedman said. Friedman was early forties, pale and pudgy, wearing jeans and a tan jacket, looking slick. For the first time Dan noticed what was on the table— an odd-looking machine resembling a tape player. He took Rick's hand off his elbow and walked quickly toward Martha Cruz.

He heard Rick's footsteps behind him. "Dan! Wait up! They're talking business over there." Rick tugged his arm. "Hey, listen, I'll give you a call tomorrow."

Dan looked down at Martha Cruz. "What is this?"

She glanced at Rick, then back to Dan.

Dan hit the eject button. The door fell slowly open, revealing a gray cassette, smaller than the usual size. The label said *Party*.

He slammed the door shut again and pressed Play. Party noises. Laughter. Voices in the background. Then rock music blared from the little speakers. Mayhem.

Joel Friedman set his drink down and stared. "Who is this guy?"

"He's my lawyer. Never mind him." Rick turned off

the music then dragged Dan several yards away. "Listen to me. This is her chance. She had to do it. We didn't have a demo."

"Had to do what?"

Rick's nervous laughter mixed with the soft background chatter and the sound of the sea. "You know. Get the tape. It was their party on South Beach last week. The girls recorded it in case we didn't get the demo tapes from Manatee Studios. Really, you should've been at the party. It was a super performance."

Dan stared at Martha, then back at Rick, who was still talking. "Friedman loved it. I knew he would. We're gonna find a new bass player—do you believe that Scott guy was DEA? Arlo's gonna do drums, Bobby's coming with us, too."

"Martha took me after the party tape," Dan said numbly.

Rick said, "Hey, whatever works, right?"

"Where is the Barrios tape?" His head felt off-balance. "Did Martha tell you about the Barrios tape?"

"Well . . . yes. It never actually existed. Kelly made it up. She had to get the DEA off her back."

It was starting to make sense. Dan managed to speak calmly. "Okay. Martha knew about me and the Barrios case from you and Kelly. She used a tape that didn't exist to get me to escort her to Salazar's place— Correct so far?" Rick nodded. "Because she couldn't go back herself to get a tape she and Kelly made of a party on South Beach. Right? And I was shot at *twice,* nearly drowned by a fucking dragline, and only by the grace of God am I standing here now."

"Dan, we had no idea Miguel was home, I swear. Then the DEA—"

"We. Meaning you helped her in this?"

Rick hesitated, then said, "This was my last chance for a deal with a major label. I thought I was going to prison, but if I could do this one thing, even if they took it all away—" He forced out a laugh. "But it worked out. Didn't it? You were great. You saved my life, man. They can't do anything to me now. Look. They had crooked DEA agents all over the place. Tomorrow with what's-his-name, Paxton, at the U.S. attorney's office, I want you to tell the guy, we're pleading not guilty. Let them take me to court, see what they get."

Dan grabbed Rick's lapels and shook him. "You knew. You *knew* what you were sending me into."

"He wasn't supposed to be home!"

"Wasn't *supposed* to be?" Dan was screaming. People nearby moved away, then scattered. "They nearly killed me! I could be *dead*, you stupid son of a bitch."

Arlo Pate unhooked Dan's fingers from the front of Rick's jacket. "Well, you're not, are you?"

CHAPTER 41

It took awhile to arrange things, but in June, with Josh out for the summer, Dan took him fishing near Islamorada for a week. Dan pulled the old twenty-foot Mako down on a trailer, and they slept in a motel at night, but Josh didn't seem to mind. He was getting brown from the sun, and he had learned how to handle the new rod and reel Dan had bought him. Dan had not replaced his spearguns and doubted that he ever would. Using a net, he and Josh had caught some nice tropicals, which they would take back to Miami and put in Dan's new aquarium.

At the moment Josh was asleep, and Dan lay on the end of the pier behind the motel looking south into the vast blackness of the ocean.

It still surprised him that he was here, and alive, thanks to Vincent Hooper. Shaken by a nonexistent recording of a phony incident, Hooper had gone off to South America, though it remained unclear exactly which country, to fight in some other battle. One where the moral ground wasn't so rocky, if such a place existed.

What surprised Dan as much, if not more, was how easily he had given up the trip to Cat Cay. Dan did not feel defeated, far from it. Being with Josh, catching a few fish and cooking them on the grill in the motel's backyard—it was enough. He had known that it would be, and he could pinpoint the moment it had become clear to him: when he was underneath that black water in the lake, feeling his way in the ooze, certain he would never see daylight again.

He had invited Elaine to come with him and Josh, meaning it sincerely, but she had declined. *You guys go.* She would be waiting for him when he got back.

Elaine still had a job, which she had said was a miracle. The newspaper had praised her: *Assistant U.S. attorney helps bust DEA killer.* This had been a subhead of a splashy story about the successful roundup of two dozen members of the Guayaquil cartel. The office could hardly have fired her after that.

Sitting up, Dan pressed the light on his dive watch: 11:36. If he went back to the room he could see Martha Cruz on *Saturday Night Live*—the motel had cable TV. But Rick had promised to send him the video clip.

Dan lay back down and locked his hands under his head. He remembered his father's boat, a little trawler used for shrimping or, in season, taking on lobster traps. They used to go south off Marathon at sundown in the winter, taking the boat out beyond the glow of the city on the horizon, halfway to Cuba, it seemed. They turned off everything but the red and green running lights, but they could see each other clearly by the light of the stars as they baited hooks and tossed them into the sea. They had no radio. They were only a speck on the ocean, so far out that if they signaled no one would ever notice, but Dan had not felt the slightest edge of fear. He saw stars wheel up out of the sea and sweep overhead. Then in the depths of the night a faint yellow glow toward the east, a pale ghost, a slice of moon.

BARBARA PARKER brings back attorneys Gail Connor and Anthony Quintana in her sizzling new legal thriller!

SUSPICION OF DECEIT

Attorney Gail Connor has made a few changes in her life since we last saw her in Barbara Parker's *Suspicion of Guilt* (available in paperback from Signet). She's left the prestigious Miami law firm where she has spent her entire professional career in order to go into practice for herself, and she's become engaged to top criminal defense attorney Anthony Quintana. At last, since her sister's tragic death and her own devastating divorce, things are looking bright again for Gail and her ten-year-old daughter, Karen. But then a former spy for the Cuban regime is found dead, and Gail fears that her fiancé knows more about it than he will admit. When a second person with connections to Anthony is murdered, Gail is wracked with doubt, and his silence feels like a betrayal. Their relationship is tested to the limits as Gail digs into the past for the truth about the crimes that can save—or destroy—the man she loves.

Turn the page for an exciting preview of Barbara Parker's brilliant new thriller!

A Dutton hardcover on sale in January 1998

PROLOGUE

Near the rear of the funeral procession, the Cadillac traveled in a cloud of mist whirling up from the expressway. It had rained heavily all morning, tapering off by midday to a light drizzle. From the passenger seat Gail Connor watched Miami scroll past under a dreary sky. Dense foliage, a palm tree here or there. Small stucco houses. Razor wire on the flat roofs of businesses.

She crossed her arms, unable to get warm, even in her wool suit. Anthony reached out to adjust the temperature control. Gold flashed on his wrist. "Is that better?"

"Thanks."

He held her hand on his lap.

She took long, slow breaths, refusing to cry. She wanted to. Wanted to lean against his shoulder and close her eyes and pretend Rebecca Dixon wasn't dead. Go to Anthony's house and get into bed with him. Go to sleep without seeing the explosion again, and again, and Rebecca screaming, and her clothes catching fire, and her hair, and then toppling over in that odd way. Slowly. Almost gracefully.

"Gail? Is something wrong?"

"On the way to a cemetery, what could be wrong?" She looked around. Anthony's eyes were on her face, gently concerned. "I didn't mean to snap at you. I didn't sleep well last night."

He squeezed her hand. A truck went by in the left lane, momentarily blurring the windshield.

"I guess . . . what's bothering me is Rebecca. I can't stop thinking about what she said. Why would she make up such a story?"

Anthony shook his head. "I wish I knew."

"To make it so real," Gail said. "It was a horrible thing to tell me. That girl, kneeling. Her hands tied with electrical wire. You with the gun—"

His sharp exhalation stopped her. "Gail, I didn't—"

"I know. I know you didn't." She entwined their fingers. "I'm sorry. We won't talk about it anymore."

CHAPTER ONE

In early January, Rebecca Dixon hosted a party to benefit the Miami Grand Opera. Gail had been given two tickets, one for herself, the other for Anthony Quintana. They had been engaged only a few weeks, and she could think of better ways to spend the evening, but since the opera had just retained her as their general counsel, she thought it would be wise to drop by.

They took the ferry from Miami Beach to Fisher Island, inaccessible by road. The night was clear and cool, and Anthony rolled back the sun roof so they could see the stars. Feeling buoyant, Gail kicked off her pumps, climbed on the passenger seat, and pulled herself carefully through the opening.

"Hey, where are you going?"

She laughed with pure delight as a gust of chilly wind blew back her hair and fluttered her shawl. She wrapped it tightly around her shoulders and leaned against the roof to steady herself. Turning slowly, the ferry pulled away from the causeway and headed east.

A hand went around her knee. Anthony leaned over to look through the sun roof. "Having a good time?"

"The best. It's Friday. Karen's with her father till Sunday

night. I don't have any cases to spoil my weekend." She poked his thigh. "Hey. Are you busy later?"

He smiled wickedly from the deep shadow of the car's interior. "*Que chévere*. People are staring at you."

"Do you care?"

"No. I think they're jealous."

Maneuvering back inside, she lost her balance and fell halfway across his lap, tangled in her shawl, laughing. Her short blue jersey dress was riding up her legs. He held her where she was and kissed her. The air outside had chilled her lips, and his mouth was warm and soft. Finally he pulled back and frowned, giving her a little shake. "You're a crazy woman, you know that?"

"You love it." A strand of hair had fallen over his forehead, and she pushed it back into place. "Without me you'd sit alone in the dark and brood."

"Oh, you think so? I'd be out having fun. Dancing, parties—"

"Don't I take you to parties? Tonight you get to hear Thomas Brandon."

"Who is he?"

"Who? The singer. Tonight's entertainment?"

"Ah. Yes, I remember."

Gail smiled. "Don't worry. We'll sneak in, mingle for a bit, then leave." She smoothed the lapel of his perfectly draped Italian jacket. Charcoal gray with thin burgundy stripes. "I should be there. The president of the board called to make sure I was coming. That's Rebecca Dixon. I introduced you at the *Messiah* concert. Brunette, very elegant, all those diamonds?"

"What does she want?"

"I don't know. We don't socialize, so it must be related to opera business."

"Are you sure you have to go?"

"Well . . . do you have another suggestion?"

"Yes. When we get to the other side, we turn the car around and catch the next ferry back. We drive to my house. It isn't far."

"And then?"

"We go upstairs. I unzip this lovely dress. Take it off."

He tilted her head back and brushed his mouth along her

jaw, then down her neck. *"Qué rica tu piel, como la seda. Eres pa' comer."*

"Oh . . . yes. Whatever it means. No, don't tell me. You could explain jury selection in Spanish, it would sound romantic." She held his face and kissed him, opening her mouth. It took her a second to realize that his hand was under her skirt, and several more to remember where they were. "Somebody's going to see us. Let me up. Anthony!" He sighed and leaned back in his seat, palms raised in surrender.

Gail flipped open the visor mirror. The light came on. Her eyes were dilated to a rim of blue. Her mouth and cheeks looked thoroughly ravished. "Oh, dear. Good evening, Mrs. Hornswoggle, I'm the new lawyer for the Miami Grand Opera."

Two months ago Gail had turned down a partnership at the big firm where she had worked since getting her law degree eight years ago. Her daughter needed her. Gail needed a life. Her new office was ten minutes from home in an office tower across from a shopping mall. Clients didn't just stroll in off the street. She had become an expert in handing out business cards. Good to meet you. I'm Gail Connor. I specialize in commercial litigation. Personal injury. Estate planning. Whatever the person she was talking to seemed to require.

Anthony said, "You know . . . I've met Rebecca Dixon before."

"You have?"

"Yes. I think it was the University of Miami. We may have had a class together. I mention this in case it comes up in conversation. She probably doesn't remember."

Gail put on fresh lipstick. "Did you know . . . that Rebecca and Lloyd Dixon have made a pledge of two hundred and fifty thousand dollars?"

"What does he do? Or is the money hers?"

"No, it's his. He owns a cargo airline, I think." Gail's mother, Irene Connor, had summed him up in words Gail didn't want to repeat: *an Alabama redneck trying to buy himself some class.* Which was entirely possible in Miami, if a man threw wads of cash at charity, at the arts, and had the good luck to find a woman like Rebecca Dixon.

"Can you imagine? A quarter of a million. And it's not the biggest donation the opera has received, either. But it certainly puts my paltry five hundred bucks into perspective." Gail sat back in her seat and smoothed her skirt. "I promise we won't stay long, but I really need to show my face tonight, maybe cultivate some paying clients. Lucky you, to be so well established."

Anthony smiled. "Ah, but my clients— I usually find them at the jail, not at opera parties."

When the ferry bumped against the dock, Anthony slid down his window and told the guard where they were going. The guard checked their names off a list, and told them to follow his golf cart. On the south side of the island was a social center that used to be a winter home for one of the Vanderbilts. Tropical trees and a fountain marked the entrance. Anthony gave the keys to the valet, and they went inside. A passing waiter in a tux pointed out the way. They could hear a piano, a torrent of notes, and a deep male voice singing in Italian.

At the door to the ballroom Gail whispered, "Let's wait till this one is over."

Anthony discreetly squeezed her backside. "We're not staying late."

She glanced around at him, told him to be quiet, then eased the door open when applause began. The attendees were mostly middle-aged and up, attired in the usual South Florida casual chic, not so many tuxes. This was a good crowd, about a hundred people, some standing, some seated at small tables. The chandeliers were turned off, except one in the front illuminating the singer and his accompanist, a young Asian man.

Thomas Brandon wore a black silk jacket and white banded shirt. His hair was tied back in a ponytail. He was somewhere in his mid-thirties, with a good build. Not a pretty guy, but definitely intense. On stage he would be gorgeous. Most of the women—and a few of the men—seemed to be on the point of swooning.

They found an empty table as the accompanist's hands came down on the keys. There were some opening chords, then Thomas Brandon took a step forward and opened his mouth. He had a clear, rich voice.

"O mio sospir soave, per sempre io ti perdei!" Someone had left a program on the table. Gail picked it up and found

the translation. *Oh, my gentle breath of life, forever are you lost to me. . . .*

After the last song, everyone stood up and applauded while Brandon and his accompanist made several bows. Gradually the applause faded away. Before Gail could turn to pick up her purse and shawl, a delicate hand touched her arm.

"Gail? Yes, I thought it was you." Rebecca Dixon stood smiling at her side, a model-slim woman in a gold silk tunic and trousers. Her heavy, dark hair swung at shoulder length. "I'm so glad you could come. Mr. Quintana, it's good to see you again. May I be selfish and borrow Gail for a few minutes? Let me introduce you to some friends of mine first, so you won't feel abandoned."

"That isn't necessary. There are people here I know."

Anthony lightly kissed her cheek, and the two women walked away through the crowd, people putting themselves in Rebecca Dixon's path, saying hello. She introduced Gail to one person after another, no name forgotten. But all the time they were moving toward an exit door.

With a billow of silk and click of heels on parquet, Rebecca led Gail along the corridor, then turned into a foyer. Past the sloping lawn and row of royal palm trees, the ocean was visible through uncurtained glass. Moonlight laid down a path of silver across the water. She took Gail's arm and walked her closer to the windows. "What do you think of our singer?"

"He's superb," Gail said.

"Isn't he."

"I read he's doing *Don Giovanni* in March?"

"Yes. The title role. Between now and then he will be teaching master classes and making various and sundry appearances, all of which have been heavily publicized. And we—the opera—have a situation on our hands."

"Oh?"

"One of our board members called me this morning. She said that two years ago last November, Thomas Brandon sang at a music festival in Havana."

"Havana, Cuba," Gail said.

Rebecca nodded slowly, her expression gone a little sour. "Our board member, who is Cuban, by the way, heard it from one of her friends who had gone to a benefit last weekend for La Liga Contra el Cancer."

"My first week on the job, I get a porcupine in my lap."

Rebecca's bell-like laugh turned to a sigh. "Yes. A porcupine."

"What did Mr. Brandon have to say? Is it true?"

"Oh, yes. He admitted it. He said, So what? I said, My God, Tom, why didn't you tell us? It didn't cross your mind that there are people in this community who are going to take offense?"

Gail tried to remember the last time Miami had blown up over something like this. Last spring a Brazilian jazz combo had been booked into a theater downtown. Nobody paid much attention, till the news hit the Spanish-language talk shows: The band had just played in Canada with a Cuban group called Los Van Van. A gross insult. A slap in the face of the exile community. The theater manager received death threats. K-9 dogs sniffed for bombs. The scene outside the concert turned ugly—shouting, pushing, the police trying to keep the crowds behind barricades. Then a bottle hit one of the concert-goers. His blood showed up nicely on TV. The second show had been cancelled, and the indignant Brazilians held a press conference that wound up on *Nightline*.

"What would you like me to do?" Gail asked, not knowing what in hell could be done.

Rebecca twisted her gold necklace around her finger, then nervously moved the diamond pendant back and forth, metal clicking. "Our general manager is in New York looking at talent. When he returns next week, I want to have a recommendation for him. Most of us are leaning toward letting Thomas Brandon go. On the other hand, what does that say about singing in Miami? You have to pass a political test?"

"How much is his contract?"

"Eight thousand dollars per performance. Nine performances."

Gail did the math, then said, "Yikes. You'd have to pay him if you cancelled his contract without cause."

"Exactly," Rebecca said. "My husband is opposed to replacing Brandon. He's adamant. Lloyd says, 'You people are a bunch of . . .' " Rebecca laughed, her ivory cheeks coloring with embarrassment. "Well. He isn't a happy camper these days." The diamond pendant was still clicking on its gold chain.

"Is Lloyd on the executive committee?"

"He's not even on the board."

Meaning he had no say in what the opera did. But $250,000 could buy a lot of clout. Gail was at a loss, not knowing what kind of advice Rebecca Dixon expected her to give.

The large brown eyes shifted to Gail, regaining some of their fire. "I've been president for four months. The first woman ever to have this job, did you know that?"

"Is that right? Congratulations."

"Some people say I bought it."

"Not what I've heard," Gail said. "Membership is up, ticket sales are strong—"

"Yes, and you'll see how fast I take the heat if something goes wrong. Oh, damn. I have so much I want to accomplish." Rebecca Dixon gripped Gail's arm. "Here's what you can do for me. Stay for the meeting and bring Anthony Quintana with you. We need his input."

"Tonight?" Obviously tonight. "Well . . . we had plans."

"Oh, don't say that. I've got to have someone who can tell us how the exile community is likely to react, once the news gets out—and it will. I'm sorry for Thomas Brandon, if he doesn't get to sing, but the opera can't be turned into a political battlefield."

Gail suspected she was about to be moved around on the Dixons' marital chessboard. Or that Anthony was.

Rebecca was still hanging on her arm. "I wanted to consult you first, of course, as our attorney, and in view of your relationship."

"You mean our engagement."

"Irene told me," Rebecca said. "I hope you don't mind. It's wonderful news." She had her social smile on again, just a few watts too bright. "Have you set a date?"

"This summer, probably, after Karen—my daughter—is out of school. Listen, Rebecca. My relationship aside, why do you need Anthony? He's not going to want to get involved. You have Cubans on the board, don't you? Ask them."

"I would, but they have no connection with the— I don't want to say the extremists. Let's say certain groups who would make a cause out of this."

"Good Lord." Gail had to laugh. "Anthony isn't into causes. He stays away from politics, particularly exile politics."

"It's his *family* I'm referring to. His grandfather is a member of every hard-line exile group in Miami. His brother-in-law has a talk show on WRCL. So who better to give an opinion? I could ask him myself, but it would be better if you did."

After a moment Gail said, "I'll ask him. What he says is up to him."

"Thank you, Gail. And don't worry about dinner. The meeting is just down the street at my house. We'll find something for you in the fridge."

When Rebecca took a step toward the music hall, Gail said, "One question. How did you come to know about Anthony's family?"

"It's common enough knowledge." Rebecca's smile was back on.

Eight years of trying lawsuits had left a mark. Gail said, "He said you and he knew each other at the University of Miami."

"Did he mention that? Well, of course. He was quite political in those days. That's why I thought he would be willing to help us now."

"Political?" Gail frowned. "No . . . I don't think he was ever . . . that far on the right. Not like his grandfather."

"God, no. Anthony had a poster of Che Guevara in his apartment."

What an odd sensation, Gail thought. As if the walls failed to meet squarely at the corners. Things just slightly off. Beams of light that curved and hit the ceiling in unexpected places.

Rebecca gestured toward the corridor. "I suppose we should go back. They'll be wondering where we are."